"You are either the most foolish diplomat who ever drew breath, or else you have a death wish!" Kang shouted, spittle flying from his mouth in a fine spray.

"Perhaps neither," Dax said. "Perhaps I merely don't wish to waste my time listening to boasts and veiled threats. If *you* are not ready to cooperate and act with honor, then perhaps the High Council sent the wrong emissaries to represent them."

Kang stared at him, and Dax imagined that he saw a spark of grudging respect flashing deep in the Klingon captain's eyes.

Behind the Klingons, Dax saw that Commander Sulu and Lieutenant Commander Cutler had exited the chamber as well, and were quickly relaying commands to their security officers. Beyond them, he saw Sarek and Dostara trying to talk with Kamarag and Baktrek and the other ambassadors, even as Captain Styles and several of his staff stood by, obviously considering their next moves, diplomatic or otherwise.

Have I gone too far? Dax asked himself as he shifted his attention back onto Kang. The whole affair had lasted less than a minute, but felt like an eternity.

And then a brilliant flash of light and a loud noise obliterated Dax's vision.

Even as the explosion from within the Korvat conference chamber rocked the air, throwing Dax and the others off their feet, Dax heard screams and several more explosions originating from somewhere else nearby. The back of Koloth's hair was burning, and as Dax breathed in, a lungful of acrid smoke and heated air told him that more than just the Klingon was afire.

Panic overtaking him, Dax grasped the one lucid thought swirling through his mind.

We've just been bombed.

OTHER STAR TREK® FICTION BY
MICHAEL A. MARTIN & ANDY MANGELS

STAR TREK®

EXCELSIOR
FORGED IN FIRE

MICHAEL A. MARTIN & ANDY MANGELS

BASED UPON *STAR TREK*
CREATED BY GENE RODDENBERRY,
AND *STAR TREK: DEEP SPACE NINE*
CREATED BY RICK BERMAN & MICHAEL PILLER

POCKET BOOKS
New York London Toronto Sydney Ganjitsu

Pocket Books
A Division of Simon & Schuster, Inc.
1230 Avenue of the Americas
New York, NY 10020

This book is a work of fiction. Names, characters, places, and incidents either are products of the authors' imaginations or are used fictitiously. Any resemblance to actual events or locales or persons, living or dead, is entirely coincidental.

This book is published by Pocket Books, a division of Simon & Schuster, Inc., under exclusive license from CBS Studios Inc.

First Pocket Books paperback edition January 2008

POCKET and colophon are registered trademarks of Simon & Schuster, Inc.

For information about special discounts for bulk purchases, please contact Simon & Schuster Special Sales at 1-800-456-6798 or business@simonandschuster.com.

Cover art by Tom Hallman; cover design by John Vairo, Jr.

Manufactured in the United States of America

10 9 8 7 6 5 4 3 2 1

ISBN-13: 978-1-4165-4716-7
ISBN-10:   1-4165-4716-9

To the memory of Kurt Vonnegut, Jr. (1922–2007).
So it goes . . .

—M.A.M.

. . .

This book is dedicated to my brother and sister
and their families, who've always appreciated
their wild and woolly sibling "Uncle Andy"
(and all of whom grew up too fast)!

For my sister, Cathleen Wilde, and her Trekkie husband,
Doran, plus nieces and nephews Cameron, Brandon K,
Ned, Becky, Desiré, Andy, and Shannon.

For my brother, Ron Mangels, and his wife,
Stacey, plus nieces and nephews Andrea,
Katie, Jon, and Lauren.

May you all live long and prosper!

—A.M.

The bulk of this story takes place late in 2289 and early 2290, approximately halfway between the time of the films *Star Trek V: The Final Frontier* and *Star Trek VI: The Undiscovered Country*. This places it about four years before *The Captain's Daughter* and eight years before *The Lost Era: The Sundered*.

We only become what we are by the radical and deep-seated refusal of that which others have made of us.

—Jean-Paul Sartre
(1905–1980)

PROLOGUE WA'

2173 (the Year of Kahless 799,
early in the month of *Lo'Bral*)

Qu'Vat

"I know you think this is the only way to reclaim your honor, Doctor Antaak," said Quv. The younger Klingon man's voice shook in a distressingly un-Klingon manner that strangely suited his unnaturally smooth forehead. "But what you are about to do isn't far short of pure insanity."

As he continued walking briskly through the throngs in the central public transport concourse of the Klingon colony world of Qu'Vat, Antaak clutched his medical bag close to his chest and cast a weary smile at his student, who breathlessly kept pace beside him.

"How little you truly understand of honor, Quv," Antaak said. "And of what it means to lose it."

Antaak couldn't blame Quv for his reticence; his student was far too young to truly understand or appreciate what Klingons were *supposed* to look like. Quv was younger than Antaak's own adult children, and thus had no firsthand memory of the time before the Change. The time before Antaak's own attempts to create genetically enhanced Klingon warriors had unexpectedly created the mutated Levodian flu virus that sentenced all of Qu'Vat's millions to a horrible death—a fate that Antaak had averted only by distributing a therapeutic retrovirus suffused with specially altered Earther DNA.

The consequence had been the creation of a new subrace that now dwelled on Qu'Vat and far beyond, Klingons whose bodies were so free of their people's traditional texture that even Kahless himself would doubtless have been unable to recognize them as his own folk. Although those afflicted with this mark of shame represented only a minority of the overall population of the Klingon Empire, a large generational cohort had grown up literally wearing Antaak's failure upon their faces.

It was an intolerable reminder, and it plagued Antaak, assailing both pride and conscience, every time he looked in the mirror. He had been determined to remedy it since it first happened, regardless of the cost. And now that both success and redemption finally lay within his grasp, he would brook no further delay.

Antaak came to an abrupt stop beside the fire fountain in the main square, which housed an obelisk that stood as tall as three large men. Rising from the center of the stone display's perpetual conflagration stood oversized cast duranium representations of Kahless and his brother Morath, locked in their eternal hand-to-hand struggle on the slopes of the Kri'stak Volcano, where legend had it that Kahless had fashioned the very first *bat'leth* out of a lock of his own hair. The complex topography of the foreheads of both brothers seemed to dance and jump in the chaotic spray of flames and sparks that framed their age-old conflict. It seemed to Antaak that the metal colossi were but pausing in their eternal combat, as though eager to watch Antaak redeem both his people and his own honor.

He reached into his medical bag and removed a small vial, pausing to watch the preoccupied crowds as they paced to and from the maglev platforms and the tube trains that were taking most of them back to their homes for the evening, while transporting a few less fortunate others back into the business and industrial districts where the night shift was about to begin.

The only one present who seemed to have any inkling that anything out of the ordinary might be about to occur was Quv, whose brow now appeared nearly as furrowed as those of his honored ancestors.

"Are you really certain this is safe, Doctor?" Quv said, his voice quavering in unmistakable fear.

Quv's continued sniveling had finally reached the elastic limits of Antaak's patience; Antaak thought it might soon snap, like a length of frayed cable suddenly placed under far too much tension.

"My senior staff is satisfied with the bioagent's preliminary tests," Antaak said, biting off his words one at a time. "So there is no reason to delay deployment any longer—especially when our financial patrons on the High Council have grown so restive of late."

To say nothing of the demands of honor far too long denied, Antaak added silently. *Besides, if I were to allow this research to drag on long enough to completely satisfy the fainthearted, I'd never live to see it reach its conclusion.*

And B'Etris, his wife of more than twenty years—a great beauty whose brow had retained the proud cranial topography of the warriors of old—might never see her husband finally become worthy of her again.

Antaak's gnarled thumbs pushed at the vial's cap, launching the stopper skyward with an audible pop. He raised the open container over his head, trusting the vial's preprogrammed internal mechanism to do the rest. A woman carrying a small child paused to eye him curiously for a moment before she walked on and blended into the milling, shifting crowds.

The vial moved slightly in Antaak's hand, the mild sensation of recoil confirming that the tiny aerosol delivery device had launched itself high above the open-air plaza. Within moments, the vial's microscopic contents would be randomly distributed throughout the transit mall before spreading swiftly beyond via the station's efficient network of maglev trains and the prevailing winds.

Antaak wondered if he dared hope not only for redemption, but also for immortality in the annals of Klingon history. There would be stories told at the *Kot'baval* festival, and songs sung, in between the celebrations of Kahless's legendary defeat of the tyrant Molor in single combat. Perhaps an achievement such as this one—the complete restoration of the pure Klingon genome, a battle won by science rather than blades—might even rate its author a statue in the Hall of Heroes.

Minutes passed as Antaak stood silently beside the fire fountain, watching the passage of the unwitting crowds. He could only wonder if the proud foreheads of their ancestors would begin to return immediately, even as he watched. Or would the mass metamorphosis these people were now carrying with them to home and workplace take hours or even days to manifest its full effect?

"I don't feel very well, Doctor," Quv said.

Antaak had finally had enough. "Be silent, you fool. Can't you see that you are witnessing history?"

Quv was indeed silent after that. He remained particularly so after he pitched forward onto the stone pathway beside the fountain, where he landed as limp and boneless as a child's rag doll.

"Quv?" Antaak knelt beside his student, whose breaths were now coming in rapid, shallow bursts. *Perhaps this is some manner of allergic reaction,* he thought, willing his jangled nerves to steadiness.

A scream pierced the air a short distance behind him, prompting Antaak to rise quickly and turn in the direction of the sound. A smooth-headed woman held a toddler— Antaak wasn't certain whether she was the same young mother he had seen watching him a few moments earlier—and the child was in obvious distress. The child, a boy who couldn't have been more than two or three years of age, appeared to be in the grip of some sort of convulsion or seizure. Like the forehead of the panicked woman who carried him, his own was smooth, though it was growing noticeably inflamed and red even as Antaak watched.

A familiar pattern of bumps and ridges was clearly beginning to appear on the child's forehead.

Then the boy screamed, vomited, and went limp. He hung apparently lifeless in the young woman's arms even as she, too, began developing facial features similar to those displayed by her son. Two other people near the woman appeared to be having difficulty breathing. A short distance behind them, a uniformed constable tore off his helmet, displaying a badly inflamed but heavily ridged forehead before he, too, collapsed onto the transit mall's unyielding stone floor.

Antaak quickly lost the ability to distinguish further manifestations of the new plague he had apparently just unleashed. He saw only flashes of mortified faces, heard only pained screams and running feet, felt and tasted only terror. Antaak's suddenly rubbery legs gave way beneath him before he came to the belated realization that he, too, could no longer breathe properly, nor even gasp. His mind flashed back to the Hall of Heroes, which he understood with resigned finality would now enshrine neither his name nor his likeness, both of which would doubtless be reviled, now and for all the ages to come.

He realized that dull, plodding Quv had been right after all. Had he the breath for it, he would have laughed.

Among Antaak's last coherent thoughts before oblivion pulled him under was to hope that his wife, his grown daughters and son, and his five young grandchildren would find a place of safety before this new plague reached them.

Along with gratitude that none of them had been immediately present to witness this final, career-defining failure.

PROLOGUE CHA'

2295 (the Year of Kahless 921,
early in the month of *Soo'jen*)

Qo'noS

There was no stillness to this night. The very air itself
seemed agitated, as if it could ignite at any moment into
a blazing conflagration. Captain Hikaru Sulu had been to
Qo'noS twice before, but never to observe so solemn a ceremony as this. And never at so damning a moment in time.

Above those assembled here, the charred and crumbled
remnants of Praxis, the Klingon moon, shone with a wan
light. The satellite had been a dead place for nearly two
years now, but the Klingons had refused to destroy what
slivered shards of it remained, and tidal forces had yet to
grind it to dust, or drag it down to Qo'noS itself. Like a
wounded warrior still engaged in some legendary battle, it
stood above them, reminding those under its gaze that it survived, and would continue to endure until a challenger rose
to reckon with its shambling remains.

A warm wind gusted past, and Sulu closed his eyes to
keep the dust from getting into them. He was glad that Kang

had chosen not to have his son's remains cremated on a funeral pyre; despite all the cultural differences Sulu had encountered in his Starfleet career, he wasn't certain that he could have maintained his composure while watching a child's corpse being immolated.

The wind calmed for the moment, and Sulu opened his eyes, even as those near him reached to retrieve their weapons. Catching the hitch in his breath before it could become noticeable to others, Sulu kept still. Despite the accords so recently signed between the Federation and the Klingon Empire, the sight of three Klingon fighting men in full warriors' garb, brandishing polished *bat'leth*s, was enough to make even a Vulcan's pulse race.

The other companion who pulled a *bat'leth* from a ceremonial satchel was not Klingon at all, but a member of the Trill species. Curzon Dax was fast becoming one of the most renowned and fearless diplomats working in the Federation, and his presence here was a testament not only to the trust the Klingons had placed in him, but also to the piece of himself that he had allowed to reside with *them*.

No example of that trust was more clear than the inscription that had been graven upon the face of the burial vault that the Klingons had erected here today. As with other such vaults, which Sulu had seen only in the form of holophotos, the lineage of the House of Kang was delineated in the angry strokes of Klingon script, hammered masterfully into a copper-colored metal. At the bottom of the list was the name of the young child who had been entombed today within the vault: DaqS, son of Kang and Mara.

It had been only five days since DaqS had succumbed to a mysterious disease; from what Curzon had told Sulu during their trip to Qo'noS, the illness had come on suddenly and had subjected the child to excruciating pain. DaqS was Curzon Dax's godson, the only Klingon that Sulu had ever heard of that had been named after an offworlder. Kang's respect for Curzon must have run very deep indeed for the Klingon to bestow such an honor upon him.

Sulu knew that his own past with Kang, Koloth, and Kor had instilled in them a trust for the Starfleet captain as well, but even that trust could not compare with the bond the three warriors shared with Curzon. It was Sulu's observance of that distinction that kept him from brandishing a *bat'leth* of his own during this somber moment, as the Trill ambassador did.

Kang was the first to stab his *bat'leth* into the sky, his sharpened teeth bared, his ridged brow taut. A powerful howl issued forth from his throat, sounding as raw and intense as though they were his own death cries. Koloth, Kor, and Dax raised their *bat'leth*s seconds later, guttural cries coming from each of them. The other mourners assembled around them raised their own *bat'leth*s—or their fists, as did Sulu—yowling into the warm night air.

The sound was an indescribable cacophony, and Sulu felt his pulse quicken even as a cold sweat broke out on his skin. He knew that the death ritual was usually performed in the direct presence of the fallen warrior or family member, generally with the deceased's eyes pried open to ensure a better view of the afterlife. But DaqS had been a mere boy, barely into the earliest levels of training, and his passing had apparently convulsed, distorted, and desiccated his body so horribly that it had not been deemed fit for viewing, even by Klingons—a species not known for being squeamish. The thought made him shudder.

So the mourning party howled to the memory of the child, whose remains were already ensconced within the vault, remembering him for what he was and for what he represented to Kang's bloodline. Sulu had never met young DaqS; the boy had been born less than a year after the last time that he had been in the presence of Kang, Koloth, Kor, and Dax. But he could empathize with the loss, had seen it etched in the faces of those in his life whose children had preceded them into death. Despite all his bravado, James Kirk had been indelibly scarred a decade ago when a Klingon soldier had murdered his estranged son David Marcus on the Genesis Planet. Others, on board both the *Enterprise* and *Excelsior,* had faced similar traumas, which had changed each of them irrevocably.

And then there had been the time not all that long ago when he'd thought Demora dead.

In the angry skies overhead, Sulu saw a meteor streak by, and he wondered for a moment if it was an omen or just another piece of Praxis that had finally tumbled into Qo'noS's atmosphere. The tumultuous cries around him continued to resound strongly for another few minutes, until Kang stopped, slashing his *bat'leth* through the air one-handed to silence all the others as well.

Sulu glanced toward Mara, to see if she would join her husband near the tomb marker, but she stayed where she was, deferential to the male warriors who had assembled around Kang. Sulu had met her only once, very briefly, when they were all much, much younger.

Kang began to sing then, his basso voice hoarse yet strong. Through his universal translator, Sulu understood the basis of the song, even as others joined in. It was part of the traditional *Ak'voh* rite, a mournful song intended to keep predators both physical and spiritual from devouring young DaqS's spirit before it could safely reach *Sto-Vo-Kor.* During the shuttle ride to Qo'noS, Curzon had told Sulu of the ritual song, explaining that if it was performed, which seemed likely, it would have to be modified, since the soul of a child would face a far more perilous journey to the Klingon afterlife than would that of an experienced, blooded warrior; thus, the more strongly the voices of his family and fellow warriors sounded, the easier young DaqS's passage into *Sto-Vo-Kor* would be.

The blood on your face is that of your foe,
The fire that burns toward you will temper your blade,
The Halls are Waiting, the Halls are Waiting!
Each carrion-eater that attacks shall lose an eye,
You will wear their teeth around your neck,
Their fur as your cloak, their spines on your boots,
The Halls are Waiting, the Halls are Waiting!
The serpent that bites you with poison will die itself,
Its jaws pried apart as you force the poison from you. . . .

For a moment, Sulu wondered precisely how the song had been altered from its original form for the child, and how much more violent the unexpurgated version could have been. But this *was* Klingon culture he was experiencing firsthand, and he compared it again to that of his own lineage. Many generations ago, his own clan had included a father and son who were samurai in feudal Japan; unlike Kang, however, their bloodline had survived to succeed them.

The *Ak'voh* song rose toward a thunderous finish, growing so loud that it seemed as if the Klingons were trying to be heard on the remains of Praxis, or perhaps even on the bridge of *Excelsior,* which currently orbited Qo'noS. He now heard numerous verses being shouted by numerous people, each layering over the others indecipherably as every mourner and warrior offered their own warnings or protections on behalf of the departed spirit.

Sulu found himself lost in the noise—and the emotions that propelled them—and began to sing himself, a *Banka* he had learned as a child, for the funeral of his great-grandmother. It was a Shinto blessing for the dead—a decidedly non-Klingon tradition—but it nevertheless seemed fitting to express the vicarious sorrow overflowing from his heart.

Once he was certain that they were alone, Curzon Dax finally decided to say what was on his mind. He suspected that he wasn't the only one present who harbored these thoughts, what with Captain Sulu here alongside the three Klingon captains. But none of them had spoken as yet of the threat their old adversary had once made.

"Kang, has anything further been learned of the cause of my godson's illness?"

The elder Klingon regarded Curzon for a moment with an inscrutable scowl before answering. "The physicians still have learned nothing. The disease is unlike anything they have encountered before."

Sulu cleared his throat. "If you'd permit me, it would honor me to take the medical records to some of the experts who work with me. With our resources, perhaps we can learn something your doctors overlooked."

Kang squinted, his bushy, upswept eyebrows and beady gaze giving the appearance of two exclamation marks. Curzon understood that Kang knew from bitter experience gained long before the Praxis explosion that there was no honor in declining Federation assistance simply out of pride. "I shall consider it, Hikaru Sulu."

Curzon waited to see if either Koloth or Kor were going to say something. When they didn't, he took the plunge. "Could this disease be the realization of the threat that the albino made against us all? He promised to one day avenge himself upon us through our children."

"That *petaQ*!" Kor spat out the words. "He does not have the spine to deliver on any such threat."

Again sparing a glance toward Kang to gauge his mood, Curzon pressed. "We all know he is a coward. And who better for a coward to strike at than those who are still unable to defend themselves?" He chose his words carefully, not wanting to upset Kang, especially after such a moving *Ak'voh* rite.

"Kang's son was struck down by an unknown disease that has no known antecedent, and no known cure," Curzon said. "From what I have heard, the disease's progression was so fast that it could *not* have been natural. And the fact that no other Klingon has been diagnosed with this disease leads to one possible conclusion: that this was a specific and targeted bioagent."

"'No other Klingon' is correct," Koloth said. "If this was an attack on Kang by the craven Qagh, then it should have been an attack on us *all*. But none of my children—or Kor's—have shown any signs of this malady, or any other."

"This tragedy may have arisen from the bite of some insect, crawled up through the ground from the bowels of *Gre'thor*," Kor said, his words carrying the embellishments of a storyteller. "Or it might have been the venom of some reptile, as yet undiscovered. The leap between this tragedy and the actions of a genetic throwback who is probably long dead is a far leap to make, Dax."

Curzon saw Kang wince almost imperceptibly at Kor's mention of Dax's symbiont name, which was phonetically identical to that of his deceased son. But he also saw a fire in the warrior's eyes, stoked by the fuel of Curzon's suggestion. Whether or not the albino *was* responsible for DaqS's death, the idea that he could be the architect of this disaster had obviously given Kang something at which he could focus his anger.

"Captain Sulu, has your Starfleet found any sign of the chalk-skinned Ha'DIbaH?" Kang asked, his voice so even and sharp that it could cut skin.

The human captain's brow furrowed. "To my knowledge, no one from Starfleet has encountered the albino since *we* faced him," he said. He shrugged his shoulders slightly, his crimson ceremonial uniform retaining its form and lines perfectly. "I'll immediately search our records to find out if there has been any recent news on the subject."

Koloth regarded Sulu, and Curzon was glad to see that the captain wasn't backing down at all in the face of the highly charged, angry atmosphere that had begun swirling about the Klingon assemblage.

"And what of *your* family, Captain Sulu? Have *your* children faced any unexpected dangers?" Koloth asked.

"I still have only the one daughter, Koloth," Sulu said. "She is, however, a fully grown woman now, and serves aboard another Starfleet vessel. I have not heard that she's faced anything other than the usual dangers of Starfleet service, but . . ." He hesitated a moment, then continued. "We have not spoken for quite some time."

"Your daughter follows your path, and yet you do not find that honorable?" Kang asked.

"It's more complicated than that," Sulu said.

"Family relations always are, Captain," Kang said gravely. "But I would give all I have to be able to watch *my* child honor *me*. Instead . . ." He didn't finish, but looked up toward the sky.

Curzon said nothing. Though the others assembled here today probably knew more about Kang than did anyone else in Starfleet or the Klingon Empire combined, they did *not* know every secret he harbored.

They certainly didn't know of the decision he had made five years ago, regarding the fleeing albino and his parting threats. . . .

Standing away from the others, Sulu opened his communicator. Its familiar chirping sound had long ago become a part of his workadáy environment, and he rarely gave it a second thought. In this windswept and emotional atmosphere, however, it sounded inappropriately bright and cheery.

"Sulu to *Excelsior.*"

A second passed, and then the voice of his longtime friend, Commander Pavel Chekov, issued from the device. *"Excelsior here, Captain. Is everything going . . . properly?"*

Sulu could tell that his executive officer had groped for a second to find the correct word, in case anyone else had happened to be within earshot. He was glad to have his old shipmate at his right hand aboard *Excelsior*, after the long succession of temporary first officers that had followed the departure of Lieutenant Commander Cutler.

"It's going as well as can be expected. I anticipate that the ambassador and I will be returning to the ship sometime in the next four to five hours, barring any unforeseen circumstances."

"Very good, Captain." Although his Russian accent was almost imperceptible these days, Chekov's "very" still sounded like "wary," and his "captain" came out closer to "keptin."

"Pavel, please ask Commander Rand to set up a remote subspace comlink to the *Enterprise*."

"Sir?"

"I need to speak to my daughter, Commander," Sulu said. Kang's words had stung him. Whatever had gone wrong between him and Demora, they still had time to fix it.

But just as importantly, he wanted to ascertain that Curzon's supposition was wrong. Other than Kang—if indeed the death of DaqS had been the work of Qagh—nobody among the quintet had experienced the brutality of the albino in quite the same manner as Sulu had. The memories were decades old, but the terror-stricken cries of Sulu's parents remained as fresh and loud as those of the mournful Klingons attending today's ceremonies.

"Captain, I have the Enterprise *for you on subspace."* That was the voice of Commander Janice Rand, another old *Enterprise* shipmate who now served on *Excelsior*. *"Captain Harriman is waiting to speak to you on channel B."*

"Thank you, Commander," Sulu said. "Please put him through."

"Hello, Hikaru," said John Harriman, Jr., his tone sub-

dued. *"It sounds like you're at a very noisy party. Can you talk away from the crowd?"*

"Hello, John," Sulu said. "It's actually a Klingon funeral." He walked several more paces away from the noise. "I apologize for the unorthodox communication, but something came up, and I didn't want to wait until I got back to the ship to contact you. Is my daughter available?"

Harriman took a bit too long to respond, and Sulu immediately knew that something was wrong.

"Hikaru, I'm sorry to—"

No. Don't say that, Sulu thought.

"—tell you that—"

Please. No. His knees felt weak.

"—Demora fell ill less than an hour ago. Doctor Michaels is doing everything he can, but he's never encountered anything like this before."

Not dead. Thank God.

"What are the symptoms, John?"

"It's not pretty, Hikaru. She's expelling liquids, her body is in some bizarre kind of twisted rigor. Doctor Michaels is keeping her as sedated as he can. I was going to call you as soon as we knew something definitive, but—"

"It may be a tailored bioweapon of some sort, targeted directly at her." Sulu nearly shouted into the communicator, interrupting the other man. "I need you to help me find out where and how she might have been exposed to it."

"A bioweapon?" Harriman sounded alarmed, and rightly so. *"What do you mean?"*

"I told you I'm at a Klingon funeral," Sulu said. "The decedent died of the same symptoms. And the one thing the Klingons and I have in common is an old enemy with a taste for biological terrorism."

He didn't want to even think it, but the words came into his mind unbidden.

Same results.

He shook his head violently, as if trying to dislodge the thought. *She's not dead. Demora's. Not. Dead.*

"Keep me updated, John," he said grimly. "And keep my daughter alive."

Before the other captain could respond, Sulu snapped the communicator shut, then sprinted toward Kor, Koloth, Kang, and Dax.

"Get your surviving children into medical isolation now," he blurted out to all of them as they looked at him questioningly. "They may be in danger."

But how could they stop the threat the albino had made half a decade earlier—especially if the threat had already been carried out?

Sulu felt his blood run cold.

PART I: DEATH AND LIFE

The woe's to come; the
children yet unborn
Shall feel this day as sharp to
them as thorn.

—William Shakespeare
(1564–1616);
Bishop of Carlisle,
Richard II, Act IV,
Scene I, Line 322

ONE

"The Lady Moj'ih grows impatient," Do'Yoj said brusquely. Her boots drumming an impatient rhythm against the stone floor as she walked, she ushered the two physicians down the dim corridor toward the sprawling villa's center, where its largest bedchamber lay.

The master bedchamber had become the sole domain of the Lady Moj'ih ever since her husband Ngoj had fallen in battle against the cursed *RomuluSngan* at Nequencia nearly four months ago. And since that unhappy time, the ornate room's tapestry-draped walls had come to mark the boundaries of the Lady's existence. Do'Yoj thought it had become a veritable throne room for her reclusive mistress, who was now the de facto head of the House of Ngoj, one of the few ruling matriarchs among the noble classes of Qo'noS.

And now, as the Lady Moj'ih's ever more complicated pregnancy advanced inexorably toward term, the chamber had become a prison in all but name.

"My apologies," said Hurghom, the taller of the two doctors, speaking a bit too obsequiously for Do'Yoj's taste as he came to a stop behind Do'Yoj just outside the heavy wooden bedchamber door. Was he mocking her? Or was he merely trying to adopt the tone most appropriate for a smooth-headed *QuchHa'* such as himself?

Dr. Nej, whose darker countenance contrasted sharply with Hurghom's owing to its prominent frame of cranial ridges, spoke a good deal more boldly.

"I am sure that the Lady Moj'ih will understand the reason for the delay," Nej said, raising to eye level the small black valise he clutched in his gnarled right hand, as if to emphasize his point. "The procedure we must undertake this day requires the utmost delicacy if we are to avoid bringing harm to the Lady's child."

"We have to be certain that we get this right in every detail," Hurghom said, his disturbingly smooth head bobbing in agreement with his colleague's words. "I'm sure you will agree that much is at stake. And what is at stake is nothing less than a male heir to the House of Ngoj."

A future patriarch of this noble House, Do'Yoj thought with no small amount of resentment. *An heir who will doubtless have as much to conceal as his parents did, if he is to maintain this House's power and prestige.*

Answering Hurghom with only a tart scowl, Do'Yoj turned and pushed on the door with her shoulder, leaning into its superbly balanced bulk so that it began to move smoothly and silently inward on its well-oiled duranium hinges.

The room beyond the threshold was dark, shrouding its sole occupant in gloom. Do'Yoj entered and stepped to the side, allowing the physicians to waste no further time before converging upon the large bed that was mounted on the raised dais in the center of the room. Do'Yoj wasn't entirely sure that the Lady Moj'ih was actually *in* the bed until she

spoke, her rounded belly moving noticeably beneath the
tangle of bedclothes.

"What is the reason for your tardiness?" the Lady said,
addressing both physicians in an imperious tone suited to
a woman of noble breeding. Do'Yoj thought it was a tone
suited to one born to the birthright of the *HemQuch,* those
who, unlike Dr. Hurghom, possessed the cranial ridges that
had been the genetic patrimony of every Klingon, from the
boldest warrior to the humblest tiller of the soil, since long
before the time of the unforgettable Kahless.

Do'Yoj, of course, knew the real truth behind the Lady's
brave façade. As the Lady Moj'ih's most trusted personal
retainer, there was no way that Do'Yoj could ignore the
fact that her haughty, proud-visaged mistress was actually
just as smooth-browed—and thus every bit as disgracefully
QuchHa'—as Dr. Hurghom and his ancestors. Do'Yoj was
all too aware that the Lady's striking brow ridges, scarcely
visible in the room's dim light, were prosthetic fakes. They
were biosynthetic implants—which required frequent cosmetic maintenance, despite having been surgically attached
to her skull—and had been used covertly by members of
the influential House of Ngoj ever since the Great Qu'Vat
Plague of 1462, a disaster that lay more than half a century
in the past.

*Maintaining the noble deception with sufficient care
from day to day is becoming too taxing for the Lady in
her current condition,* Do'Yoj thought, blending invisibly
into the blood-hued tapestries as she watched her mistress
begin conferring with her physicians, one of whom applied
a moist towel to her forehead, which the Lady held in place
with her hand, covering up her false brow ridges. If the Lady
Moj'ih would not trust even Do'Yoj to see to the upkeep of
her prosthetic forehead—perhaps she was unwilling to appear vulnerable before a social inferior whose own natural
cranial appurtenances marked her as one of the Lady's

biological betters—then it was unsurprising that Moj'ih had opted to hide her chronic shame using both a towel and a shroud of darkness.

"We came as quickly as we could, My Lady," Dr. Nej said, matching the Lady Moj'ih's brittle tones with the no-nonsense manner of a senior physician who was used to receiving more deference from his patients—even the noble ones.

Perhaps, Do'Yoj thought, *this is because he, too, knows the truth that the Lady must keep concealed at all costs.*

"The procedure we must undertake has not received extensive testing prior to today," said Hurghom, again speaking in that placating manner that Do'Yoj found so very irritating. "We had to be as certain as possible of the outcome before proceeding with the final phase of the child's genetic alterations. Especially in light of . . . the unfortunate occurrence not so very long ago on Qu'Vat."

"I should think you would be the last one to remind anyone of your failure at Qu'Vat," Moj'ih said, the moist, sharpened points of her bared teeth glinting in the room's scant light.

Though she remained standing in silence at the room's periphery, Do'Yoj was inclined to agree. How many had died on the Qu'Vat colony during Hurghom's most recent attempt to rid the Klingon people of the Earther genetic baggage with which his ancestor Antaak had saddled them during the previous century? The death toll had to be in the tens of thousands, at least. That many *QuchHa'* had died in the space of a single afternoon, the shame of their Earther-smooth foreheads—the tragic, so-far-indelible mark with which Antaak had imprinted their forebears decades earlier in the process of saving them from the Levodian plague—compounded with the shame of being denied entry into *Sto-Vo-Kor* through a warrior's honorable death in battle.

Do'Yoj reflected that Hurghom's failure could have been far worse. After all, the doctor's ancestor Antaak had inadvertently killed *millions* during his own attempts to rid the Klingon genome of the Earther taint he had inflicted upon it decades ago.

"Wisdom comes from experience," Dr. Hurghom replied in a meek voice.

"Just as experience may come from foolish errors," Nej added with an audible sneer as he set his black valise upon the foot of Moj'ih's bed and opened it. He withdrew a wicked-looking, almost *mek'leth*-sized device that Do'Yoj assumed was a hypodermic needle, along with a small handheld scanning device.

"My Lady, can we get some light in here now?" Nej said, displaying his instruments as best he could in the room's inadequate illumination. "Then we can get on with the task ridding the next head of the House of Ngoj of the consequences of Antaak's so-called cure."

Responding to a nod from her mistress, Do'Yoj moved toward the lighting controls in the chamber's southeast corner and brightened the room.

She watched in silence as Nej slowly pulled back the bedclothes, raised the needle, and leaned toward the Lady Moj'ih.

2218 (the Year of Kahless 844,
late in the month of *Merruthj*)

Qo'noS

Another contraction came, this one striking a few heartbeats sooner than the Lady Moj'ih had expected. The pain lanced through her insides like a *bat'leth* blade still white-hot from the forge. She cried out, her agony giving way to shame at her weakness, as well as to a momentary gratitude to the heedless fates that Ngoj could not be present to witness her disgrace.

She lay back and bit down on her lip until it bled freely. *Only a little longer,* she told herself yet again, continuing to repeat the phrase endlessly in her mind, like a monk performing meditation mantras in one of Boreth's monasteries.

"Keep pushing, my Lady," said the ever-loyal Do'Yoj, who was standing beside her, clutching her hand. Moj'ih clutched back nearly hard enough to shatter every bone in the handmaiden's stout forearm.

Lady Moj'ih did as her handmaiden bid her. *I can accept a smooth-headed child if I must,* she thought, acknowledging the peace she'd had to make with the high likelihood that Hurghom and Nej's retrogenetic efforts would prove to be a failure once her infant finally emerged. There was an argument to be made, after all, that the curse of being *QuchHa'* had toughened her House, forcing its members to cultivate strengths lacked even by many of their *HemQuch* cousins.

Moj'ih was well aware, after all, that the hereditary handicap that she and Ngoj shared—a trait that he had never hidden beneath prosthetics, as she had—had motivated her late husband to achieve the much-sought-after military rank of *HoD*. It had also pushed him to achieve command of the *I.K.S. Ghobchuq* and its highly heterogeneous crew—the cruiser had carried a mixed complement of both *QuchHa'* and *HemQuch*—and to retain that post for more than a decade.

Do'Yoj, by contrast, had remained for years in a servile position within the House of Ngoj, despite being a *HemQuch* with relatively easier access to the higher social classes than most smooth-headed Klingons enjoyed. Hurghom, likewise, had doubtless had to work extremely hard to stay in the same societal sphere as his colleague Nej.

The flame that burns in every Klingon's heart is all that

counts, she reminded herself, swallowing her pain as she gathered her concentration and bore down for yet another hard push. *Ngoj was as brave as any ten* HemQuch.

"I can see the top of the child's head," Dr. Hurghom said.

Moj'ih drew some solace from that, although her awkward supine posture prevented her from seeing what was right before her physicians' eyes. However this problematic pregnancy turned out, she was certain now that the worst of the waiting was finally over; very soon, she would know whether her child, the only piece of her dead, beloved Ngoj that still endured, bore the proud sagittal crest that was the birthright of the Klingon race.

Or if the infant's painstaking genetic alterations had failed, forcing her to decide whether or not to order her surgeons to attempt to disguise his smooth-headed *QuchHa'* status.

"Well?" demanded the Lady Moj'ih. Despite the hoarseness engendered by her endless hours of labor, she all but screamed her impatience.

The doctors said nothing for a protracted moment. Moj'ih was about to snarl an imprecation at them when she noticed that Do'Yoj had released her hand, no doubt preparing to catch the child that was still struggling to complete the arduous passage from womb to world. Then another fiery contraction tore through Moj'ih's insides, blinding her with agony and rendering her momentarily speechless.

No smooth-headed QuchHa' *child could cause such agony,* Moj'ih thought, drawing hope from her pain.

"The child does indeed have a pronounced crest," Moj'ih finally heard Hurghom say at length, though haltingly. Relief stirred within her nonetheless, slaking the fiery pain of the birthing bed, at least a little.

Perhaps those interminable retroviral gene therapy treatments had actually worked!

Moj'ih kept her eyes tightly shut as another contraction came and went. She bore this one better than she had the previous ones, and her spirits lifted further still when she heard the keening wail of the infant she had been carrying for a seeming eternity.

"A boy. I don't like his coloration, though," Moj'ih heard Nej say in his customary blunt fashion. "Perhaps the child is anemic."

Moj'ih opened her eyes and saw Do'Yoj rising from where she had been crouching at the edge of the unyielding birthing bed. She noticed the stricken look on her handmaiden's face before her gaze was drawn irresistibly down to the small, squirming bundle that the young woman carried before her.

A tiny, chalk-white form partially wrapped in a small, coarse birthing blanket.

Never having given birth before, Moj'ih wasn't quite sure what she had expected to feel for the child when she finally laid eyes upon it for the first time. Nevertheless, she had always entertained the vague notion that an emotional bond of some sort would form very quickly, despite the birthing ordeal. But being somewhat unsentimental by nature, she wasn't all that surprised to note that she felt no such bond.

What she *hadn't* expected was the overwhelming sense of revulsion she was experiencing. It felt almost like hatred at first sight, as though a deep and fundamental instinct at the very core of her being was warning her that something was terribly wrong with this child.

Crest or no, this child is no Klingon.

Do'Yoj bent down and tried to hand Moj'ih the sickly-looking child.

Moj'ih used what remained of her depleted reserves of strength to push her handmaiden away, nearly causing the younger woman to drop the infant onto the flagstone floor.

She ignored the horrified looks she saw crease the faces of
both Do'Yoj and Hurghom.

Nej merely nodded to her. He, at least, appeared to
understand. Whether this child was Moj'ih's only living link
to Ngoj or not, she could never allow such an un-Klingon
abomination to be a part of her House, much less its only
male heir and eventual patriarch. Better he had been born
with an Earther's smooth forehead, a *QuchHa'* as she and
Ngoj had always been. Better she had never tried to tamper
with whatever random forces governed such things.

She threw back her head, filled her lungs, and issued a
cry of grief and fury that she hoped Ngoj's soul would hear
in far-off *Sto-Vo-Kor*.

"I take it the Lady Moj'ih has not changed her mind,"
Do'Yoj said gravely. She still held the infant, which mewled
weakly in her arms.

Hurghom pushed the bedchamber door closed behind
him and stepped farther into the hallway, as though concerned that the Lady might overhear him. He nodded to
Do'Yoj, his mouth fixed in a grim slash. "She has not."

"Then the task falls to me," the handmaiden said. She adjusted the baby boy's blanket, wrapping him more securely.
She adjusted the metal clasp to hold the blanket in place.

She wondered why she was bothering to see to the
child's comfort at all. Very soon, the infant would be beyond
all such concerns.

"I will do what tradition demands," said the handmaiden,
speaking the words that custom and her job required of
her. She suppressed a brief surge of contempt for the Lady
Moj'ih, who really ought to have disposed of her own genetic
refuse, her current depleted condition notwithstanding.

"The Lady instructed me to give you this," Hurghom said
as he produced a gleaming, long-bladed *d'k tahg* from his
belt. He presented the blade to her, haft-first.

She took it with one hand, holding the restless baby with the other as she tucked the blade into the sash she wore beneath her cloak. Then she fixed Hurghom with a hard stare.

"Did the Lady specify where the deed is to be done?"

Hurghom shook his head again. "She has decided to leave that to your discretion, so long as you do nothing to compromise *her* discretion."

Of course, the handmaiden thought. *As far as anyone else on Qo'noS knows, this House's genes are among the strongest and purest in the Empire. It wouldn't do to leave behind a dead infant that proves otherwise.*

Again, she experienced a flash of hatred for her employer.

"You may take as long as you require to carry out the Lady's wishes," Hurghom said quietly.

Do'Yoj nodded, quietly considering her options for a lengthy moment.

Finally, she arrived at a decision.

"Very well, then."

Holding the infant as though it were a hair-trigger piece of ordnance that might detonate at any moment, Do'Yoj turned away from the physician and strode purposefully toward the villa's front door.

Do'Yoj clutched the crying, squirming infant in her left hand and held the long blade aloft in her right. Laying the blanket open with the *d'k tahg*'s gleaming tip, she placed the edge against the baby boy's throat and opened the weapon's spring-loaded side-blades. The child screamed and instinctively drew back from the cold metal, windmilling its tiny arms as it wailed its terror and discomfort. Several tiny drops of bright blood appeared where the child's throat had been slightly nicked; they had also spattered the blade's keen edges.

This is Klingon blood. Innocent *Klingon blood.*

Windblown, powdery snow nearly as white as the child's skin crunched under Do'Yoj's *targ*-skin boots as she drew the blade back, despising herself for what she had agreed to do. Shivering in the cold, she glanced up in time to see the hired flyer that had brought her to this remote mountainside arc overhead on the way to its next destination. It would be back for her within the hour, its pilot having been paid handsomely to reappear when necessary and to ask no questions.

There would be ample time to do what needed to be done. The only question that remained was whether or not she really ought to do the deed.

The Lady Moj'ih should have had the courage to do this herself. I shouldn't have to do the dirty work of a cowardly QuchHa', one who rightfully ought to be beneath my station.

Do'Yoj came to another decision. She allowed the knife to fall from her cold-numbed fingertips and watched it land point-first in the snow that lay piled at her feet. Then she set the wailing child, blanket and all, down in the snow a few paces away.

If a House as unworthy as that of Ngoj can be allowed to wield power over HemQuch, then why shouldn't a weakling child be allowed even the smallest chance to survive and succeed?

Now unencumbered, she reached into her cloak and removed a small audio communications device from her belt. After she withdrew far enough from the child to be certain that her comm's microphone wouldn't pick up his forlorn cries, she entered the Lady Moj'ih's personal comm frequency into its keypad.

"Do'Yoj." The Lady sounded angry, but Do'Yoj had long ago grown used to that.

"Here, my Lady."

"It's been hours."

"I needed to find a sufficiently remote place to . . . dispose of the remains."

The Lady paused long enough to make Do'Yoj wonder whether her comm signal had been interrupted.

"Then it is done?" the Lady asked finally.

Do'Yoj eyed the bundle that now lay some twenty meters away from her in the snowy wastes. The wind was gathering force, and the child's cries were now all but inaudible. She wondered idly whether the weakling infant would succumb to the cold before becoming a meal for a sabre bear or some other alpine predator.

"I have finished," Do'Yoj lied, though she supposed her prevarication would come true soon enough.

Do'Yoj thought she heard a slight catch in her mistress's breathing, though she supposed it might have simply been her imagination at work; still, she could scarcely imagine being so cowardly and dishonorable as to kill anyone by proxy.

Especially a helpless infant.

"Well done, Do'Yoj," the Lady Moj'ih said at length before signing off, leaving Do'Yoj alone except for the company of the snow, the chill wind, and the weakling baby's distant, fading cries.

The QuchHa' *House of Ngoj wields power over* HemQuch *only because almost no* HemQuch *know that the Lady Moj'ih is really* QuchHa', *and has been hiding that fact all her life.* In that instant she made yet another decision, one that she had been considering for years.

She entered another frequency into her comm, one that was used by one of the House of Ngoj's most bitter rivals on the High Council.

Within moments, an aide answered. "This is Do'Yoj, personal assistant to the Lady Moj'ih," Do'Yoj said. "Please put me through to Councillor Sturka."

"Sturka is in a Council session presently," the aide said imperiously.

"Summon him," Do'Yoj said, in the same tone that the Lady Moj'ih so often used. She began walking farther away from the infant, which was already dead to her. "I have information about the House of Ngoj that Sturka will be extremely grateful to receive. . . ."

Ganik quickly shook the snow off his boots in the landing craft's airlock, then hastily made his way aft, carrying his almost insubstantial burden toward his employer's small berth. He worked hard to suppress a mischievous grin as he handed the snow-crusted bundle of blankets to D'Jinnea, his employer. Although she nearly dropped the thing in surprise when she saw what it was, the green-skinned Orion free-booter chieftainess regained her composure almost instantly, holding the bundle before her as though she thought it might explode if mishandled.

"Why have you just handed me a dead baby, Ganik?" D'Jinnea said at length.

Ganik's grin broke partially free of its restraints. "Aren't you more interested in *where* it came from, D'Jinnea?"

"I prefer to solve one mystery at a time," the tall, broad-shouldered woman said. She was clearly nettled, but just as obviously curious as well. "But just taking a wild guess, I'd imagine you found this poor waif buried in the snow some-where outside the ship."

"Actually, a local trader found it," he said, folding his muscular, deep-green arms across his massive chest. "One of the mountain dwellers who looks too much like an Earther to make a legitimate living down in the First City, or anyplace else for that matter." He didn't need to remind her how valuable such folks were to the Orion Syndicate's itinerant trade, both legal and illicit, throughout Klingon space and beyond. The Orions couldn't care less about brow ridges or their absence; all that mattered was the trade, and the profit that came with it.

D'Jinnea's brow furrowed, a mannerism that Ganik found downright alluring, at least when she didn't have a hand laser within reach. "Don't tell me you paid good money for a dead baby."

Ganik shook his head. "Not for the *baby*. For what he's carrying. Look at the metal clasp on the child's blanket."

Holding the dead infant with one hand, D'Jinnea used her other hand to rummage carefully through the tangle of blankets that had swaddled it. Her scowl softened when she revealed a palm-sized, irregularly shaped piece of tempered *bat'leth* metal, which gleamed in the chamber's actinic blue lights as she turned it slowly from side to side.

She cast her gaze again squarely upon Ganik, her deep sea-green eyes widened in pleased surprise. "Do you recognize the pattern etched into this metal?"

Ganik nodded again. "The *tuq Degh* of a noble Klingon House."

"The family crest of the House of Ngoj," D'Jinnea said.

"One of the more influential Houses. They have a great deal of pull on the High Council. And in determining which forms of commerce are considered legitimate, and which are interdicted."

Ganik could see the flames of avarice becoming stoked behind her eyes. He felt much the same way. *There has to be some way to use this discovery to gain leverage over the House of Ngoj*, he thought.

Sobriety abruptly returned to her gaze. "The child would have proved more valuable to us if you'd found him before he'd frozen to death."

"I *didn't* find him," Ganik reminded her. "He was *brought* to me this way, remember?"

"Regardless. A living heir to the House of Ngoj could have been quite useful."

Ganik chuckled. "I can see it now. We might have adopted him."

"Or at least raised him to adulthood," D'Jinnea said. "Who knows? He might one day have provided me—

provided *us*—with the front door key to the House from which he came."

And access to all the wealth and power accorded an heir to the House of Ngoj, thought Ganik.

He moved closer to D'Jinnea so that he could get a better look at the exposed portions of the dead child's face. He could see the infant's chalk-white forehead, which was striated by a series of horizontal lines. But the little creature's cranial texture didn't strike him as particularly Klingon-looking, and neither did its skin coloration.

"We might even have found an appropriately Klingon name for him," Ganik said.

D'Jinnea offered him a somewhat sad smile, apparently willing to permit her lieutenant's bantering tone. "You have a name in mind?"

In fact, a Klingon name *had* just occurred to him. "How about 'Qagh'? It's from a Klingon word that means 'mistake.' "

"That name would have worked as well as any," she said, growing abruptly serious once more. "But it's a moot point now. He was obviously a sickly weakling, after all. And you know how the Klingons feel about the sick and the weak."

"The House of Ngoj has evidently dumped its genetic trash on our doorstep," said Ganik.

"Please dispose of it properly," she said, handing the bundle back to him.

He nodded, then turned toward the narrow hatchway that led out of D'Jinnea's berth.

The contents of the blanket shifted before he got all the way through the hatchway. Ganik stopped in his tracks, wondering if he or D'Jinnea had somehow undone the clasp that secured the blanket around the small corpse as he gathered up the blanket's edges so as not to spill the tiny albino corpse onto the landing craft's deck.

Now completely concealed by the blanket, the slight weight inside the bundle shifted again.

This time it also made a muffled cry.

He turned back toward D'Jinnea, whose look of intense surprise told him that she, too, had heard the noise.

This unlucky little waif simply won't accept death, Ganik thought. *Perhaps he really* is *a Klingon, in spite of appearances.*

Ganik cleared his throat awkwardly, a predator's grin creeping across his emerald features. "D'Jinnea, about that adoption idea . . ."

TWO

Stardate 8988.2 (Late 2289)

U.S.S. Excelsior

This damned thing came apart easily enough, Sulu thought, regarding with mounting frustration the small pile of ODN components that was spread between his elbows. *So why is putting it all back together again turning into such a pain in the stern?*

Then he heard Lieutenant Commander Meredith Cutler's acid-tinged voice before he'd even noticed that she had entered the room. "If you don't mind my asking, Commander," Cutler said in a tone pitched barely north of insubordination, "why didn't you delegate this job to Chief Engineer Lahra, or somebody on her staff?"

Taking care not to scatter his tool kit or the array of delicate helm relay components he'd just taken apart, Sulu grabbed his dynospanner and set his boots on the bulkhead-mounted ladder. Then he quickly climbed down from the narrow ceiling-access panel into which he had partially crawled.

I'd be within my rights to bite her head clean off, he thought, straightening his uniform tunic as he turned to face the sharp-featured, fortyish woman. But even though Cutler was only second officer—and therefore his subordinate—Sulu knew better than to go out of his way to antagonize her. It would be more prudent to keep trying to get on friendlier terms with her, not only because she was *Excelsior*'s chief of security, but also because of her status as a longtime personal friend of Captain Lawrence Styles.

He swallowed his pride for the moment and smiled broadly—and was immediately gratified to see that his expression seemed to infuriate her. "It's late, Ms. Cutler," he said. "Lieutenant Commander Lahra is usually off duty during the gamma watch, unless something really dire is happening to her engines."

"I guess I just don't understand why *Excelsior*'s first officer would want to be belowdecks crawling around in the Jefferies tubes in the middle of the night," she said, brushing a stray blond hair away from her eyes.

"So you're concerned that I'm doing work that's beneath my dignity?" His smile broadened. *Or maybe you're just worried that I might show you up in front of the captain,* he thought. *That might explain why* you're *up all hours prowling the bowels of the ship.*

She reddened. "I simply meant that Chief Engineer Lahra could have assigned Tim Henry or one of the junior engineers to rebuild the main navigational deflector."

"True enough," he said with a shrug. "But since this project is mainly going to affect helm efficiency, I thought it best to see to it myself, and Commander Lahra agreed. Why are you so interested, by the way? Aren't you supposed to be off duty at this hour?"

Her lips curled into a thin, humorless smile. "A chief of security is never *really* off duty, Commander. Particularly when she notices that somebody is down on deck fifteen opening up navigational deflector access panels in the dead of night when none of the authorized engineering personnel are present." He wondered if she might not be making a backhanded swipe at Captain Scott's surreptitious sabotage of *Excelsior*'s transwarp computer drive a few years earlier.

Well, you're nothing if not "by the book," Cutler, he thought, not permitting his smile to falter. "I appreciate your diligence," he said aloud, bowing his head slightly. "Next time I'll see to it that Chief Lahra sends you the signed paperwork in advance. And in triplicate."

Cutler's mien soured further, and she appeared to have to restrain herself from saying something caustic in response to Sulu's gentle barb. After a brief pause during which she evidently decided she had already pushed *Excelsior*'s first officer as far as she dared, she said, "That's all I ask, Commander." And with that, she turned on her heel and strode purposefully out into the corridor that lay beyond the nearest exit.

A familiar voice chose that moment to make its owner's presence known, startling him into nearly dropping the dynospanner he still clutched in his right hand.

"Don't worry about her, Hikaru. I think Cutler's always been a bit of a hard-ass. Captain Styles seems to see that as a good thing."

Grinning, he turned toward the source of the voice. "Janice! You shouldn't sneak up on me like that. I'm a trained martial artist, remember?"

Commander Janice Rand returned his smile with interest. "I remember. And a botanist, a physicist, a fencer, and a collector of exotic weapons. So what *is* a man with so many varied facets doing skulking around in a starship's underbelly in the middle of the night?"

Sulu frowned as he realized that Rand was essentially restating the second officer's question. "Looks like Cutler's not the only one who's been keeping tabs on me. You moonlighting in security now?"

She scoffed. "Running the communications department

keeps my hands a bit too full for that. But it also allows me to look around corners for my friends, as long as I'm discreet about it."

"So I guess I've been around here long enough for you to see that it isn't a very good idea to be seen talking to me."

"That's why coming down here during the graveyard shift seemed like a better idea than sharing breakfast with you in the crew mess. Styles and Cutler both don't seem to be huge fans of *Enterprise* alumni—especially senior officers."

A resigned sigh escaped from him, sounding in his own ears like atmosphere venting from a ruptured hull. "If you came down here in the middle of the night to warn me about *that,* then you're about three weeks too late. I figured it out for myself when I first came aboard."

"Actually, I came down because I overheard Cutler sharpening her knives a little while ago. I wanted to warn you that she might give you a hard time about your midnight maintenance work." Rand paused, and a sheepish look crossed her face. "Looks like I got here a bit too late. Sorry, Hikaru."

He offered her a small smile that he hoped she would find reassuring. "Thanks for making the effort, Janice. So do you think the captain and Cutler have it in for you, too?"

She shook her head again. "I'm not quite sure yet, which is why I wanted to see you in person instead of warning you in a way that would leave a trail on the comm grid."

Sulu grinned. "Sneaky."

"No more so than Cutler," she said, shrugging as she matched his grin. "Anyway, Cutler *has* made it pretty clear to me that she doesn't like anyone that the *captain* doesn't like. And I know that he hasn't exactly been the president of the James Kirk Admiration Society for quite a few years now. *Especially* since that little Mutara Sector caper back in 'eighty-five."

Sulu remembered that "caper" very well indeed. Outfitted with the first field-practical transwarp drive system,

Excelsior and her crew had been poised to break every warp-speed record right out of Spacedock, thereby assuring her captain an honored place in Starfleet history. *Excelsior* had also been promised to Sulu, whose promotion from the rank of commander to captain—and whose orders to assume command of this wondrous if still experimental starship, the first of her class—had been signed by Admiral James Kirk himself.

But fate, the unauthorized mission to recover Captain Spock, and an invasion by a superpowerful alien probe all had conspired to derail Sulu's plans for starship command. Sulu harbored no regrets about his participation in those events. After all, the actions of Kirk and his officers had literally saved Earth, a fact that allowed Sulu and his friends to essentially escape official punishment for multiple acts of insubordination, sabotage, assault, theft of Starfleet property—and the destruction of the *Enterprise*. Command might have come down on them a lot harder if it hadn't been for the intercession of a grateful Federation President, but they hadn't gotten through it entirely unscathed; Jim Kirk had been demoted, and Sulu's anticipated promotion was suspended indefinitely.

Nor, evidently, had Lawrence Styles forgotten the humiliation he must have felt when *Excelsior*'s transwarp-driven "hot pursuit" of the renegade *Enterprise* crew had failed so completely, as had the entire transwarp drive project itself. And when Admiral Smillie had signed the orders that most recently aborted Sulu's incipient captaincy of *Excelsior*—and assigned him instead to the starship's first officer position—Styles had made it abundantly clear that he wasn't happy with Starfleet's decision to saddle him with a second-in-command whose very presence served as a constant reminder of old humiliations.

"Maybe I've escaped the captain's wrath so far because he doesn't associate me with Captain Kirk," Rand said, dispersing Sulu's reverie. "After all, it's been a long time since I served on the *Enterprise,* and I didn't stay there anywhere near as long as you did."

"Lucky for you, I guess," Sulu said glumly. "Still, I suppose Captain Styles has his reasons for not warming up to me, even if they're completely wrongheaded. But I just don't understand why *Cutler* has such an ax to grind against me. I mean, she wasn't even serving aboard *Excelsior* when we pulled our, ah, stunt at Spacedock."

"I'm no psychologist," Rand said, "but her motivation seems straightforward enough to me."

"Then that makes one of us."

She scowled at him as though he were an obtuse cadet trainee. "Captain Styles was about to promote her to executive officer before Starfleet overruled him and stuck you into the job."

Now all the unpleasantness of the past three weeks was finally beginning to make sense, though he still preferred to find a solution to the problem other than simply pulling rank on Cutler. "I suppose I can't blame her for feeling slighted," he said. "Especially since she's lost out to someone who nearly succeeded in grabbing the center seat away from Lawrence Styles."

"Not once, but *twice,*" Rand said, grinning.

Sulu sighed and shook his head in bemusement. "Starfleet has really got to start sending psychotherapists out into deep space with starship crews."

Rand nodded. "I guess in the meantime we'll just have to content ourselves with obsessive nocturnal work sessions."

"Well, there's no better distraction from bad situations than hard work," Sulu said, quoting his great-grandfather Inomata's thoughts on the subject as he raised his dynospanner to emphasize his point. He was determined not to let himself despair over his current circumstances. "Speaking of which, I'd better get these control modules back in place before the secondary nav deflector ruins our day by smacking us into an asteroid. I wouldn't want to give Captain Styles or Commander Cutler a *real* reason not to like me."

She looked at the dynospanner and shuddered theatrically. "Next time you feel the need for 'hard work therapy,' I'd suggest you do it up in the gym," she said as she moved toward the same exit Cutler had used. "Fencing is a whole lot less frustrating than reinitializing computer modules."

Alone again, he climbed back up the ladder. As he gloomily surveyed the farrago of tools and equipment he had left piled up inside the Jefferies tube, Sulu couldn't help but agree with his old friend.

THREE

Although he had served aboard *Excelsior* for less than a month, and therefore didn't yet feel any urgent need to take shore leave, a large portion of the crew had disembarked at Galdonterre, and Sulu had joined them.

Though he didn't feel particularly exhausted by his new duties, it was a welcome diversion. He still felt ill at ease around both Captain Styles and Lieutenant Commander Cutler—especially in light of his conversation with Janice Rand yesterday—but sharing some downtime with a handful of his other *Excelsior* crewmates was definitely helping to nurture his sense of camaraderie.

He learned, for instance, that junior science officer Lieutenant Christina Schulman had a knack for haggling over the prices of the various artworks offered for sale in the city's vast open-air marketplace, and that she showed a distinct preference for items carved from trees or other organic materials as opposed to those rendered in stone or metal. Lieutenant (J.G.) Eric Braun, another member of the science crew, was apparently something of an unintentional mimic; he had picked up the accent of the locals after spending only a few minutes among them, and was now drawling his *o*'s and slurring his sibilant consonants. And transporter chief Darnell Renyck was definitely the life of the party when not on duty.

It was Renyck who had picked the bar in which Sulu's group was currently encamped, and though it was seedier than Sulu would have preferred, it didn't seem to be an overly dangerous place—if one wasn't too put off by the dozen or so noisy, heavily imbibing Klingon soldiers who were mixed in among the establishment's extraordinarily diverse nonhuman clientele. Of course, the presence of so many Klingons was hardly surprising on a world that lay on the border between the ragged edge of Federation space and territory controlled by the Klingon Empire. Thankfully, the Klingons were mostly keeping to themselves in the upper level of the bar, even though their raucous laughter, shouts, and boasts were still clearly audible just about everywhere in the building.

Sulu approached the bar to order a round of drinks for the quintet who shared his table. Schulman wanted something called a Blazing Sunburst, as did her friend, Lieutenant Heather Keith, while Braun, whose nickname at the Academy had apparently been Flyweight, wanted only a single dark beer. Lieutenant Dmitri Valtane and Renyck had more expensive tastes, opting for the Romulan ale that was still illegal on all worlds located closer to the core of Federation space. Sulu wasn't overly concerned with the cost of the drinks, however, since Starfleet provided a more than adequate stipend to officers who took their shore leaves on planets with cash-based economies.

The bartender—a gigantic being whose gender wasn't easily ascertainable—took Sulu's drink order with a grunt and busied itself pouring the concoctions with its six tattoo-covered, azure-tinted arms. Looking around the bar while he waited, Sulu found his attention drawn to a side door, through which a female humanoid had just finished making a rather unsteady and halting entrance.

Though Sulu wasn't immediately familiar with the young woman's species, her body language wasn't at all difficult to understand. Sulu watched her peer furtively about the barroom, as though fearful of whom she might encounter here. She approached the bar, turning directly toward him as she lumbered forward. Her gaze locked for a moment with Sulu's before she backed away apprehensively, melting into the shadows of the booths in the rear of the tavern.

"Yurrr drinkshhup," Sulu heard behind him, and he turned to see that the bartender had loaded the drinks onto a slotted carrier tray, which it set down with surprising grace onto the bar.

"Thank you," Sulu said as he handed the huge mixologist a wad of credit notes. The creature swiftly distributed the bills into its multiple hands and studied them for a moment before shoving them into a pouch located on the front of its shapeless, drink-spattered garment. Since the barkeep didn't glare at him—it turned away instead to help another customer—Sulu assumed that either he had tipped appropriately or he had just been cheated out of his change.

As Sulu moved back to the table, tray in hand, Renyck stood up and held his beefy arms out to grab for the drinks. "Three cheers for the commander," the transporter chief said pleasantly, his eyes widening to match his grin as he caught sight of the pale blue Romulan ale, which was only quasi-legal at best, even in this part of the galaxy. "And for his discretion!"

The others took their drinks and raised them in a salute, exclaiming "Here, here," and "To Commander Sulu."

Smiling at the good cheer being directed his way, Sulu pulled out his chair. Before he could sit, however, a sudden movement at the edge of his vision caught his attention.

Turning toward the motion, he noticed the unsteady humanoid woman again. Despite the low illumination in the room, he could see that she was staring directly at him as she swayed slowly back and forth, wobbling and trembling as though caught in the grip of a delirium. If not for the unoccupied table she was using to steady herself, she might have fallen.

"Looks like you have an admirer, Commander," Renyck said, grinning and gesturing toward the woman, whom he apparently hadn't studied quite as carefully as Sulu had. The woman responded by withdrawing again into the darkness that marked the room's shadowy margins.

"I noticed her a little earlier," Sulu said quietly. "Something's wrong with her."

"She looks more sick than drunk to me," Braun said, squinting as he looked over his shoulder. "Though I suppose I don't know what passes for normal for her species."

Still standing, Sulu pushed his chair back up to the table. "I'm going to see if she needs any help," he said to no one in particular.

"You want us with you, Commander?" Valtane asked, appearing ready to spring from his own chair.

Sulu held up his hand in an *as-you-were* gesture. "I'll let you know if I need any backup. Just don't let that ale knock you out."

The woman held Sulu's gaze as he moved toward her, though she stumbled backward into a dark alcove behind the table she had been using as a crutch. As he approached, taking care to remain in the direct line of sight of his fellow officers, the woman sat down awkwardly on a bench in the corner. Sulu helped to steady her as she propped herself up against the rough block-and-mortar wall behind her.

"You seemed to be trying to get my attention," Sulu said softly as he sat beside her on the bench. Though he effectively stood between her and the nearest exit, she exhibited no further desire to run or hide. Sulu couldn't tell whether this was a sign of trust, resignation, or simple fatigue.

"Is there something I can do to help you?" he said.

She merely stared at him with dull, unfocused eyes, and despite the low lighting Sulu could see clearly that she was indeed in dire need of help. Although he knew no more than Braun did about what passed for normal for members of her species, her tremors and profuse perspiration had to be pathological. Sweat was collecting quickly in the small stack of horizontal ridges that covered the bridge of her nose, and had begun to run like a small waterfall down her aquiline nose, spilling in fat droplets onto the barroom floor.

"You need medical attention," Sulu said. "Let me get you some help."

Her gaze focused upon him again. "It won't make any difference," she said with vocal cords that sounded as dry as kindling. "The virus has already gone too far, you see." She chuckled, then coughed.

"Let's see what Doctor Klass has to say about that." Sulu reached for his communicator and flipped it open.

She reached out with surprising strength and speed, seizing Sulu's hand and forcing the communicator's grid back down into the closed position. "It's already too late for me," she said. "But you can stop him. He *has* to be stopped."

Gently but firmly, Sulu disengaged his hand from her iron grip, pulling the communicator out of her grasp. Her hands felt cold and rough, like granite carvings spattered with icy rain. He felt chilled to his core, though he wasn't sure whether the woman's touch or the obvious nearness of death was responsible.

"*Who* has to be stopped?" Sulu said.

"The man who has forced me to . . . serve him," she said haltingly, her eyes turning alternately bright and dim as though she were struggling to maintain consciousness. "The white pirate. The man who plans . . . plans to attack the Korvat colony."

"You're a slave?" Sulu had nothing but contempt for slavery and anyone who profited from it. The institution violated every principle of the Federation. Of course, the rough outpost of Galdonterre was hardly a stronghold of Federation law and tradition. And Starfleet's sacrosanct directive of noninterference with alien societies effectively prevented him from doing very much about humanitarian outrages such as this.

At least *most* of the time.

"He captured me during one of his raids," she said, her words slurring. The stream of sweat on her face was fast becoming a torrent, and was doubtless liberally mixed with tears. "Many years ago."

"You'll be safe aboard *Excelsior.*" Sulu found it hard to imagine even the sometimes-supercilious Captain Styles refusing an asylum request from an escaped slave.

The woman coughed, her throat rasping with the sounds of dry leaves and ragged burlap. "No place will be safe for me—not since he put the virus in my veins."

"Virus?" Sulu said, horrified. "Are you saying you were forced to work for someone who uses . . . *disease organisms* against the people he's enslaved?"

She nodded, then withdrew a small, sweat-dripping medical scanner from her loose-fitting traveler's cloak. "Yes. Individually . . . tailored viruses. Designed specifically for each of his slaves. To keep us . . . in line . . ."

She trailed off, her gaze briefly losing its focus again before her fitful lucidity once again returned. "I've been scanning visitors to this world for weeks now. Looking for . . . antibodies to the virus I carry. *You* look like the most promising potential source I've scanned so far. A pity . . . it's already too late. But it's not too late . . . to *warn* you."

"Warn me?" Though he was no longer touching her

hands, the earlier sensation of extreme cold returned, this time coursing up and down along the length of his spine.

"Warn you," she repeated, then interrupted herself with a mad, rasping giggle. "After all, what can he do about it? *Kill* me?"

"What do you need to warn me about?" Sulu asked, trying to keep her focused.

"About . . . about Korvat," she croaked. Her perspiration was intensifying, and Sulu sensed that she was fading fast. Now that he knew she might be carrying a genetically engineered virus of some sort, he was no longer quite so eager as before to get her aboard *Excelsior,* where others might be exposed to whatever disease was consuming her.

"You mentioned Korvat before," he said. "Is your . . . employer planning to stage another one of his raids there?"

She shook her head. "Not merely . . . a raid. He wants . . . to shut down . . . the peace conference . . . between your people and his."

The border world known as the Korvat colony, Sulu knew, would soon play host to high-level Federation-Klingon diplomatic talks. *So this slaver, this pirate, is evidently a Klingon,* he thought.

"Why do you call him 'the white pirate'?" he said aloud.

"Because . . . because his skin looks like the winter snows back home in Janitza Province."

The chill sensation seized his spine once again as he considered the woman's description—along with some very old ghosts that still haunted his dreams, at least on occasion.

Sulu tried to focus past his own personal ruminations, since this wasn't the time to indulge them. "Tell me more about Korvat," he said, signaling to his companions with a wave of a hand. A quick backward glance confirmed that the entire group was rising from the table and approaching. "Why does this . . . white pirate want to disrupt the peace talks?"

The woman's reply was punctuated by her labored, wheezing breaths. "Peace along the border zone is . . . bad for the albino's business. So he must thwart that peace."

Sulu was immediately inclined to take the woman's warning seriously. After all, the schedule for the upcoming session of Federation-Klingon talks hadn't been finalized until shortly before Christmas, and the existence of the conference itself was not yet generally known. The talks might even have been part of the reason that Starfleet had dispatched *Excelsior* to this general region of Beta Quadrant space.

Schulman was the first to reach the alcove, her tricorder already out and scanning the stricken alien woman. The others gathered around, earnest expressions of concern etched across their faces. Startled by the new arrivals, the woman reached toward Sulu, who instinctively took the alien woman's frigid hand and squeezed it gently, offering whatever solace he could manage. With his other hand, he raised his communicator again.

"I can still get some of our medics down here," he said. He had no doubt that just about any member of the sickbay staff, including Dr. Klass herself, wouldn't hesitate to volunteer to beam down with an emergency medkit, despite the obvious danger of contagion.

But the silent, unmistakable look of resignation on the woman's face made plain the meat-hook reality of her imminent death.

Then, right before Sulu's nonplussed eyes, and in full view of the entire shore-leave party, the woman's body ceased perspiring, her skin abruptly taking on the texture and color of dry, weathered quartz. Even as Sulu realized that she must already be dead, the visible portions of the woman's flesh turned translucent, transforming into faceted, crystalline material, metamorphosed as though by some wizard's terrible and arcane alchemy. A few heartbeats later, what remained of her lifeless body adopted a granular texture and instantly began to crumble like a sand castle dried out in the sun. The woman's garment maintained her shape for perhaps another second or two until gravity and her own collapsing remains conspired to pull it all down to the stone floor beneath the bench. Within the space of perhaps twenty horror-charged seconds, the woman's disease had reduced her to a few handfuls of white, desiccated crystals.

I've seen this before, Sulu thought, speechless, his heart in his throat. Though more than three decades had passed since he'd last witnessed such an obscenity, there could be no mistaking—to say nothing of forgetting—the rare malady that had taken the lives of a Federation starship's entire crew.

"Looks like some form of flash-dehydration, Commander," Braun said, unable to keep the shock out of his voice.

Sulu nodded silently, a hard lump of carefully modulated fear forming in his throat. *This is how everybody on the* Exeter *died. After they came back from Omega IV, with a native airborne virus tagging along for the ride.*

And everyone here had more than likely already inhaled the pathogen, if this was indeed the same thing.

Sulu started when he heard a screeching roar behind him, followed quickly by another. He whirled to see a trio of young Gorn shrinking away from the carnage, upending a nearby vacant table as they hastened to put some distance between themselves and the few spadefuls of horror that now adorned the floor. *They must have seen what just happened,* he thought, almost grateful for the distraction from the terror that he and his people had just witnessed.

"Commander, we may have a bit of a problem," Renyck said. "If the other customers get it into their heads that *we* killed this woman . . ."

But Sulu knew that the Gorn wouldn't be highly motivated to make trouble with the planetary authorities, or even to alert the bartender, whom Sulu doubted would deign to give the screeching, retreating reptiloids so much as an annoyed glance. Moving with uncharacteristic swiftness, the Gorn headed toward the door, their tails held rigidly behind them. *Must be heading right back to the Hegemony,* Sulu thought. He saw another man watching the alcove where the dead woman lay, but when he caught Sulu's eye, he ducked out the door as well.

Sulu's impulse was to prevent anyone from leaving, establishing a de facto quarantine. But until he knew for certain what he was really dealing with here, he knew he couldn't justify taking any such action.

Putting aside his own revulsion and fear, he turned back to face his shaken, ashen-hued shipmates. "Form a tight ring around me, but try to avoid looking suspicious. We need to find out what really happened here before things get out of hand."

He turned to Schulman. "Do you have a specimen container in your kit?" He was grateful that the junior science officer always took an exploratory kit with her whenever she ventured off-ship, even during her shore leaves; he made a mental note to commend her later for that.

"I do, sir," she said as she extracted a small tube made of clear plastic. She unstoppered it and held it out toward him.

"I'll scoop up a sample of the . . . remains," Sulu said. He decided that if whatever had killed this woman turned out *not* to be transmitted through the air, then he was the only person who had been exposed thus far through direct physical contact; he was determined, if at all possible, to make whatever risk of exposure remained entirely his own.

As he carefully scooped up some of the woman's bone-dry remains, he reached for his communicator and flipped it open. "Sulu to *Excelsior*," he said, raising his voice slightly to make himself heard over the barroom din.

A few seconds later, the voice of *Excelsior*'s commanding officer issued from the communicator. *"Styles here. You aren't scheduled to check in for another four hours, Commander. Is anything wrong?"*

A wry smile tugged at the corners of Sulu's mouth. "You might say that, sir," Sulu said. "We may have been exposed to a potentially lethal contaminant. Possibly a strain of the Omega IV virus, or something similar. I have collected a specimen that will need to be analyzed immediately."

Several tense seconds elapsed before Styles replied. *"I'll have it beamed directly to the quarantine chamber in sickbay. Please put your communicator with the sample so we can establish a transporter lock."*

Sulu didn't have to wonder what the others were thinking at that moment, because he suspected it was exactly what was going through *his* mind as well. "Why not beam us *all* to quarantine, sir? Only six of us, at most, have potentially been exposed."

"I don't want to take any chances with the health and safety of everyone else on Excelsior, *Commander,"* Styles said. *"The Omega IV virus is nothing to take lightly. Until we know for certain what it is we're dealing with, even placing the six of you in isolation poses a risk. You are all to consider yourselves under a planetary quarantine until further notice. Keep me apprised of any change in your status. Styles out."*

Disappointed but not surprised by Styles's conservative decision, Sulu set the open communicator down on the bench on which the dead woman had sat, taking care not to touch anything. Then he placed the specimen tube beside the communicator. A moment later the two items disappeared in a brief but brilliant shimmer of light.

Braun was the next member of the group to speak. "This Omega IV virus. I take it there's no known cure for it." Even if it was phrased as a statement, it was obviously a question as well.

"Not that I'm aware of," Schulman said softly. "At least not this side of Omega IV."

"We don't know for sure that this is the Omega IV virus," Sulu said quietly but firmly, hoping to buck up the group's obviously flagging morale, in spite of his own gnawing doubts. Prime among these was the dying woman's assertion that he, Hikaru Sulu, was the best potential source of antibodies she had found so far. Was this because his blood still carried both the pathogens and the immunizing factors to which he had been exposed when he had led an *Enterprise* rescue team on the surface of Omega IV?

"Besides," he continued with all the confidence he could muster, "the woman told me that the virus in her blood had been tailored specifically to affect *her*, in order to keep her under the control of a slaver. There's no reason to assume that anybody else is at risk because of it."

But even as he watched his people nod, apparently encouraged, he couldn't help but agree with Captain Styles's choice not to wager *Excelsior*'s safety on such a slender chain of reasoning and wishful thinking.

FOUR

Dr. Judith Klass frowned as she carefully and deftly manipulated the small sample vial that had been beamed into sickbay's isolation chamber just minutes ago. Despite the sense of security the seals of isolation provided, working with any kind of potentially deadly virus demanded the strictest of protocols. There was no way she could risk handling the vial and its contents with either gloves or directed shielding; one microscopic tear in the hazmat gear, or a single energy fluctuation in the shields, might spell disaster. So she was back to utilizing retro-technology that seemed almost prehistoric on a ship as advanced as *Excelsior.*

She toggled the controls to the right, gently nudging the robotic arm closer to the stopper at the top of the vial. She had trained with robotic arms like these at Starfleet Medical nearly forty years ago; later, when the first Horta biologist came to share his species' biophysical knowledge, she had outfitted him with a set of arms very similar to these. Those had been controlled through the galvanometric currents generated on Flek's rocky exterior, whereas the ones she was using now were controlled solely by her hand-eye coordination. It was akin to playing chess while using somebody else's hands to move the pieces.

As beads of sweat began to appear on her brow, Klass momentarily regretted having sent her two nurses out of sickbay, or at least not having donned a surgical cap. She willed herself to ignore the creeping droplets, steeling her concentration to remain focused on the task before her. The stopper successfully extracted, she moved the vial over to the left side of the chamber, where a sample slide was already prepped and waiting. With infinite patience, she tilted the vial, allowing a few grains of the white powder to spill onto the slide.

From what she understood, those white grains had been part of a woman of undetermined alien origin not so very long ago. Sulu had said that she'd turned into the crystalline powder right before his eyes. Klass hoped, for his sake—and for the sake of the rest of the crew whom Styles had quarantined on Galdonterre—that the cause was not the Omega IV virus, as was feared.

She liked Sulu, and had found him charming and gentlemanly from the time they had first met, when he had come in for his initial routine physical. She had read in his file that he had originally been a physicist; as she was examining him, she asked why he had transferred from the sciences to helm duty aboard the *U.S.S. Enterprise.*

"There's more action in the driver's seat," he had responded jokingly. "I've never been happy cooped up in an office or a laboratory. I'd rather apply sciences directly, or *test* theoretical physics. Besides, if you knew Mister Spock and Doctor McCoy, you'd know that there wasn't room on that ship for a third scientific opinion."

"Oh, I know Leonard," Klass had said. "Smartest Georgia farm boy ever to make it offworld. I studied at St. George's

University in London; when he came over for a semester as an exchange student from the University of Mississippi, he made himself known to every unattached girl on campus . . . and several attached ones as well."

Seeing Sulu's incredulous look, Klass had laughed. "You probably don't think of Lenny as being a lothario, do you? Well, I don't know how successful he was with others, but he wasn't exactly my type."

"Are you still on good terms with him?" Sulu had asked.

"Well, I haven't talked to him in ages, but I'd be happy to throw back a pint or two with him if the opportunity ever came up. I remember his tastes ran to Tennessee whiskey and mint juleps."

She had studied him for a moment, a realization suddenly dawning on her. "In answer to your unspoken question, yes, I *would* associate with Lenny, despite what certain others in the command hierarchy of this ship might feel," she said, pointing to the ceiling, several decks above which was the bridge.

Klass had leaned in closer, confiding in Sulu. "I've served on a host of different ships, Commander, and one thing I've learned in all that time is that those in command break down into a few camps. There are: number one, the ones who want to be friends with their crews and have adventures; number two, the ones who want to command their people and don't much care about interpersonal stuff nor much of anything else that's fun; and number three, those who are an awkward combination of both styles. Currently, *Excelsior* has a number two," she said, smiling. "But if you do a good job, and stay away from your previous CO's cowboy tendencies, you should be okay."

In the three weeks or so since that day, Sulu had dropped in to see Klass numerous times, not for medical reasons, but just to chat. They were fast on their way to becoming good friends; this burgeoning camaraderie now helped guide Klass's hand as she began her examination of the dead woman's remains for pathogens.

The slide clicked into place under her isolated scanner, and Klass gently restoppered the vial. She wanted to clear Sulu and the others to return to the ship as quickly as possible, but she also knew that any error in her findings could cause potentially irrevocable damage and bring death to everyone aboard *Excelsior.*

Not much pressure at all, she thought with a grim smile. Still, in her forty-three years as a physician—thirty-seven of which she had spent on various starships—she'd faced pressure before. And she had always come through somehow.

Of course, there's always a first time for everything. . . .

Styles frowned and leaned forward in his chair, moving marginally closer to the small comm terminal that was mounted in the center of the conference room table. Because the incoming message was on one of the audio channels, the terminal's screen was now dark. "Would you mind repeating that, Commander? I'm not certain I heard you correctly."

"We can't leave here without knowing exactly what killed that woman," Sulu said, his voice slightly muffled but more directed, as if he had brought the communicator directly up to his lips. *"And I'd prefer not to shout about subjects that might be classified."*

"Whatever you've just done seems to have helped the situation," said Cutler, who was seated to the left of Styles. "So, please repeat what you just said, as the captain asked."

There was a pause before Sulu spoke again, and Styles imagined he could hear his first officer's teeth grinding. *"The woman told me that the person who . . . owned her was planning an attack on the Korvat peace conference."*

"Did she provide you with any proof?" Cutler asked.

"You mean other than the fact that she knew exactly where the Federation and the Klingon Empire would be

holding their top-secret talks? No. *She didn't have time before she died. She did say that this was only part of this person's plans. Hinted that he was planning other attacks aimed at disrupting any peace between us and the Klingons."*

Styles rubbed one hand over the end of the swagger stick he habitually kept tucked under his arm. "Any thoughts on who this theoretical adversary is?"

"No clue. Other than that he is an albino and that he has a crew of pirates and slaves working with him. And that he seems to be very well versed in viral weapons." Sulu hesitated for a moment before adding, *"She did mention that he wanted to disrupt any peace that might develop between our people and his. That may imply that he's a Klingon."*

Cutler gave Styles a surprised look. "An albino Klingon?" she whispered. "I didn't know there *was* such a thing."

"It's a big universe," Styles murmured.

"Will you be notifying Starfleet, sir?" Sulu asked.

"I'm certainly considering it, Commander," Styles said. "I'll have some of the crew search for any records of an albino Klingon, and Cutler and I will do a risk assessment based on whatever data we're able to compile."

"It's unfortunate you weren't able to get more information from the woman before she died," Cutler said.

There was another pause, longer than the last, before Sulu came back on the comm. *"Yeah, shame that she had to die on me so suddenly while warning us of a potential threat. What poor manners."*

That's the kind of smart-ass attitude that proves you're not a team player, Styles thought, his eyes narrowing in annoyance. He held up his hand, signaling the equally irritated Cutler not to respond to the sarcasm.

Then a beep from the tabletop comm unit spared them from any further unpleasantness.

"Klass to Captain Styles," intoned another voice.

"Commander Sulu, I have to break this off," Styles said. "Apparently Doctor Klass has found something. Let's hope it doesn't ruin the rest of everyone's day. Styles out. Go ahead, Doctor."

"Good news," Klass said. *"I've managed to isolate the virus that killed the woman in the bar. While it does appear to be a strain of the Omega IV contagion, the organism has been genetically tailored in a very specific manner. It's difficult to tell whether it was altered to affect this woman* specifically, *or to target her specific familial genetic code, or even her entire species."*

"So what does that mean for *our* people, Doctor?" Cutler asked. Styles knew that she would never acknowledge it, but she was rather fond of Darnell Renyck, the ship's transporter chief. Were shipboard romances allowed on *Excelsior,* Cutler and Renyck might have pursued one, but Styles felt that such romances were counterproductive, and had banned them in no uncertain terms.

"It means that the odds are astronomically against this virus having any affect on any member of Excelsior's *crew, or even anyone else on Galdonterre. From what I can tell of the woman's DNA, she belonged to no species we've encountered to date. Certain genetic markers show superficial similarities to some Alpha Quadrant species, but there are no direct links. If anyone else* were *at risk, it would have to be someone who belongs to her species . . . and even that wouldn't guarantee an infection."*

"So, to be clear, Doctor, Mister Sulu's team can return to the ship?" Styles asked.

"In my medical opinion, yes."

"Very good, Doctor. I still want you to inform the ruling factions of Galdonterre of the possible contamination. If there's any chance, however remote, that this single bizarre death might presage a spread into other border worlds and into Federation space generally, we would have a true calamity on our hands." Since Galdonterre was essentially a lawless outpost world, there were multiple ruling factions, each in charge of its own embattled frontier fiefdom; Styles didn't relish the idea of speaking to each of them individually, but he knew it had to be done.

"Already handled, Captain, even though it probably wasn't really necessary. Before I buzzed you, I asked Lieutenant Spiro to run a scan on the planet to see if there were any genetic matches with the dead woman present anywhere on the globe. She found nothing."

Cutler frowned. "The Omega IV virus is nothing to fool with, Doctor. I'm still a bit uncomfortable with the odds. It puts us all at risk if we beam aboard personnel infected with this virus. Captain, I recommend we place the shore party in isolation for the next day or so, at least until the medical department has had a chance to study this a little further."

"That seems a reasonable precaution. Doctor?"

"I'll make the arrangements, Captain. Klass out."

Cutler folded her arms. "What are we going to do about these rumors about the Korvat conference?"

Styles sighed and leaned back in his chair. "Put it in the logs for now. I'm sure Mister Sulu will feel more than justified taking it further once he returns to the ship."

"Not without your permission, he won't." There was a flicker of fire in her eyes.

Styles cocked his head and studied his second officer for a moment. "Meredith, don't mistake my annoyance with Sulu's past for a disregard of his abilities. I don't have to *like* the man to know that he's a good officer. More than that, he is an *Excelsior* officer. If I cannot trust my own people to be efficient, then I've picked a poor crew to captain." Styles saw no point in mentioning that Sulu's posting as *Excelsior*'s exec was at least as much Starfleet's decision as it was his own. Regardless, the last thing Styles needed right now was for his difficulties with Sulu to create problems for anyone else in the crew.

Chastened, Cutler nodded. "Understood, sir."

"I'll leave it to you to get everyone back on board then," Styles said, standing and adjusting the swagger stick that was tucked under his arm. "I'll be up on the bridge."

Word that the shore party was cleared for return to *Excelsior* came just as the dead woman's remains were being discreetly transferred to a crystal vase. Schulman had purchased the vase at a local market as a souvenir; it was now the dead woman's urn.

Back aboard *Excelsior,* Sulu had briefed Styles again, through the force field that kept his group in the sickbay isolation ward. He had spoken with Dr. Klass only briefly so far, but what he *had* heard about the virus concerned him greatly.

"What if this group is planning to direct a *customized* biological attack against Korvat?" Sulu had asked Styles. "They could direct it against the Federation delegates, or the Klingons, or any *others* who are present. That kind of disruption could cause chaos in the peace efforts."

Styles, surprisingly, had been receptive to Sulu's ideas, though skepticism had seeped in around the edges. Sulu didn't blame the captain for that. The evidence was admittedly scanty and speculative; there was little to go on other than a brief conversation with a now-dead woman and the viral traces that Dr. Klass had found within her remains.

"Until we obtain further information," Styles had said, "I don't want to raise the alarms. Few enough people know of these peace talks anyhow. If we stir up a lot of general paranoia within Starfleet or the Federation Diplomatic Corps, or among the Klingons, we risk turning a vague warning into a self-fulfilling prophecy."

Before Sulu could reply, Styles had held up one hand.

"That said, I *will* send an advisory message to the *U.S.S. Saratoga* and Captain Margaret Sinclair-Alexander. They are transporting Ambassador Sarek and his diplomatic staff to Korvat for the conference. Perhaps they will be able to consult further on this matter. Forewarned is forearmed and all that."

An hour later, Sulu lay on a foldaway bunk, tossing and turning. Too much had happened today to let him get to sleep easily, his exhaustion notwithstanding. And yet he knew he would need his rest.

If today was the warning shot, then the skirmish will be just around the corner, he thought. It had occurred to him that the woman could have been allowed to escape, and might even have been sent to her death, deliberately.

Finally, unable to quiet his thoughts, Sulu padded over to a table and retrieved a hypo that had been left there by one of Dr. Klass's hazmat-suited nurses. He pressed the cool metal device to his neck and injected the sleeping agent it contained with a slight hiss. By the time he reached his bunk, he was already feeling his limbs and mind becoming heavy with impending slumber.

But even as Sulu drifted into dreams, he felt something wicked and strange yet familiar bubbling its way up inexorably from somewhere below the level of consciousness. Against the onrushing darkness, he saw a chalk-white form moving toward him, pitiless and implacable.

And then, for the first time in decades, the white thing invaded his dreams.

FIVE

Hikaru Sulu had heard and read stories about Klingons all his young life. He'd seen photographs and holos of them as well, and often dreamed about meeting one face-to-face someday.

He just hadn't expected such a thing to happen with so little warning, and before he'd even reached his twelfth birthday.

What would Captain Hunter do in this situation? he asked himself, then immediately decided it was a silly question. If Hunter were here, she would leap out of hiding with hand lasers blazing, and all the guns and resources of the border ship *Aerfen* at her back. He assumed that *Aerfen* must be busy patrolling some other trouble spot along the Klingon border right now—otherwise, Hunter surely would have stopped the Klingons before their landing craft had gotten within twenty klicks of Ganjitsu's surface.

Crouching silently behind a bent air-conduit screen from which he could watch the intruders unobserved, young Hikaru had an unobstructed view of the entryway to his mother's lab. He noted that some of the raiders who had forced their way into the family compound didn't much resemble any Klingon image he'd ever seen or imagined. The facial hair and the bushy, upswept eyebrows looked right, but their foreheads were very different, almost as though they were merely humans who were made up to resemble Klingons for a Halloween party.

The apparent leader of the small raiding party looked odd as well, but in a way entirely different from the other four rough men who seemed to be doing his bidding. While the leader's forehead had the strange rippled texture that Hikaru had always associated with Klingons, the man's chalky skin was nearly as pale as the first snow of Ganjitsu's northern winter. He was also built far more slightly than the burly men who surrounded him; only the deference these brutes seemed to display toward the albino—or was it fear?—identified him as the one in charge.

"The woman said we'd find the lab in here, Qagh," said one of the albino's bushy-browed men, who held a wicked-looking pistol before him.

Woman? Hikaru thought, panic swiftly rising in his chest, though he somehow managed to remain quiet and still in his small hiding place. *Mom!*

When his mother and father had burst into his room and told him of the coming raid—Dad had said that Ishikawa Village's sensor station had identified them as Klingon raiders, whose predations were not uncommon on border worlds like Ganjitsu—they had told him to hide, and quickly. The notion that his parents either had not managed to hide themselves in time, or had been found by the raiders, terrified him.

As did the realization that the Sulu family's very survival might now be entirely up to him.

"*This* is an agronomy lab?" said the white-skinned raider,

his voice tinged with disgust as he craned his narrow neck in an evident attempt to survey everything in the room before walking out of Hikaru's narrow line of sight. The pirate leader's guttural language—Border Klingonese?—was evidently being rendered into intelligible Federation Standard by the universal translator built into the lab's security system.

Even without the benefit of the automated translation matrix, Hikaru had a pretty good notion of why the pirate leader sounded so disappointed; if the raiders had expected to find a greenhouse full of live, growing things, then they were clearly looking in the wrong place. Shimizu Hana Sulu, Hikaru's mother, did mostly theoretical bioengineering work, guiding the creation of new strains of Earth crops capable of thriving on this heavily forested colony world, while at the same time not threatening the existing biosphere by becoming invasive. Therefore, her primary workspace bore a closer resemblance to the Spartan study where Dad wrote poetry and worked out abstruse equations in subspace astrophysics than it did to any of the fifty-odd living, working greenhouses that dotted the verdant wilderness of Ganjitsu's northern hemisphere.

The gruff voices of the raiders, all of whom were still out of his line of sight, intruded on Hikaru's jittery reverie.

"I don't get it, Qagh," one of the pirates said. "You've never needed us to find *plant* materials before."

"What of it?" The chalky-visaged leader was speaking again, the pique underlying his words requiring no translation. "One can never predict what direction advanced bioresearch of this sort will take. Now let's focus. This is a raid, not a biology symposium."

One of the armed underlings grunted. "Doesn't seem to be much here to take. Perhaps the man and the woman in the dwelling were holding out on us. I could question them further, when they regain consciousness."

Mom and Dad are alive! Hikaru thought, his fear suddenly banished by an ebullient hope.

"Very well," the leader said. "But we have work to do here first. Even if this place contains no actual usable bioagents, there must be some records here that I can put to good use. Genetic profiles. DNA traces. Protein construction matrixes. I can't be sure what will prove useful, so download *everything* that's on these computers. And do it quickly."

The desperation in the albino pirate's voice was unmistakable, even in the tender ears of an eleven-year-old. Why was this raider in such a hurry to get at Mom's files? Hikaru couldn't help but wonder if it had anything to do with the man's apparent weakness and fragility in comparison to the men he commanded. *Maybe he's sick,* Hikaru thought. *And he's looking for a cure for whatever disease he has.*

The brief surge of compassion the notion raised was swept away by the storm of fear that was beginning to rage anew inside him.

Not to mention a rising tide of righteous anger that was rolling in right behind it. *If he needed Mom's help,* Hikaru thought, *then why didn't he just* ask?

"Get the portable memory cores ready while I go through the computer directories," the albino said. Hikaru couldn't see anything from his cramped hiding place, but he could hear the sounds of equipment being moved about, as well as the telltale bleeps that indicated that Mom's main computer had been activated.

Hikaru grinned. These creeps would never get past the password protections and data encryption routines. Dad had set them up himself.

"There," the albino said a few minutes later, after several minutes of silence had passed, punctuated only by the subdued sounds of manual keystrokes and muttered curses. "That was a fairly complex security lockout, but the dataprobe seems to have found a back way into the directory structure. Hook up the memory cores now. We should be able to start downloading soon. We'll be out of this system inside of a *kilaan*."

Although he had no idea how long a *kilaan* was, Hikaru's heart leaped up into his throat. They were going to get Mom's files, in spite of all of Dad's careful precautions. He wasn't sure what use those files would be to the pale pirate, but the sense of violation bothered him intensely.

He came to a decision right then and there. Maybe he *wasn't* able to do whatever Captain Hunter would have done to repel these invaders.

But he did know one simple way to prevent these crooks from taking things that didn't belong to them.

The junction box that brought power from the main compound to the agronomy lab was located maybe twenty meters or so from the vent inside which Hikaru had hidden himself. He reasoned that with a little luck, he might be able to crawl through the ductwork that led toward the junction and let himself out of the vent there without being noticed by the raiders.

There was only one problem: he hadn't reckoned with just how narrow the vent was in places, particularly where it turned sharp corners. And the fact that the acoustics inside the air duct seemed to amplify every sound tenfold made him nervous almost to the point of paralysis.

At least that meant that he could hear what the raiders were up to as their harsh, throaty speech reverberated along the narrow length of the metal conduit he was still attempting to transit despite the claustrophobically close quarters.

"There's the main directory," Hikaru heard the pirate leader saying.

"Might as well be written in Romulan," said one of his men.

"To *your* eyes, perhaps. But I see real potential here."
Hikaru could hear something that sounded like admiration
in the albino's voice.

"Potential for what?" asked another one of the pirates.

"Weaponization, for one thing."

Hikaru froze for a moment. Though he had never heard
it before, the word "weaponization" evoked a frightening
picture of Mom's years of careful research into plant and
microbial life being turned from its rightful purpose—
feeding the Federation's ever-increasing population—and
used instead to create pain and disease and death.

Determination not to let any such thing happen overcame
Hikaru's momentary paralysis, but only barely. He continued
inching forward, and arrived at another vent grille a seeming
eternity later. Curling into a ball, he turned his body in the
small space, braced his back against the air conduit, placed
both feet against the aluminum grille, and pushed his legs
forward with all his strength. The grille resisted. He relaxed
his muscles, took a deep breath, and tried again, taking care
not to make any noise as he strained. No good. Undeterred,
he took a breath and tried it a third time.

A moment later the grille flew free from the aperture that
held it and clattered to the hard floor tiles outside.

Although the thing weighed little and had fallen less than
half a meter, it made a clatter that could have awakened the
dead.

"What was that?" Cheb shouted from directly behind Qagh.

Startled by both Cheb's surprised exclamation and the
echoing clang that had precipitated it, Qagh nearly knocked
the portable memory core from atop the lab's main computer terminal. The noise, which sounded like something
metallic falling or being dropped, seemed to have come
from a nearby room located just beyond the far west side of
the lab.

Scowling at Cheb, Qagh moved the memory core away from the edge of the monitor and allowed it to continue downloading data. He rose from the chair where he'd been working, drew his long-barreled hand laser, and motioned with his free hand toward Cheb and the rest of his men.

"Somebody out there might be trying to be a hero," Qagh said as he walked cautiously toward the door, his weapon preceding him. "So let's give him a hero's welcome, shall we?"

The junction box that controlled the electrical power inputs to both the lab and the adjacent house was right where Hikaru remembered it, in a narrow utility vestibule just outside Mom's lab, a place that both his parents had warned him many times was off-limits. He supposed they would discover eventually that he had broken that particular rule perhaps as many times as they had reminded him of it.

It didn't take long to find the particular switches that Dad had identified as the most dangerous ones. He wrapped his sweat-slicked fingers around them. Absurdly, he found he was looking forward to stern parental lectures once this was over, as if he were anticipating Christmases that might never come.

His hands strained against the stiff metal levers, finally throwing all of them into the position that Dad had said could overload every circuit in both buildings.

A light fixture built into the ceiling abruptly exploded, showering the windowless corridor outside the main lab room in a short-lived plume of sparks.

Abrupt, absolute, total darkness followed, punctuated by Qagh's own curses.

"Hand lights!" Qagh shouted, enraged. A fumbling, confused few moments later, the beam of Horen's palm beacon speared the darkness.

"What happened?" Cheb asked.

"Lights went out," Horen said, the beam jiggling as he shrugged.

Geniuses, Qagh thought, shaking his head in disgust. "Someone overloaded the lab's electrical circuits."

Realization kicked him squarely in the gut. *The lab's computers are running off those circuits,* he thought. *My memory cores, too.* His lungs suddenly felt constricted, and he fumbled one-handed at the inhaler lashed to his belt. He sucked in a dose of his most current pharmaceutical cocktail while still holding his pistol at the ready. His breathing calmed, he tucked away the inhaler, stepped over to Horen, and grabbed the palm beacon out of his hand.

Then he began retracing his steps back to the main computer as quickly as he could manage.

Doing his best to stay silent, Hikaru listened to the raiders' angry voices from the relative safety of the air conduit. The emergency lights had just come on, casting a dim, gloomy light throughout the lab complex, and he regarded the fact that they hadn't discovered him yet as nothing short of a miracle.

"Get anything?" one of the pirates asked. Hikaru assumed that the emergency circuits must have also reactivated the automated translation matrix, or else he probably wouldn't have been able to understand a word any of them were saying.

"It's fried," growled another voice. Hikaru immediately recognized the harsh, angry tones of the pirate leader.

"You won't get anything but data fragments off that core in the shape it's in now," said another of the albino's men.

Hikaru's fear gave way, at least a little, to a sense of triumph. Fried computers and ruined data storage modules were just one of the catastrophes his parents had worried that he might cause by playing with the junction box controls. But yesterday's forbidden mischief, it seemed, had just become today's brilliant, life-saving improvisation.

"QI'yaH!" cried the albino. The translator evidently couldn't parse what was no doubt a pungent curse, but the murderous frustration in the raider's voice was abundantly clear.

"What are we going to do now?" Hikaru heard one of the pirates ask.

Several long heartbeats passed in silence as Hikaru sat in his hiding place, straining to hear the results of the pirate leader's deliberations.

"We're going back to the shuttle," the albino said at length, his voice laced with gravel and hostility. "Then back to the *Jade Lady*."

"What about the 'hero' down here who turned out the lights on us?"

"Run a scan and find him. Then kill him, along with anyone else in the compound who might still be alive."

Hikaru's heart raced. He gasped, though evidently not loudly enough to give away his position in the air conduit. But soon, no amount of stealth would be enough to hide him.

"Ghuy'," said one of the pirates, uttering what had to be yet another toxic curse. "Whatever trick our saboteur pulled also scrambled the hand scanner. I'll need at least a *kilaan* or two to recalibrate it."

"Then forget it. Let's go."

Hikaru leaned back in his narrow crawlspace, relief flooding his body like a tsunami engulfing a beach.

"We'll blow this complex to atoms from orbit," the albino said.

Fear abruptly regained its desperate grip on Hikaru's heart.

• • •

Hikaru was relieved to discover not only that his parents were still breathing, but also that they were beginning to stir. Whatever weapon the raiders had used on them must have had a stun setting.

But he also knew that he had no time to waste on rejoicing.

"Mom! Dad! We have to get out of here."

Dad blinked blearily up at him as he rose to his elbows. Mom was beside him, already rising to her feet.

"Hikaru, why are you still here?" Dad asked as Hikaru and his mother helped him get his feet beneath him. "I thought we told you to run and hide."

Captain Hunter wouldn't have just snuck off to hide, Hikaru thought, but thought better of saying it aloud. The last thing he wanted was to set off another one of Dad's "where is Starfleet when we need it out here on the wild frontier?" rants.

"We *all* have to get away from here," Hikaru said. "And fast."

"Calm down, honey," Mom said, wrapping her arms around Hikaru. Tears streamed down her cheeks, belying the carefully schooled calmness of her voice. "Are you hurt?"

"I'm *fine,*" Hikaru said impatiently, and gently broke free of his mother's embrace. He grabbed her hand, then Dad's, and began pulling them both toward the family room door and the exit beyond with all the strength an eleven-year-old could muster.

They stood rooted in place, like a pair of Ganjitsu's old-growth trees. "Are the raiders still here somewhere?" Dad wanted to know.

"No. I got up on the roof and saw them fly off."

"Then why do we need to leave in such a hurry?" Mom asked.

"Because they were pretty mad when they left. They

didn't find anything they wanted, because I . . . did some stuff to the computers."

Mom's eyes widened in surprise. Then she smiled and ruffled Hikaru's hair. "Good thing I just backed up all my data off-site."

Dad's eyes widened as well, but he looked more frightened than pleased. Hikaru could see at once that he understood the danger.

"How do you know they were angry, son?"

Hikaru tugged on his parents' hands again. "Because I heard the leader say he was gonna blast us from space."

Mom and Dad briefly exchanged shocked looks. Their feet came unrooted a moment later, and the trio ran together, still hand-in-hand, toward the door, and the forest beyond.

As the shuttle's engines roared back to life, Qagh noticed that he was feeling feverish again. Annoyed at his own weakness, he wiped the beads of cold perspiration from his rumpled brow.

He said nothing to the other members of his raiding party during the little ship's brief flight back into orbit about the border planet, whose once-promising green surface now seemed to mock him through the shuttle's forward window from over four hundred *qell'qam*s below. He sat in brooding silence as Horen deftly maneuvered the landing craft back into the *Jade Lady*'s docking port.

His raiding team and the rest of the *Lady*'s crew seemed to sense his foul mood immediately, and parted to allow him instant passage through the freebooter vessel's maze of narrow corridors as he stalked directly to the bridge.

As he entered the cramped control room, Qagh was gratified to note that neither D'Jinnea nor Ganik was present; that meant he'd be able to ask forgiveness rather than permission for what he was about to do. He grinned savagely, giving vent to but a minuscule portion of his rage as he pushed Golag out of the main gunner's chair, where he'd evidently been either drilling or daydreaming. The other young Klingon appeared to be considering retaliating, then clearly thought better of it after being swept by Qagh's glare and glimpsing the pale man's carefully sharpened teeth.

"What are you doing?" Golag asked as Qagh took his seat and began tapping a quick sequence of commands into the weapons console. A series of winking green lights made it obvious that he was powering up the forward laser cannon.

"What does it *look* like I'm doing?" Qagh growled. He paused to wipe a bead of sweat out of his eyes, irritated by the brief interruption.

"You look unwell, Qagh," Golag said. "More than usual, I mean."

Qagh ignored the other man and continued pressing buttons. "You noticed. I'm touched."

Golag grunted. "And you're getting ready to blow something away down on the surface."

"Very good. Your powers of deduction are indeed nothing short of extraordinary."

Qagh noticed a look of suspicion darkening Golag's dull brow. "Does Ganik know about this?"

"*Fek'lhr* take Ganik," Qagh said as he finished fine-tuning the coordinates on the target lock controls. "This is *my* affair."

He slapped the "initiate" button with his palm. A heartbeat later, the small tactical monitor above the weapons console displayed a swiftly spreading amber-colored blossom of fire.

That's better, he thought as he watched the complete immolation of nearly a square *qell'qam* of border-world wilderness. Anything that lived in the lab compound *wasn't* living anymore.

2248

The *Jade Lady*

Qagh had been back aboard the *Jade Lady* for less than a quarter-*kilaan* when the hatch to his small berth slid open unexpectedly. Looking up from the small workbench where he developed most of his ad hoc medicaments, Qagh was unsurprised to see Ganik's wide-shouldered frame coming through the narrow hatch.

"Hope I'm not interrupting anything important, Qagh," Ganik said, a snide edge to his voice.

"Only the usual—research that my life literally depends on," Qagh said, pushing aside the microscope and the petri dish to which it was attached. "But does that really matter? It's not as though you knocked before you came in."

The Orion grinned, though the smile didn't reach his eyes. "Don't have to knock, Qagh. I'm the boss, remember?"

Qagh shook his head. *"My* boss, maybe. But not *the* boss. Unless, that is, you want us to make your move against D'Jinnea before we reach Qav'loS."

Ganik's grin collapsed, and a shadow of fury darkened his broad face from a gentle leafy green to the color of a Romulan's blood. He quickly closed the hatch behind him and dogged it shut before turning back to face Qagh.

"Nicely done, Qagh," the Orion pirate hissed, pitching his deep voice low as though still worried that someone might overhear him even through the closed door. "Why not simply post a mutiny announcement on the crew bulletin board?"

Qagh answered with a chuckle that gave way to a momentary coughing fit. "It's bad for your blood pressure to worry so much, Ganik," he said after he'd gotten his breathing back under control.

"And if D'Jinnea discovers what we're up to before we're ready for her, it'll be very bad for us *both*."

"I tend to doubt that," Qagh said.

The older man replied in a low growl. "What makes you say that?"

Qagh turned his chair so that he faced the huge Orion, but he didn't bother to rise to his feet. "As long as D'Jinnea continues to need what my research produces, she won't be able to afford to do anything permanent to *me*," he said. "So if she were somehow to get wind of what's in store for her, I think she'd probably place all the blame on *you*."

The hulking Orion's eyes narrowed to slits. "Ungrateful whelp. I should have left you to die in the snow when I had the chance."

"That might have been a boon for us both," Qagh said, nodding. "But what's done is done. You can't get rid of me now, can you? My research has been as profitable for you as it has been for D'Jinnea. You get weaponry, plus the means to block the pheromones she produces to keep you and the rest of the males on this ship in line."

"Assuming you ever get the formula right. It never lasts very long."

"It will be perfected in time. Like all my other labors on your behalf. Like every new bioagent I've developed to allow D'Jinnea to shave more decades than I can count off her true age. Neither of you could afford to dispense with me—even if you really wanted to."

"That's quite a theory to test with your life."

"My life has been in my own hands for a long time, Ganik. The prospect ceased to frighten me when I was still in my teens. Just as *you* ceased to frighten me."

Ganik took a single deliberate step forward, towering over Qagh, his clenched fists reminding the sickly Klingon of demolition equipment.

"Just remember one thing, you spindly little freak,"

Ganik said, grabbing the front of Qagh's shirt and lifting him slightly from his chair. "The 'research' you have to do just to keep yourself alive wouldn't be possible without my protecting you from the rest of the crew."

"Don't forget D'Jinnea's bankroll," Qagh said quietly, trying to keep his countenance as emotionless as that of a grandmaster of *klin zha*. "*Neither* of us would be able to exist without her resources—which I've noticed she's been lavishing more and more on younger members of the crew lately. Have you seen the way she looks at Cheb and Golag these days?"

"What are you talking about?" Ganik said through clenched teeth.

"Oh, please. You *must* have realized by now that she wants someone younger in her bedchamber. Isn't that why you finally found the courage to make a move against her after all these years?"

The Orion's jaw muscles drew as tight as suspension-bridge cables, and he seemed to be seriously considering snapping Qagh's neck, which would have been a trivial expenditure of effort for him. In his own way, Ganik was every bit as vain and egocentric as the youth-obsessed D'Jinnea. Qagh began to wonder uneasily if he'd finally pushed the old man slightly too far.

As if on cue, the intercom unit on the bulkhead crackled to life. "*Ganik,*" said the sharp yet sultry voice of the *real* boss, the commander and namesake of the freebooter *Jade Lady.* "*I need to see you in my quarters. Now.*"

Qagh contained his sigh of relief, but allowed a grin to spread slowly across his face. Though he couldn't be certain it wasn't his imagination, he thought he could see beads of sweat starting to form near the crown of Ganik's shorn green scalp.

"Sounds like you have a serious problem, Ganik," Qagh said quietly.

"And bring that scrawny albino with you," D'Jinnea added.

Ganik set Qagh gently back into his chair, and returned his grin with a rictus that chilled the smaller man's blood.

"Perhaps we *both* have a serious problem, Qagh."

Even though her pheromonal output had never affected him quite as much as it had the rest of the *Jade Lady*'s crew, Qagh had always regarded D'Jinnea as an extremely attractive female—attractive for a green-skinned Orion, that is. Even after all the long decades she'd spent building up her various extralegal trade enterprises, she still favored the scanty garments typical of her species and gender. Though Qagh knew she had been in business for at least twice as long as he'd been alive, D'Jinnea looked extraordinarily young—perhaps thirty standard revolutions old at the outside—to have attained the degree of status and power she'd accumulated. It was only on occasions when she was truly angry that Qagh could see the faint lines that betrayed her true age.

Occasions like this one.

"Will you *please* explain why in the nine hells you blew away a lab on a world you said would be a biological treasure house?"

"Turns out there wasn't very much down there after all," Qagh said, meeting her withering stare head-on so as not to enrage her further. "Or rather, whatever *was* there wasn't nearly as . . . accessible as it should have been."

Ganik stood beside the raised settee where D'Jinnea lounged and looked down at Qagh. Qagh hated it when Ganik somehow managed to sidestep the mercurial woman's wrath. He hated it even more when the two of them set up a unified front before him, like stern parents delivering a reprimand to a recalcitrant child.

"And you found that frustrating," Ganik said.

"More than either of you can ever know," Qagh said.

After all, both Orions had stable DNA that lacked the tendency to spontaneously "wander" the way Qagh's mutated genome did. How could either D'Jinnea or Ganik possibly understand having to depend on a steady stream of new bioscience discoveries, whether generated in his own meager lab or plundered from the work of others, just to survive from month to month, or even from week to week?

"You'd be surprised, Qagh," Ganik said. "Raising you as if you were my own son ought to qualify me to conduct master classes in frustration."

"You forced us to break orbit in a hurry," D'Jinnea said. "And you may have caused Starfleet to upgrade the *Jade Lady* from nuisance to *threat*, Qagh. I'm not very happy about that."

Qagh had to admit that D'Jinnea had an excellent point. He had no good excuse for allowing his temper to get the better of him, and no viable alternative to begging his employer's indulgence yet again. In spite of himself, he felt more compliant now that he was in close proximity to her, no doubt because of the cloud of pheromones her body produced.

"Forgive me, Lady D'Jinnea," he said. "I will try to keep my passions on a tighter rein in the future."

Deep green eyes that were far older than they appeared flashed at him. "See that you do. I can't afford a repetition of your performance on Ganjitsu at our next stop."

This will be the last apology I deliver to this vain creature, Qagh thought, quietly seething. *Once we reach Qav'loS, there will be no further need.*

Aloud, he said, "The Qav'loS sector is more lightly patrolled than any of the other border regions. As far as I can tell, no Starfleet or Klingon vessels have ever come within two parsecs of the one habitable world there."

"That's fortunate," Ganik said. "I would like you to help ensure that it stays that way."

"At least until after we have taken what we need from that world," said D'Jinnea.

"Your report about Qav'loS makes it sound almost too good to be true," Ganik said, sounding neither overly credulous nor overly eager.

Just as we planned.

"The planet's humanoid natives can live for upwards of a thousand standard revolutions," Qagh said. "The reason is without doubt environmental. We merely have to send a team to the planet's surface and isolate the cause."

"I trust you are certain of this?"

Qagh suppressed a triumphant smile. "My sources of information are reliable, as always."

As is your endless gullibility concerning the quest for eternal youth, he thought.

2248

Qav'loS orbit

Qagh says the stuff is finally ready to use, Ganik thought. *He'd better be right.*

Ganik was the first of the survey team to emerge from the docked landing craft into the *Jade Lady*'s cramped shuttle-bay, where D'Jinnea was waiting impatiently for the team's return. Although he hadn't been down on the planet all that long, he saw immediately that something wasn't quite right with his employer. Of course, he was willing to allow that she might merely have been anxious about having her two most valuable crew members off the ship and out of her immediate control for the past three days. But her teal-green pallor told him that something even more fundamental was wrong.

Maybe her "immortality" treatments are finally wearing off, Ganik thought, pleased by the notion. *Or else that*

*albino bastard has been secretly altering those potions she's
come to depend on.*

As the rest of the planetary survey team began to emerge
from the landing craft behind him, Ganik cast an uneasy eye
on Qagh, who seemed more gaunt and unsteady than usual.

"We shouldn't have let him go down to the surface,"
Ganik said quietly to D'Jinnea once he'd drawn near enough
to her that no one else could hear their conversation. "I don't
like the way he looks."

D'Jinnea snickered. "You've *never* liked the way he
looks."

"That's not what I mean, D'Jinnea. I think he's sick."

She looked at him as though he'd just sprouted a second
head. "Of *course* he's sick, Ganik. How many years has it
taken you to finally notice that?"

"I mean he's *really* sick. Have you ever seen him sweat
like that before?" Ganik was willing to allow that Qagh
might merely be nervous about following through with their
plan. But he felt certain there was more to it than that.

"Qagh has always been . . . delicate," D'Jinnea said,
watching the albino closely as he supervised the other crew
members who were unloading various crates of delicate
bio-samples taken from the world below. "But maybe you're
right. Still, I needed to send him down there with you, in
spite of the risk. After all, who *else* would have known precisely what to look for?"

"Good point," Ganik said as Qagh approached.

While D'Jinnea was momentarily distracted by the intercom—Golag was calling from the engine room to explain
why he'd need an extra day at least to finish cleaning the
Bussard manifolds—Ganik exchanged a silent but significant glance with the white-skinned Klingon. Qagh acknowledged Ganik's wordless signal with a nod, then reached
under his cloak and withdrew a small vial, which he opened
with a flick of his thumb.

The trigger's been pulled, Ganik thought. Like a spear already cast through an Orion spineboar's hearts, the laboriously created contents of that vial now could not be recalled, even if he desired it; the exotic chemical compound was already making its way into the ventilation system, which would spread it quickly through the entire ship.

It's about damned time, Ganik thought. He had wanted Qagh to release the compound before the *Jade Lady* reached Qav'loS. But even though the formula appeared to have passed all the tests, Qagh had resisted doing anything with it prior to today.

Ganik experienced a moment of fear. What if Qagh was double-crossing him? He could have just released some sort of general poison or neurotoxin, dragging his feet until after their departure from Qav'loS just to cover his tracks. But the Klingon albino, always so fastidious about maintaining his own safety, would never subject himself to that sort of risk, not even for a chance at grabbing the keys to D'Jinnea's criminal fiefdom for himself. Dismissing his concerns as foolish, Ganik fell into step alongside Qagh as D'Jinnea led the way out of the shuttlebay and into the captain's quarters in the forward part of the *Jade Lady.*

Once the three were inside D'Jinnea's small but luxuriously appointed quarters, Ganik and Qagh waited in silence while their employer retreated behind a flimsy privacy screen and changed from her already abbreviated work attire to a filmy, flowing robe. Ganik knew that her behavior was motivated less by modesty than it was by a reluctance to reveal the subtle scars left by decades of surgical rejuvenation procedures. Since he'd first come aboard as an adolescent, he had seen more of D'Jinnea than he cared to.

"I want your full report about Qav'loS now," she said as she disrobed behind the screen. Her shoulders, visible over the top of the screen, looked blotchy and uncharacteristically stooped, like those of a frail old woman. "Give me everything that has even a chance of being useful."

Turning toward Qagh, Ganik said, "Your analysis, Qagh?"

D'Jinnea seemed annoyed as the feverish-looking albino stroked his wispy beard, fixed his unfocused gaze on the ceiling, and gathered his thoughts.

Ganik found her pent-up impatience understandable, if somewhat annoying. She had originally ordered Ganik to keep the shuttle in constant contact with the *Jade Lady,* transmitting every discovery and analytical result in real time. Ganik and Qagh had both worked hard to persuade her that this would be unwise, since there was no knowing who might be listening in.

"An interesting place, Qav'loS," Qagh said at length. "A humanoid-habitable environment, not all that different from Orion or Qo'noS. The humanoid population is divided primarily into two factions, mutually hostile to each other. We kept well clear of both, particularly the more violent of the two groups, whom the villagers called Yang—"

"I don't have time for a sociology lesson!" D'Jinnea snapped, interrupting. "What are the biological potentials of the place?"

Ganik noticed the authoritative tone D'Jinnea was using. Generally, her words snapped him to full attention and all but unquestioned obedience when delivered in this manner, and he had always understood why, at least intellectually: it was the Orion male's physiological response to the pheromonal secretions of the Orion female, which had a similar intoxicating effect on the males of many other species as well. It was, in fact, the entire biochemical basis for the Orion civilization's essentially matriarchal structure.

He noticed something else as well: he no longer felt any compulsion to obey this woman. Unquestioned obedience had been a part of his basic makeup for so long that its sudden absence was more than a little disorienting, despite the fact that he and Qagh had planned this together in secret more than three standard cycles earlier.

As D'Jinnea put on her robe, glowering at him and upbraiding them both from across the top of the privacy wall, Ganik saw something utterly at odds with the sexually charged dynamo—She Who Must Be Obeyed—to whom he had sworn fealty more than half a century earlier.

He simply saw an old woman, a yoke that had grown too heavy to bear. He saw an obstacle in his ambition's path.

His hand wandered slowly toward the handle of the long-bladed knife he kept in his sash.

Qagh leaned toward Ganik and spoke in a thin whisper. "Her own DNA is probably becoming nearly as unstable as mine. Probably the cumulative effect of all those rejuvenation treatments."

Ganik could only wonder how long Qagh had suspected this.

Cinching her robe about her slim waist, D'Jinnea came storming out from behind the screen until she stood in the small stateroom's center, glaring at both men.

"Well? Are *both* of my senior lieutenants suddenly dumbstruck? I'm still waiting to learn the biological potentials of the planet you spent the past three days surveying."

Ganik turned toward Qagh, who seemed to be ignoring D'Jinnea entirely. "How are you feeling, Ganik?" Qagh asked.

"I feel . . . strange. Liberated."

"Hello?" D'Jinnea shouted. "Qav'loS, remember? I need to know about every bit of exploitable biology you found down there."

Of course, Ganik thought, grasping the handle of his knife in a tight grip. *You're not getting any younger, are you?*

Suddenly looking stronger than he had in years, Qagh continued to ignore her. "The pheromone uptake inhibitor ought to be taking hold by now throughout the ship, Ganik," he said. "But there's only one way to really test it."

Ganik knew precisely how to conduct that test; he'd been rehearsing the procedure in his dreams for years.

He drew his knife, lunged toward the mortally surprised woman, and relieved her of command.

No sooner had Ganik formally taken charge of the *Jade Lady*—and announced D'Jinnea's unfortunate accidental death to the crew—than his earlier intuition about Qagh's declining health proved correct.

The albino collapsed in the control room, right in the middle of an animated discussion about whether or not further visits to the surface of Qav'loS would be necessary, and Ganik wasted no time carrying him belowdecks to the medical pod. No one was available to treat the stricken Klingon, however, since Qagh himself had always served as the closest thing the *Jade Lady* had to a ship's doctor.

Fortunately, the delirious albino had managed to remain lucid enough to guide Ganik in administering a series of injections that quickly brought him back from what had appeared to be death's proverbial door.

Qagh rallied, and he even looked marginally less pale than usual. Ganik felt immense relief, both because he hadn't lost a crew member whose peculiar expertise had always turned a large profit for the *Jade Lady,* and because he had saved a young man whom he'd raised from infancy, and whom he regarded in some respects as the son he never had. A sickly, ugly son to be sure, but one who nevertheless inspired paternal feelings that Ganik had never believed he'd be capable of experiencing.

Back in the control room less than half a *kilaan* later,

Ganik himself began to feel ill. The fever came first, making him wonder if something had gone wrong with the environmental controls. Immediately following this was a disorienting free fall–like sensation that prompted him to speculate that the grav plating might also be malfunctioning.

Cheb's sudden collapse, followed minutes later by a messy bout of projectile vomiting by Golag, convinced him that whatever had gone amiss had nothing to do with the ship itself.

As the remaining dozen members of the *Jade Lady*'s crew complement fell swiftly in an apparent epidemiological chain reaction, Ganik's earlier fear that Qagh had somehow double-crossed him returned full force.

Why did the albino, who had been near death so very recently, seem to be utterly unaffected by whatever had felled the rest of the *Jade Lady*'s personnel?

"I think I may have a partial answer to what's happening," Qagh said, interrupting Ganik's dark reverie. Ganik looked over the albino's slight shoulder at the scanners, graphical and digital displays, and microscope equipment that Qagh had linked into the autodoc's computer.

Ganik blinked as he steadied himself by gripping the back of Qagh's chair. He wasn't certain whether or not his rising fever was the culprit, but he did know that he couldn't make any sense whatsoever out of what he was seeing.

Fortunately, Qagh saved him the trouble of asking for an explanation. "We must have brought some pathogen or other back with us from the surface of Qav'loS," he said.

"How . . ." Ganik said, pausing as the deck slanted steeply beneath his feet and Qagh showed no sign of having noticed even after it righted itself a moment later. "How did your scans miss it?"

Qagh shrugged, and replied in somewhat nettled tones. "Scanners can only scan for the things they're designed to scan for, Ganik."

"Well, what's this thing going to do to us?"

"No way to tell for certain other than to let it run its course," Qagh said with another shrug.

Ganik didn't like the sound of that one bit. "You mean you aren't going to do anything?"

Qagh turned away from his displays and faced Ganik, grinning up at him. "I didn't say *that*." He picked up a small airhypo that lay in his crowded workspace for apparent emphasis.

Ganik wasn't sure whether he ought to feel relief or foreboding.

Overruling Qagh's objections, Ganik insisted on being the last member of the *Jade Lady*'s crew complement to be injected with the hastily synthesized counteragent. Ganik wasn't simply being noble; if it turned out that Qagh was administering something lethal, Ganik didn't want to learn about it the hard way. As it turned out, everyone aboard the ship seemed to feel much better almost immediately.

"How soon will we know whether or not this cure is going to take?" Ganik said, rubbing the burning spot on his left bicep where Qagh had injected him.

Qagh's sour expression told him he wasn't going to like the answer much. "It may buy us a little time. But it's insufficient."

"Meaning?"

"Meaning that the environment of Qav'loS itself will probably do a much better job of neutralizing the virus we've contracted than I can. A few *kilaan*s or so of additional exposure to the planet's atmosphere—maybe a whole standard rotation—ought to do it."

Ganik's residual suspicions recrudesced, deploying a scowl across his face. "You want to cure a disease by sending everyone down to the very place where that disease came from."

"I can't think of a better solution."

"It's insane."

Qagh folded his arms across his slight chest and returned Ganik's scowl. "It isn't my fault that the universe sometimes works counterintuitively."

A wave of weakness seized Ganik, turning his knees to water. He reached toward the bulkhead to steady himself.

"Are you all right, Ganik?" Qagh said, a vague smile on his face.

Ganik growled. "No, I'm not all right, damn it. I'm *sick,* remember?"

"And you may get a whole lot sicker, along with everybody else aboard the *Jade Lady.* Unless you authorize the treatment I've just prescribed—and fast."

"Funny that *you're* not tipping over from this infection," Ganik said.

"I've had a lot more experience than you have in coping with illnesses. Now, do I have your authorization to order the crew down to the surface?"

The albino's white face seemed to bifurcate as Ganik's vision began to blur. Reluctantly, the Orion came to a decision. "All right, Qagh. Go ahead and get started. I'll be in my quarters."

Qagh nodded. "Will you be coming down in the landing shuttle, or do you want to use the transporter?"

"Neither," Ganik said. "I'm staying aboard."

"That might not be the smartest decision you've ever made," Qagh said as he moved toward the door, clearly intent on carrying out his new orders.

Leaving the ship unattended seems even less smart, Ganik thought. "We'll see."

Qagh paused in the open hatchway and looked back in Ganik's direction, a calculating smile splitting his countenance. "Even after all we've been through together, Ganik, I still get the feeling that you don't entirely trust me."

How perceptive of you, Ganik thought.

"But it's your call," the albino added, smiling. "You *are* the captain, after all."

It sounded as if he muttered something else as he turned away, but Ganik couldn't be sure.

A pair of faces gradually resolved themselves from the swirling maelstrom of Ganik's delirium.

One of the faces was as white as Orion's north polar cap.

"I thought you left the ship, Qagh," Ganik said, confused. He struggled into a half-sitting position, and noticed only then that he was stripped to the waist, in his own bed in the berth that had formerly belonged to D'Jinnea.

He couldn't quite remember how he'd gotten back here.

"I left the ship yesterday," said the albino. "I decided to come back aboard after you stopped answering the comm."

Ganik turned toward the other face that hovered nearby, which he saw belonged to Golag. "Where is the rest of the crew?"

"They're still down on the planet, recovering," Golag said. "Qagh still insists that we all might have died from the infection had you not sent us to the surface." Though Ganik was still disoriented, he immediately recognized the sound of the gunnery specialist's skepticism.

"Half the crew already seems to be back to normal," Qagh said, apparently unfazed by his colleague's unconcealed doubts. "Golag was the first to get back on his feet, if you can believe that. The rest of the men will be back on board shortly."

Good thing I stayed on the ship, Ganik thought. He still had no concrete reason to believe that the second trip down to Qav'loS had really been necessary. And he wouldn't put it past Qagh to try to usurp command of the *Jade Lady,* her crew, and the various ongoing criminal enterprises that Ganik had inherited from his late predecessor, D'Jinnea.

The thought that he might have just thwarted the albino's plan to do to him what they had both done to D'Jinnea pleased him greatly.

Qagh turned toward Golag and said, "Do you mind if I speak with the captain in private for a moment?"

Golag frowned, then looked toward Ganik for guidance. The Orion nodded his assent; despite his weakened condition, he knew that Qagh wouldn't dare raise a hand against him with Golag standing right outside the door to his quarters.

Golag exited the room after delivering a parting shrug.

After the hatch had closed, Qagh sat on a plain, functional chair that was near the foot of the bed. "You still don't trust me, Ganik." He paused. "Well, I can't say I blame you."

Ganik nodded. "You have to admit, curing this little plague of yours could have given you a convenient means of . . . taking over."

"If you had left the ship with everybody else, you mean," Qagh said, picking up and activating a handheld medical scanner that he must have been carrying all along. He smiled. "But it looks like you were too smart for me, Ganik. And you're right. I *haven't* been entirely candid with you about the return trip to Qav'loS."

The Orion's eyebrows went aloft unbidden. He couldn't believe the little albino would admit to scheming against him.

Unless he believed he'd already succeeded.

"What are you talking about, Qagh?" Ganik said, his voice rasping in a throat that had suddenly gone dry.

The white-faced Klingon looked down at his scanner, whose readout wasn't visible to Ganik. The younger man's smile expanded. "I told you that the planet's environment would *probably* help cure the illness, Ganik. But I'm afraid I left out one important detail."

Ganik found that he could no longer speak. His mouth was as parched as Tyree's deserts. He wanted to rise to get a glass of water, but his limbs suddenly felt like they'd been hewn from granite. His heart raced, as though it were trying to break the warp barrier.

Qagh fixed his gaze back upon Ganik, his smile twisting into a rictus of pure malice.

"I neglected to tell you," Qagh continued, "that I paid good money to one of my biotechnology sources to learn that this disease organism is *always* fatal—unless the infected person remains on the planet for a few *kilaan*s after exposure, to build up an immunity. But you opted to guard the ship instead of taking the only cure. It appears, Captain, that caution has killed you."

Ganik's breath was coming in painful rasps. Lightning coursed through his limbs. In spite of his agony, he somehow found his voice again.

"Why, Qagh? You were . . . like a son to me."

The albino sneered. "You and D'Jinnea have exploited me all my life. I was your *slave*. An ugly weakling you tolerated only because I developed expertise that made money for you both—and because of where I must have come from."

Qagh reached into his tunic and pulled a small metal object from an inner pocket. Though his delirium was rapidly returning, threatening to swallow the universe whole beginning with the edges of the room, Ganik recognized the object immediately.

It was the clasp that had once kept Qagh's baby blankets in place, when the albino had been a half-dead foundling. The clasp bore the family crest of the House of Ngoj, the once-powerful Klingon family from which Ganik and D'Jinnea had always assumed Qagh had come. Though that family had suffered many reversals over the years—Ganik had heard that revelations about some sort of genetic scan-

dal some three decades earlier had brought the House low—
the House of Ngoj had been returning to ascendancy of late.
Ganik and D'Jinnea had both hoped that their albino charge
would help them leverage some of that House's wealth and
power someday.

Now Ganik knew that day was never going to come. He
tried to scream, but his breath failed him.

Then delirium took hold of his mind, even as blackness
came creeping in at the edges of his vision.

The hatch hissed open, startling Golag. "Get in here!
Hurry!"

Golag had been leaning idly against the sealed hatch,
alert for an emergency summons from Captain Ganik. He
was mildly surprised to note that the voice that called him
belonged instead to Qagh.

He wasted no time getting back inside the berth where
the captain had been recuperating from his illness.

And where he now lay on his bed, ashen-faced and
breathing in brief, wheezing gasps.

"What's happened to him?" Golag asked the little albino,
who was standing beside Ganik's bed and slowly moving a
scanning device over the stricken man's chest.

"It seems to have come over him suddenly," Qagh said.

"*What* has come over him?" Golag reached toward the
knife at his belt, then paused, realizing he would be raising his hand against the *Jade Lady*'s legitimate captain if
it turned out Ganik was succumbing to illness rather than
assassination.

"The end of the disease process," Qagh said. "I wish he
had heeded my warning and returned to Qav'loS, even for a
short time. He might have recovered by now."

"You said anyone who refused to go down to Qav'loS
might come to a bad end," Golag said. "But you never
proved it."

Qagh favored the gunnery man with a knowing nod. "Ah, yes. You were one of the skeptics. But at least you were wise enough to go to the planet, even without proof."

Golag nodded. "There's no point in taking unnecessary chances."

"Of course not. Especially not when your captain felt compelled to take those unnecessary chances for you."

Ganik's body suddenly began to convulse. The captain's huge, gray-mottled arms flailed, sending a bedside table and several drinking vessels crashing into a bulkhead as both Qagh and Golag ducked out of the way.

The albino gestured toward Ganik. "I fear you now have the proof you wanted about what the Qav'loS virus can do if left unchecked."

Ganik shuddered and stopped moving, his pleading, rheumy eyes locking on Golag's. Though he was clearly unable to speak, he nevertheless seemed desperate to say something.

Golag's spine was flash-frozen with renewed apprehension about the albino. Was Ganik trying to tell him that Qagh had poisoned him? Or was he simply experiencing whatever terrors bedeviled Orions when the *Fek'lhr* finally came calling?

While Golag knew he would never know the answer to the latter question, he could see that this death matched no poison he had ever seen. As he watched with horrified fascination, Ganik's body seemed to desiccate and deflate, like a pile of dry leaves consumed by fire. The thick, ropy muscles of his forearms shrank and retreated, and his skin became thoroughly gray, turning hard and crystalline.

A final staccato shriek of horror and agony escaped Ganik's petrified lips an instant before what remained of the Orion pirate lord collapsed into a pile amounting to a few large handfuls of mineralized, blue-gray powder.

"A pity," Qagh said distractedly, waving his scanner

over Captain Ganik's mortal remains with a dispassion that would have done a Vulcan proud.

The albino turned off the scanner, then looked directly at Golag.

"Well, Golag. It appears I will be the one setting the agenda from now on. And planning the raids. And allocating the money."

Golag was too stunned by what he had just seen to do anything but nod.

He tried very hard not to think about the fate of anyone who got in the albino's way now.

SIX

"Please don't take this the wrong way, Commander," said Dr. Klass, gazing at Sulu from across the top of one of her biobed monitors. "But you look like hell."

"No offense taken, Doc," Sulu said through a thin smile. "I didn't get a lot of sleep last night. I suppose it shows more than I realized."

Standing beside her primary workspace in the sickbay's main science lab, Klass watched him with that same sincere *I'm-listening-very-closely* expression that Sulu had seen crease the faces of many of Starfleet's best physicians over the past quarter century.

After appraising him in silence for several moments, she said, "Maybe watching that woman die right in front of you yesterday affected you a bit more than you know."

He sighed, wishing, just this once, that she wasn't so damned perceptive. But he also couldn't deny that her gift of perspicacity was the main reason that *Excelsior*'s chief medical officer had become such a close friend and confidante during his first few difficult weeks serving as Captain Styles's executive officer and second-in-command.

But despite his feelings of friendship for the doctor, he decided not to mention last night's return of his intermittently recurring dreams—at least not before he'd spent a little more time pondering the question of why a pale-visaged ghost he'd seen only once more than four decades ago had chosen last night to pay him one of its rare visits.

"It isn't every day you see someone die the way that poor woman did," he said at length, recalling the horror of watching a living being suddenly collapse into a few handfuls of vaguely crystalline residue. "Have you identified whatever it was that killed her?"

Klass released a frustrated sigh and shook her head. "I'm still running analytical comparisons, using all the data I scanned during *my* sleepless night from the tissue samples you beamed up. All I can say so far is that your initial impression may be on the right track: I can't rule out this thing being a strain of the Omega IV pathogen."

Moving with a supple grace that belied her apparent age, the gray-haired doctor approached the computer terminal that sat atop her desk and tapped its slender keypad. An image of a greenish, globular-shaped microorganism, magnified many thousands of times, appeared on the screen.

"The virus you found on Galdonterre still hasn't given up all its secrets," Klass continued. "But at least I *finally* managed to persuade the captain that it isn't casually communicable."

"Speaking on behalf of myself and everyone who was with me on Galdonterre," Sulu said, chuckling although the night he'd spent in quarantine had passed very slowly indeed, "you have our undying gratitude for that."

Klass cast a grin in Sulu's direction before turning back toward the screen. "I'm sure I could spend the rest of my life studying this virus before I get all the way to the bottom of it. But there are a few things I've been able to determine right off the bat."

Sensing that Klass was quickly shifting into lecture mode, Sulu folded his arms before himself and leaned against one of the examination tables. "Such as?"

"First, it's obvious to me that this is a deliberately tailored pathogen. And a computerized cross-comparison to known 'wild' strains with similar molecular markers revealed that the original biochemical substrate the genetic designer used is an extremely rare and potent retroviral form of the Levodian flu. Fortunately, it isn't an airborne strain like the original Levodian flu virus, or the Omega IV pathogen. So at least the captain won't have to try to enforce a general quarantine around Galdonterre."

"That's something to be thankful for," Sulu said, relieved at the news. "But are you sure about the Levodian flu connection? I had a bad bout of it as a child, but it didn't turn me into pile of rock salt."

"Of course not. Levodian flu is generally harmless to most humanoid species, especially once the fever, chills, and sniffles run their course." Klass tapped a control on the terminal's keypad, and the magnified image gave way to a schematic diagram of a familiar yet alien double-helix DNA spiral. "Needless to say, there's a lot more folded into this bug's genome than the baseline Levodian flu virus that might have kept you out of school for a day or two. My cross-checks with some generous and discreet friends at Starfleet Medical and Starfleet Intelligence have confirmed the presence of Klingon DNA—along with some extremely peculiar *human* gene sequences as well."

Sulu's eyebrows rose involuntarily. "Klingon—*and* human? Someone mixed those genes together deliberately?"

"That's a hard question to answer," Klass said with a small shrug. "After all, there are plenty of microorganisms capable of acquiring genes from one another through direct cytoplasmic transfer. That phenomenon alone might account for portions of the virus's genome."

"But not all of it."

Klass nodded. "Right. The odds against this organism arising naturally are astronomical. It has far too many points of similarity to the pathogen that devastated the planet Qu'Vat in the twenty-second century to be unrelated."

"Qu'Vat," Sulu said. "That's a Klingon colony, isn't it?"

Klass nodded again. "Just two light-years from the border of Federation space. A Denobulan physician named Phlox wrote several papers detailing the plague that broke out there one hundred and thirty-five years ago, and its aftereffects. He drew heavily on the work of a Klingon geneticist named Antaak, who used tailored retroviruses to treat the plague."

"Did these papers explain how both human and Klingon genes might have gotten grafted onto *our* virus?" Sulu asked.

"Phlox wrote extensively about Antaak's recombinant DNA techniques," Klass said, pinching the bridge of her nose as she considered the possibilities. "Of course, the genes could have jumped from one viral strain to another without any advanced lab work, especially in the original 'wild' airborne version of the pathogen. The virus we're dealing with here could have picked up DNA sequences from members of one species before being transmitted to members of another species and picking up theirs, whether or not the original virus itself had been tinkered with in other respects."

Because of his knowledge of the genetics of exotic plant life—he'd been an amateur exobotanist longer than he'd served in Starfleet, thanks in no small part to his mother's work as an agronomist—Sulu was willing to believe that random mutations and gene transfers might explain the lethality of this new virus. But the horrible death of the woman in the bar—not to mention decades of suspicions about the motives of the Klingons—wouldn't allow him to invoke pure coincidence just yet.

"Is it possible," he said, "that the Klingons *intended* this virus to be a weapon?"

She spread her hands. "I can't say for sure one way or the other. It's tough to imagine anybody perverting bioscience in such a way as to deliberately create a bioweapon that kills the way this thing can. But I suppose we can't put that past them, especially given what happened on Qu'Vat."

Sulu felt a surge of embarrassment that he wasn't better versed in the past couple of centuries of Klingon frontier history. "What do you mean?"

"Well, the Klingon scientist I mentioned—Antaak— worked on variants of his initial therapeutic Levodian flu retrovirus for years after the plague. It was as though he wasn't satisfied with the cure, despite the millions of lives he was credited with saving. So he continued his recombinant DNA research. And either because of or in spite of this work—nobody really seems to know which—several million Klingons living on Qu'Vat died from another similar plague outbreak sometime in the early 2170s. Antaak himself was one of the casualties."

Sulu winced. Despite his ambivalence toward the Klingon Empire and its aggressive, expansionist ways, he'd had personal dealings with a Klingon officer or two during his time in Starfleet. He had even worked alongside one on an important clandestine mission. He had found these men, warriors all, to be honorable; their culture seemed to demand it. Such people deserved better than to die from the ravages of some microorganism.

"It sounds almost as though everyone was wiped out," Sulu said. "Were there any survivors?"

"Of course," Klass said, though a haunted look crossed her lined face. "There always are. Several million of them, in fact. But these people suffered permanent retroviral alterations to their DNA. These changes rendered most of them sterile. There was widespread albinism, anemia, as well as just about any other chronic ailment you can imagine."

Sulu's throat suddenly went dry. He knew enough about Klingon mores to guess what must have happened next. "The Klingons must have quarantined the planet afterward. And then mass-euthanized all the sick people the virus hadn't managed to kill."

Klass nodded, her mouth set in a grim line. "With typical Klingon ruthlessness, no doubt, since they've never made it a secret that they consider only the 'strong' to be worthy of survival. For all we know, the virus I've got under the microscope right now could have been part of a secret Klingon bioweapons program that the Empire decided to test on its own 'undesirables' on Qu'Vat."

Undesirables, Sulu thought with an inward shudder. *Lepers. Outcasts.*

And outcasts frequently became outlaws.

Sulu considered the nameless Klingon albino who had so terrified the woman in the spaceport bar—and who had apparently engineered her death with a highly specific biological weapon. Then he recalled the chalk-skinned terror of his childhood, the phantasm that had afflicted his dreams yet again last night.

Despite the renowned Klingon tradition of weeding out "weaklings"—a phenomenon that could only make albinism an all but nonexistent rarity in the Klingon Empire—Sulu realized that the odds were decidedly against the dead woman's albino being the same man he had witnessed raiding his mother's lab on Ganjitsu more than four decades ago.

But last night's dreams still argued persuasively that his subconscious believed otherwise.

SEVEN

2269 (the Year of Kahless 895,
early in the month of *Xan'lahr*)

I.K.S. 'Oghwl'

Captain Koloth stalked onto the bridge, his usually smooth brow furrowed in barely contained fury.

The captain of an Earther starship had once again filled his engine room from bulkhead to beam with a writhing mass of furry, screeching *yIH*—the pestilent creatures that the Earthers called "tribbles." It was the same blight that had infested his previous command, the battlecruiser *I.K.S. Gr'oth*, which Koloth had been forced to scuttle hurriedly in order to prevent the hated furballs from spreading to the Klingon agricultural colonies in the Donatu sector and beyond.

The ignominy lay not merely in the fact of the presence of the *yIH* themselves, although that was certainly bad enough. No, Koloth's current humiliation derived mostly from the fact that today marked the second occasion in as many years when he had fallen victim to this very tactic.

Worse yet, it was the second time it had been employed against him—

—by James.

Tiberius.

Kirk.

Koloth stomped toward the command chair, which sat atop a dais in the center of the crowded control room. Commander Korax, the *'OghwI'*'s second-in-command, hastened to relinquish the seat and get out of Koloth's way.

"Ship's status!" Koloth barked as he sat, baring his teeth in a rictus that only superficially resembled a smile. He could see from the quailing reactions of the two young *bekk*s who manned the stations just beyond the command chair that his aspect couldn't have been more frightening if he possessed the proud *HemQuch* forehead crest of his noble warrior ancestors.

"Our standard offensive and defensive systems remain operational," Korax said. "But the stasis cannon we've been testing is still depleted, and will take several *kilaan*s to regenerate its power cells."

"The stasis cannon is clearly a failure," said Koloth. "It cripples us as much as it does the enemy. How is the cleanup progressing?"

"Second officer Gherud and Chief Engineer Kurr have just finished spacing the last of those miserable *yIH*," Korax added.

"They will no doubt have missed some of them," Koloth said, drawing some degree of comfort from the fact that Lieutenant Gherud was finally making himself truly useful. Such was not always the case with Gherud; it was a never-ending source of frustration for Koloth that the ambitious second officer's political connections within both the Klingon Defense Force Command and the High Council had made Gherud's position as the *'OghwI'*'s political officer an all but unassailable sinecure.

"Some of the *yIH* have probably managed to enter shielded sections of the ship by now," Korax said. "We can't scan those areas properly, or establish positive transporter locks."

Koloth suppressed a growl. "Indeed. The vermin started getting into everything—*after* you scattered them by firing your disruptor into their midst."

Chastened yet sullen, Korax thrust out his chin, tempting Koloth to tear it loose and beat him senseless with it. "The *glo'meH* can surely devour the few that remain," said the first officer.

The *glo'meH,* or "glommer," as the Earthers called it, was an artificial life-form, a prototype created by the Klingon Empire's finest geneticists for the sole purpose of eradicating *yIH,* which even now threatened to overrun at least one of the Empire's key agricultural worlds. Apparently it wasn't enough that the cursed fuzzballs that the *glo'meH* was designed to destroy had, not long ago, blown apart a carefully laid Klingon Intelligence scheme to seize the disputed Donatu-sector world of *SermanyuQ* from the ever-grasping hands of the Earthers and their *yuQjIjQa',* otherwise known as the United Federation of Planets.

Then the shrieking creatures just *had* to turn out to be more than even the hungry *glo'meH* could stomach.

Koloth shook his head. "At this moment, Korax, our prototype predator is cowering under the engine room deck plating like a frightened Regulan bloodworm. Let us hope its descendants will prove somewhat more useful." Eager to change the subject, Koloth added, "What is our current heading?"

"Archanis, Captain," Korax said. "As you ordered. Do you wish to reverse course, sir? We can still intercept the *Enterprise* well before it reaches *SermanyuQ* if we come about now."

Koloth was seriously considering doing just that. The thought of allowing Kirk's quintotriticale-laden convoy to make it intact all the way to *SermanyuQ*—the world the

Earthers insisted on calling "Sherman's Planet"—was very nearly too much to bear.

"May *Fek'lhr* boil Kirk's eyes and feast on them," Koloth said.

"Your 'dear old friend' deserves no less, Captain," Korax said, nodding and displaying a death's-head grin of his own. "And I know I would relish nothing more than teaching that swaggering, tin-plated martinet a lesson." A cold realization came to Koloth: a decision to even the score would still be a decision to pursue, attack, and destroy the *Enterprise*.

And very likely renew the state of all-out war that would have utterly engulfed both the Empire and the Federation had the energy-beings of *'orghenya'* not deigned to interfere.

With so many Klingon worlds suffering from simple lack of food and other resources of late, is this the wisest course to pursue right now? Koloth thought, unsure of how even the unforgettable Kahless himself would rule on the matter.

"Request permission to pursue and attack," Korax said, interrupting Koloth's weighty musings. The first officer's fierce expression showed a desire for revenge that seemed to occlude all else.

Koloth decided then and there that Korax's desires—and in no small part, his own—were far too personal to be allowed to jeopardize what remained of the Empire's current diminished prospects.

Koloth felt a surprising calm descend upon the fires of his warrior's soul. It was as though he was seeing the meaning of an image change just by being projected onto a much larger surface. The image in his mind encompassed the entire Empire, all the centuries that it had endured since the outrages of the Hurq invaders all the way to whatever grand destiny awaited it in the ever-shifting mists of the future.

Let the High Council decide when and how to plunge the Empire into total war, Koloth thought.

"*Fek'lhr* will take Kirk when he is good and ready," he

said at length. He leaned forward in his chair and began addressing the young helmsman, a neutral yet anticipatory expression displayed on his goateed *QuchHa'* face.

A high-pitched squeal from somewhere overhead interrupted Koloth just as he opened his mouth to speak.

"Up there!" Korax said, pointing toward one of the ventilator grills mounted in the control room's crowded and dimly illuminated ceiling.

A stray yIH, Koloth thought, shaking his head. *How long will it take to rid the* 'OghwI' *of the last of these vermin once and for all?* Unpleasant visions of the hastily abandoned *Gr'oth* being blown to atoms just *qelI'qam*s from his retreating escape pod sprang unbidden into his mind.

"Get the cursed thing down from there and dispose of it," Koloth snapped.

"With pleasure," Korax said. He wasted no time climbing toward the ceiling grille, pushing a *bekk* aside in order to use the crewman's communications console to make his precarious ascent. Korax tore the grille screen open with a resounding clang, inserted one long arm into the air conduit behind it, and extracted a single chittering, angry *yIH*. The first officer held onto the writhing, twisting creature as best he could.

And fell awkwardly to the deck with a bone-crunching *thud.*

Korax rose, enraged and in obvious pain, grasped the screaming furball in both hands, and tore it asunder. A messy deluge of hair and ruby-hued alien ichor spattered the first officer's uniform tunic, raining messily to the deck while the *bekk*s looked on.

Koloth closed his eyes and shook his head slowly.

"Thank you, Korax. Now I'd appreciate it if you'd get a mop. . . ."

EIGHT

Klass sat at the conference table with her hands folded, watching the captain intently. Not for the first time, she wondered what he'd do with his hands if he didn't have that omnipresent swagger stick to play with.

"Biochemical warfare," Styles said. "Directed at the Federation and the Klingon peace talks by a mysterious, possibly albino, possibly Klingon, possibly male sentient, who may or may not have sent a woman to her death for delivering a warning to you." Styles leaned back in his chair, a dubious expression on his face. "Have I *missed* anything?"

Before either Klass or Sulu could respond, Styles held up a finger. Looking directly at Sulu, he said, "Oh, and who may or may not be the same albino Klingon who raided your parents' settlement forty years ago, when you were a child. There, I believe *that* about covers it."

"Captain, let me show you why I believe that there may be more credibility in *Commander* Sulu's suggestions than may seem obvious." Seated next to Sulu, Klass spoke up, even as she punched data into her tricorder. She had been certain to place a slight emphasis on the word "commander" just to remind her captain that his passive-aggressive stance toward Sulu should be tempered by rank, even if not by propriety. She gave Sulu a quick sidelong glance and was pleased to see that he was masking his emotions, which were, no doubt, as high as Yellow Alert level inside: no one liked being talked down to as though he were a recalcitrant schoolchild.

The signal from her tricorder fed onto the triscreen in the center of the conference room table, allowing not only Styles but also Lieutenant Commander Cutler and Lieutenant Schulman to view the images. The monitors displayed the same magnified greenish, globular microorganism that Klass had shown Sulu in sickbay earlier this morning.

"This is the viral bioagent that killed the alien woman," Klass said. "The pathogen incorporates genetic code cribbed from the Levodian flu, the Klingon retroviruses that devastated the Klingon colony on Qu'Vat more than a century ago, as well as at least seven other genetically tailored viral elements that include assorted known human, Klingon, Orion, and Andorian viruses."

"So, you're absolutely certain that this thing is a bioweapon?" Cutler asked.

"If you'll excuse the expression, I'd stake my life on it." Klass gave Cutler a wry smile, peering in much the same way that Klass's own mother had done whenever she'd been intent on communicating something important. "This particular pathogen is heavily bioengineered. And its only purpose would be to kill."

Styles frowned. "Before I lifted the quarantine, you said this virus was not a danger to the crew."

"It isn't," Klass said cleanly. "It's not airborne, nor transferable by skin-to-skin contact. It's theoretically possible for an infected person to pass the pathogen to others through blood or other body fluids, but according to my preliminary studies it would take months of repeated exposure."

"What about ingestion?" Cutler asked.

Klass spread her hands and gave a slight shrug. "This particular virus . . . maybe, maybe not. As a bioweapon, it would be most effective if delivered to the bloodstream quickly and in high concentrations, by hypospray or some other injection mechanism."

She turned toward Sulu. "We're all concentrating too strongly on *this* particular virus, however. Put simply, whoever designed this was a biotech genius. The grafting of multiple types of alien DNA I found within this virus is truly astonishing in its complexity. If this were the work of a Federation scientist, the designer would have to be somebody at the very top of the microbiology food chain, so to speak."

Klass gestured toward Sulu, continuing. "The reason Commander Sulu is taking this potential threat so seriously—and the reason we all should do likewise, in my opinion—is that whoever designed this virus . . . if he can engineer *this,* he can probably also engineer something a whole lot worse."

"So your research shows that we clearly have discovered a bioterrorist weapon," said Styles. "But what we *don't* have, beyond hearsay from a dying woman, and Commander Sulu's hypothesis, is an actual *terrorist* . . . nor any truly *credible* threat to the Korvat peace talks."

"If I may, Captain," Lieutenant Schulman spoke up, pulling up data on the padd that lay on the table before her.

"Go ahead," Styles said, settling back in his chair again.

"Searching through both Starfleet and civilian Federation databases, I've found thirty-four separate accounts in the last fifty-plus years of border raids or attacks at which one of the raiders was identified as a pale or albino Klingon. The majority of them also identify various Orions among the raiding party—curiously, all male—and a scattered few other species, including Klingons."

"What were the raiders' targets?" Cutler asked.

Schulman tapped some keys, and highlighted data appeared on the tabletop's viewscreens. "Up until 2248, the majority of the raids followed a certain profile: people taken captive, presumably to be sold into slavery, and various supplies and technology stolen. But sometime in mid-2248, the raids began to take a turn toward scientific settlements and outposts, and even targeted some medical facilities."

Sulu cleared his throat briefly. "That's also the year that the raiders in question razed Ishikawa Village on Ganjitsu, where my parents' laboratories were. I was eleven years old. I did *not* have direct face-to-face contact with the albino Klingon at that time, but I did catch a glimpse of him and his raiders while I was doing whatever I could to . . . discourage them."

"I should also point out that there were countless raids along the Federation side of the border during that same time period in which no witnesses were left behind," Schulman said, twisting a lock of her hair around one finger near her shoulder. "The vast majority of these sightings and raids occurred in or near disputed regions of space between long-established UFP sectors and Klingon territory. It's possible that there have been significantly more raids on the Klingon side of the border that can be attributed to this albino and his cohorts."

Cutler shook her head, frowning. "It's also possible that the other raids have nothing to do with this albino. Klingon and Orion raiders have been a problem since long before any of us were in Starfleet. And we also don't know if it's all the work of *one* albino Klingon, or if there are several, all of whom could be outcasts from their society. They could even have some kind of syndicate for all we know, acting in concert with the Orions."

Styles leaned forward again, clasping his hands together and steepling his fingers under his nose, his swagger stick tucked beneath his arm. "For the sake of this discussion—and given the supporting evidence—we know that there likely is at least one raiding party led by an albino Klingon. What bothers me is that although the dead woman warned us of a planned attack on Korvat, and then died from a bioengineered virus, there's no *clear connection* between any of these elements. We have an unusually pigmented border-world bandit with a penchant for striking scientific targets. Why would he want to disrupt the Korvat talks?"

Klass couldn't argue with Styles's logic or his line of questioning, but she saw that Sulu was about to do just that. He would have been a bad poker player, given his propensity to fidget.

"If the Federation and the Klingon Empire do succeed in achieving some kind of lasting peace accord, it would certainly make border raids a more difficult proposition," Sulu said.

"And?" Styles asked simply.

"And what?" Sulu replied.

"That's the sole motivation?" Styles asked. "Space is vast, Commander. If you want to get away with skullduggery, just travel another hundred light-years."

"We don't *know* the albino's motivation, because almost nobody has had contact with him and lived to tell about it," Sulu argued. "But we do have the dying warning of the woman that put us on this trail, and—"

"Commander, I think you've just put your finger on something," Styles said, interrupting. "Just about everyone who has encountered this albino pirate hasn't lived long enough to tell anyone about it. But *you* have. And you survived an attack that threatened your family and destroyed your home—when you were a *child*. That kind of trauma stays with you for a lifetime. Perhaps you're a bit too personally involved to consider this matter objectively." Styles's expression softened, and Klass sensed that he was actually being serious and nonjudgmental, rather than simply trying to put Sulu down. "I can't say that, given an opportunity to avenge something of that nature, I wouldn't grasp at the same straws you have. But until we have something more concrete to go on, I don't see any point in taking any further steps in this matter . . . steps that might introduce unnecessary tensions and distractions into the peace talks, or maybe even derail them altogether."

Klass could almost see steam rising from Sulu's collar, but even she had to admit that Styles had a point. The facts pointed to several possible dangers, but none of them connected sufficiently to draw a complete picture.

"I will concede that I *am* personally involved, Captain," Sulu said through thin lips. "But I think that ignoring the facts that we have might be inviting a calamity."

Styles stood. "If it doesn't get in the way of your duties, Commander, you can still research this. Lieutenant Schulman will assist you. Again, *if* it doesn't get in the way of your duties. If you find further evidence, you can be certain that we'll act on it."

He put a hand on Sulu's shoulder and smiled in a gentle, almost fatherly way. "If you'll excuse the expression, don't let this become your white whale, Hikaru," he said.

"Yes, sir," Sulu said quietly.

Klass saw the first officer's jaw clench, and she wondered just what plans were hatching in his head even now. She knew that Sulu had been a part of Kirk's crew long enough that he wasn't likely to let this matter go, no matter what the captain ultimately decided to do about it.

She just hoped that he wouldn't push too far, or in the wrong manner.

"You want me to *what*?" Janice Rand asked, her voice sharp.

"Trust me on this, Janice," Sulu said. "I know what I'm doing." He hated the fact that he couldn't do this alone, but at least he knew he had one good friend on board who was in an ideal position to help him.

She shook her head, her dark blond bobbed hair moving from side to side as she did so. "If we get caught, we'll both be in big trouble."

Sulu grinned. "That's why you won't let us get caught. You're too *good* to slip up. And me, well . . . you know me."

"All right," Rand said, stepping away from Sulu, toward the turbolift to the bridge. "Five minutes, though. Or less. I'll signal you when I'm ready."

"Thanks, Janice."

Sulu turned and stalked down the corridor toward his quarters. Going around Styles was a risky move, but he knew he had to try regardless. *It's not like I'm going over his head, exactly,* Sulu thought mischievously. *Just changing frequencies on him.*

He was still simmering with frustration over the meeting they had had earlier, though he took some comfort in the fact that Styles had given him permission to continue researching the albino and his crimes. He was simply widening his search parameters by seeking a bit of outside help. He felt thankful that he had some history with one particular person who might prove more helpful than just about anyone else in the Federation.

In his quarters, Sulu took a seat in front of the viewscreen of his communications console, its monitor glowing with the cool blue-and-white logo of the UFP. He entered the proper frequency and waited.

A few minutes passed, and his wall-mounted communicator chimed three times. It was Rand's signal that she was now preventing the capture of any record of the outgoing call from Sulu's quarters, and scrambling the subspace frequency he was using to prevent detection or interception on this end. For the next few minutes, Sulu could communicate in complete privacy.

He tapped the console nervously, and moments later, the viewscreen picture changed.

The man who answered the call was a male Trill of perhaps twenty-five, judging both by his smooth skin and the spots on his neck and brow, a man whose face was unfamiliar to Sulu. *"May I help you, Commander?"* the Trill said, clearly having read the signal Rand had sent as she'd opened the private comm channel.

A wave of disappointment passed through Sulu, but even as he spoke, he saw movement behind the Trill man. "I need to speak with the ambassador. It's urgent," Sulu said. He was aware that he had now lost at least thirty seconds.

"Very well," the Trill said before moving out of view.

A moment later, a dignified older Vulcan stepped into the camera's line of sight. He was attired in simpler robes than those he'd worn during their last encounter, and his angular, upswept eyebrows now showed even more of the gray that frosted his bowl-cut hair. Still, despite the man's stern, unemotional countenance, Sulu felt his spirits lifting, at least a little.

"How may I help you, Commander Sulu?" the Vulcan asked.

"I don't have long to talk," Sulu said, "but I have a matter of grave importance to relay to you, Ambassador Sarek."

•   •   •

An hour later, Sulu was back up on *Excelsior*'s bridge, reviewing some recent duty logs with Valtane, when Lieutenant Rand called out.

"Captain Styles, I'm receiving a message from Starfleet Command."

Sulu turned to see Styles step up out of his chair, straightening his tunic slightly. "On-screen," he said.

Fleet Admiral Lance Cartwright suddenly appeared on the main viewer, his expression grave but otherwise unreadable. Sulu had had relatively little interaction with Cartwright. But he also knew that Cartwright currently served both as Chief of Starfleet Operations and the organization's liaison with the Federation Diplomatic Corps, and therefore chose to take the man's appearance as a hopeful sign.

"Greetings, Captain Styles. There's been a change in your current orders. Because the Saratoga *has been assigned to other duties, you are to immediately rendezvous with the shuttlecraft* Hedford, *which is carrying Ambassador Sarek and his retinue.* Excelsior *is to ferry them to the Korvat colony, and provide security for the peace conference there."*

"Yes, sir," Styles said crisply. "Is there anything in particular that we should be aware of regarding the conference's security needs?"

The admiral frowned slightly. *"We have reason to believe that an increased security presence may be necessary. Intelligence has reached us that leads us to believe that the location and times of the talks may have been compromised. We want to make certain that hostile parties do not make the conference an opportunity to plunge the Federation and the Klingon Empire into war."*

"Understood, sir," Styles said.

Sulu turned away to suppress the slight smile that had crept onto his face. Apparently his brief warning to Sarek had been enough to get the ambassador rattling some cages among the Starfleet brass. *Sometimes it's good to have connections,* he thought, allowing himself to enjoy a moment of enormous satisfaction.

"Please make certain that every courtesy is afforded the ambassador and his staff," the admiral said. *"And if any trouble does arise at Korvat, don't hesitate to make every effort to end it as quickly and quietly as possible."* He nodded his head, and then said, *"Cartwright out."*

Sulu saw the new coordinates from Starfleet on his and Valtane's consoles even as Styles began issuing orders, his voice steady and sure. "You all heard the admiral. Let's get to the rendezvous point before Ambassador Sarek does."

Sneaking a look over his shoulder toward Rand, Sulu saw Styles looking his way, and rather intently at that. *If he suspects anything, he'll have a hard time proving it,* Sulu thought. *And either way, we're going to be closer to the fight—if there is one—than we would have been before.*

The thought gave him some additional satisfaction, but little comfort.

NINE

The inside of Koloth's skull throbbed and pulsated like one of the old-style *targ*-hide war drums of ancient Qo'noS.

He could no longer deny that he was succumbing to the fever that had begun its inexorable spread throughout the *'OghwI'* only four *kilaan*s or so after the battle cruiser's departure from *yuQjIjQa'* space.

Koloth heard the control room doors hiss open behind him. With a painful effort, he swiveled his command chair toward the noise in time to see the lift disgorge Choq, the ship's elderly and sour-countenanced surgeon, into command center.

"I have come to make my report on the illness," said Choq, halting once he'd come within slightly more than a *bat'leth*'s length from the command chair.

"You could have called from the infirmary," Koloth said.

"Certainly. But then I wouldn't have been able to observe how well my captain is enduring this affliction," Choq said as he drew a handheld scanning device from the scabbard on his belt.

Koloth leaned toward the surgeon and swatted the annoyingly noisy instrument out of his hand. The healer suppressed a wince as the device clattered against the deck, where it landed far too loudly for the captain's taste. "*My* condition is unimportant. I need you to save my *crew*. But first, make your report."

Choq turned his head, regarding his fallen instrument as though thinking about retrieving it. Then he shrugged and fixed his rheumy gaze firmly back upon Koloth.

"Very well, Captain. The illness comes from a virus—one that the *yIH* must have brought aboard with them."

"And that fool Korax no doubt spread it about when he tore that miserable vermin apart right in this very room," Koloth said, suppressing a sudden transitory wave of nausea.

Choq nodded. "Let us hope that Korax awakens from his coma, so that he may regret having done that. But in all fairness, Captain, the virus was probably already airborne more than a *kilaan* before he cast the creature's guts to the winds, as it were."

Koloth suppressed a growl. "How?"

"Some of the smaller ones must have gotten into the ventilation system almost immediately, and more than a few of those no doubt ran afoul of the circulation fans in fairly short order. The blades and the air stream would have done the rest—which is why two of the three crew members we have lost so far were already unconscious before Korax took his frustration out on that particular unfortunate *yIH*."

PujwI'. Weaklings, Koloth thought, repelled and horrified by the notion of being felled by something as lowly and insignificant as a microorganism, and an alien one at that. His chest was abruptly seized by a rapid series of wracking coughs, making him wonder whether he, too, might face a death that would deny him his rightful place among the heroes of *Sto-Vo-Kor.* The thought crossed his mind briefly that he needed to find a battle—*any* battle—in which he might die with honor, thereby avoiding a fate incalculably worse than death.

"Have you found a cure yet?" Koloth said a few moments later, once he regained some semblance of control over his breathing.

The healer shook his great shaggy head, his smooth brow furrowing in a fair imitation of the highly textured foreheads of his ancient ancestors. "No, and I'm not likely to do so soon enough to do us any good."

Koloth scowled, and the scowl hurt like a *bat'leth* wound. "Why?"

"This virus incubates very quickly, Captain. And unless it burns itself out soon, we are all likely to be very dead in another few *kilaan*s."

Koloth heard a heavy thump behind him, and he turned in time to see the heavy body of a young *bekk* finish its insensate tumble from the railing beside the astronavigation post to the deck below. The gleaming-browed, feverish-looking helm officer rushed to take the fallen man's place. A moment later dour-visaged Gherud, the *'OghwI'*'s second officer, stepped over the fallen man's body and took over the nav station, curtly ordering the helmsman back to his own post. From the look of him, the young pilot already had one boot planted firmly on the deck of the Barge of the Dead.

"I'd better see to that man, Captain," Choq said, gesturing toward the unconscious crewman sprawled on the deck.

Koloth nodded, and Choq moved to the fallen man's side. *If very many more of my men collapse, Gherud and I will end up having to run this ship all by ourselves.*

And the blame for that belonged entirely to one man.

"Kirk," Koloth said in a low growl as his frustration began to boil over. He stepped unsteadily down from the small dais upon which his command chair sat and stalked toward Gherud, nearly stumbling over Choq and his supine patient in the process.

"Relieve the helmsman, Gherud," he said. "Bring the ship about."

Gherud turned from his console to face Koloth, confusion creasing his brow. "Sir?"

"Find '*Entepray,*'" Koloth said, using the *tlhIngan* pronunciation of the name that was both hated and respected across countless sectors of space inside and outside the Empire. "The *Enterprise,* Gherud. And Kirk." He bared his teeth.

"We are going to destroy them both."

He has taken leave of his senses, Gherud thought, though he nodded affirmatively at his captain's orders and gave every appearance of acting to carry them out. Although he knew that the '*OghwI'*'s disease-depleted crew stood little chance of prevailing against a Federation vessel as formidably armed as the *Enterprise,* he also understood how unwise it would be to defy Koloth, particularly in his current frame of mind.

Disease-addled or not, he is still Koloth.

But Gherud knew that the captain still had to be stopped, with his own *d'k tahg* if necessary. Gherud could only hope that the High Command had received his covert message about the *yIH* pestilence in time to intervene. As the ship's covert intelligence officer, he could not allow a rogue captain to risk spreading a lethal malady to any other part of the Empire—even the border regions in which the '*OghwI'* had last encountered the *Enterprise.*

He ignored the clatterings made by the half-dead helmsman who was busy helping Choq drag the fallen crewman out of the control room. Hyperconscious of Koloth's alert but feverish eyes boring into him, Gherud turned toward the helm console and deftly entered the commands required to put the ship on a heading for the Donatu sector.

• • •

"Captain, we are being challenged," said the voice.

It took Koloth a moment to realize that the voice belonged to his second officer. His cheeks blazed with shame. Had he actually allowed himself to doze off in the command chair?

"On-screen, Gherud," Koloth said, leaning forward attentively. "I want to see Kirk's ship clearly before I blow it out of the sky."

But the image that replaced the black-draped starscape on the control room's main viewer was not that of *Entepray.* Nor was it a single ship.

It was a trio of Klingon battle cruisers, their forward tubes open and glowing aggressively, revealing their amber-colored internal fires.

A gruff voice suddenly issued from the comm. "I.K.S. 'OghwI', *you are under interdiction by the Klingon Defense Force. Stand down or be fired upon.*"

They know about the illness, Koloth thought. *Did that fool Choq send a medical report directly to Command without running it past me first?*

Multihued spots suddenly swam before Koloth's eyes, forcing him to marshal all his strength merely to remain upright in his chair. A momentary wave of vertigo washed over him, with the salutary effect of focusing all of his remaining concentration on his most immediate problem.

Those ships out there.

"Sir?" Gherud had turned to face Koloth, hands hovering above his console, his expression expectant.

"Acknowledge, 'OghwI'," said the gruff voice on the speakers. *"You are outgunned three to one. Stand down. Now."*

"Do not acknowledge," Koloth said. "Maintain alert posture."

Gherud looked mildly astonished, as did the two *bekk*s

stationed at the nearby weapons consoles. But they followed their orders.

Koloth's eyes narrowed as he stared at the three ships that slowly grew larger on the screen. Fellow Klingon ships or not, they were standing in the way of his vengeance. They were therefore obstacles to his honor.

The collective superior firepower of the challengers meant little to Koloth, since cleverness mattered far more than mere weaponry. Besides, he had prevailed despite far worse odds in many prior battles.

Forcing down another wave of dizziness, he thought, *They will soon learn precisely why this vessel has earned the name* 'Oghwl'.

Devisor.

Gherud's eyes went wide with surprise, and perhaps also with fear. "The lead vessel is opening fire, Captain!"

Sure enough, the vessel in the middle of the screen issued an intense orange blast of force. A moment later, the *'Oghwl'* shook and rattled as the shields absorbed the brunt of the impact.

"We can't take many more hits like that, Captain," Gherud said, his voice quavering in unmistakable terror. "Especially not if all three ships attack us in concert."

They mean to destroy a plague ship, Koloth thought, regarding the younger officer with silent contempt. *Did you really believe they would spare* you*?*

Koloth realized then that Gherud might indeed have believed just that—if *he* had been the one who had informed Command of the outbreak of *yIH* plague.

"Return fire!" Koloth shouted, tightly gripping the arms of his command chair. "Full reply."

Though Gherud hesitated, the two *bekk*s manning the guns hastened to comply with Koloth's orders. But the *'Oghwl'*'s answering barrage seemed to have little effect on the attacking ship. All three of them now displayed brightly glowing weapons tubes, evidence that they were about to deliver a devastating triple-tandem attack.

Koloth sat back in his chair. *Perhaps this isn't Kirk's day to die after all,* he thought as the spots before his eyes grew larger, more numerous, and danced with increased abandon. *But if it is* my *day to die, at least* this *death will lead to* Sto-Vo-Kor.

The ship rattled and shuddered again.

"Return fire!" Koloth shouted.

Gherud looked bleak. "Weapons systems are off-line. Shield generators are failing as well."

As the edges of the room began growing dark, all Koloth could do was pray that incoming fire would finish him and all the sick crewmen before the illness did.

He felt drunk, like a young *bekk* plunging too quickly into his first barrel of bloodwine.

Closing his eyes, he braced for the end. He welcomed it, reveling in the intense burning sensation of molten *bat'leth*s piercing his forehead. He suddenly felt himself drifting as consciousness itself began to drain away.

"Sir! We're receiving another hail!" It was Gherud's voice again, reaching him as though from a great distance, tethering him to the material world with the slenderest of threads.

Through the haze that had gathered around him, he heard an even more distant voice coming over the comm. It belonged to another male Klingon, his tones every bit as deep and aggressive as the voice that had demanded his surrender.

But this voice was far more familiar. Koloth smiled.

"This is the commander of the I.K.S. Klolode cha'," the new voice said in inflections that brooked no debate. *"The next vessel to open fire on the* 'OghwI' *does so at its own peril. Captain Koloth's ship and crew are under my protection."*

But Koloth experienced no sense of relief. He understood that he was not only to be denied a glorious final battle with Kirk, but would also very likely miss his last opportunity to enter *Sto-Vo-Kor* via a hopeless battle against the Klingon forces that now opposed him. He felt only bitter disappointment that an old friend would so blithely risk sending his soul to *Gre'thor* for all eternity—even to conduct a rescue.

Perhaps today isn't *my day to die after all,* he thought. *At least not in combat.*

As oblivion finally overtook him, Koloth could only hope that the *yIH* virus would take that into consideration.

TEN

Sulu paused before the mirror in his quarters, making sure one last time that his maroon dress uniform jacket was both spotless and free of any conspicuous wrinkles.

He tugged at his too-stiff collar. *Why in the name of the Great Bird did the captain order all this pomp and ceremony?* Sulu thought. *We're bringing aboard a Federation diplomatic team, not a fleet admiral on an inspection tour.* He couldn't help but wonder whether the captain was unconsciously living up to the derisive description that some of his fellow flag officers had snickeringly attached to him—"Styles without substance"—shortly after *Excelsior*'s initial transwarp-engine tests had ended in failure nearly half a decade ago.

The dress uniform tunic constricted Sulu's chest like a fencing jacket that was at least one size too small. He was grateful that he'd had occasion to don formal attire only very rarely over the past few years; like the rest of his *Enterprise* crewmates, Sulu had worn an ordinary duty uniform even while standing before Federation President Hiram Roth, anxiously awaiting the statesman's decision about how Kirk and his crew might be disciplined in the immediate aftermath of the alien probe affair.

Once he was finally satisfied with the appearance, if not the comfort, of his apparel, Sulu exited his quarters and turned left down the quiet corridor. He strode toward the nearest turbolift, whose door hissed open obediently to admit him.

Only after he was sealed inside did he realize that the lift wasn't empty.

"Commander," Captain Styles said with a stiff nod, his ever-present swagger stick looking even more pretentious than usual tucked under the left arm of his medal-bedecked dress jacket. Styles's free hand was on the lift's control handle. "Main shuttle bay," he said, his gaze cast upward as he addressed the computer.

As the lift began its smooth, almost undetectable acceleration, Sulu realized that this was only the second time he'd been entirely alone with his new captain during the nearly four weeks he'd been aboard *Excelsior.*

"I know this wasn't what you were expecting, Commander Sulu," Styles had said on the last such occasion, which was Sulu's first day on the ship. *"But the top job here is no longer vacant after all."*

"I . . . understand, sir," Sulu had replied, his voice sounding unconvincing even in his own ears.

"I'll be staying aboard as Excelsior*'s CO, and I'll be in need of a new executive officer,"* Styles had said. "You *have come rather highly recommended for the job."* He'd smiled broadly, extending his right hand as he rose from behind the situation room desk.

Sulu's fingers felt numb as he'd accepted the handshake.

"Captain," Sulu said, acknowledging Styles's presence alongside him in the lift, but keeping his expression as neutral as possible. An uncomfortable silence shrouded the lift as the two men stood side by side, each looking upward, carefully avoiding making eye contact. Not for the first time, Sulu wondered whether he'd been inflicted on Styles rather than recommended to him. Perhaps Styles had offered him the exec job with the expectation that he would decline it as he had the *Bozeman* posting.

A whistle sounded over the intercom, followed by a familiar, businesslike voice. *"Cutler to Captain Styles."*

Styles released the lift's control handle and punched a button on a wall-mounted panel. "Styles here, Commander. Go ahead."

"The ambassador's shuttle is making its final approach, sir."

"Very good, Commander. Mister Sulu and I are already on our way. Styles out." Styles punched the intercom button again, closing the channel. "I hope the ambassador will appreciate the reception he's about to receive—especially in view of *Excelsior*'s having taken the *Saratoga*'s place as his transportation to the Korvat conference on such short notice."

"I know how badly you wanted this command," Styles had said on that first day, sounding sympathetic. *"But that just wasn't the way things shook out this time. I hope* Excelsior *won't turn out to be a big disappointment for you."*

"Of course it won't, Captain," Sulu had replied, determined to do his utmost not to let time make a liar of him.

Folding his arms across his chest, Styles leaned against the side of the turbolift and cast a questioning look at Sulu. "Well, it seems you'll get your chance to keep a close eye on the Korvat diplomatic meetings after all."

And you're still wondering whether I had something to do with the Saratoga*'s last-minute itinerary change,* Sulu thought.

Ignoring the captain's last comment, Sulu said, "Ambassador Sarek has never been overly impressed by Starfleet's ruffles and flourishes, sir." He paused to pull at his collar again, emphasizing his point. "So I wouldn't expect him to be very demonstrative either way."

"Why do you say that, Commander?" Styles said, his tone growing slightly brittle. "Apart from the obvious fact that Ambassador Sarek is a Vulcan, I mean."

Sulu was growing uncomfortable with the drift of the conversation—and this latest reminder of how starkly their personalities and command styles differed—but he did his best to conceal his discomfiture nevertheless. "I've . . . met the ambassador before, Captain," he said finally.

Styles nodded. "And therefore your judgment regarding how to handle him should be preferred over mine. Just like your assessment of the alleged danger facing the Korvat conference."

"I never said either of those things, sir," Sulu said.

"You didn't have to, Commander." Styles grasped the control handle again and said, "Computer, stop lift."

The lift's gentle but relentless motion came to a quick but smooth halt. Releasing the handle again, Styles turned toward Sulu and regarded him through narrowed eyes.

"Captain?" Sulu said, more uneasy now than he'd been at any other time since he'd become *Excelsior*'s executive officer.

"It's no secret that you've wanted to command this ship for years," Styles said.

Sulu nodded. "I suppose not, sir."

"And as recently as a few weeks ago, you still thought Starfleet Command was going to hand her over to you."

Again, Sulu nodded. "Admiral Kirk *had* cut the initial command-transfer orders personally, several years ago. Sir."

"But they hadn't been implemented until *after* Starfleet Command rescinded the last orders *Captain* Kirk had issued as an admiral," Styles said, obviously intent on reminding

Sulu that even after five years not everyone had forgiven the breaches of discipline that Kirk and his crew had committed, even though their actions had saved Earth from obliteration.

Sulu's collar suddenly felt too hot as well as too tight. "Permission to speak freely, Captain?" he said in clipped tones, steeling his courage to say precisely what was on his mind.

"Go ahead, Commander," Styles said with equal curtness.

"As recently as a few weeks ago, I had it on very good authority that you were going to retire, along with Commander Darby, your previous exec. Lieutenant Commander Cutler hadn't applied for the job, so *Excelsior*'s center seat would have been entirely up for grabs. You even made a public announcement that you were leaving the service."

"Changing a decision is a time-honored command prerogative," Styles said, denying nothing.

"Fair enough, Captain." Sulu could at least take comfort in this demonstration of *some* flexibility on the captain's part, whether he understood it or not. "Sir, may I ask you *why* you changed your mind about retiring?" he asked.

"That, Commander," Styles snapped, "is something that I choose to keep to myself."

It was obvious to Sulu that he had stepped on a raw nerve, which hadn't been his intention; however prickly his relationship with his captain might be, he didn't regard Styles as an enemy.

"I withdraw the question, Captain."

"Very good. Suffice it to say that I *am Excelsior*'s captain, until Starfleet Command says differently—regardless of how much more qualified you might believe yourself to be for the job." Styles grasped the lift's handle again and told the computer to resume the cabin's motion. "So suck it up, Commander."

Sulu bit back a tart response, then drew in and released

a single deep, calming breath. He told himself that he had
no reason to be angry with Styles. In fact, the captain was
probably entitled to a bit of ire, considering all the second-
guessing to which his exec had subjected him lately, justified or not.

"Yes, sir," he said.

Sulu couldn't deny that Styles was right—his own career
disappointments and the captain's evident paranoia notwithstanding.

In the observation gallery that overlooked *Excelsior*'s main
shuttle bay, Sulu watched in silence as the boxy, eight-
meter-long spacecraft moved through the hangar's wide-
open entrance, her passage marked only by a momentary
sparkling ripple of the aperture's atmosphere-retention field.
A moment later, the craft made a textbook touchdown in
the precise center of the amber markings that denoted the
vessel's designated landing space.

The *Nancy Hedford* appeared to be a standard-issue
Starfleet shuttlecraft, a fact that Sulu found mildly surprising considering the illustrious passenger he knew it carried;
he'd half expected Ambassador Sarek to arrive in a larger
Vulcan craft, though he supposed that the Starfleet shuttle's
simple utilitarian design held a certain esthetic appeal
for the austere and parsimonious Vulcan diplomat. Sulu
glanced to his left, where Captain Styles stood, watching the
shuttle's arrival with a slight scowl. Perhaps the captain was
disappointed by Ambassador Sarek's choice of such an un-
adorned vessel, and by the implication that followed—that
Sulu might be right about *Excelsior*'s reception committee
being overdressed for the occasion.

Tucking his riding crop securely under his left arm,
Styles turned and made his way down the ladder toward the
main landing level, with a dress-uniformed Cutler following
close behind. Sulu brought up the rear as the trio entered

the hangar, where two rows of six dress-uniformed security guards stood rigidly at attention, flanking a path that led away from the shuttlecraft's main hatch and toward the interior exit that led into the rest of *Excelsior*'s expansive secondary hull.

As the *Hedford*'s hatch opened, Styles took up a position at the honor guard's left side—near security officers Melinda Rebovich and Nino Orsini—while Sulu and Cutler stood facing Styles from the right.

A slightly bent figure emerged first from the shuttle. Sulu immediately recognized him as Sarek, despite the hood that covered his head and shadowed most of his face. The Vulcan ambassador was dressed in a robe that was darker and somewhat more ornately patterned than the one he had worn when Sulu had spoken with him two days earlier. His hands were folded under his voluminous sleeves.

A few meters behind Sarek was the male Trill who had answered Sulu's clandestine call to the Vulcan ambassador's office, and alongside him walked a third figure, a middle-aged Vulcan whose gender seemed indeterminate beneath a heavy swaddling of formal diplomatic robes. The pair silently followed Sarek down the ramp and onto the flight deck. The shuttlecraft's hatch remained open as the three diplomats moved along the path created by the two ranks of at-attention security personnel.

Sulu scowled involuntarily. The Lady Amanda Grayson-Sarek, the ambassador's wife, was conspicuously—and somewhat disconcertingly, to Sulu's mind—absent.

Following Sarek's lead, the diplomatic party came to a stop directly in between Captain Styles and the spot where Sulu and Cutler were standing. Using both hands in an elegant, almost ceremonial way, Sarek removed his hood, revealing his iron-colored hair as he turned toward the captain.

"Captain Styles, I presume?" Sarek said, his voice deep

and resonant despite his advanced age. Sulu knew that the ambassador was about a century and a quarter old; while this age would have been all-but-impossibly ancient for a human, it added up to perhaps late middle age for the typical Vulcan.

Sulu watched as Styles fidgeted for a moment, appearing as if he wanted to shake hands in greeting, then instead raised his right hand in an awkward attempt to make the standard split-fingered Vulcan greeting.

"Captain Lawrence H. Styles, Mister Ambassador," said the captain with exaggerated courtliness. "Please allow me to welcome you and your people aboard my command, the *U.S.S. Excelsior*. I trust that your voyage was a pleasant and uneventful one."

"We encountered no difficulties along the way, Captain," was Sarek's only answer. He gestured toward the pair that had accompanied him, indicating first the Trill and then the other Vulcan. "While the rest of our party prepares to disembark, please allow me to introduce two of my colleagues, Junior Ambassador Curzon Dax of Trillius Prime, and Dostara of Vulcan, our diplomatic aide."

The rest of his party, Sulu thought, feeling suddenly reassured at the notion that the *Shuttlecraft Hedford* was not yet completely empty. The Lady Amanda must still be aboard the shuttle.

"Very good, Mister Ambassador," Styles said. "This is *my* senior staff, Commander Sulu and Lieutenant Commander Cutler." Then, a few pregnant moments later, as if only belatedly realizing that Sarek had introduced his lower-ranking subordinate as well as the more senior one, Styles gestured toward two members of the honor guard and added, "And these are Lieutenants Rebovich and Orsini, in charge of our security honor guard."

Sulu greeted the diplomats as though he had spoken to none of them recently, lest it feed Styles's suspicions.

"Trillius Prime," Cutler said as she and the young Trill engaged in a handshake, a custom to which the Trill evidently weren't as averse as were Vulcans. "I have to confess that I'm not familiar with that planet."

The young man grinned sheepishly, using his free hand to brush back his brown and somewhat-longer-than-Starfleet-regulation hair. Sulu noted that his fair-skinned face was framed by an orderly row of almost reptilian russet-colored spots that ran down both sides of his neck and disappeared beneath the collar of his plain gray civilian suit.

" 'Trillius Prime' was a name concocted by some ancient, long-forgotten stellar cartographer, Commander," said Curzon Dax. "These days we tend to use the same nomenclature to describe both ourselves and our homeworld: Trill."

Sulu winced inwardly as Sarek raised an eyebrow; the junior ambassador was probably not scoring any brownie points with his boss by correcting him right in front of *Excelsior*'s command staff. *This kid had better learn a few fundamentals very quickly,* Sulu thought. *Or else his diplomatic career is going to be one of the shortest ones in Federation history.*

Seeming to be aware of Sulu's misgivings about Dax, Sarek spoke as though intent on dispelling them. "Junior Ambassador Dax is one of the Federation's leading experts on Klingon culture and society."

"I have made an extensive study of everything known to both Trill and the rest of the Federation regarding Klingon customs and mores," Dax said. "Including the discipline of the *Mok'bara.*"

Styles appeared impressed. "No doubt your special training will be extremely useful in the days ahead."

Let's just hope he doesn't need to trot out his Mok'bara *knowledge while negotiating with the Klingons,* Sulu thought; combat among diplomats, unarmed or otherwise, was usually a bad sign.

"Thank you, Captain. That's assuming, of course, that my, ah, *assumptions* about Klingon psychology are more or less on target," said the young Trill, punctuating his comment with a halting smile that Sulu thought instilled very little confidence.

To Sulu's mind, scholarly assumptions concerning a hostile power about which the Federation knew so very little wasn't much of a foundation on which to build a future of galactic peace. He couldn't help but feel relieved at the knowledge that it would be Sarek's experienced hand, rather than that of some green academic, guiding the Federation's side of the forthcoming discussions at Korvat. *The Klingons would eat this guy alive inside of five minutes without Sarek to back him up,* Sulu thought as he regarded Dax in silence.

"We are prepared to give you a tour of the ship before we schedule the first diplomatic briefing session," Styles said to the diplomats. "And, of course, we have made our best VIP quarters ready for all three of you."

"There are actually *four* of us, Captain," Sarek said solemnly. "We shall therefore require one additional set of quarters."

"Of course, Mister Ambassador," said Styles. "Commander Sulu will see to it immediately."

Sulu's brow furrowed as he studied the Vulcan's craggy face. "Pardon me for asking, Mister Ambassador, but isn't the fourth member of your party the Lady Amanda?" Sulu knew that it was the ambassador's longstanding custom to bring his wife with him whenever and wherever he traveled, just as it was Amanda's custom never to leave the ambassador's side unless the separation was unavoidable.

Sarek regarded Sulu coolly, raising his right eyebrow long enough to make him think that he might have asked an impertinent question. Then the iron-haired Vulcan shook his head gently, his gaunt features retaining their typical Vulcan impassivity, but in a way that Sulu found reassuring thanks to his long familiarity with the mannerisms of the ambassador's younger son.

"She who is my wife has not accompanied me on this mission," Sarek said.

"I hope she's well, Mister Ambassador," Sulu said.

Sarek nodded. "Although the passage of the years exacts a greater toll from humans than from Vulcans, the Lady Amanda's health remains undiminished. To ensure that nothing changes this, however, I insisted that she return to Vulcan and remain there for the duration of the Korvat conference."

Sulu nodded mutely, feeling simultaneously vindicated and apprehensive in the face of this clear evidence that Sarek had indeed taken his warning seriously. He was also impressed by Sarek's resolve; from what he knew of the strong-willed Lady Amanda, the ambassador must have had the devil's own time convincing her to let him face a possible terrorist attack without keeping her at his side.

"Well, then," Styles said, glancing down at the small chronometer built into the shaft of his swagger stick, "when do we get to meet the fourth member of your party?"

Dax shook his head and made a gentle *tsk* sound. "The Klingons certainly won't put up with this sort of tardiness," he said quietly, shaking his head.

Sulu suppressed a smile. *This kid has really got to learn to lighten up a bit.*

Looking back toward the shuttle and raising his voice slightly, Sarek asked, "Doctor, will you be joining us?"

A moment later a figure emerged from the small ship, and Sulu was surprised to see yet another familiar face among Sarek's staff.

"Sorry, folks," the brown-haired woman said as she closed a medical tricorder and slung it over her shoulder. "I didn't mean to keep everyone waiting."

Sarek turned back toward Styles. "Doctor Christine Chapel is our diplomatic party's physician, on temporary loan from Starfleet. She'll need to be billeted on your ship as well."

"Of course," Styles said agreeably, then turned to regard Sulu with an inscrutable stare. "Commander Sulu, I believe you're already acquainted with the doctor. I'll put you in charge of seeing to her accommodations, as well as setting her up with whatever workspace she may need."

Sulu grinned. "It'll be a pleasure, sir," he said, and meant it.

After Sulu and Cutler had shown Sarek, Dax, and Dostara to their VIP suites on deck five, near the junior officers' quarters—Rebovich and Orsini had taken charge of the party's luggage, with the help of two other members of the honor guard—Sulu showed Dr. Chapel to a nearby set of unoccupied rooms reserved for visiting diplomatic luminaries.

"These new starships are flying luxury hotels," Chapel said as she looked around the spacious but sparsely furnished central room, obviously impressed. She set her two small bags atop the otherwise bare central coffee table, which stood between a pair of low sofas.

"That's not what the junior officers tell me," Sulu said, smiling.

"Lucky them. Now let's get out of here and go for a walk before I get an attack of agoraphobia from all this wide-open space."

Sulu led the way back out into the empty but comparatively narrow corridor, and the two old friends immediately fell into step beside each other for a peripatetic conversation.

"So, how have you been doing, Christine?" Sulu said.

She shrugged. "I can't complain too much, Hikaru. Well, I *could*, but I suspect you have your own gripes to be concerned with. Besides, most of mine are about achy joints from getting older, not . . ." She paused long enough to glance up and down the corridor to make sure her next remarks weren't overheard. "Not about pains in the ass brought on by a CO's ego," she added quietly.

Sulu let out a short, low laugh. "You noticed it *that* quickly?" he said, sotto voce.

Chapel responded with a laugh of her own. "Between your secret communiqué with Sarek and the peculiar attitude that Captain Styles seemed to be exhibiting toward you back there . . . yeah, I noticed it. Besides, I've worked with Styles before, during some of *Excelsior*'s transwarp tests. And I'm familiar with the history between Styles and the *Enterprise* crew."

Sulu nodded as he led the way toward one of the turbolifts. "We're both going to have to try not to let that prejudice us."

She sighed. "Agreed."

"Styles is my CO now. And that means I have to defend him, God help me."

"Sorry, Hikaru. I didn't mean to put you into an awkward position."

He chuckled as he realized he had seldom felt anything *but* awkward since he'd assumed his current posting. "That ship has already sailed, so to speak."

They stepped into the turbolift, and the doors closed around them. "Deck seven," Sulu told the computer before it had a chance to prompt him.

"So what's our first destination?" Chapel asked.

"Unless you have an objection, I'd like to give you a rain check on the tour of the ship," he said. "I'd like you to meet our CMO right away. And there's another thing you really need to see sooner instead of later."

"Like I care about who's got the widest corridors or the biggest nacelles," Chapel said, waving her hand to one side. The lines around the sides of her eyes crinkled pleasantly as she smiled. "Give me some new medical equipment to test-drive and some new bug to diagnose, and I'll be much happier. Plus, you've got to get me schooled up about all the intrigue around here, so I can brief the diplomats."

The turbolift doors opened, and they stepped out onto one of deck seven's gently curving corridors. "Sickbay is this way," he said, gesturing to the right. "Doctor Klass will bring you up to speed on everything."

Chapel put a hand on Sulu's shoulder, stopping him, an expression of surprise and delight on her face. "*Judith* Klass? Goddess, I wonder if she'll remember me. I took one of her courses at Starfleet Medical, ages ago."

"She'll probably be a lot happier to see you if you go easy on the 'ages ago' part," Sulu said, grinning. It felt good to be around his old friend again.

Moments later, they entered sickbay. Klass was bent over a neutronoscope, peering into it intently. "Be right with you," she said. "If you're wounded, please try not to bleed on the carpet." Klass straightened and looked up, then did a mild double-take as she recognized her newly arrived colleague. "Well, as I live and breathe. *Christine Chapel.* It's been years!"

Chapel held out her hand for Klass to shake. "More than I want to try to count. I wasn't sure if you'd even remember me."

"Ah ha," Klass said, engulfing Chapel in a quick bear hug before releasing her and turning toward Sulu. "Doctor Chapel was a brilliant student, although she sometimes let herself get a little too distracted by some of the male interns for her own good. She once managed to laser-splice one of her fingers to a cadaver we were practicing on."

Sulu saw Chapel's face redden slightly. "It was nothing that a protoplaser and a dermal regenerator couldn't fix," she said in good-natured tones. Sulu quietly shuddered at the whole idea.

"The other funny thing I remember about you was the minidresses. You adored them—well, I would have, too, if I ever had legs like yours—but you were always railing on about how they were *sexist,* and that if the women were expected to wear them, then the men should at least have to wear shorts."

"That's true," Chapel said. "Still is. You don't see nearly as many skirts around these days, but I'd still appreciate seeing a nice pair of male legs in uniform once in a while."

Klass sighed heavily. "Well, maybe someday. Meanwhile, welcome aboard *Excelsior.* Has our XO told you much about what's been occupying most of my attention down here lately?"

"We weren't able to talk freely before," Sulu said. "Besides, I thought the evidence would be more compelling if Christine could see it up close."

"Well, come this way then, and let's get you filled in," Klass said, gesturing toward one of the medical lab's rear workspaces.

"There," Chapel said, pointing to a small portion of the image displayed on the large bioscreen. "It's Augment DNA. See the extra strands here and here? If you look at the composite breakdown, you'll find those same strands in the Augment sequences."

"Well, we could if it wasn't *classified information,*" Klass said, peering closely at Chapel.

The look was one that Chapel remembered well, and which abruptly took her all the way back to her undergraduate years at Starfleet Medical. It wasn't a negative look per se, but rather one of careful scrutiny, as if saying, *"Do you really know what you're doing?"*

"As you may recall, we had a run-in with the actual, honest-to-God Khan Noonien Singh and his crew of Augments," Chapel said, gesturing toward Sulu. "When I was the *Enter-*

prise's head nurse, Leonard McCoy and I gained quite a bit of knowledge about the Augment DNA resequencing. Then Starfleet put a clamp on all of it. But they couldn't exactly erase it from our memories."

"So, what you're saying is that not only is this viral DNA a potential bioterrorist weapon, it may also be linked to Earth's Eugenics Wars?" Sulu looked nonplussed as the implications hit home.

"Not exactly," Chapel said, shaking her head. "But possibly. It could be that the virus was cultured at some point inside a person who possessed Augment DNA sequences, which then simply piggybacked onto the virus as it was further bioengineered for its main purpose. We know that the Klingons experimented with viruses containing Augment DNA sequences over a century ago and its effects are still with them today."

Klass looked thoughtful. "You're talking about the smooth-headed Klingons. My research indicates that the 'smooth' trait was caused by a genetic mish-mash of Augment genes that got picked up by a Levodian flu retrovirus sometime in the twenty-second century. Or maybe it was done deliberately. Regardless, it was deadly. It decimated at least one Klingon colony, and set the 'smooth-headed' mutation in the genomes of the survivors and their descendants."

"And here we have a genetically engineered retrovirus that has both Levodian flu and Augment genes thrown into the mix," Sulu said slowly, the gravity of his words hitting all of them. "Could the albino be planning to unleash a similar disease in the Klingon Empire? Or in Federation space?"

Both notions chilled Chapel to the marrow. On the cusp of the peace talks between the Federation and the Klingon Empire, a single rogue genetic engineer fixated on terror could threaten everything. It didn't matter that most such

DNA manipulations were unlawful under Federation stat-
utes—and likely under Klingon law as well—because it
wasn't the process that was the threat now, it was the results,
and one man's decision to pursue them.

"We'd better get that briefing scheduled," Chapel said.
"We're just about to jump out of the frying pan. . . ."

ELEVEN

2269 (the Year of Kahless 895,
early in the month of *Xan'lahr*)

Koloth realized only very slowly that he was awake. Whether or not he was actually still alive, however, seemed to be an open question.

This certainly isn't the way I imagined Sto-Vo-Kor, he thought as he pushed himself up into a sitting position. Neither did the place bear much resemblance to the Barge of the Dead, or its fearsome final destination of *Gre'thor,* the eternal home to all lost, damned souls deemed unworthy of admittance to the glorious perpetual battleground reserved for the fallen heroes of Qo'noS.

He was sitting, stripped to the waist, on the edge of a narrow, threadbare cot in what appeared to be an austere but brightly illuminated infirmary room. Or perhaps it was a science lab, judging from the presence of what appeared to be several large pieces of scanning equipment, as well as several other roughly man-sized devices that might or might not have had medical applications; Koloth had never spent enough time in places such as this to learn to make such subtle distinctions.

Then he noticed the telltale blue glow of a planar force field that completely covered the threshold of an otherwise open hatchway. This aperture led off to an anteroom that lay just beyond the most distant of the bulky pieces of lab equipment.

He understood at once that this was neither an infirmary nor a lab, at least so far as he was concerned. For him, for whatever reason, this place was a prison. He digested this new knowledge stoically and without surprise; despite the fever that had felled him, he could recall having opened fire on the three Klingon vessels that had been attempting to waylay the *'Oghwl'*.

Koloth rose to his feet, gratified to note that they were steady beneath him. Likewise, all traces of his earlier vertigo had vanished. The pounding in his head and the fever, both parting gifts of the disease-ridden *yIH,* were conspicuously absent as well.

My crew, he thought as he came more fully awake. Had they fared as well as he had?

A flash of motion to his left caused him to tense into a combat crouch. He felt ridiculous an instant later when he realized that he had merely seen his own face reflected in the dull metal surface of one of the room's enigmatic machines.

But it was a face that bore an aspect he had never seen before. Wondering if some curvature in the metal was distorting his reflection, he approached to take a closer look.

Koloth scowled into the image of his own surprise-stricken face, which had somehow become attached to a high, magnificently textured *HemQuch* forehead that might have made Kahless himself proud.

He probed the front of his skull with both hands, felt the texture for himself. This was no optical illusion. And it was no artificial, surgically installed prosthetic device; he could feel his own warm, living flesh beneath his hands. His chest and shoulders likewise had changed, bulging with the characteristic ridges that were the birthright of all Klingons.

Joy warred with terror. *What has happened to me?*

"Captain Koloth?" said a voice, startling him out of his reverie.

He turned toward the room's force field–protected entrance. Just on its other side stood a pair of Klingon men, both several decades Koloth's senior. They wore nondescript civilian work clothes rather than military uniforms, and both lacked the commanding bearing of a blooded warrior. But both men possessed the alert eyes of a hunting *targ,* prompting Koloth to tag them immediately as academics of some sort, probably physicians or research scientists.

But although the two men clearly shared similar occupations and social standing, they also possessed another superficial but instantly noticeable characteristic that contrasted them sharply with one another: the man on the right had a highly ridged forehead like Koloth's own, which marked him as the product of a family line that had escaped exposure to both the First Qu'Vat Plague of the previous century, and to the unhappy genetic side effects associated with its cure. The other, slightly taller man was a *QuchHa',* whose forehead was as baby-smooth as Koloth's own had been prior to his exposure to the *yIH* illness.

"Captain Koloth?" repeated the academic who stood on the right, the proud-browed man who had first called his name.

Deciding that this man had to be the one in charge, Koloth said, "I am Koloth. And I would know who has asked."

The ridge-headed *HemQuch* man nodded and said, "Of course. I am Doctor Nej. This is my associate, Doctor Hurghom."

Koloth approached the energy field–protected entrance, coming to a stop just short of it. *"NuqneH.* I have heard those names before."

Koloth noted with interest that both men seemed a bit discomfited to hear that.

"That is no doubt because of our past association with the House of Ngoj," said the taller, smooth-headed scientist, the man Dr. Nej had identified as Dr. Hurghom.

"No doubt," Koloth said, nodding. *Of course.* Though it had occurred decades ago, the fall of the House of Ngoj, whose smooth-headed members had falsely passed themselves off as *HemQuch* in order to hang onto the perquisites of power in the High Council, had been publicized far and wide. Even now, despite the many social gains the less favored *QuchHa'* had made during recent years, the Ngoj scandal still served as a cautionary tale explicating the dangers of trying to function above one's station.

"It is also not at all relevant," Dr. Nej said, sounding nettled.

"I agree," Koloth said. "Allow me to raise some far more relevant topics, such as the reason I am being imprisoned behind a force field. And just where I am."

"You mistake us, Captain," Hurghom said. "You are not in detention."

Koloth raised his palm. He placed it just inside the doorway's threshold, thereby producing a momentary but spectacular flash of amber light that made his hand feel as though it was suddenly teeming with Talarian hookspider larvae. Both scientists jumped backward slightly in startled response, forcing Koloth to suppress a smile. It was always good to be able to maintain both unpredictability and inscrutability, especially with one's captors.

"The presence of this force field would seem to argue otherwise," Koloth said as he began massaging the feeling back into his left hand with his right.

"This is only a medical quarantine field, Captain," Hurghom said. "You are recuperating from your illness at a Klingon military facility."

"This facility obviously serves other functions as well," Koloth said. "Which is no doubt why it retains the services of the former physicians to the disgraced House of Ngoj." His eyes rolled up toward his altered brow. "Did you use the same techniques on me that you used to disguise the . . . hereditary handicap of that once-great House?"

"Not precisely, Captain," said Nej, shaking his head. His scowl made it clear that he did not enjoy rehashing this particular chapter of his past. "The House of Ngoj hid its shortcomings"—he cast a fleeting glare at Hurghom, who quailed slightly—"using cosmetic surgery, for the most part. You, Captain, are the beneficiary of a far more *permanent* treatment."

Pieces of the puzzle into which he had awakened were assembling themselves right before Koloth's eyes. "You have found a means of removing the 'Earther' taint from the genes of *QuchHa'* people."

Koloth had always found it ironic that some of the Earther DNA that now tainted so many Klingon bloodlines originated from genetically augmented humans, and therefore imparted to its bearers a certain strength, tenacity, and ruthlessness that even the magnificent Kahless himself may have lacked. Koloth had always been sufficiently prudent not to air such opinions aloud in the presence of the wrong company; he had learned very early in his career to rely on the tangible gifts his "bad blood" granted him, and to use those gifts to advance through the military ranks as quickly as possible. He exulted in the thought that the injustices he had faced all his life might soon become a thing of the past.

"We still need to conduct more tests to determine whether the changes you have undergone are of a permanent nature," Hurghom said. "But the initial signs are very encouraging. The retrovirus in your system seems to be working as planned."

Though the idea of being anybody's experimental subject angered and revolted him, Koloth chose to regard this revelation as a hopeful sign; it meant that he might not have lost his entire crew after all. Still, he couldn't deny feeling reticent about broaching that question directly with these academics, whom he assumed were unlikely to tell him anything they didn't want him to know. And he knew there was precious little he could do for his men from behind a quarantine force field—assuming they weren't already beyond all help anyway.

"There had to be a delivery mechanism for this . . . treatment to which my crew and myself were evidently subjected," he said. "It was the *yIH,* wasn't it? Or perhaps the *yIH*-devouring *glo'meH* prototype we recovered from the Earthers brought your virus into our midst."

Nej and Hurghom looked at one another somewhat uncomfortably, confirming for Koloth that he had indeed struck his target, though he couldn't be sure how close to the center he had come. He could see, however, how unsure both men seemed to be about how much more they ought to say.

"Do I need to point out that my security clearance is probably a good deal higher than either of yours?" Koloth prodded, gently but with tempered *bat'leth* steel in his voice.

"You have surmised correctly, for the most part, Captain," Nej said at length. "Both the *yIH* and the *glo'meH* prototype were carrying a new variant strain of the Levodian flu. We developed it in secret for the High Council."

Koloth knew he was anything but an expert on the Levodian flu, but he knew enough for this revelation to raise any number of warning flags inside the back of his skull. "That virus was the source of both of the Great Qu'Vat Plagues," he said.

"It was," Hurghom said. "Of course, that fact ought to

surprise no one. After all, the Levodian flu virus has been used in virtually every genetic engineering project conducted within the Klingon Empire for the past century."

"But why were the *yIH* and the *glo'meH* carrying this *particular* virus?" Koloth wanted to know. "There had to be a specific purpose."

"There was, Captain," Nej said again, almost guiltily. "We developed it as a means of restoring the Klingon people's genotypic and phenotypic characteristics to the way they were before the First Qu'Vat Plague occurred. But before we risked deploying the new viral variant generally throughout the Empire, we had to start *somewhere*. Our first secret full-up test was to be done on the small Klingon population that has been living on *SermanyuQ* for the past few years, side by side with the Earthers."

Nej's mention of the name of that long-contested world, which the Earthers persisted in calling "Sherman's Planet," made Koloth bristle. Since the disgraced spy Arne Darvin's plot to poison the Earther grain stocks bound for that world two years earlier had been foiled—by those miserable, screaming *yIH*, no less—the *'orghen rojmab*, the so-called Organian Peace Treaty, had forced the Empire to all but cede *SermanyuQ* outright to the Earthers who even now grubbed in the ground there.

"The new virus is actually a carefully tailored retrovirus, a bioagent designed to rewrite the DNA of the test population," Hurghom said. "We were using the internal metabolic processes of both the *glo'meH* prototype and the *yIH* to incubate the virus."

"We've concluded from your most recent log entries, Captain," Nej said, interrupting, "that your encounter with Jones, the Earther thief who briefly stole the *glo'meH,* and the Federation starship on which he took refuge, must have resulted in the premature deployment of the variant Levodian flu retrovirus."

"And, ah, accidentally made you part of our test population," said Hurghom. "Along with your entire crew."

Though he willed his face into expressionlessness, Koloth took a single quick step toward the force field barrier. He was pleased to watch both scientists instinctively back up a step, even though they must have known that they were in no danger so long as the field remained in place.

"And did my crew share in my good fortune?" he asked, focusing his bottled anger into a hard glare aimed at them both.

Hurghom's face fell, and Koloth suspected that he wasn't going to like whatever either of them was going to say next.

"Unfortunately, only those possessed of a particular genetic profile regained their cranial ridges," said the smooth-headed scientist. "The virus left others unchanged as it ran its course. And, unfortunately, it killed many others outright. We will furnish a list of the casualties and survivors as soon as possible."

Despite his own personal good fortune, Koloth could only hope that Gherud, the man he held responsible for alerting the High Command of the disease outbreak aboard the *'OghwI'*—and who had also cheated him out of a chance to wreak bloody vengeance against Kirk—numbered among the dead.

A disquieting thought suddenly occurred to him: these scientists might have been a little *too* forthcoming in providing answers to his many questions. Of course, that might have been because he'd managed to intimidate them into cooperating with him. Or perhaps it was because their retrovirus research had placed them at odds with the High Council, thereby forcing them to confide in him in order to cultivate an unofficial ally who might help *them* survive whatever consequences were certain to follow in the wake of their admitted failure. It was also possible that they expected him to join the ranks of the dead soon, becoming yet another victim of their botched retrovirus test.

He decided that the only way to resolve the matter was to continue asking questions. "What will become of the survivors now?"

"What the High Council does next will depend greatly upon the contents of our report," Nej said. "And that will depend on the behavior of the virus."

"And *that,* in turn, will depend upon what new mutations may have arisen in the retrovirus's genome because of its metabolic interactions with both the *yIH* and the *glo'meH,*" said Hurghom.

"We can be thankful for at least a *partial* success," said Nej, gesturing toward Koloth's newly terraced brow.

Hurghom adopted an emotional tone that Koloth could only interpret as sincerity. "Regardless of what happens to anyone else who's been exposed to the virus, Captain, your transformation represents a fundamental breakthrough in the research that we've both been pursuing for decades."

"You must also look forward to . . . correcting your *own* condition," Koloth said, his eyes squarely upon those of the smooth-headed scientist.

"Of course I do," Hurghom said, nodding. "But honor is more at stake here than vanity."

Koloth found it passing strange that a non-warrior should be overly concerned with matters of honor. "What are you talking about?"

"Antaak, the man responsible for the Earther taint in the genes of us *QuchHa',* was my grandfather," Hurghom said. "I have inherited far more than his forehead, Captain—I am also heir to his enduring shame."

Antaak. Koloth recognized the name. Antaak had not only been responsible for curing the first outbreak of the lethally mutated Levodian flu on Qu'Vat during the last century—an act that had spawned every smooth-headed *QuchHa'* alive today—but he had also inadvertently slain himself and millions of others on the very same world during a subsequent botched attempt to restore what the *QuchHa'* had lost, using techniques not unlike those that Hurghom and Nej were employing now.

"I have devoted my life to restoring Antaak's lost honor," Hurghom said. "Because therein lies my own."

"You and the survivors of your crew represent the final hope of our decades of research, Captain," Nej said. "The High Council has grown impatient with our slow progress."

Hurghom nodded somberly. "And not only with *us,* Captain. Because of the Council's unwillingness to risk the outbreak of another great plague, the Defense Force has already scuttled the *'OghwI'.*"

Koloth felt every muscle in his body stiffen involuntarily, though he kept his face free of any emotion. Losing a ship was something he doubted he would ever get used to, no matter how many times it happened. His previous command, the *I.K.S. Gr'oth,* had suffered a like fate after being overrun by *yIH* two years ago, in the very same sector of space where this latest encounter had occurred. Now, as then, every one of the horrific little shrieking furballs aboard his vessel had been vaporized. Along with every particle of virus they carried in their misbegotten bodies.

"Unfortunately, the *glo'meH* prototype appears to have been destroyed as well," Nej added.

"Which is truly unfortunate," Hurghom said. "The *glo'meH* could have been bred into an effective biological means of containing the *yIH.*"

Nej shrugged. "There are other ways to deal with those pests, as I am sure the captain is aware. I have it on good authority that the Defense Force is diligently searching for the *yIH* homeworld to employ some of those alternate methods. They want to obliterate the planet's surface, to make certain that the creatures can neither continue to endanger the ecologies of Klingon worlds, nor act as potential disease carriers."

Koloth found the thought of such a fate befalling the noisome fuzzballs immensely satisfying—as long as the *yIH* home planet was the *only* thing that was obliterated.

"What about my crew?" Koloth asked. "Are they also to be summarily dispatched because of the virus they're carrying?"

Nej stood and studied Koloth impassively. Hurghom coughed and averted his gaze, having acquired a sudden keen interest in the toes of his boots.

"We cannot lie to you, Captain," the smooth-headed scientist said after a lengthy pause. "Initially, the Defense Force wanted to kill everyone aboard your vessel outright, Captain. Yourself included."

"*Particularly* you, Captain," Nej said. "Although the High Command might conceivably take your illness at the time into account, your decision to open fire on your fellow officers did not win you any friends within the ranks of the fleet."

Koloth could certainly understand that; he had to admit that he himself would find such an offense rather difficult to forgive had he been on the other side of the transaction.

"But obviously they were somehow talked out of having us all vaporized, or spaced," he said. *At least so far.*

Nej nodded. "They have stayed their hand, pending full batteries of medical tests."

"Which will be performed under the strictest of quarantines, of course," Hurghom added. "We have to make certain that the virus all of you are carrying can indeed be rendered harmless and noncontagious before any of you can be released from this facility."

As reasonable as that sounded, something still wasn't quite adding up precisely to Koloth's satisfaction. Casting a hard, appraising stare first at Hurghom, and then at Nej, he said, "Surely the High Command would never have made this decision merely at the behest of the former servants of a disgraced House. And certainly not for men with whom the High Council has already grown as impatient as you claim."

Nej said nothing, though he continued to meet Koloth's stare with an admirably inscrutable equanimity. Koloth could only wonder whether the senior scientist was contemplating the possibility that the High Council might soon turn him and his associate out of their jobs—or perhaps execute a far more precipitous and final decision.

"It is as you say, Captain," Hurghom said, once again minutely studying his boots.

"Then who has intervened on my behalf?"

As if they had been waiting for Koloth to articulate that very question, a pair of shadows abruptly crossed the floor of the vestibule a short distance beyond the doorway where Nej and Hurghom stood.

"*We* did, Koloth," intoned a deep, familiar voice. The same voice that had spoken to Koloth through his feverish delirium aboard the *'OghwI'*. It sounded both imperious and slightly . . . happy?

A moment later, the owners of the shadows stepped into full view immediately behind the scientists, both of whom stepped obligingly aside to allow the two baldric-draped, uniformed figures to approach the plane of the quarantine field.

Koloth registered some mild surprise at the sudden entrance of Captain Kang and Captain Kor. But his surprise was supplanted somewhat by his enjoyment of the nonplussed striations that suddenly rippled across their normally smooth *QuchHa'* foreheads. They stared at Koloth in silence, gaping like a pair of landed fish at his transformed but obviously still recognizable countenance.

"My old friends," Koloth said. "Did you rescue me out of loyalty?" Then he gestured toward his new forehead. "Or were you simply looking for a way to get one of these?"

TWELVE

Captain Styles listened intently as Dr. Chapel outlined all of the results of the research that she and Dr. Klass had conducted on the DNA and protein residue of the virus that Commander Sulu had "discovered."

He had been unsurprised that Chapel and Klass requested the medical briefing for the start of the meeting; ever since the orders had come down from Admiral Cartwright that *Excelsior* was to take over unexpectedly for the *Saratoga*, placing Styles on a far more direct course for the Korvat conference than he had anticipated, he had suspected that Sulu had somehow been complicit in wrangling the new orders. Styles had even asked Cutler to check for logs that might show unofficial and unsanctioned outgoing communications from Sulu, but she had been unable to find anything.

Maybe I'm just allowing my misgivings about Sulu to color my judgments, he thought. *I could be seeing a conspiracy where there's only a coincidence. Except that this coincidence just happens to bring Sulu a lot closer to his albino bogeyman.*

As if on cue, Chapel concluded her presentation. "And it is my belief, as well as Doctor Klass's, that given the specific nature of the retrovirus's tailoring, and the highly contagious nature of the original twenty-second-century Levodian flu virus upon which this modern pathogen was based, the retrovirus is clearly a bioweapon. Its ultimate purpose is as yet unknown, however."

Styles expected Sulu to speak up then, but it was Sarek who raised his voice first. Seated beside the Vulcan around the conference table were the other ambassador, Curzon Dax, and their Vulcan assistant, Dostara.

"Regarding this matter, I have read the advisory message you sent earlier to the *Saratoga*," Sarek said, looking to Styles, one eyebrow raised slightly. "I've also consulted *Excelsior*'s logs concerning the incident on Galdonterre. The warning from the deceased woman—combined with the related subsequent discoveries about the retrovirus—gives me pause. Logic dictates that these matters may be linked more closely than any of us may have thought before."

Although his doubts remained, Styles decided to give Sulu his due. "Actually, Ambassador, Commander Sulu feels very strongly that we *should* pursue this matter vigorously, as the woman on Galdonterre warned." He was vaguely amused to see a flicker of surprise on Sulu's face. "However, without further data or leads, I felt the evidence was too sketchy to justify taking any action that might jeopardize the peace talks, which are on a fragile footing at best."

Dax leaned forward. "An actual bioweapon attack on the peace talks would be significantly more disruptive than a false alarm. Better to die of embarrassment than from—"

Sarek held up his hand, cutting the junior diplomat off. "While Dax is correct, you, too, are correct, Captain. The panic that could result from an unverified threat—and at minimum, the distrust such an incident would surely engender—could prove disastrous, though not as disastrous as a successful attack, to be certain. So it falls to you, Captain Styles, to make certain that security measures are increased on *our* side without inflaming the Klingons' distrust of the Federation and its representatives, and without allowing any attack against the conference to succeed."

Tall order, Styles thought. He knew that he couldn't back down now, and luckily, he and Cutler had been working on enhanced security scenarios already, despite his skepticism about Sulu's warning.

"We've already made plans to strengthen certain security procedures," he said, "and we *will* take these new revelations into account as well." He gestured toward Cutler, who was seated a few chairs away almost on the opposite side of the conference table. "Commander Cutler will explain further."

Cutler cleared her throat and squared her shoulders. Tapping commands into a small keypad in front of her, she looked toward the tri-screened viewer that was mounted in the table's center. Data columns and related diagrams suddenly appeared there.

"We already have strong detachments of security at the conference facilities, which will be in rotation with Klingon forces, as well as two specialized Starfleet security detachments that had already been dispatched, consisting of human, Vulcan, and Andorian officers. All of them have been briefed—and will be rebriefed—on explosives, frontal assaults, and other more conventional threats. There will be weapons checkpoints far outside the main complex, frequent interbuilding scans, and visual surveillance."

She tapped on the keyboard a few more times, and several new diagrams began a slow procession across the screen, displacing the earlier ones. "Given this new information from Doctors Klass and Chapel, we will also set up hidden sensors at every checkpoint to provide a thorough battery of scans for all known biohazardous agents."

"Be certain to input the data from the specific strain we've discovered," Klass said, interrupting. "The combination has not yet been added to the Federation biohazard database. Just most of the individual elements."

Having been quiet for most of the meeting, Sulu finally spoke again, his voice deep and resonant. "The Klingons won't like it, but I suggest a sterilization of the conference chambers, almost to clean-room conditions."

"That'll certainly put a damper on their table manners," Dax said with a mischievous grin.

"It will also be more difficult to make this seem like a traditional precautionary measure," Styles said. His own encounters with Klingons had made him keenly aware that these measures might push their already heightened distrust of humans over the brink, no matter how beneficial they might prove to be. "The more we clamp down, the more panic we can expect, or at least resentment. And we really don't need the Klingons any more on edge than usual."

"I believe I can aid with that transition, Captain," Sarek said. "Diplomacy is my arena. I will simply have to work somewhat harder to convince the Klingons that our security measures are conducive to their own goals. Perhaps I will blame it on humans and their irrational need for caution. That may both appease their warrior spirit and give them the honorable option of humoring us in our attempt to protect them better."

Cutler favored the Vulcan diplomat with a respectful nod. "Thank you, Mister Ambassador. Mollifying the Klingons will indeed be helpful. As to off-site security, in addition to *Excelsior,* we will have the assistance of multiple Klingon vessels. It's my understanding that Captains Kor, Koloth, and Kang will be present with their respective battleships, if not others as well."

As Cutler continued, Styles stole a quick glance at Sulu. The first officer listened to the ship's head of security with rapt attention, displaying no air of "I told you so" in his body language. In fact, he had been rather subdued throughout the meeting, making no mention of his hypothesized personal stake in catching the albino Klingon.

Perhaps I've misjudged him a bit, Styles thought as he absentmindedly rubbed the metal end of the swagger stick that lay on the table in front of him. *Maybe I've allowed my other feelings to fuel my suspicions.*

He didn't feel any sudden need to forgive or forget his years of more-than-justified annoyance with Kirk and his *Enterprise* crew. But he was able to resolve, at least, that perhaps the time had finally come to give Sulu some of the benefit of his many doubts.

THIRTEEN

"When nothing goes as planned, the world is in balance."
It was an old Trill saying, and Curzon Dax found it circling
through his mind every thirty seconds or so, like an annoying insect that couldn't be chased away. Though the mantra
didn't accurately reflect his high hopes for the Korvat peace
conference, by midway through the first day he had to concede that it was apropos.

Excelsior's security team had been astonishingly thorough—far too thorough for the Klingons who found the
whole screening process invasive and the facilities here at
the Korvat colony far too clean for their unrefined sensibili-
ties—and that had delayed the start of the talks for almost
two hours. Even the calming influence of Ambassador Sarek
had succeeded only in making the delays tolerable rather
than "merely" maddening for the Klingons.

Once the talks started, the posturing of the Klingons
was almost Shakespearean in nature—Curzon was familiar with the old Earth playwright's work largely through

the memories of Emony—especially that of Ambassador Kamarag, who was backed not only by a support team of junior ambassadors, but also by a trio of cocky warrior captains named Koloth, Kang, and Kor. Kamarag's voice rang loudly in the diplomatic hall, in bellicose contrast to Sarek's stolidly emotionless and subdued tones.

Dax knew that Sarek was a brilliant and enormously experienced diplomat, but he wondered just how well he understood the real cultural values of the Klingon Empire. Dax had little doubt that if even half of the boastful bluster that Kamarag had been spouting all day could be bagged and shipped, it could transform even the most barren Vulcan desert into a galactic agricultural marvel. Nevertheless, he also understood something of the substance behind the boasts; because he had made a careful study of Klingon society and biology during his undergraduate years, Dax suspected that he might understand its subtleties better than anyone present who had not actually been born on Qo'noS, Sarek included.

Dax had noticed immediately that Kor and Kang had the smooth foreheads that labeled them as *QuchHa'*; their presence here today, and their influential positions as the captains of Klingon warships, meant that despite their culturally undesirable—and fully visible—genetic aberrations, they had clawed their way to the top. By contrast, Kamarag and Koloth and nearly all the other Klingons present possessed the more traditional textured *HemQuch* forehead. But Koloth, Dax had learned, hadn't been born with *his* *HemQuch* features, having acquired them later in life, after he had already achieved a captaincy, presumably in defiance of the same ingrained prejudices that Kang and Kor had had to overcome.

Even before Dr. Klass and Dr. Chapel had conducted briefings about the bioengineering experiments of the suspected saboteur, Dax had known about the Klingons' continued covert experiments with bioagents intended to restore the traditional *HemQuch* phenotypic features, lost to large numbers of Klingon bloodlines for reasons that were not well understood outside the Empire, to all members of the Klingon species. Unfortunately for those secretly experimenting on *QuchHa'* test subjects, these efforts so far appeared to have achieved success only for those Klingons who possessed a very specific genetic profile. Dax could only conclude that Koloth had been born into this genetically favored smooth-headed group, since he had reviewed the tall Klingon captain's profile in the Federation Diplomatic Corps's intel files, which had contained both "before" and "after" holoimages of Captain Koloth.

Dax's knowledge about the Klingon biosciences hadn't come purely from Federation files, of course, nor had his knowledge of some of their societal secrets. After all, the Trill people were certainly experts at keeping secrets, about both themselves and their adversaries, and therefore did not share information indiscriminately, even with allies such as Earth or other Federation members. It was because of the closely held secret of Trill symbiosis that the Trill people had sought neither apologies nor reparations from the Klingons when a strain of the Klingon-engineered Levodian flu retrovirus had mysteriously infected a Trill colony. Although the infection had not proven lethal, it had caused a mutation not only among the Trill who were exposed to it but also among their descendants. Although the high, rippled forehead manifested by the few who carried the mutated genes differed from the classic features of the Klingons, there were those, sadly, who considered it a dangerous oddity, a prejudice that had driven many with the trait into hiding on their own homeworld. Only now that a second generation of this small minority was beginning to come of age were the Trill with rippled foreheads being seen again, and accepted, in public.

Kamarag finally sat down, but before Sarek could take his turn to speak, Koloth rose to his feet. Although the Klingon captain had been argumentative with both Sarek and Dax almost since their first exchange of words, what emerged now was an icy-cold kind of argumentativeness, somehow passionate and yet almost devoid of surface emotion. *For a Klingon, Koloth would make a pretty good Vulcan,* Dax thought.

"The Klingon Empire has never before considered a peace initiative such as this one, because we have had no need to do so," Koloth said, continuing with some of the same points that had just been made by Kamarag, as well as by Baktrek, one of the Klingon junior emissaries who had spoken earlier. "The initiative begs the obvious question: Why should we ally ourselves with those who are weaker than we are, when we could simply *conquer* them instead?"

"But you have already chosen *not* to conquer them," Sarek said, breaking in quickly when Koloth stopped to take a breath. "The Klingon Empire has not expanded significantly in more than two decades. My understanding is that this is because the High Council does not wish to overextend its already depleted resources with further conquests, preferring instead to consolidate its most recent gains and thereby strengthen the Empire domestically."

"You know *nothing* of the reasoning of our High Council," Koloth said. Though his brow crinkled more severely, no other outward sign of anger or peevishness was visible on his face. "Nor do we need to explain it to you."

"Perhaps it would help us to understand more clearly if you *did* explain it," Dax said, hoping his words wouldn't be taken as empty sarcasm even as he spoke them. "If conquest really is the virtue you seem to think it is, then why did the High Council make a trade pact with the Romulan Star Empire more than twenty years ago? Using your logic, Captain

Koloth, conquest would presumably have been simpler than cooperation."

"Bah," grunted Kor, rousing himself in his seat to lean forward. "That was purely a military strategy. It lasted no longer than it needed to."

"If you can ally yourself with the Romulans—who have antagonized all of us at one time or another—for even a *brief* time," Dax countered, "then why do you seem so unwilling to attempt to establish an even more productive, more beneficial peace with the much larger and much more prosperous Federation?"

Kamarag squinted as he leaned forward menacingly. "We are here, are we not? And we have not left the table."

"And yet, we seem to be at a stalemate, sirs," Dax said, leaning forward himself and baring his teeth as he spoke. He understood that he was adopting an aggressive posture, but he also knew that the Klingons were testing their adversaries-cum-potential-allies—and *had* been testing them for hours now. And this was only the first day of the conference.

Sarek placed a hand on Dax's arm, squeezing almost imperceptibly. Dax felt his arm go nearly numb from the light but insistent pressure. "Perhaps now would be a good time for a brief break for refreshments," Sarek said. "We can resume our talks shortly."

He gestured behind him, where Captain Styles and his retinue from *Excelsior* were stationed in a staging gallery. "I have asked Captain Styles to have his cooks prepare a kettle of *bahgol* for your enjoyment," Sarek said.

"It had best be warmed properly," Baktrek said grumpily as two *Excelsior* crew members brought forward trays of the flattened bowls containing the *bahgol*.

Dax took one of the steaming metal bowls and almost dropped it onto the table because it was so hot. He saw the Klingons grab the bowls brusquely, displaying no such aversion to the temperature of the food. Neither did any of them complain when bringing the steaming bowls to their dark lips.

"It is adequate," Koloth said, liquid dripping from the tips of his long mustache. Dax would have offered him a napkin had any been present, but he knew that no matter how formal or ceremonial an occasion might be, a sleeve was always the best friend to a Klingon in the act of drinking or eating.

Downing his drink with a speed that might have cauterized a non-Klingon esophagus, Kang slammed the bowl down on the table and stood. "You Earthers and your allies," he said, sweeping one arm toward the *Excelsior* crew before gesturing toward Sarek, Dax, and Dostara. "You have no concept of where the Klingon Empire has been, nor of what true honor is and what the warrior's life is like. Your people have been domesticated, the sight of blood making you queasy, your economies and politics and social attitudes equalized to the point of ridiculousness.

"It is no wonder that the Federation sends three aliens to negotiate," Kang continued. "The humans are the softest of all. That is why they ally themselves with others—to protect themselves against those who could wipe them out with minimal exertion. This is why they seek now to bring the Klingon Empire into their pact. We have an old saying: 'Keep your enemy as a friend, but be ready to gut him when the time comes.' This is a—"

"If you're not willing to speak civilly, and without threats, these talks are useless," Dax said evenly and sternly, his voice low. He was surprised he had said it out loud.

Kang stared down at the man who interrupted him for a moment, then resumed his tirade. "This is a negotiation that offers us nothing. The Klingon Empire should choose when it wishes to be at peace and when it wishes to achieve its ends through the warrior's arts. It is our power that terrifies others, that brings them to us, suing for peace—"

Dax stood up abruptly, the *bahgol* in front of him slopping out of its bowl and onto the table. "Your passion has blinded you," he said evenly, then turned and began to walk away.

Dax strode purposefully toward the room's main exit, hyperaware with each step away from the table that he was risking both the abrupt end of his career and of his life. *To say nothing of our chances for peace,* he thought.

But his intensive study of Klingon culture and their often violent debating techniques told Dax that his calculated but spur-of-the-moment tactic might actually get him somewhere. He wished he could explain that to Sarek somehow, but he hadn't realized he was actually going to make the bold gesture until a split second before the time to do it was upon him.

The room was deathly quiet for a few moments as he walked, and although he could not turn around to see, he imagined that Kang's mouth was probably opening and closing like that of a beached fish. Then, as he neared the door and the Klingon and Starfleet security personnel who guarded it, he heard a roar of anger rising behind him. It no doubt would have sounded utterly incoherent to anyone who wasn't conversant with the fine art of Klingon cursing.

The guards let Dax pass, and he felt steady when his hands made contact with the heavy wooden doors that separated the conference hall's inner sanctum from the outer corridor beyond. Outside stood an entire phalanx of guards—both Starfleet and Klingon—who looked at him with surprise as he strode out into their midst.

Although the time seemed an eternity, Dax knew that only seconds had elapsed before he heard Kang roaring up behind him. He turned and saw that Koloth and Kor were flanking their fellow captain, whose deep brown features had turned almost purple with near-apoplectic outrage. Even Koloth's heretofore-icy features displayed fervid displeasure.

"You are either the most foolish diplomat who ever drew breath, or else you have a death wish!" Kang shouted, spittle flying from his mouth in a fine spray.

"Perhaps neither," Dax said, his voice as steady and unquavering as he could make it. "Perhaps I merely don't wish to waste my time listening to boasts and veiled threats. If *you* are not ready to cooperate and act with honor, then perhaps the High Council sent the wrong emissaries to represent them."

Dax stood his ground in silence as he tried to force his slightly shaking knees to remain still. Kang stared at him, and Dax imagined—perhaps wrongly—that he saw a spark of grudging respect flashing deep in the Klingon captain's eyes.

Kor spoke up then. "You challenge Kang's *honor*?"

I had a feeling that might have been the wrong word to use the moment I said it, Dax thought. But he had chosen this road and now had to deal with the consequences.

"I did *not*," he said. "Those who act in concert with the *spirit* of these peace negotiations—as *agreed* to by the High Council—*do* act with honor. If Kang does not feel he is *obeying* those directives, then he is the one who would feel that he has betrayed his honor."

Behind the Klingons, Dax saw that Commander Sulu and Lieutenant Commander Cutler had exited the chamber as well, and were quickly relaying commands to their security officers. Beyond them, he saw Sarek and Dostara trying to talk with Kamarag and Baktrek and the other ambassadors, even as Captain Styles and several of his staff stood by, obviously considering their next moves, diplomatic or otherwise.

Have I gone too far? Dax asked himself as he shifted his attention back to Kang. The whole affair had lasted less than a minute, but felt like an eternity.

And then a brilliant flash of light and a loud noise obliterated Dax's vision.

Even as the explosion from within the Korvat conference chamber rocked the air, throwing Dax and the others off their feet, Dax heard screams and several more explosions originating from somewhere else nearby.

Through barely focused eyes, he saw what appeared to be Koloth toppling forward onto one of *Excelsior*'s officers, a young man who sported a small but bright red circular tattoo between his eyes. The back of Koloth's hair was burning, and as Dax breathed in, a lungful of acrid smoke and heated air told him that more than just the Klingon was afire.

Panic overtaking him, Dax grasped the one lucid thought swirling through his mind.

We've just been bombed.

PART II:
INTO THE FIRE

When all else is lost, the
future still remains.

—Christian Nestell Bovee
(1820–1904)

FOURTEEN

Hikaru Sulu could smell his own singed hair for what seemed an eternity before he felt the prickly sensation of first-degree burns on the back of his neck. He heard far-off moaning and faint screams as he struggled to get his feet back underneath him, and saw several unconscious *Excelsior* security personnel and Klingons lying sprawled all around him. Others were picking themselves up, cradling their injured limbs. Smoke and embers floated through the air.

What the hell just happened? Sulu thought groggily, but even as he turned to take in the devastation all around him, he knew. Through what was left of the conference room doors, he could see the conflagration that raged inside. *We were attacked. Despite all of our precautions.*

A Klingon warrior pushed past him to run into the center of the chamber, and in that instant, Sulu saw other movement inside the room. *Rescue them,* a frantic voice inside his mind screamed at him, making itself louder than anything else he was hearing. He moved to reenter the chamber and flipped open the communicator that had miraculously stayed attached to the belt on his dress uniform.

"Sulu to *Excelsior*! We have an emergency! The conference has been bombed!" He couldn't hear anything in response, and he could tell that his hearing had been badly compromised. As two Klingons began dragging bodies out of the hall, Sulu fumbled along the wall for one of the fire extinguishers he had seen earlier in the day. As he drew nearer to where the devices should have been, the lingering smoke and ash thickened. He tripped over a body and went down on one knee.

Through the hazy air, he could see that the body was that of Dr. Klass, her jacket melted away over her shoulder, and her right arm smoldering. He couldn't tell whether she was unconscious or dead, but he struggled back to his feet and began dragging her back toward the doorway.

Another body knocked into him, and he whirled to see Cutler, her uniform and hair disheveled, her face streaked with soot. She began yelling something at him, but he couldn't understand her. She stopped yelling and began to cough violently, then sprinted away, moving farther into the smoke-filled chamber.

Sulu felt a hand on his arm, and he turned to see Lieutenant Lojur, the Halkan navigator who had chosen to work with the security detail despite his people's pacifistic tendencies. Lojur said something incomprehensible, then stooped to pick up Dr. Klass and began carrying her outside. Satisfied that he could do no more for Klass than Lojur was already doing, Sulu turned back toward the conference tables. The initial conflagration appeared already to have burned itself out, probably already having consumed most of the oxygen necessary to sustain it. But the air remained thick with smoke and redolent of charred furniture and flesh.

As he neared the shattered, burned-out remains of the

conference table, he saw a familiar figure swaddled in ceremonial robes, struggling to rise from a pile of smoking debris. *Sarek!* Sulu was immediately at his side, but was distressed to see green blood seeping from between the Vulcan's fingers, which were pressed to the side of his neck. Sulu ducked under the ambassador's other arm and began helping him toward the exit. Keeping an eye on the floor, Sulu saw the mangled torso of Sarek's assistant, Dostara, lying in a pool of scorched green blood, clearly beyond all help. Lieutenant Commander Lahra, her face frozen in a mask of wide-eyed surprise, her neck bent almost at a right angle to the rest her body, lay unmoving on the floor nearby.

More Klingons rushed into the chamber, then nearly bowled Sulu and Sarek over as they tried to make their way back toward the exit. A moment later Sulu noticed that several other Klingon guards that had been in the hall earlier were hurriedly transporting a body out with them, moving with grace and discipline despite their many burns, bleeding wounds, and melted armor.

He recognized the body they carried as that of Ambassador Kamarag. *He doesn't look good,* Sulu thought grimly. *Nobody who was inside looks good.*

In the outer hallway, Sulu saw the smoke-distorted curtain of a transporter beam herald the arrival of a medical team from *Excelsior.* He recognized Dr. Harburg and Nurse Edwards among them, and, of course, Dr. Chapel. "Christine, take care of Sarek," he yelled, his voice sounding too loud as it resonated inside his own head; he had no clue how loud it sounded to the team, especially given the chaos that still swirled all around.

Ensign Leonard James Akaar, the Capellan junior security officer, entered the chamber alongside Sulu even as the Klingons removed still more bodies. Sulu recognized among them Joqel, a moderately inclined Klingon politician whom

Sarek had hoped to sway. With Joqel now missing a third of his face, Sulu doubted that he was even alive any longer, much less capable of conducting any diplomacy.

Akaar grabbed Sulu's arm, steering him toward the right, where the *Excelsior* staff had been stationed while the delegates were meeting. Sulu saw Cutler there, bent over a body, apparently trying to perform CPR on it. *That's not especially useful when there's so little breathable air in the room,* Sulu thought.

Then, as Akaar lifted another nearby limp body as though it weighed little more than a rag doll, Sulu saw the face of the person Cutler was working so desperately to save. Captain Styles was barely recognizable. His hair was mostly burned off, his face charred and blackened. Sulu quickly knelt, feeling at the side of Styles's neck for any sign of life. His hand encountered a jelly-like wetness instead of firm flesh.

Cutler looked up, made eye contact with Sulu, and immediately began to yell in his face. He couldn't quite make out all the words, but it was clear that she was distraught and angry—almost venomous—from the way she was screaming at him.

"Let's get the captain out of here," he shouted back.

She punched him in the side of the face then, hard. He heard a pop, and then a rush of sounds filled his head. "—your fault, you *bastard*!"

He saw that Cutler was about to wind her arm up for another blow, and quickly drove his palm upward under her chin. Cutler fell backward, her legs kicking out from under her as she thudded onto the debris-strewn floor beside where Styles lay.

"Let me help you, sir," he heard a voice say. He looked up to see the bearded Lieutenant Eric Braun squatting near Captain Styles's head. Another movement drew Sulu's eye to his left side, where he saw an Andorian crouching to grab the captain's legs. A moment later, and they had hoisted

Excelsior's grievously injured—dead?—commanding officer up and were ferrying him quickly toward the conference room door.

Sulu stood and moved over to Cutler, who was now sitting on the floor, looking disoriented. Extending his hand toward her, he shouted, "Meredith, we've got to find out what happened. And *how* it happened."

She glared up at him, her eyes twin orbs of incongruous whiteness in the soot-darkened air. "You're blaming *me*?"

Sulu reextended his hand, emphatically. "There's no blame to be *placed* at the moment. But there's plenty of chaos to get under control. We don't know if *more* attacks are coming."

Cutler grasped his hand and pulled herself up without saying anything further. Together, along with the Klingons and Starfleet security, they quickly continued to survey the chamber for more survivors . . . or more casualties.

The death toll from the attack was high. Two diplomatic aides and Joqel were dead on the Klingon side, while both Captain Styles and Dostara had died from the injuries they'd received in the explosion. Sulu was barely cognizant of the fact that *he* was now in command of *Excelsior*—or at least would be when he returned to the ship.

Many more had been injured, among them Dr. Klass, Ambassador Sarek, and Ambassador Kamarag. Surprisingly, the other Klingons had agreed to allow Dr. Chapel to beam Kamarag to *Excelsior*'s sickbay along with the other injured; being firmly indoctrinated into the Klingon ethos that granted survival only to the strong, the Korvat colony possessed substandard medical facilities, and those aboard the Klingon battle cruisers in orbit above Korvat were probably not much better equipped to handle so many burn and trauma victims.

Those that were left on Korvat now were completely on

edge and quite literally shell-shocked. Both the Klingon and Federation security teams were searching the complex with every scanning device available to find traces of the weaponry—or the saboteurs—that had caused the explosions.

The detonation in the main meeting hall was not the only destruction that had been visited on the conference complex, as the security teams had soon found out; there had been a number of smaller explosions throughout the sprawling building, including several in the adjacent chambers that had been converted into private meeting rooms and temporary quarters. Several more dead security personnel had been found as well, far away from any of the blasts.

"How did the bombs get through all of *our* security protocols, Commander?" Sulu asked Cutler, even as Kor, Koloth, and Kang glowered behind him.

Cutler shifted uneasily from foot to foot, staring down at the tricorder in her hands. "We don't know, sir. So far, we've found multiple chemical traces, all consistent with standard explosive materials, as well as the remnants of a device that might have been a small cloaking mechanism."

"Were any bioagents released?" Sulu asked. He saw Koloth give him a startled look.

Cutler's expression was more withering than startled. "No, sir. As far as I can determine, this was *not* a biological attack, but purely an act of conventional terrorism, or at least sabotage and murder."

"So, the one who threatened us might *not* be the one responsible for this after all," Kor said to Koloth.

Cutler's veiled slight immediately forgotten, Sulu whirled around. "What are you saying? You *knew* there was the possibility of an attack?"

Koloth squared his shoulders. "In some sectors of the Empire, there is *always* the possibility of an attack. But we had received a warning that somebody might strike at this conference with biochemical weapons."

Sulu thought he could feel the blood vessels in his forehead constrict as his blood pressure rose. "You *knew* about this and didn't *tell* us?"

Kang stepped forward menacingly. "*You* apparently knew about a *similar* threat and didn't tell *us*," he said. "But we are not surprised by your apparent foreknowledge, given all the extra precautions you took with security." He grimaced, looking around. "Not that it did any good."

Outside of the attacks themselves, Sulu wasn't sure what to be angrier about: Cutler's insubordinate attitude or the fact that the Klingons had played the same game with the Federation representatives that Styles had played with the Klingons.

"If the saboteur had an accomplice working among you Earthers, the odds are that it would be this Trill," Kang said, pointing toward Dax, who was standing a few feet away.

"How do you figure?" Sulu asked, trying to keep the annoyance out of his voice.

"He *conveniently* left the room just before the blast," Kor said. "He may even have triggered it remotely."

Dax stepped toward the Klingons, drawing himself to his full stature, which was still considerably less than Kang's. "There were three others who left the room when *I* did. Three others who've demonstrated that *they* don't care for the idea of peace between the Federation and the Klingon Empire. It seems just as likely that *they* could be responsible for this attack."

"Take care, whelp," Koloth growled. "You overstep your bounds at your peril. Remember, your senior ambassador isn't here to protect you now."

"So, finally the *d'akturak* shows some real emotion," Dax said, moving closer to Koloth. "I thought you were made *entirely* of ice. But I don't *need* Sarek to protect me. I can fight my own battles if necessary, or bring peace—if such a thing is even *possible*."

Sulu held up his hands. "Gentlemen! May I remind you all that *both* sides have taken losses in this attack. Neither the Federation nor the Empire is unscathed. So we have to put our differences aside and go after whoever really *is* responsible for the bombing."

Sulu watched as the three Klingons and Dax regarded him silently for an instant or two, and he thought he felt at least a little bit of the tension between them begin to wane.

"Commander, we have new information," Cutler said from behind Sulu. During the confrontation between the three warriors and Dax, Sulu had nearly forgotten the presence of his own personal nemesis.

He turned and saw that Lieutenant Braun had returned with a handheld security scanner, which he was showing to Cutler.

"Well, what is it?" Sulu asked, perhaps a bit more impatiently than he had intended.

"The other bombs also disabled the building's deflector shield and transporter inhibitors," Braun said. "And we've detected a recent transporter trace, indicating that someone may have been beamed out of the building immediately following the detonations."

Cutler swallowed. "You mean to tell me we've been *unshielded* for the last ten minutes? And that anybody, or any*thing,* could be beamed down among us, not just from *Excelsior* or the Klingon vessels?"

"I think so," Braun said, looking uncomfortable.

Sulu felt something inside him bend almost to the breaking point. "Commander Cutler, get every available person to work restoring the conference center's shield generators. *Now!*" As Cutler and Braun hastened to carry out his orders, Sulu flipped open his communicator.

"Sulu to *Excelsior.*"

"Rand here, Commander."

"We've discovered that shields are down for the entire

complex. I'm ordering an emergency evacuation, giving priority to all the injured and the VIPs."

"Understood, Commander."

"Once that's finished, I'll need you to beam down some portable shield generators and related components immediately. Commander Cutler will give you the specifics. We'll need a few volunteers to get this place's defenses back online."

As the three Klingons contacted their own ships, presumably to relay similar orders to their own respective crews, Sulu felt a chill of realization abruptly turn his spine to ice.

Whoever had attacked them—and he remained certain even without any overt signs of bioterrorism that the albino was the one responsible—apparently could finish what he'd begun at any moment. *Why hasn't he done it yet? And what's his next move going to be?*

Sulu couldn't even begin to guess at the answers. All he could do was hope that his own people and the Klingons could complete the emergency evacuation and raise the Korvat complex's defenses before a second attack completed the job that the first one had started.

FIFTEEN

Qagh felt his weight return as his atoms were finally reassembled on the transporter platform. With no support, however—and thanks to his injury—he pitched forward toward the deck. Only the quick intervention of Dr. Nej, who had operated the controls during the beam-up, prevented him from toppling face-first into the operator's console.

"Are you all right?" Nej said, concern creasing his face as he helped Qagh settle himself into a seated position on the platform's edge.

"I was injured when I set off the last charge," the albino said, wincing at the pain in his side. "And it seemed as if something went wrong with the matter stream during the transport process."

Nej paled slightly. "I'm afraid that it did. Something was interfering with the signal and the mirror relays you set up to allow your beam-out while maintaining our cloak."

"How long was I hung up in transit?"

"For nearly twelve *tups*, sir."

Qagh nodded numbly. The fact that he had reassembled at all after such a considerable length of time was probably a miracle in itself. That, combined with the fact that his mission to personally sabotage the Korvat peace talks—including setting off the bombs while he was still on-site, in order to defeat any effort on Starfleet's part to jam an incoming "detonate" signal—had gone mostly without a hitch, told him that he was riding the ragged edge of his luck.

That, of course, was nothing new for a man whose very existence had for decades depended upon frequent and repeated medical miracles.

"You're bleeding," Nej said as he reached for one of the emergency medical kits that were stowed in one of the wall cubbies.

The albino looked down to see the bloodstains soiling his right side. He gingerly pulled his shredded Klingon military tunic away from the wound. His disguise had allowed him to do his work on the planet below undetected for most of the past three days. It had only been near the end of that time, when one of the Klingon guards had apparently spotted him in his peripheral vision, that he had been caught. The resulting hand-to-hand combat had been swift and brutal, leaving Qagh not only with his facial disguise torn off but also with a deep wound in his side, scant moments before he had succeeded in both dispatching the guard and detonating the final bomb.

He stifled a groan as Nej wiped away some of the blood in an attempt to apply a pressure bandage. "Sorry," the physician said, wincing empathetically as he saw the pain on Qagh's face.

"That's fine," Qagh said. "Help me get to the main control room. I need to find out if anyone survived down there. And finish what I started now that the shields are down in the conference complex."

Qagh allowed Nej to put an arm around his shoulder, and

they made their way together along the freighter's narrow, winding corridors. At the control room door, the albino disentangled his arm and steadied himself against the adjacent wall. Although renewed waves of pain lanced through his wounded side, he ignored it and straightened his posture, unwilling to appear weak before his men, his chronic ailments notwithstanding.

The door slid open, and Qagh entered the command deck. "Give me a status report!" he barked at the four crewmen working the controls.

"We withheld firing until we were certain that Doctor Nej had exhausted all of his options in attempting to beam you back aboard," Messebs, the helmsman, said.

Qagh wondered how much longer Messebs would have held his fire had the rematerialization process taken even longer, then dismissed the issue as unimportant, at least for now. After all, Messebs's blood carried one of Qagh's designer viruses, as did the rest of the crew. Therefore the helmsman would have been powerfully motivated not to jeopardize his only source of the counteragents that prevented that virus from taking its lethal course. Such was the stuff of loyalty.

"How much damage did my bombs do?" Qagh asked Messebs and moved toward the centrally mounted command chair. He carefully controlled his facial muscles so as to avoid wincing visibly.

"According to our scans," said Koro, the Orion who was working an adjacent console, "both the Federation and Klingon contingents took several casualties, but we're reading the life signs of many survivors as well, in addition to some transporter traffic between the planet's surface and the Federation starship. The explosives seem to have caused severe structural damage to the conference chambers."

Qagh cursed under his breath. He had been hoping for far more extensive losses among both the Klingon and Federation diplomatic teams. "Lock our disruptors on the main conference chambers. Fire at will and finish them off."

Koro gulped audibly. "Sir, the facility's shields went back up about two *tups* ago. We can lock onto *other* targets on the surface, but the conference site itself is too well protected for us to do any real damage to it from orbit. At least, not without revealing our location to the Klingon patrol ships and *Excelsior*."

Grinding his back teeth, the albino considered his dwindling set of options. The fact that his bombs had not succeeded in completely destroying the conference chamber and its adjacent buildings was frustrating, to put it mildly. Both Qagh and his crew were keenly aware that a Klingon-Federation peace treaty—and its concomitant introduction of widespread law and order—would ultimately destroy their livelihood, or at least drive them out of the sectors in which they had been carrying out the bulk of their activities for years.

Worse, without the raids on scientific facilities that Qagh sprinkled judiciously among his more traditional pirating operations—such as the assault on a Mempa system facility that he planned to execute shortly after concluding his business on Korvat—he might lose access to the biomedical resources and other emerging technologies that had always enabled him, however precariously, to maintain his grip on life itself.

"Have any of the other ships scanned us yet?" he asked, his mind reeling.

Koro shook his head. "They're definitely scanning the space immediately surrounding the planet, but our cloak continues to evade their sensors, at least so far as I can tell. As far as we know, they have not yet detected us in any fashion."

An idea suddenly blazed very brightly in Qagh's brain. "Get us into position between the Federation ship and the four Klingon vessels," he said, leaning forward and ignoring the sticky wetness along the margins of the pressure bandage at his side. "One-tenth impulse power. Make sure we don't show up on their scans."

Messebs gave him a questioning look, but nodded and returned his full attention to the controls before him.

Whoever survived below will be returning to the ships above, Qagh thought. *They will have to lower their shields to do that, and since we've given them no reason to believe that we're still here, they probably won't wait much longer to make themselves vulnerable. Then I can finish the job that I started on Korvat.* He knew that his nascent plan might appear foolhardy. But he also understood that no victory could be won without risk.

Besides, he would have already achieved partial success even if he decided to slink quietly away now. *I've* already *disrupted the peace talks,* he thought. *If I succeed in inflicting even* further *damage, then that may be enough to create enmity between the Federation and the Klingon Empire that will last for generations.*

A brief time later, as the *Hegh'TlhoS* maneuvered closer to her prey, Qagh saw something—or at least he *thought* he saw something—that made his heart race.

"Magnify the image of the nearest Klingon vessel," he said.

The image on the screen was unmistakable. Along the flat dorsal section of the closest Klingon battle cruiser's secondary hull was graven the very familiar pictographic markings designating the specific Great House that the vessel represented, in addition to the ubiquitous red-and-black trefoil insignia that proclaimed her more general loyalty to the Klingon Empire's military hierarchy. The House-related markings were a perfect match with those on the iron baby-blanket clasp that he'd kept hidden for years in his quarters, the only tangible remnant of his personal family heritage.

That ship is allied with the House of Ngoj, Qagh thought. *A House whose fortunes have finally begun to improve, it would seem.*

A House whose holdings rightfully ought to be mine.

If he had needed any more justification to carry out a follow-up attack, then it had just been delivered to him, and gift-wrapped to boot. *This fight,* he thought, *has just become* personal.

SIXTEEN

Stardate 9000.9 (Late 2289)

U.S.S. Excelsior

"We've mopped up down here about as much as we're able to," Commander Sulu said, wiping soot from his face. *"But Commander Cutler and the science teams will continue sifting through the ashes for forensic evidence. Have your scans shown any further transporter traces?"*

Lieutenant Commander Rand shook her head, staring at the forward viewscreen on *Excelsior*'s bridge. "None, Commander. We thought we caught a faint glimmer of one less than an hour ago, but it was so scattered and diffuse that it could have just been random ionization in the upper atmosphere."

Sulu frowned. *"In the atmosphere? Not on the surface?"*

"Yes, sir," Rand said, nodding.

Sulu turned to speak loudly to a nearby group of Klingons. Rand couldn't see their faces, only parts of their heavily armored leather garb. *"We may be safe in assuming we're up against a cloaked ship in orbit, rather than just attackers on the surface,"* she heard him say.

"Have you found any evidence of this?" one of the Klingons said.

"Nothing definitive," said Sulu. *"But it might be wise to tell your ships to raise their shields just the same."*

Rand didn't need to wait for Sulu to give her the same command. She leaned forward in the captain's chair, tension gripping her. "Raise shields!" she said to Lieutenant Heather Keith, the helmsman on duty.

"Aye, sir," Keith responded smartly as she pressed a sequence of buttons on the console in front of her.

"Commander, a ship has just decloaked between us and the Klingons," Lieutenant Valtane shouted from his science station. "They're opening fire!"

"On-screen!" Rand barked.

Sulu's surprised face was replaced by a view of the space immediately surrounding *Excelsior,* as well as the five other ships that now shared it with her. Until moments ago, Kor's ship, the *I.K.S. Klothos,* had been the closest to them, then Ambassador Kamarag's diplomatic ship, the *I.K.S. Mev'Luh.* But now, a smaller ship had maneuvered between *Excelsior* and the contingent of Klingon vessels.

In the instant or so before the interloper fired what was apparently its second salvo, Rand tried and failed to identify the hostile ship's configuration. It had a scavenged appearance, as though it had been assembled from several vessels of disparate design. Nevertheless, it looked quick and dangerous.

"Come about!" she ordered, immediately understanding that she had but one option. "Target the attacking ship. Full phasers."

Even as Keith and the other bridge personnel scrambled to obey her commands, she saw three—no, five—plasma flares shoot out of the small ship in rapid succession. Two of them ripped into the aft end of the *Klothos,* which appeared to have been turning toward its attacker.

To Rand's horror, the other three blasts hit the *Mev'Luh,* which was already burning in one spot almost directly amidships, apparently as a result of the attacking ship's opening salvo. More explosions raged along the diplomatic vessel's hull, the escaping atmosphere igniting, then quickly extinguishing and forming clouds of fine ice crystals in the cold vacuum of space.

"Firing," Schulman called out from tactical.

Rand saw two sapphire-blue phaser blasts lance out toward the small raider, which had already begun rolling out of the way at a near-ninety-degree angle, barely evading the beams. *Shit, they're fast,* she thought.

On the viewer, the other two Klingon battle cruisers—Kang's *I.K.S. QaD* and Koloth's *I.K.S. Gal'tagh*—were both coming about, their weapons tubes glowing menacingly as they launched photon torpedoes toward the swiftly careening enemy ship. Unfortunately, their weapons proved no better at striking their target than *Excelsior*'s phasers had been.

The small ship rolled again, turning tightly so that it was headed directly toward the *Gal'tagh,* from which it couldn't have been more than a few dozen meters distant.

As the much larger *Klothos* seemed to wallow helplessly, Rand could see what the little raider was trying to do. "They're cutting toward Captain Koloth's ship," she shouted. "We have to catch them in a crossfire before they maneuver the Klingons into firing on each other."

"Locking phasers," Schulman said.

"Fire," Rand ordered.

But even as four phaser blasts from *Excelsior* arced toward the aggressor, the smaller ship sent what appeared to be a wide-scattered salvo from some sort of plasma weapon toward both the *QaD* and the *Gal'tagh.*

Two of the blasts from *Excelsior* caught the aggressor ship on her port side, resulting in an explosion on the aft section of its hull; Rand hoped she'd scored a hit on the raider's propulsion system.

Unfortunately, in trying to evade the plasma charges, the *Gal'tagh* flew directly into the path of the *Klothos,* on an apparent collision course. Rand imagined she could almost hear the scrape of duranium on duranium as the two vessels passed with scarcely any space between them, their shields interacting to form a brilliant if momentary aurora as the hostile vessel unloaded a potent salvo of weapons fire inside its opponent's shield perimeter. The ventral portion of the *Klothos*'s starboard nacelle spun away a split second later, her right disruptor cannon shattering incandescently into the void.

The *QaD* was not quite as lucky, having caught an entire plasma blast near its aft side, where Rand imagined its deflector-shield generators were situated.

Now they're a sitting duck, Rand thought. Then she saw that the attacking ship was once again abruptly changing direction, trailing hull debris and molecular flames after having avoided a mutually fatal collision by the narrowest of margins.

"Target them again," she said. "Cripple them if you can. I want to find out who we're dealing with."

"They're headed directly for the *Mev'Luh,* Commander," Keith said, the alarm in her voice as audible as a Red Alert klaxon.

Why would they risk doing that? Rand asked herself. After all, the diplomatic ship was already in flames.

Then something else occurred to her. *She's a diplomatic ship. A symbol of what the Korvat conference represents. And she's right in our line of fire.*

"Hold your fire!" she shouted. If the attacker thought it could manipulate *Excelsior* into making him a martyr and destroying the *Mev'Luh* in the process, they'd not planned very well at all.

"They're still heading straight for the *Mev'Luh,* sir," Valtane said with an urgency Rand rarely heard coming from the sedate junior science officer. "But they've powered down their weapons!"

On the screen, Rand saw the attacker moving inexorably closer and closer to the burning hulk of the *Mev'Luh. Turn away,* she thought, feeling helpless as she gripped the arms of the command chair. *Turn away!*

But the raider didn't turn away. An instant later the viewscreen emitted a momentarily blinding brilliance as a huge explosion tore through the space where the *Mev'Luh* had been.

Rand saw spots before her eyes and tried to blink them away even as the viewscreen automatically damped down the excess light. "Status?"

"They put all their power into propulsion and forward shields just before impact, Commander," Valtane said. "Even if we'd opened fire we wouldn't have been able to avert the collision."

If there really was *a collision,* Rand thought. Given the tactics she'd already seen the hostile using, she wasn't ready to dismiss the possibility that he had simply staged another near collision before opening fire once again and activating a cloaking device. "Begin full sensor sweeps," she said aloud as she rose to her feet. "I want to make sure the attacker didn't get away under the cover of that explosion."

"I'm reading debris from the *Mev'Luh,*" Schulman said. "But I can't find any sign of the attacker's vessel so far."

"See if you can find any weapons or propulsion signatures in the debris field." Rand knew that her second order was probably useless, but she had no choice other than to try it.

"Sensors show plasma weapons fire," Valtane said.

Rand nodded somberly. *Damn. I was really hoping the bastard would at least do us the favor of blowing himself up.*

"Not exactly standard issue for the Klingon military, or their diplomatic corps," she said aloud.

Ensign Ramiro Marquez spoke up from the back of the bridge. "Commander Rand, Commander Sulu wants a status report."

Rand sighed heavily before sinking back into the command chair. Today had not been a terribly good day. "Put him on the screen," she said, squaring her shoulders.

When she saw the fiercely angry expressions of the three Klingon captains who were standing around Sulu, she realized just how much of an understatement "not terribly good" really was.

"You must go *after* them!" Kor shouted, his deep voice reverberating throughout *Excelsior*'s conference room.

Sulu had begun to regret the return of his hearing. Gritting his teeth, he said, "I *want* to, Kor, but your government might see that as another incursion into Klingon territory. And *my* superiors would have some very strong words to say about it as well." Admiral Harriman had already shared a few choice ones with him on the topic via subspace radio.

"Yours is the only military vessel in this system that is undamaged and running at full capacity," Koloth said angrily. "It is your *duty* to avenge this wrong."

"My duty right now is to take care of the injured personnel—from my side *and* yours—from the Korvat conference," Sulu said. "I will place *Excelsior*'s entire engineering department at your disposal to help your crews repair your ships. Then *you* can pursue the attacker without risking war."

All three of the Klingon escort ships had been badly damaged in the fight against the small, weapons-heavy ship, while Ambassador Kamarag's diplomatic vessel, the *I.K.S. Mev'Luh*, had been completely destroyed. Luckily, *Excelsior*'s science teams had managed to find a trail left by the attacking ship, beginning some fourteen light-minutes away from the explosion, leading away from the Korvat system on a northerly outbound trajectory. Apparently the raider's once-working cloaking device was no longer operational, but the vessel had sped off quickly regardless—its warp capability apparently unharmed—on a heading that would take it deeper into Klingon territory.

"We do not need the assistance of cowards who are afraid to make a move without permission," Kang said dismissively. "If you cannot be a warrior even when attacked, then you are *useless,* even to your own craven Federation."

Curzon Dax, who was filling in as head of the Federation negotiating team while Ambassador Sarek remained critically injured, chose that moment to stand up. *"Ylmev!"* he barked, crying, "Stop!" in what could only have been *tlhIngan.* At least that was what Sulu *hoped* the young Trill had just said as all three Klingon captains turned to regard the junior ambassador with angry, smoldering eyes.

"You ask the commander to *dishonor* his ship and his crew by disobeying his superiors?" Dax asked with an admirable touch of bluster. "To risk war with the Empire over an attack by a third party? A war that could bring shame on *all* of your Houses if begun for the wrong reasons? Consider instead how much *more* honor you could all accrue by allowing Commander Sulu to assist you in repairing your vessels so that *you* may capture the attacker *yourselves.*"

Sulu was pleased to see that Dax's words seemed to be getting through to the Klingons. *At least they don't look as if they want to break him in half anymore,* he thought. He had considered Dax a bit reckless just before the explosion in the Korvat conference chamber, but now it seemed as though the young man was beginning to build a very narrow but almost serviceable bridge of trust.

But would that bridge bear the weight of one Trill diplomat and three Klingon captains?

"Commander Sulu has lost much as well," Dax continued. "He has even lost the captain of his ship to whoever committed this act of wanton murder and sabotage, as well as other members of his crew. But he is *not* running away from this battle. Rather, he is offering to help *you* to win the greatest honor available to you—the chance to track down and stop the person responsible for this cowardly sabotage."

A long period passed, perhaps an entire minute during which no one spoke.

"We will return to our ships and accept your help," Koloth said finally, giving a sidelong glance toward the other two captains. "And we will *have* our vengeance."

Despite the horrors of the day, Sulu thought he felt a small, astonished smile coming to his lips. Dax had reasoned with the Klingons.

And they had *listened*.

SEVENTEEN

Stardate 9001.0 (New Year's Day, 2290)

U.S.S. Excelsior

I've wanted this ever since the first time I laid eyes on this ship, Sulu thought as he stood in the bridge's raised center, staring contemplatively at the sleek, blue-padded, ergonomic chair that dominated it. *But not like this.*

Never like this.

"Have a seat, Hikaru." Janice Rand, speaking so quietly that her voice was nearly lost amid the low background hum of the various bridge instruments, had sneaked up on him somehow. She now stood directly behind the empty center seat, as though she had just materialized there. "It's where you belong now."

Though it was immediately in front of him, the command chair had suddenly taken on the aspect of an impossibly distant mountain peak. And he knew that he had been scaling that mountain, in some fashion or other, for his entire Starfleet career.

The summit he had worked so hard to reach belonged to him now—unless and until Starfleet Command told him differently.

Very slowly, and with a deference that bordered on reverence, he sat.

Of course, this wasn't the first time he had occupied *Excelsior*'s center seat; as the ship's executive officer, he had logged quite a few hours here during Captain Styles's absences from the bridge. But this was very different.

"How does it feel?" Rand asked quietly.

Sulu swiveled the chair slowly, taking in most of the bridge in a single sweeping glance as he moved. The officers who toiled attentively at their various stations appeared neither to be eavesdropping on his conversation with Rand nor to be even aware of it.

"Ask me again later, Janice," he said. "After things settle down around here." It occurred to him that his abrupt transition from exec to commanding officer might have been easier to manage had Lawrence H. Styles been someone he'd actually liked.

"By the way, Captain," Rand said, "Happy New Year."

He studied her quizzically for a moment, as though she had just sprouted a second head that sang Gilbert and Sullivan. Then a quick downward glance at the chronometer in the arm of his chair confirmed that she hadn't delivered a bizarre non sequitur. Back in San Francisco, his birthplace and the home of Starfleet Headquarters, the midnight hour had just struck, ringing in the Gregorian year 2290.

Being addressed as "Captain," however—a courtesy that tradition accorded any senior officer in overall command, regardless of actual rank—would probably take a little longer to get used to.

Sulu smiled gently. *"Ganjitsu,"* he said, using the Japanese word for "New Year's Day," which never failed to make him think of the namesake border world where he and his parents had lived for a few short years during his childhood.

Before he could satisfy Rand's quizzical look with an

explanation, the portside turbolift doors hissed open behind him. He turned in time to see Cutler step onto the bridge.

"Situation report, Commander," he said to her as she approached; the simple positive act of getting down to business immediately seemed to be the best therapy he could ask for right now.

Rand retreated quietly to her starboard aft communications station as *Excelsior*'s de facto executive officer took up a position facing Sulu from the command chair's starboard side.

Cutler nodded. "I've just come back from sickbay, so that's as good a place as any to start. Doctor Chapel is running things while Doctor Klass is injured, but she has her hands full down there."

"How is Doctor Klass?"

Cutler sighed. "She took a good deal of blunt force trauma from the blast. She's in a coma."

"Judith's a strong woman," Sulu said, for his own benefit as much as for the morale of the crew. "She'll pull through."

"Let's hope so." Cutler's brow furrowed deeply. "Unfortunately, despite the help of Doctor Hurghom—that's Captain Kor's chief medical officer—the trauma teams haven't been able to stabilize Ambassador Kamarag yet. He's still in pretty touch-and-go shape, and Chapel says he can't be moved."

"Kor and Kang and Koloth might not want to accept that," Sulu said.

"That's their prerogative, I suppose," Cutler said. "But judging from what I've seen so far, even the toughest Klingon might want to think twice before getting between Doctor Chapel and her patients."

"What about the rest of the Klingon delegation?" Sulu wanted to know.

"Lower-ambassador Kishlat is in essentially the same

condition as Kamarag. Chapel and Hurghom are keeping him alive, but he's sustained such extensive injuries that Hurghom tells me that he'll probably take his own life if he ever regains consciousness."

"What?" Sulu asked, perplexed.

"Evidently it's a warrior thing, at least according to Ambassador Dax."

"What about Ambassador Sarek?"

"He's doing better, but not by much. He's stable at least, but he's been burned very badly. The fire scorched his lungs and vocal chords as well."

Sulu nodded gravely. "What's the mortality report so far?"

Cutler shook her head. "Since the bombing, we've lost three more of the Klingons who were down at the conference, plus another one of our guards. This is in addition to Captain Styles, Chief Engineer Lahra, and two other *Excelsior* security personnel. Plus Joqel, the two Klingon diplomatic aides, and Sarek's own aide, Dostara."

Sulu felt as if a tremendous weight were crushing him— the weight of a command he had long anticipated and for which he nevertheless still felt unaccountably unprepared. Of course, even with Styles's death, he was keenly aware that his command of *Excelsior* might end the moment he set foot on a Federation starbase. Or perhaps sooner, if he didn't immediately take every action necessary to clean up the disaster that the Korvat peace talks had become.

Cutler continued making her report in crisp, business-like tones. "Lieutenant Commander Henry is leading the engineering teams in assisting the Klingon escort ships with their repairs. The teams have all been deployed, and the work should be substantially complete in another eighteen to twenty-four hours, depending on variables related to Klingon technology. And behavior."

"Good," Sulu said. He felt enormous empathy for Tim

Henry, whose situation was very much like his own; Henry had been forced to take over *Excelsior*'s engineering department immediately after Chief Engineer Lahra's death down on Korvat.

He leaned forward, staring ahead at the viewer, which displayed the planet's ocher, pockmarked face, bisected by the terminator that divided night from day. "Commander Rand, please open a channel to our team down on the surface."

"Aye, Captain," Rand said.

It suddenly occurred to Sulu that Cutler had yet to address him that way—as "Captain." For the sake of discipline within *Excelsior*'s newly revised chain of command, he hoped that wasn't going to become a problem, though he suspected that was probably too much to hope for. After all, she had already all but accused him of having a hand in Captain Styles's death. *She's mourning her captain,* he reminded himself, cutting her some slack. Cutler was in shock, though Sulu doubted she'd admit it under any circumstances.

A resonant basso voice boomed over the intercom. *"Ensign Akaar, Captain."*

"Has your team found anything new down there, Ensign?" Sulu wanted to know.

"We have discovered how the attacker got his weapons into the building," said the young Capellan security officer. Over the comm speakers, he sounded much more authoritative than his twenty-two years should have made possible.

"I thought we already knew that," Sulu said. "Didn't you already find traces of a small cloaking device?"

"That is how the weapons *were hidden, Captain,"* Akaar said. *"But not the saboteur or saboteurs. We have found the residue of a biomimetic compound on some of the wreckage. We believe our bomber used it to disguise himself."*

"But everyone in the Klingon party had to have undergone identity scans," Sulu said. "Even with a really good cosmetic disguise, a saboteur couldn't have gotten in."

"I doubt that cosmetic disguises were the only tools the bomber had at his disposal, Captain," Akaar said. *"We have also found organic traces in the bombs' remnants, which may explain why they were not detected by our earlier security scans. We have found nothing else so far, but we shall continue searching for whatever other forensic data the rubble will yield for as long as possible."*

"Good work, Ensign. Carry on. *Excelsior* out."

"Biomimetic materials, miniature cloaks, organic bombs . . . our saboteur seems to be awfully proficient in the sciences," Sulu said, stroking his chin thoughtfully. "Or at least in technology."

"And it's all pretty cutting edge stuff, too," Valtane said from the bridge's main science console, sounding almost impressed. "Whoever did this broke several Federation laws just by assembling the tools of his trade, let alone carrying out the actual attack. Who knows what sort of biotechnology Klingon scientists are developing, though, or whether they try to control trafficking in materials like this the way we do?"

An idea suddenly occurred to Sulu. "Would any DNA traces be left in the biomimetic compound?"

"We're already searching for DNA strands," Valtane said. "Unfortunately, whatever nucleic acids might remain in the residue have been pretty thoroughly torn apart by the heat released by the detonating bombs. But if we do find enough to replicate into measurable quantities with a polymerase chain reaction, we should be able to tell a lot more about our mysterious attackers. At the very least, we'll know their species. And we might even learn a lot more than that."

"How soon before we have an answer?" Sulu asked.

Valtane looked glum. "It might take a while, sir."

Sulu turned toward Cutler, who was watching him with a

hard-to-read expression that Sulu decided was one of quiet appraisal. He decided then that the best way to keep her in line was to keep her engaged—not to mention *busy.*

"Commander Cutler, I want you to continue overseeing the forensic investigation and report directly to me on its progress. And keep looking for any sort of warp trail that the attacker's ship might have left when it fled. We can use that to pinpoint the vessel's present location, which is more than likely somewhere in Klingon territory."

She scowled. "Aye, sir. But we're under orders not to pursue the hostiles into Klingon space."

"Yes, we are, Commander," Sulu said, allowing a sly smile to play across his lips. "Admiral Harriman cut those orders himself. But old 'Blackjack' never said a thing about helping the *Klingons* chase the bad guys while we stay right here at Korvat."

"Fair enough," she said, nodding. "But how can we help the Klingons find the trail if we're not able to follow where it leads ourselves?"

"If I'm not mistaken, Commander, we've recently taken aboard several palletloads of highly advanced scientific matériel. Am I right?"

Her scowl deepened. "If you're talking about the equipment for our upcoming survey of gaseous planetary anomalies in the Beta Quadrant, you already know the answer. You supervised its arrival and storage yourself when you were the exec."

He nodded. "So I did. And now, as acting captain, I want to get some use out of the stuff a little earlier than originally planned—before whatever's left of the bomber's trail goes completely cold."

"Permission to speak freely, sir?" Cutler said.

He spread his hands in a *by-all-means* gesture. "You wouldn't be doing your job if you didn't, Commander."

Her eyes widened somewhat in surprise; since Captain

Styles had never been one to encourage his senior staff to bring alternative points of view to his attention, she must have found Sulu's determined openness a bit off-putting.

"*Excelsior*'s new sensors were designed to detect very specific types of gaseous phenomena," she said. "They were never intended for use in ship-to-ship track-and-chase situations like this one."

"Granted. But the new sensors are an order of magnitude more sensitive than anything else we have. And that makes them *way* more powerful than anything the Klingons might be carrying. Even a cloaked ship will leave some sort of particle trail, particularly at warp. Those new sensors are our best hope of finding it."

"They'll have to be completely recalibrated," Cutler said, sounding both doubtful and unhappy. "And then recalibrated *again* to restore their original settings before the Beta Quadrant survey begins."

He offered her a smile that he intended as equal parts encouragement and warning. "I can't think of anybody better qualified for the job, Commander. Get on it, and report back to me the moment it's done. We've got a terrorist to track down."

"*Whose* terror are we talking about, sir?" she said very quietly, obviously aiming her words at his ears alone. He could almost hear Captain Styles whispering in his ear, *Perhaps you're a bit too personally involved.*

Sulu's jaw clenched involuntarily. He had no intention of discussing his motivations, particularly here on the bridge.

"Your objection is noted, Commander. Now get the hell off the bridge and get to work."

Moving her fingers with the deliberate delicacy of a surgeon, Meredith Cutler slowly traced the tip of the microlaser along the hair-thin duotronic circuit patterns on the tiny sensor components that lay on the worktable before her. She labored in silence in the quietly thrumming engine room alongside acting chief engineer Tim Henry, who was similarly occupied, no doubt drawing upon his considerable expertise in nanotechnology to modify and recalibrate the internal configurations of *Excelsior*'s precision scanner array.

Then something cold and merciless gripped Cutler's heart for perhaps the hundredth time since the bombs had detonated on Korvat. She set the circuit board and microlaser down and tried to regain control of her breathing.

"Is something wrong, Meredith?" Henry said, setting his own work aside, at least for the moment. His deep frown of concern told her that she was doing a damned poor job of keeping her emotions reined in.

"It's nothing, Tim," she lied, forcing a smile onto her face and shaking her head. "It's just that this wasn't quite the way I thought we'd ring in the New Year."

He sighed and nodded, offering her a thin but sympathetic smile of his own. Then he cast his gaze back down upon his labors, and retreated to the quiet stronghold of his own thoughts.

Despite her bland denials, Cutler knew there was no getting around it. *He's dead because of* me, she thought as she resumed her work, finishing the first of her circuit recalibrations. *If not for* me, *the captain would still be alive.*

It was a struggle to remain focused on her task—enabling *Excelsior* to locate and follow an impossibly diffuse warp trail that might or might not even exist—rather than on the certain knowledge that failure would not only enable the Korvat bomber to escape justice entirely, but might also even prevent the resumption of the nascent and interrupted Federation-Klingon peace talks.

The odds of Commander Sulu's blue-sky plan meeting with success seemed as remote as the uncaring stars themselves. But failure would make the death of Captain Lawrence H. Styles count for absolutely nothing.

That was something she simply couldn't accept.
Because I'd be responsible for that *as well.*

Cutler's almost contrite admission, which arrived nearly six hours later, just might have been the sweetest sound to reach Sulu's ears since he'd first come aboard *Excelsior.*

"You were right, sir," she said, punching up a stellar map on one of the bridge's aft displays. "There's definitely a warp trail that corresponds to the hostile ship, leading straight from Korvat and deep into the Mempa sector of Klingon space."

Sulu thanked her without succumbing to the temptation to gloat. Then he turned his chair forward so that he faced the helm/navigation consoles.

"Lieutenant Lojur, plot the most efficient intercept course and bundle it with Commander Cutler's new data set. Forward the resulting astronavigational matrix to Captains Kang, Koloth, and Kor immediately. They'll be eager to put it to use as soon as they can get their ships under way."

"Aye, Captain," said the Halkan navigator, the traditional red clan tattoo in the center of his forehead crumpling slightly as he concentrated on the task before him.

"You want to catch him very badly," Cutler said quietly, not asking a question. Her observation startled Sulu with its simple honesty—as did the total absence of rancor behind her words.

"More than I've wanted anything for a long, long time," he said, deciding that she deserved an equally unvarnished answer.

She leaned toward him so as not to broadcast her next words across the entire bridge. "You can't really believe that this . . . albino could really be the same man who attacked your family forty years ago."

He fixed her with a hard stare. "You know better?"

"All I know is that you may have allowed some very old

ghosts from your past to cloud your judgment today," she said, not flinching from his gaze in the least. "Your white whale. Sir."

A tart response sprang to his lips, but the whistling tone that signaled an incoming communication interrupted it.

"Chapel to bridge."

Sulu turned away from Cutler and leaned hard on the comm button at his right-hand side. "Sulu here, Doctor. Go ahead."

"I've just finished my analysis of the organic traces Ensign Akaar recovered from the surface of Korvat, Captain."

Sulu was impressed. Although she was still spending much of her time and energy caring directly for those who'd been injured on Korvat, she had nevertheless insisted on being kept up to date on Mr. Valtane's investigation into the bombing, giving the matter as much priority as her other medical duties would permit.

"What have you found?" he said.

"A reliable DNA fingerprint of the bomber, for one thing."

His heart raced. "What can you tell me about him?"

"Quite a bit, I think. So much, in fact, that I think you're going to want to take a good, close look at this yourself."

"On my way." He closed the channel and rose to his feet in a single fluid motion.

"May I come with you, sir?" Cutler said.

Pausing in midstep on his way to the starboard turbolift, he considered ordering her to take the conn and remain on the bridge. After all, why should he risk humiliating himself in front of her in the event that Christine Chapel presented them both with definite proof that the Korvat assassin was *not* the albino?

But there was also nothing to be gained by revealing his self-doubt to her, or by becoming overly defensive. *Maybe this is one of those times when valor is the better part of discretion,* he thought, deciding simply to let the chips fall wherever they would.

"I wouldn't have it any other way," he said as he led the way into the lift. "Commander Rand, you have the bridge."

Sulu watched with a mixture of eagerness and trepidation as Christine Chapel activated the computer terminal on her desk. He stole a glance at Cutler, who had taken a position on the desk's opposite side. The blue light of the quarantine field from the adjacent main area of sickbay shaded her face as she watched the screen impassively, leaning against the biolab wall with her arms crossed primly before her in a classic skeptic's pose.

"Computer, display graphic Korvat Epsilon," Dr. Chapel said. The screen's star-sector-and-laurel-leaf UFP logo vanished, instantly replaced by a complex computer rendering of a long, coiled double strand of multicolored DNA.

While he'd never laid claim to serious expertise in the biomolecular sciences, Sulu knew he had seen this exact pattern before.

"Using DNA traces I found amid the remnants of the bomber's biomimetic disguise," Chapel said, "I've determined that the attacker is definitely Klingon. A male."

"Were you able to tell whether or not he was Commander Sulu's albino?" Cutler asked in a doubtful tone that somehow stopped just short of ridicule.

"You can both decide for yourselves after I walk you through the math," Chapel said with a slight shrug. "Let's start by shedding a little light on the bomber's age."

"How?" Cutler asked.

"After running the Klingon equivalent of a polymerase chain reaction, I managed to generate enough DNA from the residue left by the bomber to take precise measurements of his telomeres."

Cutler frowned in incomprehension. "Telomeres?"

"They're the portions of the DNA molecule that govern the aging process," Sulu said, beginning to see where Chapel was heading. "In most life-forms, the telomeres shorten as the organism ages."

Chapel nodded, clearly pleased to hear that she wouldn't have to conduct a comprehensive molecular biology primer just to make her report. "And Klingons appear to be no exception to that general rule. A count of the rings on this individual's molecular tree, so to speak, yields an age range of seventy to seventy-five standard years."

A chill quickly crept up Sulu's spine and crawled back down again. The Korvat bomber was certainly old enough to have participated in the Ganjitsu raid. Still, that fact alone was anything but conclusive.

"Now back to the question about 'Commander Sulu's albino,'" Chapel said, glancing at Cutler. "This individual's genome possesses some highly unusual genetic markers— markers that precisely match the Klingon gene sequences Doctor Klass found in the tailored Levodian flu samples the captain recovered from Galdonterre."

Suddenly, Sulu not only felt certain that he had seen these gene sequences before, he also remembered exactly where he'd encountered them: in Dr. Klass's original forensics report, four days ago.

"So this proves that the person who bombed the Korvat conference and the man responsible for the murder four days earlier are one and the same," he said.

"It proves it to a fare-thee-well, at least in my book," Chapel said. "Given the fact that our culprit is too young to have picked up his rare retrogenetic traits directly from the mass disease outbreaks on Qu'Vat—where either vaccines or the disease itself sterilized virtually everyone who didn't die outright, by the way—there's only about a one-in-half-billion chance of him even *existing* in the first place. And on top of all that, his genome is at least circumstantially consistent with the murder victim's description of her killer as an albino Klingon."

"What do you mean, Doctor?" Cutler asked.

Chapel pointed to several specific loci on the DNA diagram displayed on the screen. "Here, here, and here are specific markers that correspond to the known effects of the deadly Levodian flu outbreaks on Qu'Vat during the twenty-second century. Thanks to several papers from that time written by a Denobulan physician named Phlox, we know that this disease was catalyzed by a retrovirus that caused permanent changes to the victims' DNA. These genetic changes caused a whole cluster of deleterious effects. Some of these were relatively minor, like albinism. But most would have been far more debilitating."

"What were some of the more serious effects?" Cutler asked.

"Chronic anemia, along with numerous congenital circulatory and pulmonary problems. The Klingon equivalent of diabetes. Various metastatic cancers. A number of degenerative neurological conditions. Any one of these syndromes would likely necessitate a lifetime of heroic medical intervention."

Cutler cast a confident look in Sulu's direction. "So is it really at all likely that a Klingon afflicted with these particular genetic markers would even *reach* his seventies, Doctor?"

Chapel frowned. "No, it's not, Commander. In fact, it's highly likely that *any* Klingon cursed with this sort of genetic profile wouldn't survive *infancy*, given that society's attitudes toward sickness."

The chill that had touched Sulu's spine earlier returned as though propelled by gale-force winds. If Cutler had thought she was toppling his solidifying belief that the architect of the Korvat attack was the same man who had terrorized him as a child, she had achieved precisely the opposite result.

Chapel had not only established sufficient proof to satisfy even the most skeptical Klingon that the Federation bore no responsibility whatsoever for the Korvat bombing, she had also demonstrated something else that Sulu found intensely disquieting.

The albino—*his* albino—remained at large, and was still dealing death.

EIGHTEEN

"If we must continue to meet aboard *your* ship," Kang growled, shouldering his way through the door to the conference room, "then we can at least have a barrel of blood-wine brought over."

Sulu smiled, realizing that despite the Klingon's gruffness, Kang had, perhaps, just made a joke. *I think.*

He decided to play it safe. "I haven't had a good blood-wine for at least five years. I was looking forward to . . . I *look* forward to sharing some with you in the future." He had almost said, "once we've celebrated the resolution of the Korvat conference," but realized he would have been picking at a still-bloody scab that covered a wound that still afflicted everyone present.

"What news do you have for us?" Koloth asked. None of the three Klingons was sitting, leaving Sulu, Chapel, Cutler, and Curzon Dax to stand awkwardly around the conference table.

"Have a seat, and Doctor Chapel will tell you who our

attacker was," Sulu said, gesturing toward the chairs nearest the three warrior captains. He was grateful when they finally sat, though they looked uncomfortable in the plush chairs.

Chapel activated the three-sided viewer built into the table's center, and began to explain the findings of Akaar and the forensic team, and the results of her own analyses. As she spoke, Sulu scrutinized the Klingons as closely as he could, studying their reactions.

Not surprisingly, the trio appeared genuinely shocked to learn that the Korvat bomber was a Klingon, and Sulu also noticed that Kor seemed especially shaken at the news that this particular Klingon was a seven-decade-old albino.

Chapel finished her briefing and looked toward Sulu. It was only then that he realized that she had just given the floor to him.

"The Federation has files on an albino Klingon and his cadre of raiders," he said, barely missing a beat. "They're based mostly on incomplete reports, some of which are little more than rumors. Until this week at Galdonterre, we had little more to go on than hearsay, and therefore we had no real concept of the kind of threat we now face."

As he spoke, he became aware of the intense gaze of Cutler boring into him. He was unable to parse the meaning of this particular look, but it somehow didn't seem quite as overtly hostile as before. Undistracted, he related the story of his own personal experience with the albino on Ganjitsu more than forty years earlier, and laid out for the Klingons the exact sequence of recent events since the death of the alien woman on Galdonterre.

By the time he finished, the three Klingons seemed about to burst, and yet none of them said anything for a good twenty seconds. Finally, Koloth broke the ice, if not the tension.

"It is *inconceivable* that a Klingon would do these things," he shouted. "There is no honor in piracy."

"He is a coward!" Kang said. "A *deviant*. You said yourself that the creature has genetic anomalies. He is *not* one of us."

"The albino does indeed have the anomalies I showed you, but functionally, he *is* Klingon," Chapel said, pushing a wisp of stray blond hair off her forehead. "What doesn't make sense to *me* is why he chose to target the Korvat conference. It seems to me that a man afflicted with such a life-threatening genetic condition would *support* the concept of peace; a prosperous Klingon Empire sharing technology with Federation planets would bode well for finding a cure for his condition."

Koloth raised his left eyebrow and regarded Chapel as if she were an annoying child. "We are not interested in 'curing' his condition, regardless of any agreements that may be forged between our Empire and your Federation. Freaks of nature such as this creature should simply be destroyed out of hand."

"I suppose that's a fundamental difference between the two societies," Dax said, speaking up from further down the table. "Most Federation cultures work to *overcome* prejudice against those elements of their society that differ from the norm. After all, once each society reached the stars and began encountering the vast number of inhabited worlds beyond their own, the concept of 'normal' began to lose much of its meaning."

"Bah!" Kang swept his hand in front of his face dismissively. "Such egalitarian notions have made far too many races weak and soft. The culling of weaklings is why the Klingon Empire stands stronger today than ever before."

"Be that as it may," Sulu said, trying not to scowl in distaste, "it appears that one of your so-called 'weaklings' has survived the culling. And now he's striking back."

He wondered for a moment what the albino must have faced during his childhood if he had been rejected so early and so completely by his society, or if he had even had a childhood in the traditional sense. But humanizing the albino held little interest for him. Not after the outcast had caused the deaths of Captain Styles and so many others, both here and on countless other raids. *Not to mention the one that nearly wiped out my family.*

Kor finally leaned forward and spoke, uttering his first words since he'd entered the room. "You say that the records of this albino and his raids on Federation border worlds center mostly around medical or scientific facilities?"

"Those that we know of," Sulu said. "As I witnessed on Ganjitsu, the albino was very clearly looking for biomedical technology and related information. I wonder, if you queried the proper law-enforcement agencies on Qo'noS, you might find *more* evidence of similar raids on the Klingon side of the border."

"Perhaps what this albino wants is related to his long-term survival," Kor said. "Doctor Chapel has shown us significant evidence that his genetic code has been altered more or less continuously all his life. Perhaps the biomedical technology he seeks is in an effort to extend what would otherwise have been a very brief life by a few weeks or months at a time."

"That would support a motive to stop the peace talks at Korvat," Cutler said, breaking her own silence. "Any change in the prevailing political and legal structure—or lack thereof—in the Klingon-Federation border region, could put a severe crimp in his banditry. As it is, he can raid a laboratory in Federation space and escape into Klingon territory, or attack an outpost on the Empire's side of the border, and then escape into Federation space."

"The motives of this *jay'mu'qaD* do not matter," Koloth said, pounding his fist on the table, then rising to his feet. "What matters is punishing him for what he has done *today.* Talking endlessly about *why* he attacked us leads nowhere.

It is a *targ* eating its own tongue. Honor demands that we *act*. We must track this cowardly aberration down and dispose of him—and all who serve him—to avenge those he slew on Korvat!"

Sulu rose to his feet, followed quickly by everyone else in the room, including the Klingons. "I would be remiss in my duties not to point out that the Federation would prefer to see the albino and his raiders captured and brought before the bar of justice. But since he's operating in Klingon jurisdiction, I understand that we can't demand that outcome."

Kang grinned wolfishly and leaned toward Sulu. "He *will* stand trial and face justice, Commander. As he dies on the end of our blades."

"Captains, one more thing before you return to your ships," Chapel said quickly, addressing the Klingons. "We know that the albino infiltrated the conference on Korvat, using either a disguise or some other method. He could have acquired samples of the DNA of anyone—or possibly even *everyone*—who was present. Given the kind of pharmacological and scientific ingenuity he has displayed so far—and my studies of the retrovirus Commander Sulu recovered from the alien woman on Galdonterre—it seems to me not only possible but probable that he will target others with the same kind of individually tailored retrovirus that killed the woman on Galdonterre. I can't rule out his going after anyone—including the three of you."

"And?" Kor said.

"I've been working on synthesizing a defensive agent as a precaution," Chapel said. "It's designed to block retroviruses developed from both the Levodian flu and the Omega IV viruses. Commander Sulu survived exposure to both viruses decades ago; I've cultured a sample of his blood to create the vaccine."

Sulu had known that Chapel was working on the antiretroviral agent, but not that she had used his blood. The concept was jarring; he didn't object per se, but neither had he anticipated that elements of his own blood might be injected into the Klingons. *On the other hand, they probably aren't very keen on having "Earther" blood in their veins either.*

Dax looked worried. "Doctor, excuse me if I'm speaking out of ignorance, but haven't many vaccines caused the very diseases they were designed to avert? And in this case, you're mixing two diseases that have been genetically spliced . . ."

Chapel shook her head. "I'm taking great pains to make certain that this vaccine will help protect our Klingon allies rather than infect them. Kor's own CMO, Doctor Hurghom, has aided me with the research."

"So, you may *think* you know how it works on humans and Klingons, but have no idea how it could work on a Trill?" Dax asked.

"All the biomolecular simulations show it as safe and effective," Chapel said, "as well as compatible with human, Trill, and Klingon physiologies."

"All right," Dax said, nodding in apparent satisfaction.

But despite Dax's nominal acquiescence to Chapel's inoculation plan, Sulu could tell that the young diplomat was still grappling with a real underlying fear that he wasn't articulating clearly. He wasn't at all certain he understood it, though he suspected it had to do with some yet-unrevealed aspect of Trill biology, a subject that the Trill people were known to be reticent about discussing with outsiders.

"If you have this vaccine ready when our ships are prepared to leave—and Doctor Hurghom will vouch for its effectiveness and safety—we will accept it," Kang said.

"Very good," Chapel said. "I'll be certain to prepare enough vaccine for all three crews."

"We will return to our ships now," Koloth said to Sulu as the trio stepped toward the door. "Perhaps if you discover *further* information about the albino after our vessels are sufficiently repaired to begin pursuing him, you will share it with us via the subspace bands."

Dax stepped forward. "Captain Kor, I'll be accompanying you to aid in further repairs to your ship."

Sulu shot Dax a look that said "Are you crazy?" but the young diplomat ignored it. It wasn't that Sulu distrusted the Klingons—after all, the majority of his own crewmen that had engineering expertise were already helping them—but he hadn't recalled anything about engineering experience in Dax's diplomatic dossier. And given that on Korvat, the Trill and the Klingons had nearly come to blows just prior to the explosion, allowing Dax to go with them seemed a little like lighting a match next to a barrel of gunpowder.

"Come along, then," Kor sighed, as if talking to a child. Sulu was surprised that Kor had raised no objections to Dax's idea.

With no direct power—or good reason—to stop Dax, Sulu watched the quartet march down the corridor, preceded by a few of the security personnel that had been stationed outside the conference room door.

Dax is planning something, he thought. *And hiding something.* And all his instincts told him that Kor was hiding something as well.

I hope I haven't just allowed Daniel to walk alone into the lion's den, Sulu thought soberly.

NINETEEN

Curzon Dax was surprised to discover that even the cumulative experience of five previous hosts seemed to do little to blunt his initial impression of the Klingon ship. He found the place almost overwhelmingly alien. He was struck first by its too-warm, too-humid air, the omnipresence of its dim, reddish illumination, and the oppressive closeness of its cramped passages, which he didn't consider wide enough to qualify to be called "corridors." Given the width of most of the warriors on board, and the thickness of their heavy armor, Dax wondered how they managed to function at all during emergency situations.

Then there was the farrago of intense odors that assailed him as the Klingon engineers and technicians led him from the transporter room through the various sections of the vessel that were already undergoing repairs under the ministrations of mixed teams of Klingon and Starfleet personnel. Many of the smells were intensely unpleasant, as one might expect after a damaged vessel's internal atmosphere had been compromised with higher than trace amounts of coolant gases and acrid, nostril-singeing ozone. Even the sections that he was told housed the Klingon crew's ascetic living quarters retained a strong aroma that hovered somewhere between the stench of spoiled food and the scent of the lilacs that Emony had encountered during her time on Earth. He didn't even want to contemplate the horrors that probably awaited him when the time came for his first meal in the crew galley.

But he quickly decided it was the sporadic salvoes of derisive Klingon laughter, which erupted behind him repeatedly as he followed Chief Engineer Q'Lujj around the *Klothos* on his inspection rounds that got under his skin the most. To the men and women who served aboard this ship, all of whom he had to assume were blooded warriors, Dax was simply not to be taken seriously. He was neither old enough nor *Klingon* enough for that, and there seemed to be little prospect of changing those perceptions any time soon.

Especially not among the ranks of the *Klothos*'s lower-decks personnel, for whom no amount of evidence would suffice to prove that the Federation wasn't to blame for the attacks on the Korvat colony and the Klingon vessels in orbit above it.

Q'Lujj led the way into an unexpectedly large, high-ceilinged chamber that was the largest space aboard the *Klothos* that Dax had seen so far. Near the room's center sat a complex bank of machinery that was tied into a two-story vertical cylinder that glowed with potent yet restrained energies. A small team of junior officers busied themselves around this tableau, monitoring various regulators, gauges, and displays. A pair of devices that lifetimes of cumulative experience helped him recognize as antimatter injectors lay in pieces on the deck while the engineers inspected the various disassembled components and engaged in guttural, desultory conversation about technical specifications and procedures.

Dax needed recourse to neither Tobin's nor Torias's memories to recognize the entire assemblage before him as the vessel's warp core. With those experiences at his disposal, however, the equipment and tools that lay spread across the deck nearby made it plain enough which tasks needed to be done most urgently to get the entire system back up and running.

Finally, a chance to prove his worth to these people had presented itself. His spirits buoyed by this hopeful notion, he began striding straight toward the core.

Q'Lujj's large, unyielding form glided into his path with surprising speed, stopping him cold. At least a head taller than Dax, the dour chief engineer stared down at him with dilithium-hard eyes that looked as black as space and only half as forgiving.

"Where do you think you're going, *toy'wI'*?"

Dax understood the meaning of the engineer's last word, which translated approximately to "servant" in Federation Standard. He swallowed hard and avoided breaking eye contact as though his very life depended on it—because he knew that it very well might.

Why did I insist on coming here? he thought, his earlier ebullience suddenly dashed. He found himself wishing he hadn't succeeded in persuading Captain Sulu not to keep him aboard *Excelsior* for security's sake. *I am in way,* way *over my head here.*

"I am here to assist you in getting this vessel under way, am I not?" he said, since he knew he had to say *something*. But what he had intended to come out like impressive Klingon bluster had instead sounded weak, even in his own ears, and probably merely served to confirm his *toy'wI'* status in the chief engineer's eyes.

"So I am told," Q'Lujj said, his deep voice nearly matching the low thrum of the partially disassembled warp core. "But your Earther captain has already lent me as many of his trained engineers as I can use, and you are hardly that. And it is my responsibility to protect my engines from being damaged by inexperienced hands."

Dax felt umbrage that more properly belonged to both Tobin and Torias, which was bound up tightly in the statesmanlike restraint that had always been the province of Lela, Dax's first humanoid host.

But the grin that spread across his face now belonged to no one other than Curzon. *Klingons appreciate bold gestures,* he told himself, restoking his confidence with a supreme act of will. *Looks like now is as good a time as any to make one.*

"How much would you like to wager that I can cut your repair time in half?" he said, folding his arms across his chest in an unmistakable gesture of challenge.

The Klingon engineers working around the warp core laughed dismissively. Dax fervently hoped Q'Lujj would answer his challenge with a spanner rather than with a knife.

"Mevyap!" shouted the chief engineer, who stepped out of Dax's way with a grace that Emony, the trained gymnast, might have envied. Apart from the background hum of the impulse engines, the engine room fell as silent as a tomb.

Dax continued toward the partially disassembled warp core, hoping with every step that he hadn't just confused "bold" with "foolhardy."

I.K.S. QaD

Kang still could scarcely believe his ears. But since the story had come directly from Kor's chief engineer, a veteran of three Romulan wars who had once overseen Kang's own engine room, he had no choice other than to take it at face value.

"Kor's chief engineer told me that you have done well,

Curzon Dax," he said as soon as the oddly young-looking Trill reported to the *QaD*'s busy bridge immediately after completing his tasks aboard the *Klothos*.

Kang was surprised to see a look of relief cross Dax's smooth but spotted features.

"I'm happy to hear that," Dax said. "Q'Lujj seemed almost eager to get rid of me."

Kang chuckled. "Perhaps he feared he might have to kill you to prevent Kor from giving you his job."

"Anybody could have missed finding those microfractures in the starboard nacelle coupling," Dax said.

Kang nodded. "That's true enough. But it was Q'Lujj and his men who missed them. And it was you who manually bypassed the damaged components in time to prevent a core breach."

"I'm impressed that Q'Lujj admitted that."

"Lies are dishonorable," Kang said. "Besides, such things never remain hidden for long. Not with so many eager junior officers looking for an opportunity to find fault with a superior, and thereby advance in rank and status."

Dax looked relieved. "I wasn't out to get anyone in trouble. I was just trying to help get Captain Kor's ship warp-ready again as quickly as possible."

"You have succeeded admirably. Now all three vessels will be under way within the *kilaan*."

"That's good news. Maybe we stand a real chance of tracking down the hostile who attacked the Korvat conference and your fleet."

"Why are *you* so eager to help us catch the terrorist?" Kang wanted to know.

The junior diplomat appeared surprised by the question. "I'm a diplomat by trade, Captain. My Federation and your Empire have finally begun making serious mutual peace overtures, something that hasn't happened in over a century without the effective equivalent of divine intervention."

"You refer to the *'orghenya'ngan,*" Kang said, sniffing in indignation. "They hardly qualify as gods, I should think." Kang couldn't help but wonder if that first encounter with the meddling energy-beings more than two decades ago might have turned out differently had he overseen it rather than his old friend Kor.

Dax shrugged. "Whatever they are, or were, they stopped two great nations from annihilating each other when those two great nations wouldn't stop themselves."

Kang did not much care for the implied criticism of his "great nation," though it did not escape his notice that Dax had waxed equally acerbic about his own Federation.

"We need no such enforced guidance," Kang said. "Whether it be from gods or superbeings or aliens. We Klingons slew our gods in ancient times for this very reason."

"I certainly hope you're right, Captain. We'd both be pretty foolish if we were to count on the Organians—or anybody else, for that matter—to come to our rescue again the *next* time both our civilizations stray too close to the brink. We have to build our own peace, working *together.* And whoever attacked the Korvat conference is a direct threat to that effort—and, frankly, I want his head for that."

Kang grinned. "That is a remarkably Klingon sentiment, my young friend. For a man of peace, that is."

"Peacemaking is not a craft for the fainthearted," Dax said solemnly.

"I've always found it difficult to distinguish your Federation Standard words 'peacemaker' and 'appeaser.'"

Dax smiled, a mannerism that made him look both wistful and unaccountably older than his years. "Captain, I have encountered a number of officials in both the Federation government and in Starfleet who labor under the very same confusion."

Kang chuckled, realizing that he wasn't quite sure how

best to interpret Dax's words. *Very good.* Was it possible that this whelp was really nowhere near so callow and inexperienced as he had first appeared?

"You have been willing to go a good deal further in assisting us than has Captain Sulu," Kang said. "Why?"

"Captain Sulu provided you . . . provided *us* . . . with a nice, warm trail to follow."

"While *Excelsior* herself remains safe, undamaged, and immobile."

Dax rubbed his smooth chin in what Kang took to be a thoughtful gesture. "Captain Sulu's hands are bound a bit more tightly than mine are," said the Trill. "By Federation politics as well as Starfleet regulations. So I have a good deal less responsibility than he does."

"But, conversely, a good deal more freedom to act," Kang said.

"It appears to be one of the eternal paradoxes of interstellar diplomacy," Dax said, nodding.

Maybe he actually understands Klingon honor, Kang thought after Korod, his own chief engineer, had escorted the young Trill off the bridge for a technical consultation of his own. Was it possible that Dax was actually trying to earn some measure of honor on behalf of a Federation that had, at best, only scant appreciation of such things? Kang was more than a little nonplussed by the notion that a non-Klingon might somehow have achieved such a keen insight into the Klingon soul.

Still, he couldn't shake the suspicion that the Trill diplomat was actually pursuing some private agenda of his own.

TWENTY

"I thought my previous orders were perfectly clear, Commander," Admiral Harriman said, his scowling visage moving slightly closer on the comm screen. *"Excelsior is not to leave the vicinity of Korvat. You are to guard against further attacks against the colonists there. You are not to proceed any farther into Klingon territory at this time. Does that remove any lingering ambiguity?"*

Seated at the desk in his quarters, Sulu hoped his cheeks hadn't reddened as much as he felt his ears had. Harriman's tone sounded better suited to addressing a recalcitrant child than the acting commander of Starfleet's most advanced ship of the line.

"I had hoped that there might have been some further word from the Klingon High Council," Sulu finally said, keeping his low voice measured and even. "Or perhaps a reconsideration on Starfleet Command's part."

"The Klingon High Council has not responded, except to note they are looking into the . . . situation," Harriman said.

"They want to launch a complete investigation into what went wrong at Korvat, which is precisely what you *should be doing as well."*

"We *are* doing that, sir," Sulu said. "We've already learned how the saboteur got past both our security protocols and those of the Klingons, and how his bombs were constructed. We've even uncovered genetic material that identifies *who* the bomber is, and traced his ship *after* he made his follow-up attack run against us and the Klingon vessels. His residual warp trail is steadily dissipating, and *our* sensors are far better able to follow it than the equipment the Klingons are using."

Harriman frowned, peering down at something on his desk. *"Given that both the saboteur and his vessel were cloaked or otherwise hidden initially, you have no way to be certain that the Korvat colony isn't at risk of further attacks, do you?"*

"Sir, the attacks weren't against the *colonists*," Sulu said. "They were specifically targeted at the peace talks. Just as the warnings we received beforehand predicted. *No* other locations on Korvat were targeted. And the saboteur's ship went on to attack the Klingon vessels, and even destroyed Ambassador Kamarag's diplomatic ship. That tells us pretty clearly that the Klingons and the peace talks *were* the target. Not the Korvat colony. Not the colonists. In my opinion, further attacks here are highly unlikely."

"But you can't rule it out, can you?" Harriman asked, his eyes glinting a steely gray that closely matched the color of his severe crew cut.

Sulu clenched his fists so hard he thought his knuckle-bones might pop through the skin. "No, sir, we can't." He wanted to pursue the albino's ship along with Kang, Koloth, and Kor, and not for merely political or diplomatic reasons; no matter how hard he tried to fight it, he couldn't deny that his business with the chalk-white pirate was personal.

He decided to try a different argument. "Have you considered, sir, that by *not* helping to pursue the person who attacked our peace conference, we may create an even *bigger* diplomatic problem with the Klingons than any technical violation of their border might cause? After all, the Klingons are the product of a warrior culture. Kang and the other Klingon captains clearly feel disdain toward us for our decision not to pursue the albino alongside them. Aren't you concerned about the Federation looking weak in the eyes of the High Council?"

Harriman settled back in his chair, clearly giving Sulu's words some thoughtful consideration. But his gaze hardened again almost as quickly as whatever internal debate the admiral had undertaken resolved itself. *"I will have the matter brought up with the High Council again, Commander. But we cannot afford to try to force their hand if they have decided on their own not to allow* Excelsior *to join the pursuit. And if the ball is in their court, we cannot override their wishes. If we were to do that, they wouldn't see it as an act of cowardice or weakness — they would call it an act of naked aggression on our part."*

The admiral leaned forward again, his eyes boring into Sulu's from across the light-years. *"Let me once again try to make myself perfectly clear, Commander Sulu. The chain of command is in place for a reason, regardless of how you or I might feel about particular command decisions at times. Your previous captain on the* Enterprise *may have delighted in flouting Starfleet regs—and he may have even gotten away with doing so—but make no mistake here:* your *command career will be an exceptionally brief one should you violate your orders to stay out of the Klingon territory beyond Korvat prior to obtaining the High Council's explicit authorization to do so."*

Letting his breath out evenly through nearly gritted teeth, Sulu worked hard to keep his face blank, devoid of emotion. "Understood, sir. Will there be anything else?"

Harriman looked down at his desk again, then directed his hard gaze back to the screen. *"Yes, actually. I trust that you're already aware that Captain Styles did not wish to have his body committed to space."*

Sulu nodded. "I am, sir. I had planned to transport his remains to Earth, after we hold our memorial services aboard *Excelsior,* and finish up any remaining business related to the Korvat attack."

"Very good, Commander. In fact, Starfleet Medical may wish to examine the remains of all personnel lost in this horrible attack."

Sulu wasn't thrilled with any second-guessing of *Excelsior*'s crew, whether it was being done by "Blackjack" Harriman or Starfleet Medical. But he understood how to follow orders, despite what the admiral might think of his regard for military discipline. The shipboard memorials for the dead would go forward as scheduled for the sake of crew morale, but there would be no burials in space.

"Understood, Admiral," Sulu said.

"Assuming you require no further clarifications about your orders, Commander, I have other matters to attend to," Harriman said. *"And one of those involves sending another request to the Klingon High Council."*

Sulu allowed himself a small but gratified smile. It was a relief to know that the admiral wasn't simply out to foil him arbitrarily. "Thank you, sir."

"Then I wish you a better day, Commander. Harriman out."

The screen suddenly reverted to its default display of the blue-and-white emblem of the United Federation of Planets, though the tranquil colors did little to assuage Sulu's overall annoyance with the current situation regarding the albino and the Klingons. Harriman's intransigence was understandable, if frustrating. The political ramifications of taking action or not taking action both held pitfalls, though the ones on Harriman's side of the argument seemed far less obvious than those on Sulu's; while Harriman's course was arguably safer politically, Sulu could only see it as damning, at least for himself.

He suspected that if push came to shove, even Cutler would want to chase down the albino for killing Captain Styles, Chief Engineer Lahra, and the security personnel she had lost on Korvat. *I'm just not sure she would support me defying Starfleet's direct orders,* he thought. *She seems to be barely this side of having me declared unfit for command as it is.*

He poured himself a new cup of green tea from the pot on the desk, and inhaled the subtle aroma of the blend. It was small comfort, but at this point, he would take whatever succor he could. *If I ever* do *get permanent command of* Excelsior, he thought wryly, *I may prescribe a mandatory teatime.* The thought of his command staff sipping tea on the bridge brought a small smile to his face.

A few minutes later, having collected his thoughts, Sulu called Rand to patch in a call to the *Klothos* and pipe it onto the screen in front of him. Moments later Kor's face appeared, though the Klingon seemed to be speaking from somewhere other than his ship's bridge, perhaps from his quarters.

"Captain Kor, I'm afraid I can't give you the good news I'd hoped to deliver," Sulu said. He quickly recounted a severely edited version of his conversation with Harriman, but tried to make certain that Kor understood that he, Sulu, was more than willing to accompany the Klingon fleet into battle, and would certainly do so if only his hands weren't figuratively tied.

"This doesn't surprise me," Kor said, his voice gravelly.

"In the midst of a political struggle, true warriors are often the first to chafe against the chains of enforced restraint." He actually looked thoughtful for a moment. *"I suspect that had this attack happened in Federation space, we would have been similarly barred from taking action without clearance from your authorities."*

Sulu tried not to let his surprise at Kor's perspicacious comment register on his face. "Very wise, Captain. I suspect that you are correct. As it stands, we *will* aid you in whatever manner we can, whether that be through Doctor Chapel's inoculations, or by sharing whatever intelligence our long-range sensors and probes may be able to pick up."

"Our repairs are nearing completion," Kor said. *"I expect that we will be on our way within a few hours. Do we need to evacuate Ambassadors Kamarag or Klishat from your vessel?"*

Sulu shook his head lightly. "No, I think it's best for their health if they remain in isolation right now. Doctor Chapel assures me that it's still touch-and-go for both of them. And *we* don't consider it any inconvenience to continue their treatment here. However, we will want to be certain that all our personnel return to *Excelsior* soon, including Ambassador Dax."

Kor's expression changed slightly at the mention of Dax's name, but Sulu couldn't quite read what that meant. *"I will let you speak to the ambassador privately,"* he said.

The screen blanked and several moments passed until Curzon Dax's image appeared on the monitor, a tangle of power conduits and engineering components visible behind him. *"Captain Kor has brought me up to date on the situation, Commander, as well as on your orders,"* Dax said. *"Unfortunately, I won't be returning to* Excelsior.*"*

For the second time in minutes, Sulu was surprised. "You are aware, Ambassador, that Starfleet's orders not to enter Klingon space apply to you as well."

"I'd say that's debatable, Commander, since I answer to my superiors in the Diplomatic Corps and the Federation Council rather than to Starfleet Command," Dax said, sounding both resolute and regretful. *"And I am also aware that if we have no representation among the Klingons as they beard this particular albino dragon in his lair, the High Council will ultimately not only take offense, it will view our absence as a sign of weakness on the Federation's part."*

"I just made the same argument to Admiral Harriman," Sulu said, feeling a twinge of pleasure that he and the young Trill ambassador had assessed the situation so similarly. "It didn't fly with *my* superior. Do you think it'll fare any better with Sarek?"

Dax raised an eyebrow in a fair approximation of a Vulcan's wordless interrogative glance. *"I hadn't heard that Ambassador Sarek had regained consciousness yet."*

"He hasn't. Doctor Chapel says he's put himself into a Vulcan healing trance, which means he could come to at any time, ready to get right back to work. Do you really think that he would approve of your undertaking a risky mission deep inside Klingon territory?"

"Possibly not, Commander. But until such time as he actually does regain consciousness, I am charged with making all the on-the-ground diplomatic decisions."

Including, evidently, making the decision to be insubordinate, Sulu thought, suppressing a chuckle at the Trill ambassador's bravado. "Then I trust that you are also aware, Mister Ambassador, that I could have you beamed back over to *Excelsior,* your on-the-ground diplomatic decisions notwithstanding." It was a statement, not a question.

Dax cocked his head, regarding Sulu. *"If you feel that I am making an error in judgment, then by all means, abduct me from this ship. In this matter, I feel that direct action on my part is not only appropriate, but prudent."*

He's definitely got the courage of his convictions, Sulu

thought, noting that Dax was taking the exact kind of action he would have taken if the option were open to him; he would have traded places gladly with the young Trill at this moment if he could have. *Looks like my first impression of him was a little off the mark.*

"I hope you know what you're doing, Ambassador," Sulu said, taking a sip of his tea. "And I hope that you and the Klingons find the saboteur, with or without our direct help. He has a *lot* to answer for.

"Godspeed, Curzon Dax," he said. "And good hunting."

PART III: AMONG THE LIONS

Each friend represents a
world in us, a world possibly
not born until they arrive, and
it is only by this meeting that
a new world is born.

—Anais Nin (1903–1977)

TWENTY-ONE

Kor looked up from the data that was scrolling slowly across his desktop terminal when the buzz of the visitor alarm intruded brusquely upon his thoughts.

"Enter."

The door to his quarters rasped open long enough to admit Dr. Hurghom, who immediately crossed to the desk where Kor was working.

"I see you are studying the data from *Excelsior*," Hurghom said as he looked over Kor's shoulder at the terminal. Only one favored by his House for decades would dare take such a liberty. But Kor no longer paid much heed to such intrusions on the part of his chief medical officer; after all, he could have easily blanked the screen before Hurghom caught a glimpse of its contents had he wished to do so.

Kor froze the scrolling data. "I have already all but committed it to memory. When we finally catch up with our quarry, I want to be ready for him."

He was determined to know the albino's secrets, particularly those that directly affected the volatile fortunes of Kor's ancestral House. Fortunately, the *Klothos* carried an old-style mind-sifter, which Kor was eager to apply to that purpose, using whatever intensity level might prove necessary. Having developed these psionic interrogation aids more than a century ago, the Klingon military had employed them much more commonly during earlier times, when the front-line service of large numbers of smooth-headed *QuchHa'* warriors was still a novelty that the High Council feared might be vulnerable to infiltration by Earther spies and saboteurs.

"Have you also examined Doctor Chapel's medical information, Captain?" Hurghom asked.

Kor frowned. "Only the broad summary, which has a rather disturbing implication. I forwarded the data to your office in the hopes that you would examine it in depth."

"I have already done so," the elderly physician said, nodding as he deposited himself on one of the hard, severely right-angled chairs that fronted Kor's desk.

"I am hoping you will tell me that I have come to the wrong conclusion," Kor said, though he could sense already that this was a forlorn hope.

Wearing a grave expression, Hurghom shook his head. "I only wish that I could, Captain. However, the genetic profile that Doctor Chapel assembled from the DNA remnants gleaned from the conference hall on Korvat leaves absolutely no room for doubt: the hostile we seek is a son of the House of Ngoj, born in the Year of Kahless 844, according to sealed court records that the mother, the Lady Moj'ih, had failed to have destroyed. The child had always been presumed slain as a weakling."

Kor sat back in his chair and took in the news in contemplative silence. A defective male child—a weak, anemic albino whom the official records showed had been euthanized, according to time-honored Klingon tradition—had indeed been born to the House of Ngoj that very year, now some seven decades gone. But the odds against that infant having somehow survived until the present day seemed all but insuperable.

"Is there no possibility you've misinterpreted the data?" Kor said.

The scientist once again shook his head. "Only one in approximately five hundred million Klingon children is born with this particular cluster of genetic defects. Besides, I monitored the child's *in utero* development myself. I was present when he was born, and have maintained copies of his medical records until this very day—including his DNA profile. There is no mistake."

"But how can this be, Hurghom? All such weaklings are euthanized at birth. Klingon law makes no allowances, or exceptions."

"True enough," Hurghom said with a shrug. "But if someone merely spirited the child away rather than killing it as legally prescribed, it would not be the first time someone had seen fit to set aside the law in favor of some other agenda."

"So the albino brigand who disrupted the Korvat conference—and may yet have killed Ambassador Kamarag while he was about it—is really a new-found scion of my disgraced great aunt."

Though he still could scarcely believe it, he knew he had no choice other than to accept another related and equally incontrovertible truth: control of the recently rehabilitated House of Ngoj—the very House that Kor had labored all his life to rebuild after the scandals of decades past had crippled it nearly irreparably—might well be wrested from his grasp by an older cousin, a *yur* blood relative long thought dead.

"This albino's very existence is a blot on the name of your House," Hurghom said, unnecessarily stating the obvious so far as Kor was concerned.

Kor focused a gaze of laserlike intensity on his old friend. "Not as long as the unfortunate facts surrounding his origins remain known *only* to the two of us."

Hurghom's smooth brow crumpled slightly. "I am, as always, the soul of discretion. Did I not help the Lady Moj'ih conceal the source of her greatest shame for most of her life?"

Though Hurghom had not mentioned it explicitly, Kor knew that he was speaking of his great aunt's Earther-smooth *QuchHa'* forehead. It was a characteristic that both Kor and Hurghom still shared, even in an age when many other *QuchHa'*—including Koloth—had found gene-alteration therapies capable of restoring their cranial birthright.

But in the House of Ngoj, the genes responsible for the hated smooth-forehead trait remained entrenched in the family genome, having proved stubbornly resistant to Hurghom's every retroviral remedy. As with all *QuchHa'* families in the Empire, this condition had gained its so-far unbreakable grip on the House of Ngoj's gene pool during the Plague years, though the Lady Moj'ih had managed to keep it hidden with prosthetics throughout her life in an effort to preserve the *HemQuch* prerogatives of power that her clan had enjoyed since time immemorial.

Prerogatives that Kor had spent his entire career working to regain for his House, in defiance of both societal prejudice and the persistence of his disconcertingly Earther-like appearance.

Kor favored Hurghom with a weary smile. "I will continue to rely upon your discretion. And your loyal service." He knew, after all, that his continued support of Hurghom's ongoing genetic research constituted his House's best chance of ridding itself of its Earther genetic baggage. It was the surest chance of regaining the legacy of Kahless without recourse to the subterfuge the Lady Moj'ih and her parents had employed.

The House of Ngoj had already labored long and hard over the past several decades to restore a significant fraction of its lost honor; how much faster might it rise in both power and prestige if its members no longer bore the burden of the *QuchHa'*?

"Though the High Council has never mentioned any knowledge of the brigand's ancestry, they have offered a sizable bounty in exchange for his capture," Hurghom said, interrupting Kor's musings. "Do you intend to collect it?"

Kor sighed. There was no denying that the House of Ngoj was still nowhere near as wealthy as it once had been, despite his best efforts to recover his family's scattered holdings and lost prestige. And he certainly could not deny that riches frequently compensated for all manner of other deficits.

After a long pause, he announced his decision with an emphatic shake of his head. "As much as I have to admire such a one simply for surviving in the face of such very long odds, I have only one choice open to me: to kill him. I can afford to forgo the Council's bounty better than I can afford to risk airing the albino's secret."

"So we will simply track him down and kill him," Hurghom said, sounding vaguely disappointed. "A prudent option, to be sure. But also wasteful."

"If at all possible, we will capture him first. Perhaps he can be used to advance your research before I send him to *Gre'thor*."

Hurghom seemed to relax at that, though he still looked skeptical. "And what will be your cause for killing him, Captain? The honor of a family that must deny any association with him?"

Kor grinned. "Certainly, though that rationale is for your ears alone."

"Then what cause will you invoke for killing him rather than handing him over to the Council for trial and execution?"

"Why, the preservation of galactic peace," Kor said. He grinned ironically, remembering how the skies over *'orghenya'* were once black with the massed fleets of both the Klingon Empire and James Kirk's *yuQjIjDIvI'*, the Federation.

"After all, Hurghom, what higher cause is there?"

TWENTY-TWO

"When do you expect him to wake up, Doctor?" Cutler asked.

"Vulcan healing trances run their own course," Chapel answered, forcing a slight smile. "No buzzer rings when they're done."

"Is there any danger if we interrupt his trance?" Sulu asked. He looked as if he hadn't slept much in the last few days since the attack on Korvat, and Cutler didn't look much better off.

Chapel reached over to a countertop nearby and grabbed a large hypospray. "I'm fairly certain Sarek is about ready to regain consciousness," she said. "We're just going to help give him a kick-start."

She adjusted the control mechanisms on the hypo, and was rewarded by the sight of several liquids swirling into a mixture in a clear vial set within the device. Turning, she pressed the hypo against Sarek's neck. The Vulcan lay prostrate on the table, small, fine-tuned proximity sensors attached to his head and chest, feeding data into the overhead biobed monitoring equipment. His breathing was barely discernible, but visible all the same thanks to the slight rise and fall of the linen sheet that covered him from the torso downward. Chapel depressed a button, and a short hiss was audible near the entry point where the hypo met Sarek's neck.

"The clarinoxamine and gebatex should help stimulate Sarek's norepinephrine levels, while balancing his serotonin, chlorotonin, and dopamine output against his neuromodulators," Chapel said as she put the hypo back on the counter. Unless the delicate parliament of neurochemical messengers that drove the Vulcan brain could be "booted up" in an orderly fashion, the neurophysiological consequences could be grave, ranging from stroke to cardiopulmonary shock to complete neural collapse.

Staring down at some controls next to the biobed, Chapel tapped in several sequences of precise commands. "The rest of the work will be done through electronic neurostimulus. If all goes well, the ambassador should be fully conscious within a few minutes."

"Looks like you've upgraded your methods for reviving Vulcans from their healing trances since we were on the *Enterprise*," Sulu said.

Chapel made a face. "Slapping a patient awake was never something I was comfortable with. After the day I watched Doctor M'Benga revive Spock, I worked on developing a technique that didn't involve assault." She glanced back at Sarek. "If this doesn't work, though, perhaps we'll have to give the old-fashioned way one more try."

"Chemicals and electrostimulus are certainly more humane," Sulu said, mustering a smile. It was a sight she hadn't seen on his face since she first had come aboard *Excelsior* a week ago.

"Keep it up, Hikaru, and you'll find out just *how* humane," Chapel said. She almost regretted being so familiar with Sulu in front of Cutler—who seemed lost by their banter anyhow—but decided against it. *I'll be damned if I'm going to let her discomfort alter my relationship with one of my oldest friends.*

"It appears your treatment has worked, Doctor," Cutler said, nodding toward the ambassador.

Chapel turned to see that Sarek's eyes were fluttering open. A moment later he was regarding them with a reserved equanimity that didn't quite conceal his underlying bewilderment.

Not for the first time, she wondered about the contents of Vulcan dreams.

Sulu wasn't quite certain how he had expected Sarek to react after being informed of everything that had transpired since the explosion on Korvat, but the quick briefing seemed to leave the ambassador surprisingly unruffled, even for a Vulcan.

"Commander, I am eager to contact the Klingon High Council myself," Sarek said. He was now seated in a chair in Chapel's office, facing the low sofa on which Sulu sat and beside which Cutler paced like a caged panther. One of the nurses had fetched the diplomat a black robe from his quarters, affording him some additional comfort and dignity during whatever might remain of his rehabilitative period.

"Do you think you can persuade them to allow us to pursue the bomber into Klingon territory?" Sulu asked, allowing a small spark of hope to kindle in his breast.

Sarek looked at him as if he had just sprouted a pair of Andorian antennae. "That is where our priorities differ, Commander. My principal concern is to reinforce or reestablish the desire of both sides to continue with these peace talks. I plan to begin by assuring the High Council that although this attack has been a setback, it is only a temporary one, and must not endanger the larger goal of our respective governments."

Sulu nodded. "Ambassador Kamarag is still in critical condition."

"I do not need Kamarag to speak for me," Sarek said. "The fact that we and the Klingons were attacked simultaneously—and that *both* sides have sustained losses—gives me firm ground upon which to stand with the High Council. As deplorable as this attack was, it *can* be used to promote détente."

"When life hands you *plomeek*s, you make *plomeek* soup," Sulu said with a quiet sigh. Cutler stopped pacing near the door and scowled.

Sarek raised a single interrogative eyebrow. "I beg your pardon, Commander?"

"I was paraphrasing a human proverb about optimism," Sulu said, suppressing a smile.

"Ambassador, we can send your order to Ambassador Dax to return to *Excelsior* immediately," Cutler said, shifting her weight from one leg to the other.

Sarek waved his hand almost dismissively. "First, Commander, I doubt that any of the three Klingon captains would allow anything to dissuade them from their current course of action, short of losing their quarry's trail entirely. They certainly would *not* turn one of their vessels around merely to return Dax to us. Secondly, despite his breach of protocol and orders, I am content to defer to Dax's experience. He possesses wisdom and influence beyond what his years might imply."

Sulu was surprised to hear that. According to his diplomatic dossier, Curzon Dax wasn't exactly green, but he certainly hadn't yet put in the years required to rack up a level of experience that might impress someone as accomplished as Sarek.

He wondered fleetingly whether the injuries the Vulcan had sustained during the Korvat attack had impaired his judgment on some subtle, subclinical level that no doctor could quantify.

TWENTY-THREE

Moving with care to avoid brushing against the smoldering ruin of the doorjamb, Dr. Nej passed through the blast-charred threshold and entered the laboratory. He shuddered involuntarily when he saw what lay within: the burned bodies of five slight, long-limbed humanoids, scattered across the floor. He gathered from their surroundings—which were replete with antiseptic metal work surfaces that supported an array of small computers, microscopes, scanning devices, and cell-culturing jars—that the dead creatures had been researchers, people engaged in much the same work that took up the *targ*'s share of Nej's own time.

He couldn't tear his eyes away from the still, disruptor-burned forms sprawled on the floor, even as a trio of Qagh's burly raiders worked with methodical urgency to pack every tangible trace of the dead men's labors into antigrav-equipped shipping canisters.

Nej realized too late that Qagh's feverish but alert eyes were upon him.

"It's only death, Nej," the albino Klingon said, his words tinged with disdain. "I thought by now the two of you would have become much better acquainted."

The doctor's impulse was to point out that he, Nej, had probably forgotten more about death than Qagh had ever learned; his stint as a battlefield medic for the Klingon Defense Force alone had put him on a first-name basis with death. Of course, he couldn't deny that his direct participation in the dealing of death was a rather more recent development; it followed the time of his discommendation from legitimate Imperial service two decades earlier, which had been a consequence of his lamentable failure to duplicate a one-off artificially designed pest-eating predator known as a *glo'meH* before the prototype organism's untimely death. His discommendation had forced him into an underground existence, giving him little choice other than to place his scientific expertise in the service of the highest bidder.

The fact that the current highest bidder had turned out to be the weakling whelp of the late dishonored warrior Ngoj stood as vivid proof that the universe was a far smaller place than Nej had previously imagined.

Rather than verbalize any of this, he decided to remain focused on matters of a more practical nature.

"Killing them all may have been a mistake, Qagh," he said, keenly aware of the irony behind his last utterance even as it left his lips; "mistake," after all, came from the very same Klingon word root that underlay the albino's name, an oddity that long ago led Nej to the conclusion that Qagh's earliest caretakers must have possessed considerable gifts of perspicacity.

Except, as Nej surmised from many years of underworld rumor, they had evidently lacked sufficient perceptivity to prevent their albino foundling from engineering their deaths and commandeering their various criminal enterprises.

"They left us little choice," said Qagh, who was watching his men as they continued gathering and packing up data-pads and beakers for later scrutiny aboard the *Hegh'TlhoS*. "They were trying to destroy their work rather than surrender it to us."

Nej nodded. "I suppose *jeghpu'wI'* such as these have few options available to them other than surrender or self-destruction." Like many sentient races native to this sector and those immediately adjacent to it, the Mempans were essentially weaklings; they had been conquered subjects of the Klingon Empire for as long as anyone could remember. The sight of an incoming raiding party consisting mostly of Klingons, *HemQuch* or otherwise, must have set them into a fight-or-flight panic.

Balancing out the Mempans' obvious deficits as warriors, however, was a well-earned reputation for expertise in genetic engineering, endeavors with which the Empire had never seen fit to interfere unduly so long as the Mempan Elders deployed no bioweapons and delivered tribute to the Empire in sufficient quantity and frequency to satisfy the local military governor.

Today's raid was far from the first time that Qagh and his men had availed themselves of the Mempans' bio-science knowledge, which occupied a broad pallet ranging from enhancing various humanoid traits to increasing crop yields. During recent years, Mempan genetic research had advanced with sufficient rapidity that repeated visits were warranted—so long as Qagh's raids did not come regularly enough to attract the unwelcome attention of the Klingon military, which arguably loved piracy even less than did the peace-obsessed weaklings of the Federation.

"Let us hope, then, that these dead *jeghpu'wI'* left suffi-ciently clear notes to allow us to reconstruct their work," Nej added as he studied the pale, perspiration-slicked latitudinal striations on Qagh's forehead; Qagh had not sufficiently exerted himself during the raiding party's brief orgy of killing, nor was the room warm enough, to have caused him to break into a sweat. And then there was the none-too-subtle tremor in the albino's hand, which Nej was certain he would have spotted even had he not been a trained physician.

He couldn't help but wonder just how close to *Gre'thor*'s black gates Qagh's perpetually wandering and unwinding DNA had brought him this time. His health was doubtless as close to the edge as it had ever been, or perhaps closer; otherwise, he never would have undertaken a raid such as this one so soon after the attack on Korvat, which had surely placed the Klingon military, and possibly Starfleet, on high alert.

"I fail to see how your standing there staring at me will help us discover any such information," the albino said, clearly annoyed, his eyes aglow with unnatural inner fires that gave off no warmth that Nej could perceive.

Nej gestured toward one of the microcomputers that had yet to be packed up by Qagh's musclemen. "I will sort through all the data in detail as soon as these devices are linked to my biocomp back aboard the *Hegh'TlhoS*—giving priority, of course, to stabilizing locus Q56 of your fourteenth chromosome."

Qagh nodded, his feverish eyes flashing like twin pulsars as he moved. The albino suddenly froze as his gaze locked onto something located in the space somewhere beyond Nej's shoulder.

"Isomiotic hypodermics," Nej thought he heard the albino say.

"Excuse me?" Nej said, put off by Qagh's apparent non sequitur.

The albino brushed past him, nearly knocking him over as he passed toward one of the metal work surfaces, from whose gleaming top a pair of the raiders were dumping a box of what appeared to be medical supplies into one of their antigrav containers.

The raiders stood aside to allow Qagh to reach into the container, from which he retrieved a slender metallic cylinder about as long as a man's index finger.

"Isomiotic hypos," he said again, confirming that Nej had indeed heard him right the first time.

Nej approached the albino so he could get a better look at the object in his hand, as well as the rest of the contents of the open antigrav container.

"These are isomiotic hypos, all right," Nej said. He understood that isomiotic hypos could be useful in treating certain cancers and neural disorders, and could cause death if applied in large doses. "But I fail to see how such things will be of any use in stabilizing your genome."

Qagh looked at him as though his forehead ridges had just sprouted a face of their own.

"Of *course* they can't help me repair my DNA," he said. "But they *can* be weaponized, with the appropriate modifications. There's no need to fight only defensively against those who must be pursuing me even now, after the Korvat affair. After all, they'll surely be ready for our plasma flares and disruptors at our next encounter."

Putting aside the issue of Qagh's deteriorating condition, Nej gave the matter of the isomiotic hypos some thought. The albino, whom he had to admit was a rather accomplished biochemist in his own right, was indeed onto something here; the hypos actually could be used as the basis of a significantly destructive bioweapon, one that had farther-reaching implications than fending off those who would avenge Korvat.

How fitting it would be to unleash such a thing against the High Council itself, he thought. After all, Nej was bitterly aware that he owed his discommendation to the inflexibility of both future chancellor Sturka and a majority on the Council. These were the same individuals, in fact, who had brought the House of Ngoj down decades earlier, treating him like a lowly, smooth-headed *QuchHa'* in the process.

Nej allowed a predatory smile to spread slowly across his face. *It will be easier to help you save your life yet again, Qagh, if we both have something compelling to live for.*

And what could be more compelling than the prospect of serving an ice-cold helping of revenge onto the plates of one's enemies?

Once he felt satisfied that repairs to the freebooter *Hegh'TlhoS* were well under way—a process that would be greatly accelerated by some of the matériel his raiding party was still carrying out of the Mempa II lab complex and into the holds of the temporarily grounded freighter—Qagh entered his vessel's cramped infirmary to take a gene alteration treatment that he and Nej had developed in haste from some of the Mempan lab's biomaterials. As he lay supine on the narrow examination table after injecting himself, feeling weightless and afloat on a chemical and radiological cloud despite the table's unyielding hardness, Qagh dozed—

—and dreamed he was on another raid, one not unlike the mission of plunder he had just completed on Mempa II. But unlike that world, which was dominated by deserts, grasslands, and glacial terrain, vast swaths of this planet consisted of wild, untrammeled jungle, and yielded a profusion of more shades of green than he had ever imagined possible. The Klingons called this untamed border-region planet Veqlargh, after one of the evil spirits from the myths of ancient Qo'noS. But the Earthers, who had effectively laid claim to this remote world along with its incalculably vast array of biological wealth, had their own name for the place:

Ganjitsu.

It was an uncontrolled and chaotic planet, overgrown and all but ungovernable, a cosmic analog to his own mutated, constantly drifting DNA. Perhaps that was why the verdant border world terrified him still, having served as the setting for more nightmares than he could count over the past four decades.

Just as on Mempa II, Qagh's dream-self once again stood in a spotless, well-equipped bioscience laboratory. But unlike the Mempan facility, this place was illuminated only dimly, populated by shadows behind which hid malevolent ghosts, jatyIn *intent on thwarting him, determined to force him and his men to withdraw in frightened haste to the relative safety of their landing craft.*

Just as he had done four decades earlier, he returned to his shuttle, hurriedly piloting it back into orbit about the green world. His heart pounding nearly loudly enough to cause the hull to vibrate in sympathy, he rained death onto the lab from two hundred qell'qams *skyward in order to regain some small measure of calm.*

He watched through the forward window as his disruptor fire reduced the entire compound to atoms—along with the bioscience secrets it had so stubbornly refused to disgorge.

He awakened still feeling the residue of the rage and satisfaction he'd originally experienced on that long-ago day, comforted at least a little by the knowledge that no one else could use whatever cure had eluded him then.

He sat up on the biobed, feeling stronger than he had in weeks, secure in the knowledge that he would continue to survive, just as he always had, no matter what cruel setbacks fate might deal him along the way.

Nej, who must have entered the room while he had been dozing, stepped toward him and raised an interrogative eyebrow along with the marked second hypo that Qagh had already prepared in advance. In response to Qagh's affirmative nod, the doctor injected the hypo's contents into the albino's neck. The shot stung slightly, but made him feel even stronger still.

"How long do you think the results of this round of treatments will last?" Qagh said, rubbing his neck.

Nej shrugged as he set the hypospray down on a nearby table. "Perhaps weeks. Or months. Or perhaps only days. But we've bought you enough time, I think, to acquire still other new treatments. Again."

Qagh nodded. "And time enough, I trust, to acquire a few other things as well."

"What do you mean?" Nej asked.

Qagh considered the House that had abandoned him all those long decades ago, and whose kinsmen were even now doubtless trying to follow his trail because of the Korvat affair.

He considered how satisfying it would be to do more than simply elude the members of that House.

He pondered how the isomiotic hypos he had found in the Mempan lab might help him attain that satisfaction, once he'd assembled a few other critically necessary components to complement them. It made sense. After all, why should he be forced to confine his offensive capabilities to the ability to kill only a few people at a time—especially at a time when he might need to gain serious leverage over one of the oldest Houses on Qo'noS?

"I mean," he said at length, "that you are going to do more than simply help me scrounge yet another few additional weeks or months of life, Nej.

"You are also going to help me engineer and assemble a rather formidable weapon."

TWENTY-FOUR

**Early 2290 (the Year of Kahless 915,
late in the month of *Doqath*)**

I.K.S. Klothos

"What do you mean you cannot follow the trail?"

Kor's voice rose to a roar nearly loud enough to be heard in the vacuum of space, making Dax glad he was seated at a station in the aft portion of the *Klothos*'s bridge.

"Our sensors no longer reveal any trace of the target vessel's warp trail," said the Klingon helmsman, his tone surly but not mutinous.

"Then recalibrate them!" Kor ordered. He glowered as he turned, momentarily catching Dax and several assorted Klingon bridge officers in his withering glare before seating himself in the center-mounted command chair.

"Incoming hail, Captain," the communications officer shouted.

A moment later, the equally perturbed visage of Kang filled the forward viewscreen. *"Tell me that your ship hasn't lost the trail as well,"* Kang growled.

"Ghuy'cha' qI'yaH qovpatlh!" Kor said, rendering what

Dax could only interpret as an artfully wrought stream of Klingon profanity. "I was hoping at least that *your* luck would prove better than mine."

"No. And Koloth has just informed me that he is faring no better."

Dax moved over to one of the tactical stations that served double duty as a science station, even though it bore little resemblance to any Starfleet console he had ever seen. The buxom Klingon woman who sat there—he thought her name was Ma'kella—stared up at him as though he had just pulled his symbiont out of his abdomen.

"Do you mind if I try to reestablish the trail?"

Ma'kella bared her finely sharpened teeth at him and growled something that Dax couldn't quite make out, but which nevertheless required no translation.

"Let him try!" Kor thundered behind him.

Although the Klingon woman moved aside quickly, Dax noticed that she was watching him intently as his hands moved deliberately over the unfamiliar controls. "We might be able to track it indirectly using harmonic resonances in the lower subspace frequencies, assuming that the hard-radiation trail itself hasn't degraded too far." He watched the data scrolling across the screen and frowned at it.

"Well?" Kor asked.

"I'm not seeing anything," Dax said. He continued adjusting the controls, but none of the new settings he tried seemed to give him the result he was hoping to see.

He stood and turned toward Kor and the image of Kang that frowned across the bridge from the forward viewscreen. "Your tacticians are correct as far as I can tell. The trail does seem to end here."

"How can that be?" Kang said, his upper lip twitching slightly as if he were about to snarl.

"Maybe another ship picked them up," Dax said, spreading his hands. "Or maybe they discovered that they were leaving a detectable trail and found a way to mask it."

"Dor'sho'gha!" Kor cursed. "Then we must split up and redouble our efforts to find him."

"I think I may have a better idea," Dax said. He was aware that the Klingons might not like what he was about to say, but he hoped that his best diplomatic manner would make it more palatable. "As powerful as your warships are, they weren't built with scientific exploration in mind the way *Excelsior* was. Even at this distance, her high-powered sensors might be of significant use to us in this chase. *Excelsior* may not be able to pursue the albino alongside us, but she can at least give us a reliable map."

On the screen, Kang nodded. *"It is a good plan. They have honor to regain as well, for the losses they took on Korvat. Even if the Federation won't allow Sulu to fight, he and his vessel may still be of service to us."*

Dax knew that the Federation wasn't necessarily the only obstacle in *Excelsior*'s path; there was the sometimes capricious and always vehement Klingon High Council to consider as well. But he knew that now was not the time to raise *that* particular point.

"Very well," Kor said, settling back into his command chair. "We will see what *Excelsior* can offer us."

Minutes later, with subspace contact initiated, Dax brought Commander Sulu up to speed on the particulars of their situation. As if to point out that the bridge was still his, Kor stalked behind Dax as he spoke, occasionally interjecting comments.

"Lieutenant Valtane is already working on ways to help you pick up the trail again," Sulu said, sitting ramrod straight in his bridge command chair, though his parsecs-distant image rippled and wavered slightly on the main viewscreen. *"In the meantime, please keep us apprised of whatever progress you're making on your end."*

"Thank you, Captain," Dax said, recalling what he'd been told of Starfleet's tradition of addressing a ship's commanding officer as a captain, regardless of the CO's actual rank.

"Before you sign off, Mister Ambassador, I have someone here who wishes to speak with you," Sulu said.

Dax gave a quizzical look to Kor as Sulu rose from his chair and moved out of the viewscreen's frame. Moments later another figure stepped into view in the center of *Excelsior*'s busy bridge.

"Greetings, Captain Kor, to you and your esteemed crew," Ambassador Sarek said with apparent sincerity. *"And to you, Curzon Dax."*

Dax felt conflicting surges of relief and trepidation, his delight over Sarek's renewed health wrestling with his apprehension over the Vulcan's likely response to his decision to enter Klingon space.

"Mister Ambassador," Dax said, nodding. He felt tongue-tied, his cheeks reddening as he realized how lame he sounded.

"You seem to have recovered well," Kor said. It seemed to be both a question and a statement.

"I was very fortunate," Sarek said. *"Your own ambassadors Kamarag and Kishlat are mending as well, though not as quickly as I, unfortunately. Their injuries were evidently more extensive than mine."*

Kor grunted, but said nothing more.

Dax cleared his throat, ready to make his apologies to Sarek, though he had no wish to make himself appear weak in the eyes of the Klingons. "Sir, I realize that my decision to accompany the Klingon crew was—"

"You chose the option you thought best under the circumstances," Sarek said, interrupting him. *"We each do as we must, guided by both logic and conscience."* Sarek paused, raising an eyebrow as if to signal that he would choose a more propitious time to deliver either reprimands

or praise. Or perhaps he was merely acknowledging that he had no real power at the moment to force his will upon Dax. *"I trust,"* the Vulcan continued, *"that we will discuss both at considerable length upon your return."*

Sarek held up his hand, parting his fingers in the center in the familiar V-shaped Vulcan greeting. *"Live long and prosper, Curzon Dax and Captain Kor."*

Dax returned both the salute and the salutation, and the screen went black a moment later. Only then did he allow the tension that had gathered within him to leave his body.

Here I was certain that Sarek would call me on the carpet right in front of Kor and his crew, Dax thought. The fact that his superior hadn't done so spoke highly of the trust he had invested in his junior ambassador. Perhaps it meant that Sarek assumed he might accomplish some tangible results with the very same Klingon captains who had been ready to rip his throat out only a few days before, and who were now allowing him to serve aboard their vessels, if only begrudgingly at first.

Concealing the faint glimmerings of a smile, Dax realized that if one lone diplomat could gain the respect of three of the most accomplished warriors in the entire Klingon Empire, then perhaps galactic peace was attainable after all.

TWENTY-FIVE

Stardate 9010.6 (Early 2290)

U.S.S. Excelsior

"Since Mister Dax's subspace resonance idea still hasn't panned out, we have to find some other way to get the Klingons back on the trail," Sulu said, looking over his own tented fingers at the conference room monitor, which displayed the somewhat worried-looking countenance of Curzon Dax.

"But without, obviously, violating our orders not to enter Klingon space," said Lieutenant Commander Cutler, who sat at the table's opposite side, between Dr. Chapel and Ambassador Sarek; the only senior diplomat not present, either physically or virtually, was Kamarag, who remained stable yet comatose in sickbay, in essentially the same condition as Dr. Klass.

Sulu cast a narrow gaze at his exec. "Let's take that as a given, Commander." *At least until we've completely run out of better ideas,* he added silently.

"Whatever we do, we'd better get it done while there's still a trail left to follow," said Chapel.

"That's definitely our biggest limiting factor at the

moment, Doctor," said the young Trill diplomat, who was participating in the conference via a scrambled subspace frequency. His image, which originated on a Klingon vessel located many light-years inside Klingon space, wavered and rippled slightly on the triple-sided monitor. *"If there's any way to reestablish the trail, we're going to have to do it soon. Otherwise, we won't get another chance at this terrorist ringleader until after he commits some other high-profile crime."*

Ambassador Sarek, who had been sitting still and silent, finally broke his silence. "I quite agree."

Cutler shook her head emphatically. "Lieutenant Valtane is busy double-checking the sensor returns now, but he's already hit the wall in terms of sensor efficiency. Whatever particle trail the hostile's ship left behind is already *way* too attenuated for us to work with at this distance—our new sensors notwithstanding."

"Unless you can find a way to move those sensors closer to the trail somehow, Commander," Dax said.

Sulu's jaw muscles tightened involuntarily as his frustration mounted further. "Let me point out, Mister Dax—*again*—that doing that simply *isn't* one of our options."

"Indeed, Captain," Sarek said. "We must instead explore an alternative strategy."

"What do you mean, Ambassador?" said Dax, looking somewhat chastened.

Sarek raised his right eyebrow, a gesture Sulu recalled having seen the Vulcan diplomat's younger son use frequently. "I mean that since we cannot simply follow our quarry to his next destination, we must instead *anticipate* that destination."

"Respectfully, Ambassador, that's a great deal easier to say than to do," Cutler said. "This is a *very* big galaxy."

"Granted, Commander," Dax said. *"But it's all just a*

matter of narrowing down the search. The only question is 'how?' "

Cutler raised a skeptical eyebrow, folding her arms before her as though daring the Trill diplomat to go on. "I, for one, am dying to hear the answer to that question, Mister Dax."

"We already know our fugitive has an agenda," Dax said, apparently unfazed by the exec's doubts.

Sulu nodded. "A chronic medical condition."

"A condition that requires continual monitoring and treatment," Sarek said.

"And treatment of a very specific kind," Chapel said. "I haven't seen a lot of serially progressive DNA mutations like this one before—hell, it doesn't even have a name in the medical literature, unless you've been trained in the Klingon language—but it's a safe bet our albino has an ongoing need to develop new therapeutic compounds that are rich in chromadiacetine."

"Which is what, exactly?" Cutler asked, frowning.

"Chromadiacetine is an amino acid. According to my preliminary tests, it's the best candidate for creating compounds capable of arresting or delaying this particular genetic disorder. It could take a lifetime to work out all the permutations, though."

Sulu nodded. "Our fugitive may well have spent his whole life doing just that, Doctor: slowing down the drift of his DNA just long enough to develop another drug that will do the same job the next time his genome spontaneously mutates."

"But chromadiacetine doesn't figure into the metabolic processes of most known humanoid species," Chapel said. "Or most M-class ecologies, for that matter."

"Perhaps that is to our advantage," Sarek said.

"Maybe," Sulu said, nodding. "Particularly if the stuff is

rare enough to be conspicuous when somebody goes after it in large enough quantities."

Cutler brightened, uncrossing her arms and leaning forward enthusiastically. "So all we have to do is find whichever planet has enough of this stuff for our raider to find useful. There can't be all that many places that fit the profile, can there?"

Sulu released his breath with a hiss that he realized belatedly had morphed into something perilously close to a frustrated sigh.

"In Federation space that's true enough," he said. "Maybe even along our border with the Klingon Empire as well. Unfortunately, we just don't know enough about the planets beyond to point the Klingons in any specific direction."

A pensive silence draped itself across the room like a shroud as Sulu considered his current range of options, which continued to narrow.

"Are we still connected?" Dax said, shattering the silence. Returning his gaze to the screen, Sulu noticed that the Trill's image was wavering even more than it had only moments before, as the distance between him and *Excelsior* grew at a pace that exceeded the speed of light itself by many orders of magnitude.

"We're receiving you, Ambassador," Sulu said.

"Before we lose contact completely, please send me everything you have on this chromadiacetine stuff, Captain," Dax said, grinning with an almost haughty confidence that Sulu had a great deal of difficulty squaring with reality. *"I'll—how do you humans say it?—carry the ball from here. Curzon Dax out."*

The Trill's image fluttered momentarily before being replaced by the neutral blue-and-white star-sector-and-laurel-leaf logo of the Federation.

Sulu stood, signaling that the meeting was at an end. Cutler and Chapel rose, as did Sarek, who moved with surprising suppleness for a man who had been so near death so recently.

"I certainly hope Mister Dax knows what he's doing," Sulu said.

The Vulcan surprised him with a subtle but fleeting facial expression that might have been mistaken for a half-smile had it lasted a fraction of a second longer.

"He has never given me reason to doubt it," Sarek said, and excused himself from the conference room, followed by Chapel and Cutler.

There's always a first time for everything, Sulu thought.

Early 2290 (the Year of Kahless 915, late in the month of *Doqath*)

I.K.S. Klothos

"Your own planetary database has narrowed our search down to a single world," Dax said, handing the datapad over to Kor, who sat in the command chair in the center of the cramped control center.

"Mempa II," Koloth said, watching from the chair's left side as Kor scowled down at the datapad. "How can you be so certain that is the world we seek?"

"Indeed," said Kang, who stood at the chair's opposite side looking askance at Dax. "We cannot afford to be led down a false trail. Should that happen, we may never find our quarry again."

Dax took a long, deep breath. *Speak loudly and confidently,* he told himself for perhaps the hundredth time since he'd made his decision to accompany these warriors in their quest for the albino. *These are Klingons, after all.*

"Do you *really* need me to brief you on Doctor Chapel's findings yet *again*?" he said with as much angry authority as he could muster. "Not only is Mempa II the sole known source of easily accessible chromadiacetine in the entire sector, it's also home to one of the most advanced bioscience labs in your Empire. Neither piece of information is likely to be a secret from the raider; he'll be drawn there like a *mreker* pup to a prong flower blossom."

The three Klingon captains regarded Dax in unreadable, stony silence for a protracted moment that felt at least half as long as eternity itself. Then Kang and Koloth both turned their gazes upon their comrade who occupied the *Klothos*'s center seat.

As the flagship commander, Kor would make the decision that guided the actions of the other two Klingon captains.

"Very well," Kor said at length, his dark, intense eyes settling upon Dax. Addressing Kang and Koloth, he added, "Unless either of you has reason to object."

Kang and Koloth exchanged a wordless glance punctuated by a curt mutual nod.

"We will return to our vessels, Kor," Kang said as he began moving toward the hatch in the control room's aft section.

"Lead the way," Koloth said to Kor. "To Mempa II."

**Early 2290 (the Year of Kahless 915,
late in the month of *Doqath*)**

Klingon space, near Mempa II

The repairs completed—using parts scavenged from the few Mempan shuttlecraft stationed at the laboratory settlement—the *Hegh'TlhoS* rose into orbit, surmounting the orange-tinted atmosphere and entering the inky darkness of space. Qagh felt better than he had in days; his wounds from Korvat were healing well, and Nej's latest treatment had returned him to nearly full strength. Now, both he and his ship, as well as his crew, were operating at close to peak efficiency.

The Mempan raid had been particularly fruitful, yielding not only a large quantity of isomiotic hypos, but also a wealth of data and a nested storeroom containing canisters of cobalt, selenium, and rhodium nitrate. Qagh had wasted no time ordering his men to "liberate" the entire hoard from the care of the facility's now-dead complement of Mempan scientists and lab workers. He looked forward to digesting the new scientific information he'd acquired; his men would need a short furlough soon, but Qagh rarely allowed himself that luxury, preferring instead to study and adapt any new research data or nascent technologies that he and his people had managed to plunder.

Most specifically, he had plans for the isomiotic hypodermics his men had recovered from the Mempa facility. His mind had been working overtime lately on how to adapt the genengineering technology with which he kept his followers in line, combining it with elements of germ warfare and targeted DNA sequencing. He wasn't certain if the grand design in his head could actually be accomplished, but he knew at least that he was assembling the various puzzle pieces one by one. *And with each new piece I find, the picture becomes that much clearer,* he thought.

The comm unit on his desk let out a shrill sound, followed by the voice of one of his Orion navigators. *"Captain, three Klingon warships have just entered orbit around the planet!"*

Qagh stood bolt upright. "Are we cloaked?"

"Yes, sir."

"On my way," Qagh said as he exited his onboard laboratory and stormed into the narrow warren of corridors and passages that linked the various crew compartments to the engine room and the forward command deck. A few moments later, he arrived at the latter location, where he found several of his people working the consoles with bustling yet focused intensity. Qagh surveyed the three floor-to-ceiling viewscreens that filled the forward quarter of the bridge; he saw Mempa II receding beneath them on the portside monitor, the three arriving Klingon battle cruisers on the central screen, and star-filled space—the direction opposite their incoming pursuers—on the starboard viewer.

"Have they detected us?" Qagh asked.

"No, sir," one of the navigators said. "They've shown no sign of awareness that we are here."

"Are any of our people still down on the surface?" Qagh wanted to know.

"The last of them just came back aboard a few *tup*s ago," said someone else, a smooth-headed female Klingon named Yoqala.

"Should we arm weapons, sir?" said the navigator.

"Ready them, but do not arm them," Qagh said. He activated the intercom on the arm of his chair, slamming the button with the palm of his hand. "Technician Thraq, are you certain that you repaired all the plasma leaks from the damage we took at Korvat?"

"Yes, sir," Thraq's voice came back after a delay of a few *lup*s. The shouts and clatterings of workers in the engine room were audible in the background.

"Triple check *everything,*" Qagh ordered. *That* has *to be how they tracked us,* he thought. Despite all the precautions they had taken, one tiny mistake had evidently brought these lumbering but dangerous sabre bears sniffing at his doorstep. But that was not an unfamiliar feeling; although he retained no memory, other than through the tales of long-dead Ganik, of his near death in the frozen wastes of Qo'noS as an infant, Qagh knew he had survived the violence of both weather and predators *then*—as well as every attack since, from without or within—and he had no doubt that he would do so again *now*.

"Give me a closer view of the Klingon ships," Qagh said

to one of the bridge technicians, a fierce Rigelian woman named Gnara who could best almost any warrior in combat despite the loss of one of her eyes.

A moment or two later, the image on the center screen changed, showing the three incoming ships at a higher magnification. The lead ship's hull bore the same markings that Qagh had seen above Korvat: the emblem of the cursed House of Ngoj.

His eyes narrowed, and a smile crept across his face. He knew that *someone* would likely be pursuing him after Korvat, no matter how well his people had hidden their tracks. He had thought that more damage had been done to this particular trio of battle cruisers, but with the exception of some plasma-fire scorches on the hulls, they seemed to be in perfect working order. *That, of course, can be remedied,* he thought, almost chuckling aloud.

"Activate the emitters on Mempa," Qagh said, his voice low. The trap they had set below would buy him time to finish assembling the ingredients necessary to bring the House of Ngoj to its knees.

Along with all the Federation-lovers on Qo'noS.

I.K.S. Klothos, near Mempa II

"Still no sign of the albino's ship, Captain," said one of Kor's bridge officers, a young male *bekk* who had transferred aboard only recently. "But we *are* showing life signs on the surface of Mempa II. It's a sparsely populated world notable mostly for its isolated science outposts."

And, no doubt, for its sad lack of proper police or military protection, Dax thought, hoping the *Klothos* would arrive in time to rectify that deficit.

Dax watched Kor stalk over to the *bekk*'s station. "What kind of life signs are you reading?"

"Mostly Mempan, at least in the towns and villages," the *bekk* said. "But their primary research facility shows no Mempan life signs at all. Instead I'm reading a few Klingons, a dozen or more Orions, and a handful of others."

At his adopted station on the *Klothos*'s bridge, Dax studied the readings. "We're getting some odd interference, Captain Kor, but I can verify those sensor readings. It's *got* to be the albino and his raiders." He felt silly using the word "albino" as if it were the Klingon saboteur's actual name, but absent any more definitive nomenclature, it would have to do.

A portion of the forward viewscreen flickered to a different picture: the scowling face of Koloth. *"Are you reading the life signs down on the planet?"* he asked gruffly, his long mustachios moving back and forth like twin scythes.

"Of course we are, Koloth," Kor said. "But what we *aren't* reading are any signs of his ship."

"It's got to be cloaked," Koloth said. *"No doubt they know we are here and will attempt either to flee or to engage us again in battle."*

Kor shook his head. "They won't attack. They know that we're expecting it now."

"But we *can* trap them on the planet," Dax said, looking up from his console. "They probably can't beam up—much less attack—without de-cloaking first. And if we send out a series of nucleonic pulses at the right frequencies, we might be able to jam their transporter." He looked back toward Kor for permission.

"Do it," Kor said, a slight grin edging onto his scowl.

As Dax hurriedly entered the specifications of his idea into his console and relayed the data to the other ships to enable all three vessels to work in tandem to trap the pirates on the planet, Kang's image appeared in another portion of the forward viewscreen.

"Before springing our trap, the three of us should beam down to the surface with our best warriors, so that we may cut this abomination down decisively," Kang said.

"Agreed," Koloth said quickly. *"My warriors are assembling now for a N'yengoren stealth ground attack."*

As he monitored the engineering team's progress in preparing the ships' deflectors to throw a "net" of synchronized nucleonic pulses across much of the planet, Dax paused to send a brief summons down to Dr. Hurghom in the medical bay. He felt his heart pounding. He wondered if his symbiont's nervous system was as on-edge as that of its humanoid host. At least he had heard nothing from the imagined ghosts of his symbiont's past lives in the last few days, a fact that he could only find encouraging.

Minutes later, the aft portion of the *Klothos*'s bridge was filled with armed Klingons, each carrying disruptors, each of them with a *bat'leth* strapped to his broad back. Kang, Koloth, and Kor began to strategize their attack on the albino and his soon-to-be trapped raiders.

Dax rose from his station and stepped toward Kor. "I will need some weapons as well," he said.

Kor looked at him strangely. *"You?* You plan to accompany *us?"*

"It is a matter of honor," Dax said, playing the highest card he knew of in the Klingon cultural deck.

"But not a matter of your *honor, Curzon Dax,"* Kang said, glowering from the main viewer. *"We have allowed you to accompany us this far as a courtesy, but you may show cowardice below. We cannot afford to risk that."*

Dax glared at Kang. "Cowardice? How *dare* you? I have shown you nothing but strength and courage."

"Hunh," Koloth said, half-grunting, half-laughing. *"You feared taking the* Excelsior *doctor's vaccine, even though she was on your own side. What kind of bravery is that?"*

I knew that was going to come back to haunt me, Dax thought. He hadn't wished to explain that he had hesitated only until he was certain that the drug wouldn't damage the symbiont that dwelled inside him. On further study of the vaccine's effects, he *had* allowed himself to be injected. Still, a small part of him wondered whether the recent sudden dormancy of some of Curzon Dax's unusually talkative predecessors might, in fact, have been vaccine-related.

But that was a small worry compared to what lay before him now. Dax knew he needed to prove himself to these warriors if he was going to maintain and build upon the fragile trust that he had already built with them. *I'm treading on dangerous ground here,* he thought, wishing that this once, he *could* directly interrogate a few of the previous Daxes for a little sage, clear-eyed advice.

"Captain Koloth, do *not* mistake caution for cowardice," he said, putting enough steel in his voice to demonstrate his sincerity. "If any of you doubt my nerve or my abilities," he said, gesturing toward the small landing party of warriors, "I will cross my *bat'leth* with yours without hesitation. And we shall see who emerges with honor."

It seemed for a moment as if the entire bridge had gone silent, until Kang began to laugh. The others soon joined him.

Dax wasn't sure whether they were laughing at his impudent challenge or at his earnestness, but he kept his stance rigid and his jaw set like day-old thermoconcrete.

"Very well, Curzon Dax," Kang said. "If no one else objects, I will allow the strangest ambassador in the galaxy to join our company of warriors. If this man of peace is so eager to fight, then who are any of *us* to deny him?"

"Issue him weapons," Kor said begrudgingly, addressing a member of the bridge crew who was not outfitted for assault-team duty. The man hurried to comply.

"There's one other thing we need to do," Dax said, as

he saw Dr. Hurghom enter the bridge. "A final precaution before we disembark."

The Klingons regarded him with narrowed eyes, but Dax returned only a devilish grin.

Curzon Dax had never much enjoyed using transporters, which more often than not tended to stress the Dax symbiont. The Klingon version of the device proved to be no exception.

The tingling, disturbingly vertiginous sensation that always accompanied the transition from energy back into matter passed with merciful quickness, however. Dax suddenly noticed that Kang, Koloth, and Kor had already begun leading their dozen or so armed warriors across the scrubby plain toward the cluster of low buildings that lay some twenty meters ahead. Their disruptor pistols raised and ready, they cast long shadows as they advanced through the light of the waning afternoon. Once he'd satisfied himself that his body—and the symbiont within it—had rematerialized intact, Dax hastened to catch up to the rest of the assault team.

But the transporter had been only a minor source of anxiety compared to whatever unknown they might face next. Raising his tricorder, he scanned the building for life signs and tried not to think about what he'd do if the team encountered something inside the building that the Klingons weren't prepared to handle.

"No sign of anything alive inside the building," he said after pausing for a moment to study the device's display. *But that doesn't mean there's nothing in there that's capable of killing us all where we stand.*

"Perhaps the albino and his troops managed to slip away in spite of your nucleonic pulses," Kor said after Dax followed him cautiously but quickly around a corner.

Dax shrugged. "Or maybe the nucleonic pulses are throwing off my tricorder readings."

"Perhaps," Kang said. "Or perhaps the albino has simply used false life signatures to lure us into a trap."

Koloth pointed toward the lab complex. "There is only one way to discover the truth with certainty."

With or without a tricorder, it was impossible not to notice the heavy metal door that had been melted to slag amid the rubble of one of the low exterior walls. The charred wreckage had fallen inward, making it obvious that someone had used extreme force to get inside the structure rather than to create an exit.

Moving deliberately but as quickly as he dared, Dax followed the three Klingon commanders and their assault team through the ruined entrance. After spending a few minutes transiting through darkened interior corridors that were empty but for a pair of dead, disruptor-charred humanoids—security guards, perhaps?—the landing party came to a large central chamber in which the lights were still functioning. The door to the white-tiled chamber that lay beyond had also been blasted away by some sort of particle-beam weapon, a deed that Dax's tricorder revealed had been done about as recently as the destruction of the outer entrance and the murder of the two guards in the hallway.

Dax surmised from the remains of their apparel that the alien bodies that lay on the room's floor belonged to Mempan genetics researchers. He checked for life signs even though the corpses seemed to be in only slightly better shape than the exterior door.

"Dead," he said a moment later. "Every last one of them."

"This must have been a laboratory or research center of sorts," Koloth said.

Kor kicked aside a stray chair, making no attempt to conceal his frustration. "When did this happen?" he wanted to know.

Dax shook his head. "Maybe a few hours ago. A couple of *kilaan*s at the most, since whatever passes for local law enforcement doesn't seem to know what's happened here yet."

"I doubt the place could have been this empty when the killings took place," Kang said, gesturing with his weapon toward a nearby series of bare metal tables and empty shelves.

Koloth nodded, his manner as calm and icy as Kor's was livid. "Whoever did this appears to have helped himself to whatever was here. Empty shelves would hardly have been worth the effort."

After muttering a low but pungent Klingon curse, Kor ordered the troopers to secure the rest of the complex. The men immediately dispersed to carry out Kor's instructions.

"This was our last lead," Kor said, now fairly vibrating with restrained fury. "Our quarry has escaped us without leaving another trail for us to follow."

"If the Council would allow *Excelsior* to come here, her sensors might prove that not to be quite true," Dax said as he began scanning the room with his tricorder.

"Perhaps," Kor snarled. "But that doesn't help us much in the here and now, does it? We don't even know precisely what was taken from this place!"

Dax's tricorder, which he had left in scanning mode, chose that moment to beep. The Trill looked down on its primary display.

He was pleasantly surprised. His spirit lifting as though borne aloft on antigravs, Dax looked up from the device in his hand. Regarding the three Klingon captains with a wide grin, he recalled an expression that Emony had picked up long ago, during a gymnastics competition on Earth:

It ain't over till it's over.

Dax raised his tricorder so that it faced the nearest wall.

Holding the instrument before him, he walked toward an innocuous-looking ODN jack that was set into a recess in one of the metal tables.

"Follow me, gentlemen," he said.

The freebooter ship *Hegh'TlhoS*

"The Klingon landing party is inside the complex, Captain," said Gnara, the one-eyed Rigelian who manned one of the sensor stations. "And they're all concentrated into a fairly small area."

A rare feeling of delight tugged at the edges of Qagh's face. There would probably be no better time than now to spring his trap.

"You may transmit the 'go' signal now, Gnara," he said, grinning.

The Rigelian woman nodded, then keyed in a brief command string with her two huge hands. The console responded by displaying several blinking orange lights, and issuing an unmelodious buzzing sound.

Her single frustration-narrowed eye focused tightly upon Qagh. "The signal isn't getting through. The Klingon ships seem to be blanketing the vicinity of the Mempa lab with interference of some sort."

Qagh growled quietly. "What about simply snatching the Klingons up from the surface with the transporter?"

Gnara shook her head somberly. "Not unless something changes those EM interference patterns."

"We could simply leave the Mempa system undetected," said Yoqala.

Certainly, we could, Qagh thought. *Only to allow my kinsman to chase us to our next planetfall. And the next. And the next.*

The albino bared his teeth and addressed his entire

command-deck crew in his most dangerous tone. "Find a way around that interference. *Now*!"

"Looks like our culprit got sloppy this time, Captain," Dax said, his image dominating the bridge's main viewer. *"He evidently took all the computer workstations with him when he raided the Mempa lab, but he missed the ODN data backup system built into the structure of the lab itself. That's how we got our hands on the manifest of materials the lab was working with just prior to the raid."*

Seated in *Excelsior*'s command chair, Sulu nodded as he stared at a datapad that displayed the very list Dax was describing. Most of the lab's contents seemed unremarkable, except for two item categories that Dax had flagged for particular attention.

Foremost among the noteworthy materials plundered from the lab was a series of retroviral vaccines—just as Dr. Chapel had predicted.

And then there was a large quantity of isomiotic hypos, which could not be constructed without access to substances that were customarily kept under tight control, both in the Federation and, presumably, in the Klingon Empire as well.

Damn, he thought, struggling to put down a nearly overwhelming sense of rising helplessness. *The albino got away with this stuff. And there's nothing we can do about it while we're stuck here at Korvat, other than keep lists.*

"I'm sorry we weren't able to give you more than the after-the-fact police reports," Dax said, sounding more than a little frustrated himself.

Sulu set the datapad down on the arm of his command chair and looked across the light-years into the young diplomat's bright, alert eyes. "I know you're doing everything you can, Mister Dax."

"Which is precious little," the Trill said with a sad shake of his head. *"Since we can't reestablish the trail without bringing* Excelsior *closer to us, we're back to trying to anticipate the albino's next target. In spite of everything we've learned about him and his medical condition, he's been fairly unpredictable."*

Sulu nodded, recalling the volatile nature of the man who had nearly murdered him and his family on Ganjitsu four decades ago. "Unpredictable" was a fitting descriptor of the desperate, mercurial soul who even now sometimes came calling in his dreams.

It occurred to him then that there might be an easier way to anticipate the raider's next destination than by cataloguing and analyzing his medical weaknesses.

After Dax signed off, Sulu touched the comm channel on the right arm of his chair. "Commander Sulu to Doctor Chapel and Commander Cutler. I need to see both of you immediately."

Raising his steaming teacup carefully to his lips, Sulu stared through the panoramic window of deck three's observation lounge, which was located just aft of the main bridge module. The graceful sweep of *Excelsior*'s warp-drive nacelles, illuminated by the starship's running lights, tapered away into the distance, framing the dark limb of Korvat between them. Millions of stationary stars, jewels mounted in the eternal night, filled the vastness that lay beyond.

Sulu took a seat between Chapel and Cutler at the meeting table. Because this room was generally regarded as a private conference space for senior officers, no one else was present.

"You've described our fugitive's DNA as 'wandering,'" he said, addressing Chapel.

She nodded. "I suppose that's accurate enough, Captain. Without getting too technical."

"Then let's *get* technical, Doctor. Is there any way this 'wandering' might be predicted?"

Sulu watched Chapel's thoughtful scowl appear and deepen as she considered the matter. "You mean, can we work out in advance exactly how the DNA might drift?" she said. "And see in advance what sorts of new disorders he might suffer, and which cures he might need?"

"Sounds like forecasting a future map of the galaxy based on known stellar motion," Cutler asked.

"Exactly," Sulu said, nodding. "If we can somehow calculate ahead of time in what direction the raider's DNA might wander, we might be able to work out his future biochemical needs."

"And from that we could figure out which planets he might be headed toward next," Cutler said.

Sulu grinned. "Right again, Commander. Doctor?"

Chapel sighed, scowled again, and shook her head. "The concept makes sense, Captain. But the progressive genetic drift we're talking about here makes even ten billion years of stellar drift look like pretty simple stuff. I simply don't have enough data about the exact present state of the raider's DNA to make an accurate prediction of how it's changing from day to day. And even if I did have that sort of information—which I don't because he's probably therapeutically adjusting his own DNA in ways I just can't foresee—there probably isn't enough computational power in the whole known universe to crunch the numbers in time to do us any good."

Sulu bit back a curse. "Then the short answer is 'no.' "

"So we hit yet another brick wall," said Cutler, deflating Sulu's spirits further.

"I'm not sure I said *that,* exactly," Chapel said, her thoughtful scowl giving way to a small, sly smile. "Maybe we should try attacking this problem from another angle."

"What do you have in mind?" Sulu asked, still unwilling to let his hopes gutter out entirely.

"For starters, let's put aside the whole matter of chronic genetic troubles for a minute and look at our man's other motivations."

"All right," Cutler said. "We know he's something of a weapons enthusiast."

"That's certainly true," Sulu said, nodding. The raider had been partial to high-powered weapons even decades ago on Ganjitsu, when he'd destroyed the Sulu family compound from orbit.

In fact, the albino was easily the best-armed privateer that Sulu had ever encountered; not only had he come to Korvat equipped with highly destructive plasma flares capable of crippling even well-armed Klingon warships under certain circumstances, he had also employed biomimetic compounds to attempt—and commit—assassination, and had set off organic explosives. Not to mention that he had recently murdered a woman using a weaponized retrovirus that he had tuned to his victim's specific DNA.

Most recently, at Mempa II, he had acquired a large supply of another commodity that might have as many applications for violence as it did for medicine.

"Isomiotic hypos," Sulu said.

"Excuse me, Captain?" Chapel said.

"Along with the retroviral vaccine materials the albino stole from the lab on Mempa II, he got away with a hefty supply of isomiotic hypos."

Chapel whistled, as though impressed by the raider's achievement. "That's pretty heavy-duty medicine. But I'm not sure how he'll be able to apply isomiotic hypos to his particular condition."

"What if that's not his plan?" Cutler said.

Sulu nodded and reached for the computer terminal on the tabletop.

"Computer, cross-reference isomiotic hypodermics with all known biogenic weapons applications, under my security authorization."

Precisely six and one-half minutes later, Sulu almost wished that Curzon Dax had never told him about the isomiotic hypos in the first place.

TWENTY-SIX

They won't be staying down there forever, Qagh thought as he stared at the central forward viewer on his command deck. The planet was shrouded in darkness, except for the bright crescent of its eastern limb. *They'll return to their ships, sooner or later. And then the chase will continue.*

And continue.

It was intolerable.

Qagh moved toward the console where Gnara was working. "Any change in the interference coming from the Klingon ships?"

Gnara focused her one eye on the relevant displays before her.

The eye widened in surprise. "The landing party on the surface is receiving a tight-beam subspace signal, Captain."

Qagh scowled. "What of it? Can you intercept it?"

"I don't think so, sir. But the 'go' signal we tried to transmit earlier . . ." Her voice trailed off as she tried to organize her thoughts.

"*Yes?*" Qagh prodded, his scowl deepening as his reservoir of patience ran nearly empty.

"I think we can get it through the interference field," she said, flustered. "All we have to do is piggyback the 'go' signal onto the subspace carrier they're using."

A malicious euphoria seized him. "Do it."

Mempa II

Commander Sulu's serious-looking face filled most of the large computer console in the alien lab, and Kor watched attentively alongside Kang, Koloth, and Dax while crew members from the *Klothos,* the *QaD,* and the *Gal'tagh* continued their security and cleanup operations at the site of the albino's latest massacre.

"*Unfortunately, I have no news about Ambassador Kamarag,*" the human said. "*He's still comatose, but stable.*"

Trapped between Gre'thor *and* Sto-Vo-Kor, Kor thought, shaking his head in glum resignation. *I would not wish such a fate upon my worst enemy.*

For he intended to send that enemy to a berth aboard the Barge of the Dead, and thence to the eternal darkness of *Gre'thor,* as expeditiously as possible.

"*But I do have some new information about our fugitive,*" Sulu continued. "*I think you might find it useful.*"

Kor's eyebrows went aloft without his volition, and he exchanged a quick glance with Curzon Dax and the other two captains.

"Indeed," Kor said.

"What sort of information, Commander?" Kang asked.

"*My senior staff and I have concluded that he's after*

more than just therapies for his various genetic disorders," Sulu said.

"It's no revelation that our quarry seeks weaponry," Koloth said with a dismissiveness that matched the sneer that adorned his robustly textured head.

Already disappointed by the substance of Sulu's latest communication, Kor said, "This *Ha'DIbaH*'s lust for arms is already well known to us, Commander. It explains why he has become as formidable as he is presently."

"Of course," Sulu said, apparently unfazed even by such vehement Klingon skepticism. *"But as far as we can tell, he's never before had the capability of poisoning whole planetary biospheres in a single attack. We think he might soon be able to do just that, if he can't already."*

"What are you talking about, Commander Sulu?" said Kang, his usually smooth forehead wrinkling even more than Sulu's.

Sulu paused, apparently gathering his thoughts. Then he leaned forward, as though he was entering commands into a console that wasn't visible on the screen.

Kor noticed only then that he didn't recognize the background that was indistinctly visible behind the human. Was he transmitting from his personal quarters rather than from the bridge of his ship?

"I'm transmitting an information packet to the Klothos *now,"* Sulu said, *"using our secure frequency to avoid outside interception. You'll find that it contains a . . . recipe for a truly terrible biogenic weapon."*

Kor frowned, not quite believing his ears, though he understood now why Sulu was evidently calling from a place of solitary secrecy. "Why would you do this? Why would you compromise the security of your own Federation in this way?"

"I've done it because I trust the three of you to do the right thing with the information," Sulu said. *"And because I*

believe our fugitive is trying to build this very weapon, prob-
ably with the intent to use it—against one of your planets."

Kor saw a sly smile begin to spread itself across Kang's face. "I imagine that you also determined before calling us that our own intelligence service already knew about this particular Federation 'secret.'"

"If our own scientists haven't already discovered the means of creating this weapon on their own," Koloth said, no doubt insulted at the implication that Klingons must necessarily resort to spying to advance their knowledge of weapons. "Not that true warriors would ever resort to the use of such cowardly devices."

"Regardless of what your people may or may not know already, I'm reasonably certain that my superiors wouldn't approve of my unilateral decision to share this information with you," Sulu said with a wry smile of his own. *"But our fugitive has forced my hand. Whether his ultimate targets are planets in the Federation or in Klingon space, I can't in good conscience take the chance that he might succeed in deploying this biogenic weapon anywhere."*

Kor pulled his communicator from his belt and barked a few terse orders to his communications officer, then retrieved a thick datapad from a nearby tabletop. He paused momentarily to activate the padd and link it to his communicator, to enable it to unscramble and display the secure databurst he'd just received from his ship.

The padd displayed a list of the biogenic weapon's various components. Kor read through it in deliberate, thoughtful silence as his three companions crowded around him to do likewise.

Isomiotic hypos.
Cobalt.
Selenium.
Rhodium nitrate.
Kor knew, of course, that their quarry already possessed

the first item on the list. Whether he had already gathered the remaining material, or how long it might take him to finish doing so if he hadn't, had to remain subjects of uneasy conjecture for the moment.

"Commander, do you think he already has all the necessary compounds and elements in his possession?" Kang asked, turning his eyes from the padd back to the image of Sulu's face.

"There's no way to know for certain," Sulu said. *"But I don't think so—at least not yet. This stuff isn't all that easy to find, especially in weapons-grade form, and it's almost never found together in the same place. It could take years, even for a dedicated, well-resourced criminal enterprise."*

"If the materials in question *were* in his possession already," Kor said, "then surely he would have used them against Korvat."

"There's no way to know for certain what he may be holding in reserve," Sulu said. *"At least not until* after *it literally explodes in our faces."*

"I believe you mean *our* faces, Commander," Kang said acidly, clearly unhappy that *Excelsior*'s new captain had not seen fit to violate his own superiors' cowardly orders or to challenge the will of the frequently temperamental High Council. Like Kor, Kang was an ill-favored *QuchHa'* who naturally lacked Koloth's *HemQuch* standing with the Council, and thus had cause to resent both that body's occasional inaction and its tendency to issue arbitrary edicts; nevertheless, Kor thought it strange for Kang to expect an Earther to have the courage to do what the vast majority of Klingons would not or could not do themselves.

"I suppose I'll simply have to err on the side of caution and leave it at that," Sulu said, showing no sign of having taken offense at Kang's interjection. *"I'm simply not going to assume that the albino hasn't developed a world-ravaging biogenic weapon just because he didn't happen to deploy it*

against Korvat. If he really wanted to wreak havoc in the Klingon Empire over the long haul, he wouldn't necessarily tip his hand at this stage of the game."

"You think he might have this weapon, and merely be waiting for the chance to deploy it against Qo'noS itself?" Koloth demanded.

The notion filled Kor with more dread than he thought his jaded soul had the capacity to experience.

"Aren't you taking a rather large leap, Commander?" he asked, though something deep in his own gut told him otherwise.

"Perhaps. But with the stakes so high, we'd all be damned fools not to at least consider the possibility. We know our raider already has a highly advanced knowledge of genetically tailored retroviruses. With a weapon like the one we've been discussing to distribute those materials throughout a planet's atmosphere, he could completely wipe out the biosphere of the Klingon Homeworld itself."

"Now you're being paranoid, Earther," Koloth said.

Once again, Sulu remained admirably unruffled. *"You sound a lot like my executive officer, Koloth. But nobody 'just imagined' the bombing of Korvat and the destruction of Kamarag's ship. It's not paranoia if someone really is out to get you."*

"Gentlemen," Dax said, his bearing erect and businesslike as he faced the three Klingon captains and the image of the human commander. "I don't think Commander Sulu is being paranoid in the least. I've read through all the relevant medical reports filed by Doctor Klass and Doctor Chapel, so I have a pretty fair idea of our fugitive's bioweapons capabilities."

"I had no idea you were also an expert on biological warfare," Koloth said with a smirk.

"There's a lot you don't know about me, Captain Koloth," Dax said, unintimidated.

I don't doubt that for a moment, Kor thought. He was

still impressed by the surprising depth and breadth of Dax's engineering knowledge; once again, he wondered how one so young could have amassed so much expertise.

"Our marauder doesn't have to wipe out an entire biosphere if it isn't strategically necessary," Dax continued. "According to *Excelsior*'s reports, he's able to tailor his retroviral attacks so precisely that they can be genetically 'tuned' to kill only particular individuals. I see no reason why he couldn't widen his focus slightly, targeting entire Klingon Houses—say, those that supported the Korvat meeting or the Houses that back Klingon-Federation détente in general."

"Wouldn't he have to obtain genetic samples from members of those Houses in order to calibrate such an attack?" Koloth asked.

Dax nodded, as did Kor.

"That could have been accomplished easily enough on Korvat," Kor said. "The raider was there in disguise, remember? He could have posed as one of Ambassador Kamarag's low-level functionaries."

"Which means he easily could have taken DNA samples from the drinking vessels at the conference tables," said Dax.

Kor stood in silence, trying to digest all that he had heard. Given everything they already knew about the terrorist—and what Kor alone had discovered about the man's unfortunate origins—Kor could not help but wonder whether his target was actually somewhat narrower than even the short list of pro-détente Klingon Houses.

What if the killer sought specifically to punish *Kor's* House—the former House of Ngoj—for abandoning him during his infancy?

"I wish we could do more than just hand you the fugitive's shopping list, so to speak," Sulu said, forcing Kor to set aside his personal reverie, at least momentarily. *"You have no idea how much it frustrates me to have my hands tied like this."*

"Even if *Excelsior* and all her resources were here with

us, Commander Sulu," Kor said, "you would not know precisely where in Klingon space to seek the remaining items on that 'shopping list.' We are in a significantly better position to do that than you would be."

"You have served the Empire well this day, human," Kang said, nodding toward the human's image as if to make up for his earlier brusqueness. "And your Federation as well."

Even dour Koloth seemed to agree. "*MajQa'*, Commander Sulu," he said. "Well done."

"*Qapla',*" Kor said, crossing his chest with his closed fist in salute.

"*Success,*" Sulu repeated in Federation Standard before the lab's computer terminal abruptly blanked itself.

Kor turned to face all three of his comrades-in-arms simultaneously. All of them, Klingon and Trill alike, looked toward him with expectation in their eyes.

"You all heard the human's words," he said. "A great deal of work awaits us."

Koloth pulled out his communicator. "I will instruct my science officer to begin cross-referencing the new data from *Excelsior* with the Klingon Defense Force's planetary database immediately."

Dax nodded grimly. "Then maybe we'll have a fighting chance to keep him from crossing anything else off his shopping list."

Kor opened his communicator. "Captain Kor to the *Klothos*. Alert the transporter room that I am ready to beam back up. . . ."

The freebooter ship *Hegh'TlhoS*, near Mempa II

"The subspace carrier has shut down," Gnara said.

"Did the 'go' signal get through?" Qagh said, though he already knew the answer.

"No, sir. But the Klingon vessels have just modulated a gap in their interference field."

Qagh recognized the maneuver immediately. "That means they're starting to beam personnel back up to their vessels. Transmit the 'go' signal through the gap. *Now!*"

The trap, the albino thought, *is sprung at last.*

Mempa II

"Transporter locked on, Captain," said the guttural voice that issued from Kor's communicator.

"So," Dax said, apparently addressing all three Klingon captains at once. "Which one of you am I hitching a ride with?"

Before anyone had time to answer the Trill ambassador, Kor noticed a blinding brilliance issuing from the ceiling above. *The light fixtures,* he thought as he covered his eyes with his arm. He realized, too late, that the laboratory's lights were probably the only things the assault team hadn't taken apart during several booby-trap sweeps.

Kor simultaneously felt a supremely energetic jolt seize his body, instantly setting his entire nervous system ablaze.

The pain, though tolerable, was thankfully brief. Blackness engulfed him, embracing him as tightly as the arms of a lover.

TWENTY-SEVEN

"Tlhab jIH DaH, bI'par'Mach Ha'DIbaH puqloD!"

Kor heard the hoarsely shouted expletives, though he wasn't certain he was entirely conscious. He felt he was burning alive, his skin crawling, his muscles twitching uncontrollably. Slowly, he opened his eyes, but regretted it instantly when the harsh light beyond his eyelids blinded him.

The lights, Kor thought, recalling his last moments of consciousness on Mempa II. *He must have laid a trap in the ceiling light fixtures and triggered it remotely.* Kor could only wonder why his kinsman had waited so long to draw his snare closed. Had he run afoul of the measures Kor and the others had taken to inhibit transporter use at the Mempa lab?

Something hard smashed abruptly into the side of Kor's face. His zygomatic bone shifted slightly, accompanied by a sickening crunch, and he could feel at least one of his teeth dislodge from his jaw. His mouth immediately began to fill with blood.

"The last of you *petaQ* are finally awake," a male voice said. It dripped with hatred, and its *tlhIngan* was accented by the dialects of various species from across the Empire and beyond.

Despite being immobilized by some sort of head restraint, Kor spat out a tooth, along with a mouthful of blood. He did his best not to flinch as he very gingerly opened his eyes again. "Who dares to strike me?"

"This is why I wanted to save the introductions until all of you were awake," the hostility-steeped voice said. "I *hate* repeating myself. Especially to the walking dead."

Noting that his body spasms seemed to be lessening in intensity, Kor struggled to turn his head in the direction of the voice, fighting the heavy forehead strap that pinned his head to the cold slab beneath him. He saw Koloth and Curzon Dax strapped to nearby tables, similarly restrained at the forehead, chest, forearms, wrists, and midsection. Each of them was stripped to the waist, bodies and faces covered in bruises and freshly bloody cuts.

The room appeared to be a laboratory of some sort, though it currently bore a stronger resemblance to an abattoir. A standing figure stepped forward, blocking Kor's view of the other captives. Kor looked up at the man's face and saw him, their saboteur, their quarry, and for the moment, their jailer.

The sickly albino Klingon, an abomination born of Kor's very own ancestral house.

"Captain Kor of the House of Ngoj," the albino said in malice-saturated tones. "Here are the rules of *my* interrogation room, gentlemen. I will tell you anything I choose. I will *ask* you anything I choose. If you don't answer any given question to my satisfaction, I will torture you. If you ask something of me, I may answer you, but I will also torture you. If you shout out some chest-thumping threat, I will torture you for that as well. Do I make myself clear?"

"Only a coward would torture a captive!" It was Kang's voice, coming from Kor's left.

"Interesting point, that," the albino said, crossing out of Kor's sight but brandishing a small, gleaming metal object just before he did so. A moment later, Kor heard five small thudding sounds, delivered in quick succession, followed immediately by Kang's barely restrained groans.

He's just stabbed Kang, Kor thought. Since he didn't know whether or not the blows had been fatal, he decided to focus instead on testing his bonds, looking for any opportunity to break free.

"You see, *not* having been raised in Klingon society," the albino said as he returned to Kor's line of sight, "I have not been inculcated with all the high-sounding noble rhetoric about Klingon honor and the warrior spirit and so forth." He set the small, blood-streaked blade he had just used on Kang onto a nearby counter, from which he picked up a towel to wipe the lavender fluid from his bony, pallid hands. "This, despite the fact that, as you can see, I *am* a Klingon. Just not the right *kind* of Klingon."

He smiled down at Kor, and in that instant Kor knew that the albino knew the truth of his heritage, and the secret of their linked bloodlines.

"When the Orion slavers took me on board as their mascot—or perhaps I was their pet—they considered me just as much an aberration as Klingon society no doubt would have found me. They named me Qagh, considering it humorous that I would forever be known as a 'mistake.' " He turned toward Koloth, spreading his hands. "Did you know that I had reached the age of sixteen before I even learned what my name truly means?"

"Where are the other warriors that accompanied us to Mempa II?" Koloth shouted angrily.

The albino tilted his head and smiled. "Either you weren't listening to the rules, you don't believe what I say, or you actually *like* torture," he said, his voice greasily smooth. "Personally, I prefer to believe it's the latter."

The albino moved out of view for several moments, then returned, holding a heavy metal spanner in one hand, and a handful of purplish goo in the other. "Your men will probably end up in *Sto-Vo-Kor,* even though they were disintegrated where they lay before they regained consciousness," Qagh said. "It's a pity, though, that they won't be able to see it when they get there." He opened the goo-covered hand and dropped the pulpy mess it carried squarely onto Koloth's bare chest.

Horrified, Kor recognized the shredded remains of several eyeballs within the bloody clump of tissue and fluid. Though his warrior's spirit screamed its need for vengeance, it could not prevent his gorge from rising.

"But that's not quite all," Qagh said, bringing the wrench down several times in quick succession on Koloth's forearm and hand. Though the sound of breaking bones was clearly audible, Koloth didn't utter a sound, instead maintaining a rigidly stoic mien. Qagh quickly scooped up some of the mess he'd left on Koloth's chest and stuffed it into the Klingon captain's mouth.

"I warned you," Qagh said, as Koloth spat out the horrid mouthful, which rolled down the side of his face. "But at least I *also* gave you the answer to your question. Don't you feel good about that?"

Qagh turned away. "Although this is the first *direct* contact I've had with you, I was there on Korvat. In disguise." He paused for a moment, looking thoughtful, then continued. "I have to confess that I'm at something of a loss as to why three such distinguished military captains would chase after me—other than *you,* Captain Kor—as well as this young Trill diplomat and his traveling companion."

He's going to reveal our mutual secret, Kor thought, a notion that almost made him feel relieved at the prospect of dying shortly thereafter. *At least the shame I face will likely die in this room. But what did he mean about Dax's "traveling companion"?*

"I'm also impressed by your resistance to my bioagents," Qagh said, once again moving out of sight. "I had assumed that the four of you would have been reduced to handfuls of granulated dust long before now. I suspect—" He paused, and Kor heard the unmistakable hiss of a hypospray coming from his left.

"I suspect that some clever Federation scientist must have worked up some kind of counteragent with which to inoculate you," he said as he crossed back into view. He pressed something cold and metallic against Kor's skin, and despite a burning sensation like that of hungry *targ*-mites devouring his nerve endings, Kor felt something new invade his body.

Qagh crossed over to Koloth, a large hypospray in his hand. "It *had* to have been someone on the Federation side. It's not like most of *our* scientists to have worked out a counteragent, and I know what most of the Empire's allies, colonies, and client worlds have been working on." He chuckled coldly for a moment. "After all, I've raided a significant proportion of their research laboratories over the last few decades."

The albino now moved toward Dax, who had remained nearly still since Kor had regained consciousness. He was clearly awake and in pain, but had apparently not provoked the Klingon throwback as had the other captains.

"I studied you all quite closely while you were unconscious, and my crew was getting us under way in our cloaked vessel," Qagh said, addressing Dax. "My scans were surely less invasive than any of the injuries that either I or my men have inflicted on you. And yet they revealed far more about you than I suspect you would ever have told me voluntarily—even if you thought doing so might save your life. Or should I say, 'lives,' Mister Dax?"

He injected Curzon Dax with the same hypospray he had just used on Kor, and then placed his hand, palm down, on Dax's lower abdomen. Addressing his other prisoners, the albino said, "For instance, did the good ambassador ever tell you that he shares his body with some manner of parasite? Not just *any* parasite, mind you, but one that contains a complete consciousness, and seems able—at least as far as I can tell—to *communicate* with its host in some subtle manner. No, 'communicate' is not the right word. 'Commune' might better describe the phenomenon." Qagh eyed the supine diplomat with malicious curiosity. "I wonder whether *all* Trill are joined to nonhumanoid life-forms in this fashion, or if this fusion is unique to our esteemed Ambassador Dax?"

Kor felt far too traumatized to be shocked any further. He saw that Dax was regarding Qagh stoically, even though the muscles in his abdomen were tensing and moving. *Is that his fear of what the albino might do next? Or is that where the parasite lives?* Kor was beginning to doubt that he'd live long enough to answer either question.

As if reading his mind, Qagh turned and looked directly into Kor's eyes. "Hmmm," the throwback said, grinning. "And you, oh ruler of the House of Kor, son of Rynar of the House of Ngoj . . ." He left Dax unmolested and moved back into the center of the chamber, nearer to Kor. "I can see it in your eyes. You already *know* the truth. When did *you* discover it, I wonder? When did the great and noble Kor learn that the two of us have more in common than anyone else here could possibly be aware?"

He turned back to Koloth and grabbed him by the jaw, forcing his head into a direct line of sight with Kor. "Did he tell you that we were *cousins*? That *I* am the rightful heir to the house of Ngoj, from whose residual wealth Kor's own House was built?"

Kor felt shame burning him now, an internal immolation

far more intense than the sensations caused by whatever bio-agents Qagh had just injected into him.

Qagh shook Koloth's jaw. "*Answer* me, Captain. Or I will . . . feed you again. Or perhaps take your *own* eyes as trophies. Did you *know* Kor's shameful secret?"

"No, I did not," Koloth said in a dead, lifeless voice.

Kor saw something change behind Koloth's eyes as the other captain regarded him. Hatred? Disgust? Anger, certainly. But were those sentiments aimed at Kor or the albino? And would it even matter in whatever scant time remained before Qagh murdered them all?

"I did not tell them," Kor said to Qagh, his shame outstripping his dread of whatever further pain the crazed throwback might deliver. "I had heard stories of your birth, but only as rumors, cautionary tales designed to scare members of my House as children. It wasn't until I learned of your age—and then saw the genetic evidence from your sabotage on Korvat—that I was able to guess that you might be the shame of my House, made flesh."

"Very good," Qagh said, smiling and releasing Koloth's chin. "You answered without asking a question. And I actually believe you *are* telling the truth. No doubt you intended to kill me *before* my heritage became known to your fellow warriors."

"Your heritage doesn't matter!" shouted Kang, filling Kor with relief that his old friend still lived. "I would kill you *now,* if you had the courage to face me like a warrior."

"Has the loss of blood made you so *forgetful,* Kang?" Qagh asked. "I said before that the way of the warrior has been denied me all my life." He sighed heavily and moved back out of Kor's field of vision, no doubt to torture Kang once again. "Besides, it is a philosophy in which I have no real interest anyway. I prefer to gather influence and power through means of my own."

Kor heard Kang gasp, and felt a spray of something wet

splatter across his own bare torso. "Enough, Qagh!" he shouted. "We will give you *no more* answers, nor feed your sadistic desires. *Kill us now,* and be *done* with it!"

Qagh suddenly loomed over him, staring down into his face from mere *SanID'qam*s away, close enough so that Kor could smell the rankness of the pirate's breath. A spray of dark purple blood spattered the chalky skin of his cheek. "Nothing would please me more than removing this obstacle that stands between me and my control of a noble Klingon House. And to do the honors, allow me to present *another* ghost from out of Qo'noS's checkered past."

Kor looked over his chest and was shocked to see the Klingon who stepped forward in answer to the albino's introduction. The last time he had seen Dr. Nej was at the central military infirmary on Qo'noS, where Koloth had regained his *HemQuch* forehead ridges. He had heard rumors subsequently that the physician had been disgraced shortly thereafter, evidently as punishment for some failure related to the creation of a biodesigned life-form, the *yIH*-eating *glo'meH* predator.

Nej said nothing as he neared Kor, his expression unreadable. In his hand was a large, wickedly sharp scalpel, crusted with purplish grue.

An electronic beep came from elsewhere in the chamber, followed by a female voice. *"Captain Qagh, we have a problem."*

The albino withdrew from his discomfiting proximity to Kor. "What is it?" He sounded impatient.

"We show an unauthorized launch of one of the small, warp-driven shuttles."

"Who launched it?" Qagh asked, his voice rising in evident anger.

Kor saw a strange look flicker across Nej's features for a moment, as if he was remembering something—or concealing it.

"Unknown, sir," the woman responded.

"Destroy it!" Qagh ordered.

"We targeted it immediately upon launch, sir. Unfortunately, it cloaked itself before we were able to open fire."

The albino roared in displeasure, and brought his fist down hard onto Kor's crotch.

His gorge again rising, Kor's muscles strained in response to the blow. He barely heard the next words of his long-lost cousin.

"I don't know how you did it, but you won't live long enough for it to matter!"

Qagh angrily snatched the scalpel out of Nej's hand and slashed it down toward Kor's exposed neck.

TWENTY-EIGHT

The scalpel slipped effortlessly through Kor's neck, but to Qagh's surprise, this was not because the tissue was soft or the blade was sharp; it was because Kor had disappeared in a cascade of green-gold sparkles of light.

Roaring in anger, Qagh looked up toward Kang, then whirled to see the spots where Koloth and Dax had recently been restrained. All he caught was a brief afterimage of Koloth as he disappeared, his broken fingers raised in a rude Klingon gesture.

"They've beamed out!" Nej said, startled into stating the obvious.

Qagh whirled toward him, wielding the scalpel. His bloodlust and anger might have ended the physician's life had the *Hegh'TlhoS* not violently shuddered to one side at that moment. Half the tools in the infirmary slid across the countertops, many of them clattering to the far-from-sterile floor that tilted beneath the freebooter captain's feet.

"Captain, we're under attack!" the voice of the *Hegh'TlhoS*'s Orion navigator said, slightly distorted by the ship's comm system. *"They're firing at us even though we're still cloaked!"*

"Raise shields! Evasive maneuvers!" Qagh shouted, steadying himself against one of the room's medical tables as the ship rocked again. He heard a loud, rumbling sound coming up from one of the lower decks, followed by a brief roar. *The hull's been breached,* he thought ruefully. "I'm on my way to the command deck."

Nej hurried after him, following at a respectful distance. "The prisoners must have been carrying hidden transmitters of some kind," he said. "There's no other way their rescuers could have pinpointed their location."

"Obviously," the albino snapped. "Despite all of your searches and scans, they apparently went unfound."

"I am a physician and a biological researcher, Captain," Nej sniffed as the pair made haste toward the forward section of the modified freighter. "I am not a subspace radio engineer. I respectfully suggest you focus your attention on the problem at hand rather than on blame. For instance, how do we know that our guests didn't leave more small transmitters behind? If one of their ships could achieve a transporter lock, they may be able to continue targeting us in spite of our cloak."

"Then I shall make sure that *nothing* gets left behind," Qagh said, punching the pad on the wall next to the command deck's entrance. The door slid open obediently.

The vessel's cramped bridge was in chaos, and Qagh could see on his viewscreens that the three Klingon battle cruisers were indeed firing purposefully, rather than blindly, at the *Hegh'TlhoS*.

If they can see through our cloak, then simply running will do us no good, the albino thought. *I must confront them.*

"Keep the cloaking system running at all costs!" Qagh barked. "Continue evasive maneuvers. And get a scrub team to make certain that our other recent Klingon guests really left nothing behind after they were disintegrated."

The eyes he'd taken would have to be disintegrated as well, of course. Qagh hated to lose any of the trophies he had just gone to so much trouble to collect. But if his crew performed up to his expectations, the sacrifice would prove more than worthwhile. *We'll have control of their ships—and their lives—soon enough,* he thought with a rueful smile.

"They know we're here, Captain!" exclaimed one of the Orion helmsmen. "We no longer have the element of surprise in our favor. Shouldn't we be retreating?"

"I have something else in mind," Qagh said in a tone that made clear that he would brook no further argument. Despite his crew's fear of the Klingons, the albino felt confident that his people would neither quibble nor complain. After all, they lived or died by his decisions, regardless of the outcome of this particular battle.

I.K.S. Klothos

"Continue firing!" Kor shouted as he retook his place in the elevated chair that dominated the center of the *Klothos*'s bustling bridge. Since there had been no time for him to attire himself for battle, he remained stripped to the waist, his many livid if superficial injuries somehow enhancing his authority as he led his men into battle yet again.

"We've lost our weapons lock on them just after beaming you back aboard," said Kat're'q, a female *bekk,* barely sparing a glance in Kor's direction as she worked at one of the starboard duty stations. "We must have lost our lock with the other transponder signals when they raised their shields."

"I don't give a *HIvje'* of warm *targ nIj* why you lost the target!" Kor exclaimed. "We know where they *were.* Some of our weapons fire *has* to have hit them, so there must be some debris out there that we can follow back to them. Find *something* that you can lock onto!"

"I have conveyed the same instructions to the *Gal'tagh* and the *QaD,*" Koloth said from the rear of the bridge. Hurghom, the *Klothos*'s chief medical officer, was doing his best to treat Koloth's broken forearm and fingers with a handheld osteoregenerator, despite the captain's adrenaline-fueled pacing. Curzon Dax was nearby as well, helping Dr. Hurghom's semi-capable assistant to patch the stab wounds and cuts on Kang, who had also insisted on coming to the bridge rather than wasting precious time in the *Klothos*'s infirmary. Kang's treatment consisted mostly of quickly sterilizing and closing the thankfully superficial wounds, then covering them with an antiseptic foam that sutured most such wounds cleanly and quickly without depriving a warrior of whatever braggable scars he may have earned.

As he watched the Trill ambassador work, Kor had to admit that he owed the young man a great deal of credit. Dax's idea of having subcutaneous subspace transponders inserted into their jaws prior to their mission to Mempa II had saved the lives of four members of the assault team. Without Dax's precautions, the entire landing party would have been butchered. The tactic had also greatly increased their chances of finding and defeating the wily albino. Kor wondered for an instant whether the idea had originated in Curzon Dax's humanoid brain or if it had come from the sentient parasite he apparently carried with him. They'd had no time to discuss this surprising revelation—or Kor's own dark secret—since they'd been beamed back aboard the *Klothos.*

"Captain Kor, we've got a lock on *several* additional signals now," the helmsman said, drawing Kor's distracted attention back to the matter at hand. "And they're coming from *our* men's transponders!"

The freebooter ship *Hegh'TlhoS*

The albino grinned at the images that filled his viewscreens. The three Klingon ships were falling right into his trap. They had expended considerable firepower shooting into the volume of space where the *Hegh'TlhoS* had been, and now they were making it clear that they had trained their sights toward the region where he had just dumped the last traces of the Klingon assault team. He felt certain that nothing remained aboard the cloaked freebooter ship that might reveal its position to the searching Klingon warships.

Qagh knew that his people remained nervous, if still obedient—after all, they were still well within weapons range of the Klingon vessels—but none of them had dared to give voice to their fears. After all, they knew as well as the albino did that as long as the ship's cloak continued to hold, they would be safe from detection on their new heading.

At least until such time as he decided to play the next card in his hand.

He hadn't forgotten the unauthorized shuttle launch that had distracted him earlier—and which might even have revealed the presence of the *Hegh'TlhoS* to the Klingons' sensors—but investigating that matter would have to wait until after he'd resolved the current crisis. Right now, Qagh knew he had to keep his attention focused tightly on exploiting his next clear opportunity to lessen the odds against him—or perhaps even to eliminate his pursuers once and for all.

"Are all torpedoes armed?" he asked, not even bothering to look over toward his ordnance chief.

"Yes, Captain," came the crisp response.

"Tell Bront to transfer all the power he can spare to the forward shields now," he said.

"And on my mark, we move."

I.K.S. Klothos

"Still nothing, Captain," the navigator said, scrutinizing the computer panels in front of him.

"It has been nearly thirty *tup*s since we last detected any traceable signal from the albino's ship," Koloth said, growling. "From the trajectory of the corpses, it is clear that the albino dumped them in great haste—just before fleeing like a whipped *targ*."

Kor nodded as he continued studying the forward viewscreen. All three of the warships had launched fusillade after fusillade into the empty space where they had first detected the presence of the albino's vessel, in addition to firing in almost every direction save directly at each other. And yet they still had found no evidence of debris from the pirate ship, no vented atmosphere, no radiation, no warp trail, and no bodies save those of their own warriors.

"He is cunning," Kor said finally. "He has waited patiently before, like a sea *pochtoQ* waiting for a *ghargh* to wriggle into its open maw. I don't believe that he has left the system."

"Then where *is* he?" Kang shouted. He had been noticeably more irritable than usual since returning to the *Klothos*. Despite Dr. Hurghom's expert but hasty medical ministrations, he seemed to be sweating profusely, as though battling a fever. "How long do you intend to wait to find him, when he may well already be on the way to his next raid?"

"I agree with Kor," Curzon Dax said, stepping forward. "The absence of any kind of warp trail at all leads me to believe that the likeliest possibility is that he is still here."

Kor watched closely to see how the other two captains were reacting to Dax's suggestion. Irrespective of whatever might be living inside him, the Trill had shown significant bravery and intelligence so far, well in excess of any of their expectations. Perhaps because of this fact, neither Koloth nor Kang reacted negatively to Dax now, although neither of the other Klingon captains seemed willing to give his supposition much credence.

"If you wish to stay *here*, Kor, then *you* certainly may do so," Koloth said, pointing toward him with his already half-healed hand. "I will return to my ship and find a way to *chase* this aberration, rather than remain idle."

"I shall do the same," Kang said. He approached one of the communication consoles and toggled open a particular channel. "*Gal'tagh*, lower shields and prepare to beam me over."

As Koloth gave a similar command to the *QaD*, Kor silently considered his options. Other than the demands of the albino's terrorist ambitions, and those imposed by his chronic medical condition, nothing about the actions of Kor's unwanted kinsman had been predictable; not only did he appear to defy the laws of nature merely by existing, he seemed to survive by defying both luck and logic as well.

Kor rose from his chair and was about to speak when a brilliant fireball erupted on the main viewer. A missile of some sort, a plasma torpedo from the look of it, had just exploded in extremely close proximity to Kang's vessel, the *QaD*, blowing away much of the *K't'inga*-class battle cruiser's starboard wing in the process.

Perhaps half a heartbeat later, the *Gal'tagh* exploded in a massive blast, plasma and atmosphere igniting and reigniting in cascading bursts as hull metal and internal components arced away from the conflagration in a shower of tiny fragments.

The shockwave produced by the *Gal'tagh*'s sudden

demise rocked the *Klothos,* but in the one or two *lup*s that it took the three Klingon captains and Dax to regain their footing, the albino's ship hove up from below the rapidly expanding debris cloud where the *Gal'tagh* had been mere moments earlier.

Qagh's vessel had barely cleared the debris field's fluid perimeter when it began to slowly re-cloak, its image shimmering like a very deadly mirage. In the last moment before the freebooter ship vanished from sight, Kor saw its engine nacelles ignite as it prepared to go into warp, fleeing from all the torture and murder and sabotage its cowardly master had wrought.

Kor was barely aware that he was automatically yelling orders to fire on the albino's ship, even as the cacophony created by alarm klaxons, and his busy bridge crew, and Koloth's blood-chilling howl to *Sto-Vo-Kor* on behalf of his abruptly slain subordinates, all competed for his attention.

With a calm born of countless previous life-and-death struggles undertaken in the unforgiving cold of space, Kor assessed the tactical situation. The *Gal'tagh* was destroyed, though its captain still lived; the *QaD* was crippled, but was probably repairable; and the *Klothos* was altogether unharmed.

He purposely saved my *ship,* Kor thought, his rage rising well past anything he had ever experienced before. He actually felt shooting pains in his heart.

He saved my ship because it carries the markings of the House of Ngoj.

And he intends to take that house back.

TWENTY-NINE

Early 2290 (the Year of Kahless 915,
late in the month of *Doqath*)

I.K.S. Klothos

Dax expected the tensions between the three Klingon captains to bring them to physical blows at just about any moment. Seated in the *Klothos*'s surprisingly spacious captain's mess, he watched in silence as a thoroughly healed-looking Kang pointed an accusing finger across the slate-gray tabletop at Kor. Koloth, who also appeared to be recovered from the physical wounds he'd sustained at the albino's hands, simply sat nearby, quietly glaring at the still bruised-faced Kor from across the wreckage of the countless eel-like bodies they had all just eaten. Dax had partaken of the alien meal as well, despite his lack of enthusiasm for the live and energetically wiggling creatures.

"You've known all along that the albino was your kinsman," Kang snarled, rising from his chair. "Haven't you?"

"What of it?" said Kor, also getting to his feet. Dax felt his stomach lurch, only in part because of what he'd just eaten.

"What of it?" Koloth replied with icy mockery, while

remaining in his seat. "He could challenge you for control of your House. He might even succeed, should he prove wily enough."

"The affairs of my House need not concern *either* of you," Kor said. Glaring at Dax, he added, "Nor are they the business of any outworlder."

"It is a matter of the gravest concern for *all* of us, Kor," Kang said, the knuckles of both his large hands supporting him as he leaned forward across the table. "My people, and Koloth's as well, came out here to work alongside *your* crew in the search for the albino. Koloth's crew have given their lives for this purpose. Until now I had believed we were all acting on behalf of the Empire—without regard to the power or prominence of any particular House."

Kor's eyes narrowed. When he spoke, his voice was very quiet, which Dax regarded as an extremely bad sign.

"Kang. Do you accuse me of putting the fortunes of my own House ahead of those of the entire Klingon Empire?"

Kang answered coolly, but without hesitation. "I *do*, Kor."

Koloth finally rose and took several deliberate steps away from the conference table. Though he arguably had more reason than anyone else present to be angry with Kor— Koloth had lost both his ship and his crew, after all—he merely leaned against the far wall, folding his arms before him in a gesture of disdain, evidently content to watch what Dax feared was about to unfold between the other two Klingon captains.

He knows how foolish this is, but he's not going to lift a finger to stop it, Dax thought. He was horrified not only by the notion that Kang and Kor might kill one another, but also that in doing so they might destroy whatever store of trust he had built up between their Empire and his Federation over the past several days.

The smooth foreheads of the two old friends had both

become corrugated with rage, while a third, possessed of a skull whose prominent ridges recalled those of the great Kahless himself, looked on.

Dax knew he had to do something, even if that something placed him between a pair of erupting volcanoes.

Two right hands reached for daggers.

Someone shouted *"Mevyap!"* in badly accented Klingonese.

Both right hands froze in mid-motion. The daggers remained in their scabbards, though tense fingers hovered nearby. No one else spoke. Three pairs of dark, hooded eyes sought Dax out, pinning him down with angry curiosity. Dax felt like an insect about to be consigned to an entomologist's killing jar.

He realized only then that he, Dax, had been the source of the badly articulated Klingon cry—and that he'd used a term he had picked up in the engine room of this very ship.

Another voice, a wisp of memory centered as much down in his belly as up in his hindbrain, spoke, using words that had to be intended for Dax's ears alone.

"Well, say *something, dummy,"* Emony said.

Sound advice for a diplomat, he thought. He took a single deep breath and continued over the precipice, though he supposed he'd already crossed the point of no return when he'd first entered Klingon space.

"The great Houses of the Council are balanced on a *d'k tahg*'s edge right now," Dax said as the three Klingons continued watching him closely. "Particularly with regard to whether the Empire should seek peace with the Federation, or renewed war. Any sudden, unexpected power shift within or between any of those Houses could decide the course of history with far greater finality than any number of Korvat conferences could. As long as the albino remains free to disrupt our governments' efforts at détente, the future stands a very good chance of turning out very badly."

"You have made my point for me, Dax," Kang rumbled.

Dax shook his head emphatically. "Then I must not have made *my* point particularly well. I'm trying to make you understand that the political stakes are just too high for you to be allowed to place the future in jeopardy simply because you're feeling slighted. That is both petty and unworthy of Klingon warriors."

"Take care, stripling," Koloth said as he took a single ominous step toward the table. "Kor should not have kept his kinship to the albino a secret from us. At the very least, it has cost me my command."

"That may be so," Dax said. He gestured toward Kang and Kor. "But if these two end up killing each other over Kor's family secret, then it soon won't be a secret from *any-one.* And what do you suppose will happen *then*?"

Three pairs of dark eyes regarded him with pensive sullenness. None of the souls behind those eyes, however, seemed eager to argue against his point.

"Until the albino himself decides to do something irrevocable with this information, it's in the best interests of both the Empire and the Federation that we all work to keep it from spreading any further," Dax said, pressing his advantage. Addressing Kang and Koloth specifically, he continued. "I know that Kor can trust you both to keep the albino's lineage a secret, just as I trust the three of you to respect *my* secret." He placed a hand against his abdomen, where symbiont and humanoid had joined to become a single, entirely new creature. "The three of you want to do right by your Empire, because you're all men of honor—even when you're behaving like petulant schoolchildren."

"You dare much," Kor said in a tone that closely matched the one he'd used to address Kang just prior to their abortive knife fight.

Uh-oh, Dax thought, half expecting Kor's thirsty blade to emerge after all. *Sarek always said I tend to talk too much for my own good.*

"He *does* dare much," Kang said, addressing his fellow Klingons. "But for the right cause."

Koloth nodded, and the sudden appearance of his icy grin might have chilled the blood of even the most battle-hardened Romulan. Addressing Kang and Kor, he said, "His personal observations aren't wrong, either. Particularly the part about the two of you being petulant schoolchildren."

I think I said all three *of you were petulant schoolchildren*, Dax thought, knowing better than to push his luck by saying it out loud. Instead, he said, "But schoolchildren who fought like warriors against the Romulans almost twenty years ago in the Briar Patch conflict."

Dax watched the three Klingon captains carefully as they considered his words. All four men were now engulfed in a silence that was quickly transforming the almost unbearable tension in the room into something that felt nearly companionable.

"Klach D'Kel Brakt," Kor said quietly, interrupting the moment.

"Excuse me?" Dax said.

"It was called the Battle of Klach D'Kel Brakt. Not 'the Briar Patch conflict.' "

"Of course," Dax said. He allowed the silence to descend again, at least for a few moments.

"Now that we've settled that," he said at length, "the four of us really ought to get back to work."

And to Dax's gratified surprise, they did.

Stardate 9014.6 (Gregorian date: January 6, 2290)

U.S.S. Excelsior

Sarek sat silently at the conference table in the observation lounge, accompanied only by Commanders Sulu and Cutler.

Right on schedule, the junior ambassador delivered his daily report via the subspace bands.

Like Sulu and Cutler, Sarek listened attentively, saying nothing during the youthful Trill's harrowing tale of capture by and escape from the assassin of Korvat; of the unexpected destruction of the *I.K.S. Gal'tagh;* and of the launch of a mysterious cloaked shuttlepod from the perpetrator's ship—an act that appeared to have been carried out without the freebooter's knowledge by a rogue element within his own crew.

About halfway through this recitation, Sarek had become convinced that his decision not to put an early and decisive stop to Dax's Klingon sojourn might one day rank among the bigger mistakes of his lengthy diplomatic career.

He decided that the time had come to put that error right.

I.K.S. Klothos

At first, Dax was certain that he must have misunderstood the ambassador's words. After all, it wouldn't have been the first time that random interference had garbled a signal making a near-instantaneous transit of the parsecs-deep ocean of night that separated him from *Excelsior.*

"I said you are ordered to return immediately to Excelsior *for a detailed debriefing,"* said the dour Vulcan, who sat at a conference table beside *Excelsior*'s acting captain and first officer, both of whom watched Dax in silence. *"The situation you have just described is far too volatile."*

Dax turned toward Kor, who sat in his command chair, flanked by Kang and Koloth while a complement of six junior officers paused in their duties, plainly curious as to how Dax was going to handle this not-insignificant setback. In order to allay any lingering fears his hosts might have had that his mission in Klingon space might involve espio-

nage, Dax had agreed early on to deliver his daily reports to
Ambassador Sarek and Commander Sulu in the presence of
either Kor, Kang, or Koloth.

Now all three of the Klingon captains were studying him
with barely restrained amusement.

*Sarek is going to make me look like a weakling in front of
people who respect strength above all else,* Dax thought. *As
well as discipline and the chain of command.*

He knew he was between a rock and a hard place here,
and would have to move very carefully to avoid being
squashed flat.

"Respectfully, Mister Ambassador," Dax said, "I believe
I should remain aboard the *Klothos* precisely *because* the
situation here is so volatile."

Unfortunately, Sarek remained true to precedent and
showed no willingness to give ground. *"There has already
been too much death and injury on this mission. The dangers you are facing would be better assigned to more . . .
experienced personnel."*

Though he knew it would do no good to display anger to
a Vulcan, he was suddenly finding it almost unbearably difficult to avoid doing just that. "Ambassador Sarek, after the
past five days, who else in the entire Federation Diplomatic
Corps has as much practical experience dealing directly
with Klingons as *I* do?"

Across the gulf of light-years, the Vulcan's gaze held
Dax's fast, like a pair of tractor beams. Silence stretched.

*"I do not relish the prospect of having to explain to the Trill
government your death in some remote part of Klingon space,"*
Sarek said at length, pointedly evading Dax's question.

"That is *my* decision, Mister Ambassador."

"But my *responsibility. And need I remind you that your
career is no less at risk than is your safety?"*

Dax knew he had to concede the ambassador's last point.
On the other hand, he had doubtless placed his career in

jeopardy the moment he'd disregarded Starfleet's general order to stay out of Klingon space in the first place.

"I will arrange your transportation back to Federation space, Curzon Dax," Kor said, startling Dax out of his reverie. He turned toward the Klingon captain, who was regarding him with an air of cool appraisal. Kang and Koloth did likewise as silence enfolded the room, disturbed only by the persistent chirping and humming of the control center's various banks of consoles and instruments.

They'll think me a coward and a weakling if I leave before we've finished our business with the albino, Dax thought. *I might hold on to my safety by doing as I'm told. Maybe I'll even get to keep my career.*

But in the eyes of these three men, I will never have any honor. And if he'd learned one thing about the Klingon Empire over the last several eventful days, it was that honor was the true coin of the realm here.

Considering the rickety condition of the narrow bridge he'd just begun to build between the Federation and the Klingon Empire, Dax knew that only one valid option was available to him.

"Thank you, Captain Kor," he said. "But I don't wish to leave the *Klothos* while so much of our mutual business remains unfinished."

"Very well," Kor said, nodding. The expressions of all three Klingon commanders remained neutral, but Dax thought he saw a faint glint of approval somewhere in the depths of each man's stony gaze.

Dax turned back toward the forward viewer, from which Sarek and the two Starfleet officers regarded him with a far less sanguine mien. He addressed the three of them and hoped he wasn't about to deliver his final farewell.

"Live long and prosper, Ambassador. Commander. Captain."

Dax then made a quick slashing gesture in the direction

of the *bekk* who was running the comm station; the junior
officer responded immediately by cutting off the channel.

Now the mreker *scat's finally hit the ventilator,* Dax
thought, and idly wondered whether the Klingon commanders might consider letting him use them as references for
future employment. . . .

U.S.S. Excelsior

The monitor atop the conference table went abruptly dark
for a moment before resuming its default display of the UFP
logo.

"Well, I can't say that exactly surprises me," Cutler said,
turning toward Sarek. "Your junior ambassador has been
something of a loose cannon since this mission began."

Sulu was forced to agree, though he really couldn't fault
the young Trill's instincts—even if he couldn't endorse
them officially.

Sarek nodded, his expression a study in Vulcan stoicism.
"You have no idea. In all my life, I have had only one student who was more difficult."

As much as the ambassador's remark intrigued him, Sulu
did his best to stay focused on the business at hand. "I may
be able to justify bending Starfleet's order against entering Klingon space long enough to drag your brash young
protégé back here," he said as he rose to his feet, followed a
moment later by the ambassador and Cutler. "After all, the
launch of that cloaked shuttle from the albino's ship could
certainly be interpreted as a clear and present danger to
worlds on our side of the Klingon border."

"Thank you, Captain," Sarek said as he finished smooth-
ing his ornate diplomatic robes and folded his hands before
him. "But that will not be necessary. Such overreactions are

generally counterproductive. Besides, Mister Dax's instincts are generally correct."

"Even when they've led him to defy a superior's orders, and maybe even violate interstellar law in the process?" Cutler asked as Sarek led the way toward the observation deck's exit.

Sarek paused in the open doorway for a moment to consider her strident but undoubtedly rhetorical question. "Under such unalterably unfavorable circumstances as these, we can only hope that Mister Dax's judgment proves to be *particularly* reliable.

"And, of course, we must wait."

And waiting, Sulu thought as he followed the Vulcan out into the corridor, *has got to be the most damned difficult thing of all.*

THIRTY

Curzon Dax could almost feel both Tobin and Torias looking over his shoulder while he worked on calibrating the new sensor configurations. He was thankful, at least, that his two most technical-minded predecessors-in-symbiosis hadn't whispered encouragements into his ear as he'd imagined Emony had done a few hours earlier. *When this is finally all over and I'm safely back home on Trill, maybe I'd better have a long talk with Doctor Dareel,* he thought. Accessing the memories of previous hosts was one thing; hearing them talk to him like phantoms perched on his shoulder was something else entirely.

He had spent the past five hours toiling nonstop alongside Chief Engineer Q'Lujj to refine the search for whatever vestiges of the albino's warp trail might remain detectable to the sensor equipment available to them. Thanks to narrow-band subspace bursts, *Excelsior*'s considerable computer resources had assisted greatly with the signal-processing chores.

Dax had been tasked with helping Q'Lujj increase the sensitivity of the combined sensor capacity of both of the remaining Klingon warships. The crews had accomplished this largely by increasing the distance between the *Klothos* and the *QaD,* whose respective navigational officers were now keeping station nearly one tenth of a parsec apart while maintaining real-time subspace network links between the computers and sensors of both vessels, as well as with those of distant *Excelsior.*

After Q'Lujj finally threw the switch on this hastily improvised system—Dax had dubbed the process "tandem parallax triangulation"—Dax found the initial results both surprising and satisfying.

"That's a warp trail," Dax said, using his right index finger to trace the orange-outlined frequency profile as it appeared on the monitor at the engine-room station he was running next to Q'Lujj's console. "It's faint, but it's definitely there. And it matches the albino's engine profile out to six decimal places."

Q'Lujj grunted a brusque acknowledgment as he squinted at the data that scrolled across his own station's displays. "But there's still no sign of the cloaked auxiliary vessel that his people launched," he said.

Leave it to Q'Lujj to focus on the uninvited insects instead of the picnic, Dax thought. *Then again, maybe that's one of the qualities that makes him such a competent engineer.*

Dax entered the command that transferred the new heading data forward to the *Klothos*'s command center, then looked up again at his perpetually scowling colleague.

"I think we might get an opportunity to ask the albino about that in person soon enough," he said.

Because the *Klothos* was significantly faster than the still-damaged *QaD,* Kang had remained aboard her along with

Kor and Koloth, just in case an opportunity to confront the albino arose too quickly to afford the *QaD*—and her captain—a sufficiently fair chance at making the kill.

When Kang reached the *Klothos*'s command deck just prior to the climax of the chase, he was unsurprised to see that Koloth and Dax had already joined Kor there. Kang noted, also without much surprise, that Koloth was his usual cold, distant self, staring quietly into the central viewer's image of the vast but steadily diminishing volume of star-strewn blackness that lay between the *Klothos* and her prey; though Koloth had lost much on this voyage, he had never been given to demonstrations of emotion—sometimes even when his own knife was striking at his enemy's heart.

Kang was momentarily taken aback, however, by the easy camaraderie that seemed to have developed between Kor and the young Trill diplomat. It was difficult to imagine a more mismatched pair becoming friends, although Kang himself could not deny the increasing degree of trust he himself was feeling for Dax. Kang's surprise passed, however, when he considered what Kor and Dax had in common, despite the all-but-unbridgeable gulf of mutual alienness that still separated them.

Both these men have become used to carrying burdensome secrets, Kang thought. *Secrets that only now are beginning to see the light of day.*

With Kor, those secrets had proved to be vexing and troublesome things, and not merely for Kor himself. Dax's secrets differed, at least, in that they had concealed an extensive storehouse of remembered knowledge that had made the young Trill useful far beyond his apparent years. Perhaps decades, or even whole lifetimes, of stored experience.

No longer able to contain his curiosity about such things, Kang approached Dax and gestured toward the young man's belly.

"Tell me, Dax. What is the exact nature of your joined existence?"

The Trill seemed unsurprised by the question. "I was beginning to wonder when one of you would ask me that question straight out."

"After all we've been through together so far, you can hardly blame us for being curious," Koloth said.

Kor grunted in agreement. "Especially when *you* have become privy to so much that had once been secret—even among us Klingons."

The half-dozen or so control-center personnel who were present busied themselves going about their various tasks, all of them studiously ignoring the conversation in their midst, in accordance with long-standing Klingon traditions regarding the affairs of one's social betters.

Dax nodded to Kor, conceding his point. "All right. But you have to understand that my—Curzon's—symbiosis is only about five years old, so I'm still finding my way as a joined Trill. But it goes essentially like this: the Trill diplomat you know as Curzon Dax is a combination of the man you see standing before you—Curzon Antrani—and an extremely long-lived symbiotic organism called Dax. The Dax symbiont is sentient and vermiform, and carries within it the memories of all who have preceded me as the creature's host. After the Curzon part of me is dead, *my* memories will in turn live on in the symbiont's next host."

Koloth sneered faintly as he considered Dax's explanation, as though repelled by the idea of a joined creature. Kor, on the other hand, looked unabashedly fascinated.

Kang wasn't quite certain how he himself felt about the notion, though he certainly couldn't deny the respect he felt for Dax's many obvious talents, regardless of the means by which they might have been obtained.

He wondered briefly how much of that respect Dax's Federation deserved to receive; he decided that the answer to this question would depend greatly upon Curzon Dax's actions during the forthcoming battle with the albino.

Kor mirrored Kang's gesture toward Dax's abdomen. "So just how many others are in there right now?" he said.

"Six, including Curzon," Dax said quickly, then hesitated as an odd expression crossed his features, as if for a brief instant he doubted his own answer. For that fleeting moment, the young diplomat appeared as callow and inexperienced as Kang had first mistook him to be back on Korvat.

"Are you unwell, Curzon Dax?" Kor said.

The Trill looked bemused. "I'm fine. Just a little vertigo, I think."

Kor scowled good-naturedly. "The creature within you, no doubt. Perhaps it sees Koloth's ugliness through your eyes."

"Hab SoSlI' Quch," Koloth muttered, and punctuated his response with a rude hand gesture.

Had Koloth's utterance come from a member of Kor's crew, a lethal duel with *d'k tahg*s would have been required, by custom if not by specific Klingon Defense Force regulations. But since all three Klingon captains were at least theoretically social equals, Kor merely threw his head back and laughed.

"Yes, Koloth," Kor said around a deep chortle. "My mother does *indeed* have a smooth forehead. And yet she is still not as ugly as you."

Kang and Dax joined in Kor's laughter roughly simultaneously. Koloth might as well have been one of the many scowling, silent statues that stood as sentinels in the Hall of Heroes back on Qo'noS.

A flashing amber light on the helm console suddenly caught Kang's eye. Further questioning of Dax would have to wait until a more propitious time.

"Is the target vessel within the reach of our long-range sensors?" Kor said as all trace of hilarity abruptly vanished from the room, like a warship disappearing behind its cloak.

"It should be by now, Captain," said one of Kor's junior officers. She was a female *bekk* whose impressively sharpened teeth and highly textured *HemQuch* forehead made her appear capable of successfully taking on any three of her male *QuchHa'* counterparts. "But the ship still appears to be running under cloak. Our only means of detection remains the vessel's warp trail, as imaged over the long-range network we've established with the *QaD* and the *yuQjIjDIvI'* vessel."

"Has the target detected *us* yet?" Koloth asked.

"Our own cloak remains engaged. The target vessel has made no evasive maneuvers nor changed its speed or heading in over a *kilaan*," the *bekk* said. "Assuming we aren't detected, we will enter weapons range in a mere thirty *tups*, perhaps sooner."

"Very good," Kor said. "Advise me immediately of any changes."

"Yes, sir."

"I heard the name of the albino's vessel when we were aboard her," Kang said, staring hard into the impenetrable black void displayed on the forward viewer as though he might compel the freebooter's ship to appear by sheer force of will. "It was called the *Hegh'TlhoS.*"

"'Dead'?" Dax said, sounding tentative as he attempted to translate the *tlhIngan* word roots of the proper name into the language the Earthers called Federation Standard.

"*Hegh'TlhoS* means 'almost dead,'" Kor said. "'Almost, but not quite.'"

"I like Dax's definition better," Kang said.

Koloth released an icy smile. "Then let us make it so."

THIRTY-ONE

Back in San Francisco, the city where he was born, it was 4:17 A.M. But Hikaru Sulu wasn't at all certain what time it was in the corridors of power on Qo'noS. Moments ago, Janice Rand had called him urgently from the bridge, interrupting his fitful slumber. Now Sulu was hurriedly pulling on his uniform jacket, hoping to make himself relatively presentable to his VIP caller.

Sulu sat behind his desk and keyed the bridge intercom button. "Put him through now, Janice," he said.

A moment after Rand acknowledged his order, the screen on Sulu's desk flickered to life, first displaying the laurel-leaf-framed-starmap symbol of the Federation, followed by the red-black-and-gold trefoil of the Klingon Empire, which was quickly replaced by the scowling visage of an elderly but extraordinarily tough-looking, ridge-headed Klingon.

"Commander Sulu, I presume?" the Klingon asked, an undercurrent of something akin to annoyance clearly evident in his tone.

"Yes, Chancellor Kesh," Sulu responded. "I appreciate your taking the time to contact me."

Kesh raised an eyebrow. *"I might not have done so, Commander. But you appear to have friends possessed of enough influence to make it unwise for me to simply ignore you altogether."*

Sulu tried to conceal his surprise at this revelation. Who had intervened on his behalf, and with the highest official of one of the Federation's oldest adversary nations? *Maybe one of Ambassador Kamarag's political attachés down in sickbay has recovered enough to start pulling some very special strings,* he thought. *Or maybe Sarek has more pull with the Klingons than anybody ever realized.*

"I wanted to be certain that the members of the Klingon High Council—and *you,* in particular—had gotten *all* of the news about the Korvat bombing and everything that's happened since," Sulu said. "And while KDF captains Kor, Koloth, and Kang are preoccupied with tracking down the man responsible for the attack, I wished to make sure that you were kept apprised of everything my people have been doing to assist with the search effort."

"Commendable," Kesh said, nodding and stroking his beard, which was knotted in a trio of braids. *"So, Commander—inform me."*

For the next twelve minutes, Sulu spelled out as many details about the attack on Korvat, its aftermath, and the albino saboteur—whom he now knew was named Qagh, thanks to Curzon Dax's periodic reports—as he could. Although he knew he was verging on breaking protocol, he stepped right to the edge in providing details that might be considered proprietary or classified. *If we don't start trusting them with the truth, then what was this whole Korvat peace conference for?* he thought, though he had little doubt that certain Starfleet brass wouldn't see it that way.

"Sto-Vo-Kor *will no doubt shake to its foundations when*

the crew of the Gal'tagh *arrives at its gates,"* the chancellor said in a wistful yet martial tone once Sulu had finished. *"So, the* Klothos *and the* QaD *will continue the hunt for this . . . Qagh?"*

"Yes, Chancellor," Sulu said. "As soon as they complete whatever repairs they can make to the *QaD* on the fly. But their sensors cannot track the fugitive's ship as easily as *Excelsior*'s can."

"If, indeed, the pirate can be tracked at all. He does seem to have eluded every pursuer for decades now," Kesh said, revealing what sounded like a sneaking admiration for the bloodthirsty outlaw. *"And what about this cloaked shuttle that was launched from the freebooter's ship?"*

"Nobody has any idea why it was launched, Chancellor," Sulu said. "Or what its target might be. According to Ambassador Dax's report, the albino seemed as surprised as the Klingon captains were when it happened. But I have to point out that Qagh's reaction could have been just a ruse. The shuttle could be carrying one of the albino's genetically engineered bioweapons straight toward some Klingon or Federation world even as we speak. It could even be targeting Qo'noS itself."

Kesh's dark eyes narrowed in apparent contemplation of Sulu's words. After half a minute or so of thoughtful silence, the Klingon chancellor finally spoke again. *"It would seem, Commander, that your purpose in telling me all of this is not solely to aid the Klingon Empire. You obviously have a personal stake in this matter. Qagh killed your captain, as well as other members of your crew. Doubtless you want revenge, and you further wish to save face for your Federation in response to the attack against the Korvat conference."*

"I won't deny—" Sulu started to protest, only to be interrupted.

"You don't need *to deny anything, Commander,"* Kesh

said. *"Honor, along with its defense and maintenance, are concepts as ingrained into the Klingon psyche as breathing and mating, either of which are arguably of less importance than honor. I fully understand and support your position. However . . ."* The chancellor paused, apparently gathering his thoughts.

Here's where the politics get in the way of simply doing the right thing, Sulu thought, trying not to allow his face to reveal his immediately crestfallen spirit.

"However," Kesh resumed, *"I will not allow Excelsior to advance into Klingon space any further than the Korvat system. At least not before the matter can be put to a full vote of the High Council, and that has not yet occurred. And the High Council will first wish to decide whether or not to allow the interrupted Korvat talks to continue."*

"I understand your position, Chancellor," Sulu said. "But consider everything that this *one man* has destroyed over the past few days. And if he really is using that cloaked shuttle to attack the worlds beyond Korvat, then think of how much more damage and destruction he could cause. Respectfully, Chancellor, no one on the High Council would want to allow that to happen. Please at least let me help look for the shuttle, to prevent that."

Kesh nodded soberly, his eyes narrowing as if to warn Sulu not to continue. *"I will press the Council to speed up its timetable for a vote, Commander,"* he said, his tone making clear that he would brook no further discussion on the matter. *"But that's the best I can do, especially with so many Council members currently away from the First City celebrating the Festival of* Qu'batlh. *In the meantime, the Klingon Defense Force will be put on full alert status. I am certain that it will prove more than able to protect any significant target within the Empire's boundaries."*

Kesh's face softened slightly for a moment. *"Thank you for your candor in this matter, Commander. It will* not *be forgotten. But for now, however, you will have to continue to wait."*

A moment later the monitor went black, a heartbeat or two before the blue-and-white emblem of the UFP returned.

Sulu let out a low growl of frustration. *I'm no better off than I was before,* he thought, feeling no small amount of bitterness at the failure of his gambit. *And I let out information that might come back to haunt me someday.*

Although he had little to do now other than wait through the remainder of the long night, Sulu knew that sleep would be a long time coming.

THIRTY-TWO

"How far are we from the H'Atoria system?" Qagh asked.

"Another four *leS*," Kurga said from behind the helm console. "Three, perhaps, if we drop our cloak and divert additional power to the warp drive."

Four leS, Nej thought, worried that the time it would take Qo'noS to turn on its axis four times might be beyond his employer's physical capacity, not to mention his patience. He turned toward Qagh, who was standing in front of his raised command chair, apparently far too restless and nervous to remain in one spot for any significant length of time.

He could only hope that whatever biomedical resources might await them at H'Atoria wouldn't send the albino into another disappointed rage—and that the next round of injections would calm the pirate chieftain's rebellious cells, tissues, and organs.

"When we get there, Nej, I'll expect you to get a survey

team together," Qagh said, wiping the sweat from his striated, chalk-white brow. "I will lead it."

Nej could see how unsteady the albino already looked and frowned. Then he nodded toward the much younger, much stronger Klingon who stood monitoring the long-range scanners on the cramped control room's port side. "Why not send Choq down instead?"

Qagh wasted no time considering his response. "Because Choq is nowhere near as well motivated as I am to find what needs to be found."

If Choq was insulted, he betrayed no sign of it. Instead, a look of surprise creased his smooth features as he sat behind one of the scanner consoles. "We're being pursued, Captain. It may be one of the Klingon Defense Force vessels we encountered earlier. Sensors show he'll come within weapons range in under a *kilaan*."

Qagh's energies seemed to rebound at this news, though his foul mood showed little improvement as he stomped quickly across the small control room to Choq's station. "How did he get so close to us without being detected?"

Choq shrugged, long used to his employer's mercurial and frequently abusive temperament. "Our pursuer must be running under cloak, as we are."

Nej found that perplexing. "If he's cloaked, then how did you manage to detect him at all?"

"I mined many of the surrounding systems with passive sensing equipment and hundreds of small subspace relays long ago," Qagh said as he entered a string of manual commands into one of the consoles. "Now that they've detected the ship that's following us, perhaps they can positively identify it."

"But how could they have seen through our cloak?" Nej said.

"Perhaps the same way we saw through theirs," Qagh said. "Or maybe our engine repairs were sufficiently imperfect so as to leave a hard radiation trail they were able to follow."

"The pursuing ship's warp signature matches one of the Klingon warships we evaded earlier," Choq said.

"The *Klothos,* no doubt," Qagh said. He smiled grimly as he turned toward the forward screen, squinting as if hoping to tease the invisible approaching vessel into plain view. "My kinsman and his friends are a persistent lot, I'll give them that. I may have underestimated them."

"We destroyed one of your kinsman's ships, Qagh," Nej said, trying to sound hopeful. "We don't know that he wasn't aboard it when it blew apart."

The albino shook his head. "Being a survivor runs in the family." He turned toward Choq. "Drop our cloak so we can increase our speed. Then lose them."

Choq blinked in undisguised skepticism. "Lose them *how,* Captain? There's no way we can outrun that ship for any length of time, even with the cloak down."

"You won't have to evade them for very long," Qagh said. "At least not once you get us a little closer to Qul Tuq. I noticed that our present course takes us very close to the system's outer belt of ice bodies."

Nej didn't particularly like what he was hearing, though he couldn't see a better alternative at the moment. "Qul Tuq? You'll lead him right to one of our best safe houses, Qagh. That's a rather expensive risk—"

"Facing a Klingon warship that's not susceptible to another sneak attack is far riskier," the albino said, interrupting. "Besides, we still have other safe houses. And we can count on Qul Tuq herself to even the odds for us."

If she doesn't cook us and devour us before we've reached safety in the eye of the storm, Nej thought, recalling why Qagh and his organization used this particular safe house so infrequently. He wondered if even the spectral helmsman of the Barge of the Dead possessed sufficient courage to face the *veqlargh*-forsaken hellhole the *Hegh'TlhoS* was about to enter.

He could only hope that the commander of the pursuing vessel would demonstrate the good sense to break off his pursuit once Qagh's destination became clear.

"Dropping cloak," Choq said, nodding as his large but surprisingly nimble fingers quickly entered commands into his console. "And we're now on course for the second planet in the Qul Tuq system."

Nej watched as Qagh strode toward the hatchway in the aft section of the room. "Come with me, Nej. I may need your help to present our pursuer with a proper welcome."

Nej followed Qagh through the hatch and into the narrow corridor that terminated at the entrance to the albino's small but efficient personal workspace. He watched as his employer walked to the table at the back of the room and touched the security-recognition pad built into the top of the large black case that sat there. The hinged metal lid responded by folding backward with a faint mechanical whirring sound.

Four stoppered glass vials, each one about as long as a man's hand and perhaps half as wide, stood upright inside the open case, held by delicate metal clamps.

"Nothing says 'welcome' quite like a lethal, custom-made retrovirus," Qagh said, smiling a smile that chilled Nej's bones.

I.K.S. Klothos

Dax waited anxiously while another half hour passed uneventfully. *Too* uneventfully, he thought more than once as the members of Kor's ever-efficient bridge crew continued stalking their prey in silence.

"He knows we're coming," Koloth said, looking up

from the station he had taken over during the chase. "He's changed course, and has begun accelerating away from us."

I really, really *hate being right all the time,* Dax thought as he did his best to stay out of the way of the frenetically busy bridge personnel; they had suddenly begun moving at double time in response to the newly altered tactical situation.

"Ghuy'cha'!" Kang said sourly from the station beside Koloth's. "How did he detect us?"

Kor remained seated in the command chair at the raised center of the control room. Scowling as he leaned forward, he said, "Does it matter? Pursue them, helm, and intercept. Drop our cloak and ready all weapons."

A chorus of terse acknowledgments rebounded across the room as the crew hastened to perform their various tasks. Dax could feel a subtle shift in both tension and vibration in the deck beneath his boots, signaling that the ship had abruptly changed both its speed and heading, executing a hard turn at hundreds of times the speed of light.

"The albino cannot outrun us," Kor said, leaning forward in his chair and staring into the gradually changing stellar panorama arrayed before him.

Koloth grunted in terse agreement. "He appears to be aware of that now. He has deactivated his cloak, no doubt for the benefit of his engines."

As if taking Koloth's words as a cue, the image of a beat-up, heavily modified freighter appeared on the central viewer.

Dax frowned. "Something's not right about this."

Kor's gleaming, battle-keen gaze struck him like a spear. "What do you mean?"

"He must know that he can't outrun you," Dax said, pointing toward the motley vessel on the screen. "So why isn't he at least *trying* to hide?"

"Because if he continues on his present heading, he won't

need a cloak to hide himself," Kang said, looking down at the data on his console. "He is on a course for Qul Tuq."

"Qul Tuq?" Dax asked. He wasn't embarrassed to admit that his knowledge of the Klingon Empire's star charts left much to be desired. "That means 'house of fire,' doesn't it?"

"A suitably dramatic name, don't you think?" Kor said, a death's-head grin splitting his swarthy face. "It comes from the title of one of our most highly regarded operas. I'd call that a good omen for the glorious battle that lies ahead."

Dax wasn't so sure about that. Moving toward Kang, he said, "Isn't 'only a fool fights in a burning house' one of the Klingon people's most revered proverbs?"

Kang answered only with scowling, brooding silence, prompting Dax to recall the Klingon aphorism about revenge being a dish that is best served cold.

Dax turned back toward Koloth and Kor. "What else can you tell me about Qul Tuq?"

"Your scientists would probably describe it as a neutron star," Koloth said. "Though it is a neutron star of a most peculiar type. Qul Tuq possesses a magnetic field roughly a quadrillion times stronger than those that act as shields to most inhabited worlds, such as Qo'noS."

"Then it's a magnetar," Dax said, recalling Audrid's studies on the subject. The almost unimaginably intense magnetic fields created by such dead, ultradense stars actually slow their rotation, creating surface "starquakes" that release potent showers of intense radiation, ranging from gamma rays to delta rays to berthold radiation all the way down to the less exotic, if no less spectacular, ion storms. He moved toward one of the bridge computer terminals, filling the time that seemed to stretch between the initial course change and eventual interception by reading further on the topic of Qul Tuq in particular, and Klingon magnetars in general.

"Approaching the inner system," the *bekk* at the helm station reported a short time later. "The stellar magnetic field is already pushing our shields close to their limits. And there's a lot of debris and ion stórm activity all around us as well."

Of course, Dax thought. *All the better for a pirate ship to hide in.*

The deck suddenly rocked beneath his feet, heaving him violently into a nearby unoccupied console; he clutched at its edge to avoid toppling all the way to the deck.

"Meteoroids, Captain," said the hulking young officer who manned the tactical station. Dax was relieved to hear that they hadn't fallen victim to yet another sneak attack.

"Reinforce the shields!" Kor shouted.

"Shields are failing, Captain," the tactical officer replied in a rumbling voice. "The more closely we approach Qul Tuq, the more such difficulties we will experience."

Dax didn't need to be told that without the constant protection of the shield generators, the magnetar's intense magnetic field could very quickly and efficiently fry every system aboard the ship, including life support.

Kor slammed his clenched fist onto the arm of his command chair. "Q'Lujj! All emergency power to shields and weapons systems!"

The chief engineer's voice came over the intercom, already sounding weary. *"Understood, Captain. But life support may become compromised."*

"Maintaining life support means nothing if we fail to maintain honor," Kor said before snapping the channel closed.

Dax wondered how long two lungsful of honor would sustain him once the magnetar out there finished immolating the ship's electronic guts.

"Keep the enemy in your sights," Kor said to the tactical officer, who nodded stoically.

"The albino's vessel is headed for the second planet in

the system," Kang said, looking up from one of the scanners adjacent to the main tactical console.

"The reason for that should be no mystery," Koloth said.

Kor raised an eyebrow. "Oh?"

"The planet is a dense, metal-rich world with a circumference several times that of Qo'noS. Consequently it produces an appreciable magnetic field of its own, which cancels out much of the influence of Qul Tuq, at least locally."

"The surface gravity would have to make such a place uninhabitable," Kang said.

"No doubt," Kor agreed. "So the albino will probably seek refuge on one of the planet's moons rather than on its surface."

"Closing to weapons range, Captain," the tactical officer said.

Kor nodded. "Very good. Lock on with main disruptor banks. Fire when ready."

"At once, Captain."

Dax grabbed the console, bracing himself. A moment later, the deck shook and rumbled again as the *Klothos* expended enough energy to vaporize a small city in the space of a few too-swift heartbeats.

On the viewer, the enemy vessel continued serenely dropping toward the rapidly growing gray-brown, aurora-spangled world that now lay beneath it. The image on the screen rippled and wavered intermittently, creating numerous reflections and double images as streams of magnetically accelerated ions interfered randomly with the sensor returns and the *Klothos*'s other systems.

"Nothing happened," Koloth said, neatly underscoring the obvious.

"Weapons lock is nonfunctional," said the tactical officer, looking scandalized at having missed such an apparently easy target.

A bright crimson beam lanced out from the aft section

of the fugitive ship. Though it must have been intended as a counterattack, it missed its mark by an even wider margin than had the salvo from the *Klothos*.

"Qul Tuq appears to have made blind men of us both, my esteemed cousin," Kor said quietly and dangerously.

Dax felt the vibrations in the deck shift subtly yet again. Before he could determine the reason, the helm officer said, "We've dropped out of warp, Captain."

Turning toward the tactical officer, Kor said, "Systems status report."

"Qul Tuq's magnetic field will no longer allow us to sustain a warp field at this proximity to the star," the tactical officer replied sheepishly, as though expecting to be ordered to fall on his *d'k tahg* in shame at any moment. "It has even cut into our impulse power by more than two thirds."

Kor appeared to take the news philosophically. "If it has happened to us, then it has also no doubt happened to him as well," he said, gesturing toward the static-laced image of the other vessel displayed on the bridge's central screen.

Just past the dark limb of the planet, the deceptively small and dim disk of Qul Tuq flashed, strobing faster than the eye could see as it made its thousands of revolutions every second, its churning metal innards forming a colossal cosmic dynamo that spread the magnetar's innumerable grasping electromagnetic fingers throughout the system.

"Qul Tuq has greatly slowed this chase, then, for both hunter and hunted," Koloth said, his words dripping with frustration. "It could take a whole day for either of us to actually make it all the way to the second planet."

"Longer, I would venture," Kang said.

"The star's radiations have also compromised all major shipboard systems to some extent, Captain," the tactical officer continued. "Chief Engineer Q'Lujj reports that he can keep the shields up using emergency power for perhaps another three days, assuming we sustain no serious additional damage in the meantime. But we cannot trust our weapons locks, long-range sensors, or transporters as long as we remain this deep inside the star's magnetic field."

"So either we get away from here very soon on what little remains of our impulse power," Dax said, addressing no one in particular, "or else we close in for the kill over the next couple of days and hope we can bring down the albino with a lucky shot or two."

Kor favored him with an ugly scowl, but the tactical officer interrupted before he could attach any words to it. "The other vessel is now on a precise heading for the planet's innermost moon."

"Are you certain?" Kor said.

"I've compensated for the sensor ghosts, reflections, and double images, Captain. I have no doubt as to his heading."

Koloth nodded sagely. "Where better to seek a respite from the never-ending storms of Qul Tuq? He must believe he can hide from us there."

"Well, we probably won't be able to find him from orbit if he makes it all the way down to the moon's surface before we intercept him," Kang said. "Even with the second planet's magnetic field calming some of Qul Tuq's rage."

"We can't use the transporter, in any case, with all the magnetic interference," Kor said. That the *Klothos* couldn't land on any planetary surface, of course, went without saying. "We'll have to board his ship the way the warriors of old did such things."

"Assuming we can catch up to him before he makes a landing," Dax said.

Kor stroked his beard as he considered his ever-narrowing gamut of choices. "In that event, we would still have the option of chasing him down to the surface in one of our shuttles."

"That would certainly neutralize whatever tactical advantage we might still have over the albino's ship right now,"

Dax said, not sanguine about the idea of exchanging the relative safety of a Klingon warship for the cold comfort of a much smaller—and far more vulnerable—auxiliary craft.

"Bah," the tactical officer said dismissively. "The tantrums of Qul Tuq have done that already."

All three Klingon captains then turned as one to gaze upon Dax, looks of stern expectation—and, perhaps, of incipient disappointment?—etched onto their hard, careworn faces.

"Do you fear to continue, Curzon Dax?" Kang said.

Dax swallowed hard. *Of course I do. What sane man wouldn't?*

But he knew that every second's delay would give the albino a substantially increased chance of getting away. And if the pirate escaped, he might actually succeed in creating and deploying a truly horrendous biogenic weapon.

If he or one of his people hasn't managed to do it already, he thought, recalling the launch of the still-unaccounted-for shuttle from the albino's ship.

None of those possibilities boded very well for the prospects of Federation-Klingon détente.

Mustering every iota of bravado he possessed, Dax grinned. "Don't underestimate my enthusiasm, my fine trio of warriors. We might not be able to run fast enough to catch this *targ* before he goes to ground.

"But we can't just let him get away without finishing the chase."

THIRTY-THREE

Stardate 9025.2 (Early 2290)

U.S.S. Excelsior

"I can't keep the channel open much longer, Captain," Rand said as she frantically made adjustments to her console's frequency and modulation settings.

The Trill ambassador's image wavered and danced on the bridge's central viewer, tugged and torn at the edges and stretched in the middle into taffy-pull distortions by the magnetic interference generated by the Qul Tuq magnetar.

All Sulu was able to gather before the already tenuous subspace connection broke up entirely was that Kor's ship was continuing to pursue the albino, bringing the chase dangerously close to the powerful magnetar, which was already playing hob with every system aboard the *Klothos*. The ships of both pursuer and pursued could be rendered all but blind, or even disabled entirely. The albino might even find a way to use these extreme circumstances to turn the tables, thereby escaping from—or perhaps even destroying—the vessel that continued so doggedly to close in on him. The *Klothos* might lose its life-support capabilities, along with all life aboard her, either to the magnetar or to the albino.

And neither Starfleet Command nor the Klingon High Council would authorize Sulu to take any direct action to help, even now. Sulu bristled at the notion that the bogeyman of his childhood nightmares might very well get away, while all he was permitted to do was sit light-years away and let it happen.

Cutler stepped directly behind the aft starboard communications console at which Rand sat. "Reestablish signal," said the acting exec.

Rand turned her head and fixed Cutler with a momentary but nevertheless hard glare. "The comm system can't find any signal to lock onto," she said, then turned her chair toward Sulu. "Sorry, Captain."

Sulu acknowledged Rand's report with a silent nod. *Captain,* he thought, mentally repeating the title Rand had used as he stared forward into the vast ocean of night that separated *Excelsior* from Dax, the Klingons, and their quarry. The enforced sitting and waiting made him feel less like a captain and more like a glorified caretaker, someone whose only function was to keep the big chair warm until Starfleet Command finally got around to selecting somebody—somebody other than *him*—for the job.

Sulu wondered how long even a CO as risk-averse as Captain Styles would have put up with this.

Turning his chair back toward Rand, he said, "Has the High Council sent us any further word yet about my request to enter Klingon space?"

"Not so much as a peep, Captain," Rand said as she quietly shook her head.

Captain, Sulu thought yet again. *A captain, even an acting captain, has to make hard command decisions from time to time. Even decisions that might toss a whole career straight into the recycler.*

He made one of those decisions, right then and there. "Mister Lojur, plot a course to Qul Tuq."

"Aye, sir," said the Halkan, apparently both surprised and pleased.

Sulu noticed that the helm officer was watching him expectantly as well, her long-fingered hands spread across her console like Talarian hook spiders waiting to pounce. Cutler hovered silently nearby, watching with a neutral expression, neither protesting nor making any overt sign of approval. Then, almost imperceptibly, she nodded toward him.

They all want to go after the captain's killer, he thought. *Even if that means violating orders.*

"Lieutenant Keith," Sulu said, and discovered that he had no difficulty sounding resolute while he violated Starfleet orders. "Engage the helm as soon as the course is laid in. Maximum warp."

Early 2290 (the Year of Kahless 915, late in the month of *Doqath;* Gregorian date: January 12, 2290)

I.K.S. Klothos

Dax experienced real, heartfelt delight when he realized that his Klingon hosts had largely stopped babying him; they had all apparently shared so much mutual danger already that Kang, Koloth, and Kor no longer tried very hard to talk him out of exposing himself to the same front-line perils that they themselves were willing to face in the course of pursuing the albino.

Of course, Dax recognized that this heady feeling of newfound acceptance had its drawbacks. As the *Klothos* drew steadily nearer to the albino's fleeing vessel—the Qul Tuq magnetar's energetic, particle-rich fields rendering the sensors, shields, and transporters of both vessels essentially useless all the while—the amount of danger that lay ahead seemed to be increasing at a nearly geometric rate.

And as Dax stood with the three Klingon captains in the ventral launch bay of the *Klothos,* examining the pair of bulbous, cramped-looking, barrel-shaped craft that Kor was planning to use for the next phase of the chase, the Trill diplomat found himself almost beginning to regret his easy bonhomie with the Klingons. On the other hand, it gave him the discretion to freely voice his doubts and confusion; even with the benefit of the memories of Tobin and Torias, Dax found the new strategy Kor was about to employ obscure.

"These things look suspiciously like escape pods," he said uneasily as he paced between the two stubby craft that had been brought to the center of the launch bay in preparation for deployment. "Are you already making plans to abandon ship?"

Neither of the little modules appeared spacious enough to hold more than perhaps two or three people. And the impressive array of grapples, hooks, and coils of high-tensile-strength cable mounted on their hulls made them appear better suited for mountain-climbing expeditions than for escaping imminent doom.

"They are no longer mere escape pods," Kor said in tolerant tones as he began checking the cache of disruptor weapons that lay on a nearby table. "At least not since Q'Lujj retrofitted them so that they may serve as *breach* pods as well."

Dax frowned, understanding now the nature of Q'Lujj's hasty modifications, which, coupled with the unfamiliar terminology, dredged up a few pertinent memories from the career of Tobin Dax, who had worked as an engineer more than a century and a half earlier—well before the time when hostile vessels could be boarded using the neat and tidy expedient of transporter technology. Although Dax was impressed by the ingenuity of Kor's chief engineer, he still wasn't entirely comfortable with the whole breach pod concept—not even after two more days of agonizingly slow searching and pursuit revealed the location of the albino's freighter.

Nor after the dimly illuminated, claustrophobically small breach pod he shared with Kang announced with a jarring lurch and a hollow, resounding *clang* that it had dug its duranium claws into that vessel's radiation-pocked outer hull.

"Magnetic grapples engaged," Kang said, crouching as he examined one of the small backlit readouts mounted on the pod's gray, tightly curving interior surface. "Contact torches have already begun cutting into the outer hull of the albino's vessel."

"Any signs that they've seen our approach?" Dax asked, trying to force the nervousness out of his voice without entirely succeeding.

Studying his displays, Kang did not appear to notice Dax's jitters. "None yet. Ready your weapon." Kang raised his *bat'leth,* aiming one of its razor-sharp points toward the pod's single narrow hatchway, beyond which lay the interior of the albino's ship. Had the Qul Tuq magnetar not interfered with the operations of both shields and transporters, such a brazen entrance—a tactic reminiscent of those employed millennia ago by the pirates who plundered Trill's wooden, oceangoing ships—would not have been possible. Under the current circumstances, however, this was the only workable means of boarding available.

"Ready," Dax said, raising his own *bat'leth,* wishing all the while that Qul Tuq had seen fit to spare their hand disruptors while it was crippling or compromising most of their other systems. Since the magnetar was also interfering with communications, he could only hope that the breach pod that carried Kor and Koloth had also succeeded in reaching its destination.

The pod rocked brutally a few tense moments later as the little vehicle's small cargo of shaped, directed explosive charges detonated, slamming Dax's jaws together with an intensity that made him fear for his teeth. But as the pod's exit fell open before him—creating, in effect, a fully atmosphere-sealed airlock-and-hatch assembly where no entrance had existed before—Dax decided that his dental worries could wait until after the pirate's ship had been taken and secured. He felt a small breeze, his ears popping as the small pressure differential between the pod's interior and that of the ship equalized.

Kang wasted no time stepping into the narrow corridor that snaked past and beyond the now-sealed wound that the breach pod had gouged into the pirate vessel's innards. Taking care not to catch his blade on any of the ductwork, conduits, or other low-hanging protrusions that extended downward from the corridor's low ceiling, Dax hastened after the Klingon captain.

"Mevyap!" cried a deeply guttural voice some distance behind Dax, who recognized the Klingon imperative word for "halt."

Dax did indeed stop moving forward, as did Kang; instead, both men turned in almost perfect synchronization toward the source of the command.

The slender form of the albino, armored in a leather-like, formfitting combat suit—and armed with a *bat'leth* that looked incongruously heavy juxtaposed against his slight frame—stood a dozen or so meters away, between a branching passageway and the gash in the hull created by the breach pod. Beside and slightly behind him stood the elderly Klingon scientist who had been at the albino's side during their previous up-close encounter.

As the scientist fairly cowered behind him, the albino regarded the intruders while sighing and shaking his head. "What must I do to finally be rid of you?" he said, as though he perceived an armed boarding party as more of an annoyance than a threat.

His *bat'leth* raised and poised to strike, Kang began moving resolutely toward the brigand, while Dax followed perhaps two paces behind Kang. The scientist who accompanied the albino appeared to be considering either the options of flight or of soiling himself, if not both.

"Nothing short of killing us all will accomplish that," Kang said. He twirled his blade several times in the confined space, impressing Dax with both his ferocity and his precision.

The albino grinned, his smile as icy and pitiless as the stormy Tenara cliffs on Trill.

Quick, heavy footfalls clattered harshly on the metal deck plates immediately behind Dax, who turned to see the narrow corridor suddenly surging with perhaps eight large, dangerous-looking armed men, all of whom had evidently entered the corridor through yet another nearby branching passage.

Dax cleared his throat as the motley assemblage of Orions, Klingons, a towering, fang-faced Kaylar, and assorted members of other, less recognizable humanoid species briefly took his and Kang's measure with a mixture of haughty contempt and cautious but determined malevolence.

"Might need a little help here," Dax said quietly to Kang, who continued staring in silence at the albino's musclemen.

Fortunately, the narrowness of the corridor forced the albino's defenders, all of whom carried edged weapons of various lengths, to line up in ranks two abreast.

The deck shuddered, and thunder reverberated through the vessel's walls. *Either our reinforcements have just arrived,* Dax thought, *or else this ship just got hulled by a meteoroid.* The stillness of the air in the corridor convinced him that the former possibility was far likelier than the latter.

Taking immediate advantage of the distraction, Kang stepped straight into the melee, hacking the nearest of the pirates down before anyone else could raise a weapon. Dax readied his blade as the remaining brigands surged forward

in pairs. He turned as he deflected the downward slice of a
curved sword that whistled just millimeters past his ear; as
he turned he saw that the albino and the scientist were both
retreating rapidly down the corridor behind them.

"They're getting away!" Dax cried as he and Kang continued transacting the urgent business of survival. Although
the Klingon captain had scored first blood, the initiative
was inexorably shifting to the pirates, driven by the relative
weight of their numbers.

As Dax and Kang steadily fell back down the corridor
under the advancing onslaught, it occurred to the Trill
that they both might very well die here, and in fairly short
order. And if more armed men hemmed them in from the
other end of the corridor, their deaths would be all but
certain.

After backing alongside Kang around a bend in the corridor, Dax felt a mixture of puzzlement and relief when the
advancing pirates abruptly ceased their two-by-two forward
motion. The men in the middle ranks appeared suddenly
distracted by something just around the corner and behind
them. Tempered steel struck tempered steel just out of Dax's
sight, and men screamed in rage and pain.

Kang bared his teeth, all thought of falling back now
apparently forgotten. He surged forward again, gutting
an Orion and head-butting a strong-browed Klingon into
unconsciousness before stepping over their bodies to re-
join whatever remained of the retreating melee. His hopes
buoyed, Dax followed, *bat'leth* in hand.

Around the corner he found Kang, Kor, and Koloth holding their ichor-stained blades and standing triumphantly
over a jumbled heap of silent, blood-smeared bodies; some
of these were breathing, while others already lay as still
as the grave. The sheer savagery of the tableau before him
caused Dax to shudder.

And, to his somewhat shamed surprise, to exult.

"Thank you for leaving some for us," Kor said with a predator's feral grin.

Stardate 9027.2 (Gregorian date: January 12, 2290)

U.S.S. Excelsior

Despite Dr. Chapel's stern directive that he get at least six hours of sleep during *Excelsior*'s unauthorized journey to the Qul Tuq magnetar, Sulu remained wide awake in his quarters. Having given up rest as a lost cause at least four hours earlier, he rose from his disheveled bed and stood beside the bureau in his quarters, where he exchanged his rumpled uniform for fresher attire.

As he started to don a clean undershirt, a familiar metallic gleam in the bureau mirror caught his attention. Holding the shirt, he turned toward the reflection's source.

On the wall, mounted between a pair of Sulu's most prized target pistols, a *bat'leth* hung like a silver-horned moon. The blade was the only tangible trace he possessed of the Beta XII-A entity, the noncorporeal creature that had forced humans and Klingons into bloody combat in order to generate the hatred that nourished it. The nightmarish apparition that had used the thoughts of Kang and his crew to forge this blade still drifted into Sulu's dreams on occasion.

Lately, however, another ghost from the past had taken the Beta XII-A creature's place. It was a ghost that Sulu knew he needed to bury, once and for all.

Sulu pulled the shirt over his head, threw on a fresh maroon uniform jacket, and crossed to the companel on his desk. "Sulu to bridge," he said. "Update our ETA at the Qul Tuq magnetar."

He was answered by the familiar flat tones of Lieutenant Lojur, the Halkan navigator, who was very possibly the only person aboard *Excelsior* who got less sleep than either Sulu or Commander Cutler. *"We're only minutes from establishing orbit around the second planet, Captain. That planet remains our best guess as to the current location of both the Klothos and the hostile vessel."*

"Can't you confirm their whereabouts at this range?"

"Not with all the magnetic activity coming from Qul Tuq, sir. But we should have better luck after we establish orbit around the planet. With or without sensors, we can still use our eyes."

"Very good, Lieutenant," Sulu said as he fastened his jacket's shoulder clasp.

Another voice cut in. *"Captain, we've been running these engines too hot for too long,"* said Lieutenant Commander Tim Henry, *Excelsior*'s acting chief engineer. *"We've got to give them some downtime, sir. And soon."*

Sulu couldn't help but agree—he could feel the almost pained throbbing of the ship's warp drive as it permeated the bridge deck plates, and that had been one of the factors that had conspired to scuttle Dr. Chapel's "get some goddamned sleep" order—but he also knew he couldn't afford to slow down. Not while the *Klothos,* and by extension Federation-Klingon détente, was in mortal jeopardy. And certainly not when he had finally come so close to catching the man who had threatened his family and killed his captain.

"The engines will get all the downtime they need and more," Sulu said. "Once we get where we're going."

"Henry's right, sir," said Commander Cutler. *"Excelsior can't take much more of this—not with the extra demands we're having to make on our shield generators the closer we get to the Qul Tuq magnetar."*

"Unfortunately, we don't have an alternative to riding the shields hard," Sulu said. "Not if we want to avoid shipwide system failures." He seriously doubted that either Kor's battle cruiser or the albino's battered freighter could do better, which made *Excelsior*'s alacrity even more critical.

"Understood, Captain," Henry said in grumbling acquiescence.

"Will we be able to use the transporters?" Sulu wanted to know.

"I wouldn't recommend it, sir," Henry said. *"Even with the shields reinforced against the worst effects of the magnetar. It looks like we won't be able to count on our hand phasers either."*

Sulu glanced across the room at the glass display case where he stored his small collection of ancient Earth firearms, as well as his supplies of target-shooting ammunition.

He grinned as he decided that the lack of hand phasers didn't have to be an insuperable problem.

"We'd better ready a pair of shuttlecraft," Sulu said. "The *Klothos* is almost certainly going to need both medics and engineers. Commander Cutler, I want you to assemble the appropriate teams and put them aboard the *Shuttlecraft Rickover.*"

"Aye, sir," Cutler said.

"As soon as you've done that, meet me in the hangar deck with a security team. In the meantime, I'll start prepping the shuttlecraft *Von Steuben* for immediate launch."

"Sir?"

Sulu modulated his voice into a tone that brooked no further discussion. "The minute we locate the albino's ship, Commander, we're going to board her."

THIRTY-FOUR

Still exulting on the adrenaline rush of a battle well-ended, Dax reminded himself not to get cocky.

But that decision came only *after* five more armed and angry pirates appeared in the corridor, once again halting Dax and the three Klingon captains in their pursuit of the fleeing albino. Before Dax could react, Kor and Kang surged forward, both Klingons dispatching a brigand apiece with deft thrusts of their slick and glistening blades.

One of the three surviving pirates swept the tip of his long weapon, a slender metal pole that Dax had at first mistaken for a sword, across Kor's armored side. Kor roared in fury and pain, and the air was at once sickeningly redolent with burnt leather and scorched flesh as he stepped backward, narrowly avoiding what could easily have been a killing blow. One of the remaining defenders turned to flee. The last man, an Orion, drew a thin, finely serrated knife and threw it with startling precision.

The flying blade buried itself deep into Kor's left knee.

The knife thrower looked as surprised as Dax felt when Kor calmly extracted the blade and threw it back, making up for any lack of finesse with sheer rage-fueled force.

The pirate crashed lifeless to the deck, the haft of his own knife protruding from his throat, and Dax wondered whether he'd had time to realize what had hit him before he died.

Although neither Kang nor Koloth seemed to pay any attention to their colleague's injuries, Dax rushed to Kor's side to offer assistance. Kor angrily waved Dax away, raising his *bat'leth*, perhaps as much in warning as to demonstrate that he didn't intend to allow his injuries to slow down the chase.

"My wounds will only make our victory taste sweeter," Kor said as the quartet continued along the same corridor down which the albino had fled.

Then the ship rocked again, jerking nearly hard enough to knock Dax off his feet. The Klingons glowered, but continued undeterred, passing Dax.

So much for being treated as an equal, he thought as he tried to force down a thoroughly undiplomatic surge of resentment.

Dax hastened to catch up, and wondered whether the sound and tumult they'd all just heard signified victory, or something else entirely.

A moment later, when the group turned a corner and found themselves facing no less than a dozen more armed men, he was fairly certain that he'd found his answer.

Shuttlecraft *Von Steuben*

"I'll handle the hard-dock maneuver myself," Sulu said, staring through the shuttlecraft *Von Steuben*'s forward windows. The battered freighter steadily increased in apparent size as the shuttle slowly matched distance and velocity with it.

Although the Qul Tuq magnetar had effectively neutralized sensor scans as a tactical asset, it hadn't been difficult for both *Excelsior* and the *Von Steuben* to confirm visually that the albino's freighter was indeed located near the second planet of the system—as was Captain Kor's battle cruiser, whose medical and repair needs were already being addressed by the hand-picked crew of the shuttlecraft *Rickover*.

"Are you sure you wouldn't rather delegate the docking job to me?" said Cutler, who tended the copilot's station beside him. Sulu could hear metallic clicks and ratcheting sounds as the security team seated behind her in the central crew compartment completed their final weapons checks in preparation for boarding the hostile vessel.

"Sure as gravity," Sulu said as his fingers danced across the flight control console. Since the proximity of the magnetar still ruled out any use of *Excelsior*'s transporters, this method—using orbital mechanics techniques as old as the Gemini missions conducted more than three centuries ago, at the dawn of Earth's First Space Age—was the safest and most expedient option for boarding the albino's ship. Having spent as many years as he had with his own hand directly on the tiller, Sulu wasn't about to delegate this task to anyone.

As the details of the freighter's scorched and beat-up hull became steadily more visible in the dim reflected glow of the second planet and its moons, Sulu noticed the two old-style breach pods that were attached, barnacle-like, to the vessel's pockmarked skin. He concluded that the Klingons must have already succeeded in getting themselves aboard, or had at least made a good attempt.

Let's hope my fellow captains are keeping Qagh too busy right now to look out the window and notice that more company is coming, Sulu thought as he began making his final approach.

A moment later the two hulls came into contact rather abruptly, with a resounding force that brought to mind asteroid impacts. The interior of the *Von Steuben* reverberated like a bell.

After taking a moment to study the environmental panels—probably to make certain that the craft wasn't venting atmosphere—Cutler turned toward Sulu with a grin.

"Remember, I *did* offer to drive," she said.

Sulu considered quoting the old saw about any landing that a pilot could walk away from being a good one, but instead looked down again to check the docking control readout. As he'd hoped, the shuttlecraft's expanding-and-contracting iris aperture had established a sufficiently tight fit with the freighter's outer airlock to allow the boarding party to get safely inside without the use of environmental suits—once their explosives had blown open the exterior hatch.

"You can drive the *next* time we board a pirate ship," Sulu said, then turned his attention to the security team.

The wound in his head was bleeding freely, obscuring Kang's vision and staining what little of it that remained with livid, pinkish-purple hues.

Today is *a good day to die,* he reminded himself as his attacker drove him inexorably backward, and finally tripped him. Kang felt the deck plates flex beneath him as he crashed flat onto his back. He raised his *bat'leth,* only to feel it wrenched from his grasp by a blunt, forceful impact. The blade clattered to the deck a short distance away.

The petaQ *must have kicked me,* he thought, struggling to rise even though he knew full well that he couldn't see well enough to stave off a well-placed killing blow.

He heard frantic shouts then, as well as the urgent crash of opposed metal blades, the latter generating a breeze that caused the congealing blood on his temple to spatter. From elsewhere in the freighter he heard several sharp reports, like the sounds made by the explosives used to blow open sealed hatches during shipboard emergencies. He took a moment to wipe a sleeve across his eyes, clearing his vision somewhat.

Blinking in incredulity, Kang saw Commander Sulu standing over him, a bloody *bat'leth* in his hand as he regarded the huge male Orion corpse that lay sprawled across the deck, apparently quite dead even though it still clutched a wicked-looking short sword in its large, lifeless hands. Still struggling to focus his blood-spattered eyes, Kang belatedly realized that the *bat'leth* that had killed the Orion was Kang's own weapon; Sulu had evidently picked it up from the deck after the Orion had kicked it from his grasp.

Sulu knelt beside Kang, who struggled to a sitting position, hoping all the while he wasn't allowing the human to see how much pain the movement was causing him.

"Are you all right?" Sulu said, laying the *bat'leth* down at Kang's side.

"Never better, Commander." Kang grinned as he wrapped his fingers around the blade's blood-slicked grips. "In fact, I have rarely felt so very much alive."

Sulu's female second-in-command, flanked by a pair of youthful Starfleet officers, bounded toward Sulu from around a corner. All of them carried unfamiliar-looking metal pistols that exuded a pungent chemical odor.

"What manner of weapons are those?" Kang said, pointing toward the pistols. He noticed that a similar gun was tucked into Sulu's belt. "They do not appear to be of Starfleet issue."

Sulu favored him with a chuckle and an incongruous smile. "You're right. But they'll get the job done once you learn to deal with recoil and the possibility of projectile-caused hull breaches."

"Indeed," Kang said, impressed. "Such a weapon would make a fine addition to my own collection."

"We can discuss that later," Sulu said, grinning. "For now, let's just say that this vessel has just been secured by Mister Smith, Mister Wesson, and Mister Colt and leave it at that."

The human captain turned toward his officers. "Report."

"The control room remains secure, Captain," said Commander Cutler, Sulu's executive officer. "As well as the engine compartment. We've captured several more hostiles in the past few minutes, in addition to seizing a large quantity of what appears to be bioweapons contraband. The rest of the security detachment is continuing to search for anyone else who may still be aboard and trying to evade capture."

"Most of the hostiles had already been killed or otherwise pacified before we came aboard," said the younger male officer. "Someone seems to have beaten us to them."

Kang chuckled, though the motion sent a jolt of agony through his rib cage. "Someone indeed."

As if on cue, footfalls sounded from down the corridor somewhere behind Kang, and Sulu and his officers tensed, pointing their weapons toward the source of the noise. Painfully, Kang turned his head in time to see Kor, Koloth, and Dax approaching, all of them looking distressed but relatively uninjured, if one discounted Kor's blood-soaked knee and his rather pronounced limp.

Dax beamed at the human captain. "What's that Terran expression, Commander?" he said. "'Fancy meeting you here'?"

But Sulu now appeared to have little patience for frivolities. "Have you found the albino?" he asked bluntly.

"We did," Koloth said. "But the coward turned and ran from us shortly before you arrived."

Sulu's expression took on a grim intensity that Kang had never seen before on a human face. "*Damn*. I was just up on the control deck. One of the consoles recorded the launch of a pair of small auxiliary vessels only a few minutes ago."

"Headed where?" Kor wanted to know.

"Judging from the recorded launch trajectory alone, I'd have to put my money on the second planet's big inner moon," Sulu said.

Dax nodded. "It has a substantial atmosphere," he said. "I suppose it would make a good hiding place."

"Then that's where we're going," Sulu said.

"Sir, assuming that the launch records weren't faked to throw us off," Cutler said, "I still have to point out that you have no way to know what might be waiting for you down there."

Sulu nodded soberly. "Granted. But the most efficient way to resolve either question is to go down to the moon's surface and start scouring the place."

"In my opinion, it's too risky," Cutler said. "Not to mention the fact that you are far too personally involved in this to be objective, in my opinion. Why not send me and part of the security team instead?"

"Because I need you to keep things secure *here* until I report back," Sulu said sharply. "And because the albino is *mine*."

"Sir—"

Sulu was finally beginning to look truly angry. "I'm finished *discussing* it, Commander. The matter is decided. *Understood?*"

She paused, her jaw muscles flexing like those of a sabre bear before it strikes.

"Completely, sir," she said, and glowered off into the middle distance.

"I am coming with you," Kor declared, his face a mask of utter ferocity despite the smoothness of his brows.

Sulu studied Kor for a lengthy, silent moment, as though contemplating asking him why he seemed so determined to press on in his pursuit of the albino.

"As will I," Koloth said, lifting his *bat'leth* toward the

corridor's low, conduit-festooned ceiling as he interrupted whatever question might have been about to spring to the human's lips.

"I shall come as well," Kang said. Focusing past the excruciating pain that lanced his torso, he steeled himself to rise, first pushing himself up onto one knee, then rising haltingly and getting both feet beneath him.

He immediately toppled back to the deck, his cheeks and neck baking in abject shame at having proven himself so weak in the presence of aliens. He was grateful, at least, that both Dax and Sulu had proved themselves sufficiently knowledgeable about Klingon culture to refrain from shaming him by offering to help him stand.

"You're not going anywhere, Kang," Sulu said. "Except to visit my medics."

"*I'll* go down to the moon in Kang's place," Dax said, raising his *bat'leth* in a smart Klingon military salute. "Just try and *keep* me away."

Sulu stepped toward the young Trill and placed a gentle hand on his shoulder. "As a matter of fact, Mister Dax, I *will.*"

"Excuse me?" Dax said, looking crestfallen.

Sulu remained resolute. "You're a diplomat, not a warrior. And the mission ahead will have nothing whatsoever to do with diplomacy."

Sulu turned back toward Kang. "*I* will go in Kang's place," he said, his dark gaze locked with Kang's, though he was obviously addressing everyone in the corridor.

Kang sighed in resignation and wondered if the loss of blood he had suffered had made him somehow more tractable or had simply weakened him past the point of uselessness. He decided that it didn't matter, since he knew that in his current injured state he could only be a liability to whoever was going to lead the next direct confrontation with the albino.

He picked his *bat'leth* up off the deck plates and handed it up to Sulu. "You may borrow it," he said. "So long as you do me the honor of bringing it back stained with the blood of your captain's killer."

Sulu stood holding the ichor-splotched blade in both hands, saying nothing.

But the silent, cold fire that Kang saw blazing in the depths of the human's eyes spoke as loudly as the war trumpets of mighty Kahless.

THIRTY-FIVE

Early 2290 (the Year of Kahless 915, late in the month of
Doqath; Gregorian date: January 12, 2290)

Shuttlecraft *Von Steuben*

For a fleeting moment, or perhaps even a little bit longer, Sulu regretted his decades-old decision to transfer out of astrophysics and onto the arduous career track of starship command. He hadn't come quite this close to succumbing to motion sickness since entering advanced flight training at Starfleet Academy.

He did his best to ignore his distress, focusing his attention instead upon the instruments arrayed about him in the *Von Steuben*'s relentlessly unsteady cockpit. Narrowing his concentration like a laser being channeled through a rubidium crystal, he guided the shuttlecraft steadily downward through the moon's dense atmosphere, continually adjusting the small vessel's attitude, pitch, and yaw.

"It's just our luck that this little moon has almost as thick an atmosphere as Venus," Sulu said as he continued compensating for turbulent convection currents and buffeting wind shear effects, both of which seemed to be conspiring at the moment to tear the *Von Steuben* to tiny, suborbital pieces.

"Venus?" Kor said, adjusting the bandages on his knee and around his ribs while Koloth stared into the indistinct gray nothingness of the high-pressure carbon dioxide atmosphere that was visible through the shuttle's wide forward windows.

"Venus is Earth's nearest neighboring planet," Sulu said wryly. "You'd probably love it there."

The cloud deck beneath the shuttlecraft suddenly parted, revealing the atmosphere-distorted vista of rilled, rocky landscape that lay only a handful of kilometers below. Lit in subdued sepia tones accented by the faint but angry amber glow of some of the orange rocks, the slate-gray ground rushed up to greet them with alarming speed, until Sulu leveled off the shuttle's descent. Sulu's stomach found its horizon just as the shuttlecraft did.

"There!" Koloth said, pointing toward the sensor-generated images being displayed on the console just beneath the forward windows.

It took Sulu another few minutes to confirm visually what the passive sensors had discovered: the fact that there was indeed another ship on the ground, a mere two kilometers or so distant and yet difficult to see because of the distorting effects of the moon's dense, heavy atmosphere.

The albino's auxiliary vessel had reached the surface and was still in one piece.

"Do you detect any life signs aboard that ship?" Koloth wanted to know.

More than a little curious about that himself, Sulu had already begun consulting the passive scanning equipment, since active scans were still proving less than reliable in spite of the partial shielding from Qul Tuq that the second planet's magnetic field provided.

A moment later he shook his head, both disappointed and frustrated. "There are no life signs aboard the albino's ship.

I *am* reading something underground, though. Faint humanoid bio-signs, refined metals . . . and a great deal of nitrogen and oxygen as well."

"They must have taken refuge in a prearranged safe house," Kor said.

Sulu frowned, incredulous. "A safe house? In a place like *this*?"

"The perfect hiding place for one such as the albino," said Kor. "Who would think of looking for him in a system such as this? And who would want to chase him here?"

"Maybe somebody who doesn't mind strolling right into a trap," Sulu said as he landed the shuttle just out of sight of the albino's vessel.

And certainly nobody who most people would consider sane.

The fact that nobody had reacted as yet to the presence of the *Von Steuben* struck Sulu as strange. As he took turns with Kor and Koloth in donning pressure suits—someone, after all, had to keep an eye out for any sudden attack while the other two members of the team were suiting up and preparing to leave the shuttlecraft—he found the continued quiescence of both the albino's auxiliary craft and his safe house increasingly disturbing.

It was the silence of the grave—or the quiet that concealed a carefully baited trap. *Or maybe both, unless we're damned careful.*

"Damn this suit to *Gre'thor*!" Koloth grumbled as he awkwardly pulled the garment over the cartilaginous ridges that ran from his forehead all the way down the torso he had stripped of its armored Klingon military tunic in order to fit into standard Starfleet-issue EVA garb. For obvious reasons, Koloth had more trouble getting his helmet in place than did either of his two smooth-headed compatriots.

Nevertheless, within ten minutes of landing, Sulu and the

two Klingon captains made their way onto the rugged terrain just outside the main airlock of the shuttlecraft, whose systems were now in the able hands of the ship's computer. Sulu could only marvel at the delicacy with which both Kor and Koloth handled the handsome, razor-sharp curved *bat'leth* blades all three of them had brought along in anticipation of the showdown that they all knew was coming. Each Klingon wore his blade slung across the back of his pressure suit, somehow managing to avoid slicing the garment open. Moving with extreme caution and deliberation—which wasn't easy, given the oppressive crush of the moon's atmospheric pressure—Sulu followed suit.

As the outer airlock door closed, Sulu watched the shuttle's markings—specifically the letters that spelled out the name *Von Steuben*—as they rippled in the thick, poisonous air. He couldn't tell for certain if the paint on the hull was beginning to succumb to the moon's harsh and hot reducing atmosphere, though the effect made him briefly contemplate rechristening *Excelsior*'s entire complement of shuttlecraft, a task which was every new captain's prerogative. When and if Starfleet Command made him *Excelsior*'s permanent commander, he just couldn't see maintaining the late Lawrence Styles's penchant for naming his auxiliary craft after military figures, even seminal ones like General Friedrich Wilhelm von Steuben, who had written the field manuals for George Washington's Revolutionary War–era army, or Admiral Hyman Rickover, who had pioneered the same nation's nuclear submarine fleet nearly two centuries later. He'd always thought that Starfleet shuttlecraft should be named after explorers, scientists, and diplomats.

But now isn't the time to think about shuttle names, he told himself as the three men carefully picked their way over a low, rocky rise and carefully traversed a boulder-strewn defile toward the albino's ship, handheld phaser and disruptors as ready as their blades, despite the fact that the

360 MICHAEL A. MARTIN & ANDY MANGELS

interactions of planetary and solar magnetic fields had rendered them essentially useless as anything other than crude grenades.

Which was precisely how the trio had planned to use them against the albino's parked ship, since the defenses built into the *Von Steuben* seemed to be in roughly the same operating condition as the landing party's energy weapons.

Sulu moved gingerly as he tried to adjust to the slightly higher than Earth-normal gravity that prevailed on this ultradense moon. The weight of the long, curved blade on his back felt alien, yet somehow reassuring. He hoped his years of foil and saber training would serve him in good stead if he actually had to use the thing in combat.

As they reached the albino's ship, Sulu noticed that something didn't look quite right on the port side of her hull.

"Get away from that ship!" he shouted, allowing instinct to take over.

A moment later, all the furies of Hell came streaming forth in a gale of hot death.

Thanks to the round of injections Nej had given him during the harried flight to the Qul Tuq safe house, Qagh was feeling stronger than he had in months. The burning and swelling at the injection point on his right bicep had begun to recede, but was easy to ignore in any case.

When he felt the vibrations rumbling beneath the safe house's polished stone floor, he felt even better still.

"They would seem to have taken the bait," Nej said.

"That decoy ship was one of your better ideas, Doctor," said the albino, smiling broadly. "If our pursuers noticed we launched more than one shuttle, they must have thought they were seeing a sensor ghost caused by Qul Tuq."

The floor rumbled again a few moments later, this time accompanied by a change in air pressure that was extreme enough to make Qagh's ears pop.

Someone had forced one of the airlocks open from the outside.

"Bring in the men," he said, wondering if they would stand and fight or try to bolt; they were all presently engaged in the business of either maintaining or loading the small vessel, after all. Without Qagh's voice codes, however, anyone who tried to flee in the shuttle wouldn't get very far. "And prepare the large pyrotechnics to cover our exit. But go about it quietly, so our . . . guests don't panic unnecessarily."

Nej had turned so pale that Qagh thought he was looking into a mirror. Then the physician nodded mutely and disappeared through the stone chamber's rear door.

Qagh walked toward the bare granite desk, behind which he kept several edged weapons hanging from one of the rough-hewn walls. The polished blades gleamed in the light of several softly glowing fixtures that were bolted directly into the rock of the ceiling.

A pity that simple disruptors won't work properly in this hellhole, he thought as he took down the half-moon-shaped *bat'leth* from the pegs that held it on display between a pair of ornate long swords.

He heard a soft, barely audible footfall behind him, and knew instantly that it had not been caused by any of his men; his own people knew better than to try to sneak up on him, especially when he held such a keen, well-balanced piece of metal in his hands.

"Turn around slowly." The voice behind him was smooth and deep.

And angry.

Keeping his blade flat across his chest, Qagh did as he was bid. After all, he would have to stall for only another few moments before help came.

A single glance at the bedraggled men who confronted him confirmed that he might indeed have little to fear, despite the fact that the intruders outnumbered him three to one. Not only were the pressure suits they wore scorched and battered, each of these men seemed to be dependent upon the same simple edged weapons that he, Qagh, carried. At any rate, if any of them had possessed a weapon capable of striking him down from across the room—a chemical projectile pistol, say, or even a throwing knife—then they would be fools not to have used it already, when his back was turned. He lifted his blade.

"My decoy vessel contained a rather large cargo of explosives," Qagh said. "But you seem to have reasoned that out in time to avoid taking the brunt of it. How?" He forced his voice to remain even, keeping it almost at a monotone; he hoped his guests would find that unnerving—at least until reinforcements arrived.

Unfortunately, the three intruders seemed to be anything but unnerved. Two of them removed their carbon-splotched helmets, drew their *bat'leth*s, and began approaching from the sides, like a pair of carnivorous, heavy-breathing *bregit* closing in for the kill. He immediately recognized his kinsman Captain Kor, who was walking with a pronounced limp, as well as Captain Koloth, though he had to admit to feeling some surprise at their having managed to find him again so soon.

The third man doffed his helmet, revealing unfamiliar human features. Unlike his fellows, his *bat'leth* remained hanging from the back of his pressure suit.

"I pay very close attention to ship markings," the human said in the same deep voice that had ordered Qagh to turn around. "It's been a hobby of mine ever since I was a boy living on the Klingon border. To this day, I tend to notice small discrepancies—which is a great help in spotting decoys and traps."

This is very bad, Qagh thought, a membrane-thin film of perspiration beginning to dew his forehead. As strong as he felt right now, he knew he was no match for an armed human accompanied by two extremely angry armed Klingons.

Where in the Nine Hells are my men? Qagh thought, panic slowly rising within his soul like the tide-stirred magmas that roiled beneath the surface of this moon. Perhaps someone among his crew had broken his voice codes in the shuttle's computer and had seized this opportunity to get rid of him. If he survived this, he would have to institute yet another disloyalty purge, posthaste.

"Stop!" the human shouted.

Qagh suddenly recognized this man as one of the Starfleet officers who had attended the Korvat meeting.

The Klingons paused in their tracks, though they both regarded the human as though he'd just gone utterly mad.

"He's mine," the human said. "I recognize him."

Perplexity widened Qagh's eyes. "You recognize me? And how might *that* be possible?" Although he knew that everyone now in the room had also been present inside the Korvat conference hall, Qagh remained confident that no one could have seen through the biomimetic disguise he'd been wearing at the time.

The human raised a soot-smeared glove and thrust an accusing forefinger directly at Qagh. "It's been over forty years since the last time I caught a glimpse of you," he said. "But you never forget the face of the man who tried to murder your whole family."

"Your . . . family." Try as Qagh might, he could muster no recollection of an encounter with this human prior to the Korvat meeting. "My friend, I have killed *lots* of families throughout my life," he said, hoping to provoke the younger man into losing the struggle he was obviously having with his emotions.

The human's eyes suddenly grew colder than a pair of outbound comets. "It happened on a border world where I lived for a while as a child. The human colonists called the place Ganjitsu. Does that little detail jog your memory?"

Keep stalling him, Qagh thought. "Never heard of it."

"Then I suppose you also don't remember the agronomy lab you raided, either. I was only eleven years old then, but I managed to fry all the computers in the entire compound before you and your crew were able to make off with anything. Then you and your pirates went back to your ship and lifted off—and then blew the whole place up from orbit."

Qagh remembered.

He recalled slapping the *Jade Lady*'s fire-control button with a shaking, sweat-slicked palm. He remembered how angry he had been, how thwarted he had felt. His frustration with a universe filled with happenstances that seemed collectively bent on his destruction.

And he remembered how very close to death he had come that day—all because someone had sabotaged the computers in that border-world lab before melting away into the shadows like some intangible, cowardly ghost.

"So that was *you,*" Qagh said quietly.

"Hikaru Sulu," the human said. "Commander in Starfleet. Now acting captain of the Federation *Starship Excelsior.*"

"Commander Sulu," Qagh said. "Your interference might well have killed me that day." He stepped out in front of his desk, stopping when he came to within a tall man's body length from the human and his Klingon escorts. He held the *bat'leth* before him, hands tightly fastened to the leather grips wound about the handles on either side.

"And yours almost left me an orphan," Sulu said, his body tensing as for combat, although his *bat'leth* still dangled uselessly from the back of his suit.

"My apologies for my poor aim, Commander," Qagh said. "My intention wasn't to cause you lingering emotional pain. It was to kill every last living thing in that lab compound."

"So," the Klingon named Kor said to the human. "*Your* family honor is at stake here as well."

"I'm here to bring a criminal to justice," Sulu replied. "Not to carry out a vendetta."

It was clear that neither of the Klingons believed him. Kor grinned unpleasantly and took an uneven limping step forward. Pointing toward Qagh with one of the gleaming tips of his *bat'leth,* he said, "I hope that doesn't mean you expect him to agree to just come with you quietly, Commander."

"No," Sulu said. "I don't suppose he will."

"Regardless," Kor said, twirling his blade as he took a step back, "Koloth and I most certainly do *not* intend merely to arrest this man."

"Indeed," the Klingon named Koloth said to the human as he mirrored Kor's gesture, making room for Sulu and Qagh to engage one another without hindrance. "So make sure you leave some for us when you're finished. Remember, I have a crew and a ship to avenge."

Qagh watched as the human drew his *bat'leth.* His movements were slow and tentative, bordering on awkward, as though his previous experience with Klingon blades was very limited. He had not yet even raised his weapon into a proper defensive posture.

Recognizing a clear opportunity to whittle down the odds against him very quickly—while obtaining some measure of revenge of his own against the little human ghost who had nearly ended his life more than forty years ago—Qagh suddenly spun, aiming his *bat'leth*'s right edge straight at the human's stunned-looking face.

THIRTY-SIX

Early 2290 (the Year of Kahless 915, late in the month of *Doqath;* Gregorian date: January 12, 2290)

Qul Tuq

Though the albino's sudden move caught him by surprise, Sulu managed to get his *bat'leth* up between his face and his assailant just in time to block the blow, redirecting it slightly to his left. Sparks leaped from the blades as they made contact, and the surprising power behind the assault forced Sulu backward, nearly toppling him over completely.

"Revenge delayed tastes all the sweeter for being aged," the albino said, grinning as he regained his own temporarily skewed balance. He twirled his blade slowly as he began very deliberately circling Sulu, his booted feet moving in a surprisingly graceful grapevine motion for someone so sickly-looking.

Raising his own blade into a defensive position, Sulu crouched, turning in a slow, tight circle in response to the albino's relentless movements. As he revolved to keep his flank away from the albino, he saw that Kor and Koloth continued to stand motionless on opposite sides of the cavern-like room, like a jury formulating a dispassionate evaluation of his performance. Or perhaps they were merely waiting for him to ask for their assistance.

Something in their dour expressions, however, told him that they would think less of him—and by extension the Federation as well—if they decided he was expecting rescue.

Meeting the albino's hard stare squarely, he said, "Just what makes you think *you're* entitled to revenge?"

The joyously psychotic expression on the brigand's chalky face collapsed into something that Sulu found even more dangerous-looking. "You denied me information that I needed very badly when you sabotaged that lab, Commander. Life-sustaining medicine, in effect. I came very close to dying because of it."

"You seem to have survived well enough without whatever you thought you might find in my mother's lab. And I *definitely* would have died, along with my family, if I hadn't overheard your plans in time to do something about them."

The albino swung his blade as though it were an ax, telegraphing the maneuver sufficiently to allow Sulu to sidestep the blow while countering with a two-handed parry and riposte of his own.

A lengthy series of similar parries and ripostes followed before the two fighters separated once more, catching their breaths as they studied and reevaluated one another. However thin and weak the albino might seem, Sulu understood viscerally that he couldn't afford to underestimate this man.

"It sounds almost as though *you* feel entitled to some measure of vengeance, Commander," the albino said as the two *bat'leth* wielders resumed their slow and wary mutual circling.

"Starfleet officers aren't big fans of vengeance," Sulu said, though he doubted such lofty pronouncements would succeed in fooling anybody here. He couldn't deny his struggle to remain calm as a steady and irrepressible tide of anger rose within him. This was, after all, the raider who had violated his family home four decades ago; this was the pirate who would have casually murdered him, or orphaned him by killing his parents without so much as a second thought.

"I had no idea that you Earthers were such determinedly virtuous folk, Commander," the other man said, smirking. "Maintaining that air of Federation superiority must be exhausting."

Sulu's eyes narrowed involuntarily. "At least I have no regrets. What I did that day in that lab I'd do again in a heartbeat."

"I don't doubt that a bit," the albino said with a wide but humorless grin. "Especially now that you are in a position to inflict a good deal more damage than you could have done all those long years ago. But tell me, Earther, honestly: Can you really be content with merely *arresting* me?"

Though he wanted nothing at the moment more than to plunge the tip of his blade straight into the albino's leather-clad chest, Sulu merely kept his blade steady, raised, and ready as the two men continued moving like a pair of co-orbiting planets, partners in a stately dance of death.

"Because of what you did at Korvat," Sulu said at length, "my duty is to bring you in alive—unless *you* choose to make that impossible for me."

That damnable grin only grew wider. "And what of my alleged actions on your precious border world?"

Sulu spun his blade once, though he never broke eye contact with his adversary as he returned the weapon to what amounted to a standard en garde position. "Let's just say I feel privileged to finally have the chance to do what I couldn't do when I was eleven years old."

Then he lunged forward, swinging the half-moon-shaped blade upward and down, like a scythe turned on its side. Despite being surprised and slightly off balance, the albino saved himself with a clumsy parry sixte.

Still more sparks flew as the blades collided loudly, again and again. Sulu feinted and jabbed, nicking the albino twice on the arm and lower torso before the pirate's blade bit into Sulu's upper right arm, just below the shoulder. The pressure suit absorbed so much of the blow's force that Sulu didn't think he'd actually suffered a cut. On the other hand, he might not have been hit at all but for the relatively bulky, movement-hampering garment.

The albino clearly regarded this as an opportunity to go in for the kill, but Sulu once again redirected the other man's charge. Their blades locked together briefly before the pirate took a single long and eminently sensible backward step.

"You handle the *bat'leth* better than I would have thought possible," the albino said, sounding winded. "At least for an Earther."

Sulu had to admit that he had been thinking much the same thing about his opponent. He paused for a moment to catch his breath, though he remained alert for any sudden movements on the other man's part. "I had a good teacher," he said, trying to waste as little breath as possible as he nodded toward Koloth.

Koloth had indeed shown Sulu some of the fundamental *Mok'bara* combat forms when their paths had last crossed more than two years earlier, including some crash instruction in basic *bat'leth* handling. But that hadn't been Sulu's first exposure to the ancient Klingon weapon; he had first encountered the crescent-shaped warrior's blade more than twenty years earlier, amid a pile of Klingon swords that lay discarded aboard the *Enterprise* immediately after the Beta XII-A entity had been driven from the ship.

But other than during his most recent previous encounter with Koloth—and the occasional polishings he gave the *bat'leth* he'd kept as a souvenir for the past two decades—Sulu hadn't actually trained all that much with Klingon blades. But he had always made a point of maintaining the skills that had won him the Inner Planets all-around fencing championship during his Starfleet Academy days, albeit with standard Earth weapons. And he knew that his current opponent, however ferocious and determined he might be, was a good deal older, lighter, and less robust than he was.

The albino charged again, roaring as he feinted low with his blade before turning completely around and aiming the opposite tip of his *bat'leth* straight at Sulu's temple. Sulu twisted and dodged the blade, which literally whistled past his ear. Continuing his motion, he turned and stepped inside his opponent's reach, forcing the albino to back up in haste.

Sulu suddenly dropped one end of his blade, then pulled the other end up with both hands, sweeping the albino's feet out from under him without doing any real damage. The brigand landed flat on his back with a sickening thud that the stone floor deadened only slightly. Sulu planted his left foot firmly on the albino's right wrist to prevent him from raising his blade. He brought his whole weight down on the other man, forcing his hand open so that the blade clattered uselessly to the floor.

Kicking the other *bat'leth* just out of reach, Sulu placed the tip of his own blade against the albino's pale throat.

"You are under arrest in the name of the United Federation of Planets."

The pirate only glared up at him, supine and helpless, yet still insolent. Contemptuous. Unrepentant.

Murdering bastard.

Kor and Koloth approached then, startling Sulu slightly; during the last few moments, his perspective on the universe had so narrowed that he and the albino had effectively become its only occupants.

"Why not simply slay him now, and have done with it?" Kor said as he moved a few paces closer. His eyes blazed with battle fervor even though his limping gait showed him to be in less-than-optimal condition for combat.

"That would be rather convenient for you, would it not, Kor?" Koloth said, looking as though he might kill the albino himself at any moment.

"We're taking him into custody," Sulu said, puzzled by Koloth's remark. It had been Koloth, not Kor, who had lost an entire ship and crew to one of the pirate's sneak attacks. So how would killing this man be "convenient" for Kor rather than Koloth? He recalled Kor's earlier comment that "family honor" formed at least part of his reason for chasing the albino. Had Koloth just made another oblique reference to that?

Staring into the albino's hate-filled visage, Sulu could not help graphically recalling all the havoc that this man had caused on Ganjitsu, as he had doubtless also done in myriad other places before and since—including Korvat, where he'd assassinated a Starfleet captain. And he had yet to be brought to book for that crime.

How easy it would be to just end this here and now, Sulu thought as he held his blade at the throat of the man who now lay winded, wounded, and helpless at his feet. The man who had so callously slain *Excelsior*'s original commanding officer.

The man who had, in essence, forever changed Sulu's destiny, once long ago on Ganjitsu, and once again much more recently on Korvat.

He wondered if Kor might not be right.

No. I'm not killing anyone in cold blood, he thought, disgusted with himself as the moment of temptation rose, peaked, and then passed.

Mostly.

"Your experiments in biogenic weapons are finished," he said to the man he was now trying very hard to think of as a prisoner in Starfleet custody, and therefore under Starfleet protection.

"You really think so?" the albino said, and then reached clumsily for Sulu's blade.

Sulu pushed the *bat'leth* harder against the albino's throat, causing the prisoner to gasp and let his pasty hands drop away from the weapon.

"I know so," Sulu said. "Whatever contraband you were carrying on that freighter of yours has been either captured or destroyed. Along with most of your peop—"

Sulu heard loud footfalls coming from the rear of the chamber. He looked past the albino in time to see eight or more large, grim-faced people enter, most of them smooth-headed Klingon males, with a pair of hulking green Orions and a tall, lithe Klingon woman thrown in for good measure. The pirates were all dressed in a motley array of mostly dark, paramilitary clothing. To a person, their belts were adorned with edged weapons of all sorts, ranging from daggers to swords of various descriptions.

But clutched in their hands were large, dangerous-looking alien pistols that might have been Klingon projectile weapons.

Sulu had brought one of his own old firearms along with him, but it had taken some damage when the albino's explosive trap had detonated; he didn't want to risk firing it, even if he could have gotten it free of the storage pocket in his suit's right thigh before being shot dead for his trouble.

The albino spoke in eerily calm tones. "Unlike your particle-beam weapons, Commander, *these* firearms are immune to electromagnetic interference. And I have far fewer compunctions about firing them down here than aboard my ship."

Sulu's back teeth ground together.

"Drop your swords!" shouted one of the Orions, his pistol leveled straight at Sulu's head in a two-handed grip. Like the Orion, the rest of the pirates stood in similar combat crouches, the barrels of each of their weapons trained squarely upon either Sulu, Koloth, or Kor. Across the six meters or so that now separated Sulu and his teammates from the most distant of the guns, there was precious little chance that any of the shooters would miss his or her chosen target.

Neither Sulu nor Koloth nor Kor laid down their weapons. The albino favored all three men with a smile fashioned from pure, distilled malevolence.

"These weapons fire lead projectiles propelled by explosive chemical reactions," he said. "Needless to say, they're every bit as lethal as military-issue disruptors. And, at the present moment, they are considerably *more* dangerous than any of your *bat'leths.*"

Sulu scowled in puzzlement over the albino's pedantic explanation of his weaponry. Then he remembered that the pirate had fled his own ship before Sulu's party, carrying essentially the same sort of firearms, boarded his freighter.

He launched two auxiliary craft when he left his ship, Sulu reminded himself, silently cursing himself for letting himself get caught with his pants down. *He blew one of them up just to try to kill us, and he doesn't seem all that torn up about having lost his freighter and its contents. Maybe he's got a much larger and better-resourced criminal organization than any of us gave him credit for.*

Sulu was willing to believe the latter notion at least as much as the former, since it certainly helped explain how the albino had managed to keep himself alive for so many long, desperate years, in spite of a chronic life-threatening medical condition.

He also thought he wasn't likely to be alive much longer to wonder about it if he and his comrades continued defying the orders of the albino's rescuers.

Sulu gazed at his two Klingon companions. "Better to die on one's feet than to live on one's knees," Kor snarled, his blade raised defiantly in his gauntleted fingers. Koloth stood in silence, holding his weapon at the ready as well.

It'll be a very bad day for détente if either of these guys gets killed on my watch, Sulu thought, imagining the Klingon government posthumously blaming him for the incident—and then taking out its ire on the Federation, thereby undoing decades of the arduous ongoing diplomatic work that had been accomplished by Sarek, Kamarag, Curzon Dax, and others.

"Is it better to be summarily shot in the skull?" Sulu said, addressing both Kor and Koloth. "Or is it better to live to fight another day?"

If our host plans to offer us that option, he thought before letting his *bat'leth* fall to the stone floor with a slightly echoing clatter.

The blades of Kor and Koloth remained in their hands, as firmly attached to each man as were their own limbs.

"Drop your swords! Now!" the other Orion shouted, his pistol leveled straight at Kor, as other gun barrels chose either Kor, Koloth, or Sulu as targets, seemingly at random.

Covered by the remainder of the pirate rescue party, the second Orion male approached and helped the albino get his feet beneath him again. Another one of the brigand's people—the tall Klingon woman, Sulu noted—knelt briefly, scooped up the albino's fallen blade, and handed it to him.

"Let these estimable Klingon warriors keep their precious *bat'leth*s," the albino said to his people as the standoff continued unresolved, growing steadily more tense as the seconds stretched and lengthened. "After all, if you were to shoot them down where they stand right now, they'd need to keep their cutlery in their hands to be allowed into *Sto-Vo-Kor.* We wouldn't want our guests to die as anything other than honored heroes, now, would we?"

"What would the likes of *you* know about such things as honor?" Kor said.

The albino chuckled as he walked directly toward Sulu. Apparently still addressing Kor, he said, "Cousin, whether you like it or not, the likes of me *are* the likes of you."

Cousin?

But Sulu had to put aside his bewilderment when the

albino suddenly swung his *bat'leth* toward him, stopping
short of landing a blow, yet pressing one of the weapon's
razor-sharp edges hard against his cheek. Kor and Koloth
both seemed about to spring into action in response, but
they held themselves back nevertheless, perhaps persuaded
by the half-dozen or so handheld projectile weapons that
were still aimed straight at them. Or by the keen metal
edge that pressed within a few centimeters of Sulu's carotid
artery, which was accessible just above his environmental
suit's open neck ring.

"Don't worry," the albino said, almost soothingly. "I
needn't kill any of you. At least . . . not *today.*"

Sulu felt a slight nick against his cheek, but no real pain.
It wasn't until the albino suddenly backed away, stepping
behind the protective line of his armed subordinates, that
Sulu saw the delicate tracery of his own blood on the tip of
the other man's blade. In response to the pirate chieftain's
sharp commands, his people covered his escape, their firearms at the ready as they exited en masse through a rear
door.

Now he has a sample of my DNA, Sulu realized, suddenly
chilled to the marrow. *He can take his time killing me now.
The same way he killed the woman in the bar on Galdonterre.*

"They're retreating," Kor said, still clutching his *bat'leth*
before him.

Koloth shook his head. "No. He's merely toying with us."

"That was foolish of him," Kor said. "He left us armed."

"But not nearly as well armed as *he* is," Sulu said, wishing that Klingon outrage didn't make it so necessary to state
the obvious.

The solid rock beneath Sulu's boots shuddered, like the
deck of a starship that had just taken a heavy phaser barrage.

"Autodestruct device?" Koloth wondered aloud. Sulu was

impressed by the cool detachment with which the Klingon seemed to contemplate the prospect of his own imminent death.

"Or perhaps he merely wants us to *believe* he has an autodestruct device," said Kor. "So that *we* will retreat as well."

The ground spasmed again, harder this time. Sulu didn't like it one little bit. While he had to question the logic of demolishing such an inaccessible and obviously expensive hideout when the albino possessed far simpler means of disposing of his enemies, Sulu wasn't willing to wager his life on the motivations of such an obviously unstable personality.

"What is that proverb you Klingons have about not fighting in burning houses?" he said.

Without saying another word, Sulu recovered his helmet and led the way back toward the same doorway through which the team had entered in the first place. He was gratified to see that both Kor and Koloth had quietly decided to exercise the better part of valor by doing likewise.

There'll be other chances to get this guy, Sulu told himself, reaching into the pocket on his left thigh for his ruptured suit's emergency patch kit as he walked. *And maybe sooner rather than later.*

PART IV: SIFTING THE ASHES

The real voyage of discovery consists not in seeking new landscapes, but in having new eyes.

—Marcel Proust (1871–1922)

THIRTY-SEVEN

The door before him slid obediently open, and Sulu stepped inside. "Hello, Gertrude," he murmured to the carnivorous Delvin cat trap plant that sat in a planter atop the dresser on the wall opposite his bed. The plant seemed to wave its thorny gold and crimson fronds at him in response to his voice, like a small, sessile dog eagerly greeting its returning master.

Exhaustion finally moved in for the kill as the door closed behind him; sprawling across the bed without bothering to remove his uniform jacket, he felt blissful sleep beginning to enfold him almost before his body had finished settling on the mattress.

The door chime buzzed with skull-piercing sharpness at that precise moment. *There had better be a damned good reason for this,* Sulu thought, sitting up slowly, as though struggling to escape the fierce gravitational pull of a neutron star. *Like all-out galactic war.*

"Come," he said with as much pleasantness as he could muster.

The door to his quarters slid open again, to reveal Lieutenant Commander Cutler standing in the corridor beyond.

"Commander," she said, speaking with an uncharacteristic tentativeness.

As much curious as concerned, Sulu stood. "Come in," he said.

Cutler dutifully stepped inside, only to stand at parade rest, awkwardly silent.

Sulu tipped his head in puzzlement. "Is anything wrong, Cutler?"

She looked almost scandalized, or at least vulnerable in a way he'd never seen before. "No. Sir. The opposite, in fact. Doctor Klass and Ambassador Kamarag are both finally conscious, and Doctor Chapel says that the prognosis looks good for both of them."

"That's great news," Sulu said, truly delighted for the first time since circumstances had thrust command of *Excelsior* upon him. He gestured toward the couch beside the wall near Gertrude. "Why don't you have a seat, Commander?"

But Cutler remained standing stiffly as she continued. "The shuttlecraft are stowed, and Henry's crew is checking them both for damage from the Qul Tuq magnetar. And all three of the Klingon captains have consented to Doctor Chapel's request that they come aboard for a medical debriefing—in the interests of the mutual security of both their Empire and our Federation."

"Doctor Chapel has always been a very persuasive woman," he said, genuinely admiring the doctor's creativity in marketing physical examinations—from which most Klingon warriors would vehemently demur—as debriefings that were critical to galactic security. "Let me know when the Klingons are finished in sickbay. I want to talk with them before they ship out."

She nodded. "Of course, Commander."

She's still just not comfortable addressing me as "Captain" yet, is she? he thought, wondering if she was going to hold out until she actually saw the captain's bars on his shoulders before forcing herself to utter the title in his presence.

Of course, there was a good chance that that simply wasn't going to happen, given all the toes he had stepped on over the past two days.

But Sulu could see from Cutler's posture that something else was on her mind. Something that seemed to trouble her greatly.

"Is that all, Cutler?"

"No." She hesitated. "Yes. Sir. I wanted to . . . I wanted to compliment you."

Sulu's eyes widened involuntarily in surprise, but he made no move to interrupt her.

"I've seen how much you've risked since you . . . took over for Captain Styles," she said. "I know that it would have been a lot easier and safer for you to have stayed on our side of the border."

"Safer, maybe," he said, shrugging. "But sitting still is never easy. At least it wouldn't have put me sideways with my orders from Starfleet Command, though."

"Exactly," she said, nodding. "But you saw what had to be done, and you did it. You were committed enough to the idea of building a practical détente with the Klingons to get off the safe road and take a more dangerous one instead."

"Don't congratulate me yet, Commander. It's a road that still might lead straight to a penal colony, at least for me. Depending, of course, on how cranky the top brass are feeling after reading our reports."

He had always imagined her relishing the prospect of Starfleet Command shooting him down in flames. Instead, a somber expression descended across her features.

"What I'm trying to say," she said, "is that I owe you an apology. I practically accused you of abetting the murder of Captain Styles. Then you put everything on the line to try to bring his killer to justice."

Though this hopeful moment of rapprochement with Cutler had begun to buoy his flagging spirits, thoughts of the albino created a powerful emotional downdraft.

"The operative word is 'try,'" he said, his jaw muscles stiffening into immobility as though they'd been set in thermoconcrete. "*Succeeding* is something else entirely."

"The albino has been surviving out on the frontier for decades, Commander," Cutler said, her tone going from sympathetic to gently chiding. "You've been on his trail for less than two weeks, and you've helped capture a couple dozen of his people, as well as what has to be a huge proportion of the biogenic contraband he controls. It may take some time to bring him down entirely. Even the civilization in Star System 892 wasn't built in a day."

Sulu allowed himself a wan smile at that last observation. Still, it bothered him intensely that neither he nor the Klingons had managed to capture or kill the albino himself during the confrontation on the moon of Qul Tuq II.

"Besides," Cutler continued, "it's entirely possible that he died when his compound blew apart."

Sulu folded his arms and shook his head, all thoughts of sleep now banished. "What was it you just said about him being a survivor?"

The intensity of Cutler's momentary answering glower told him that she, too, was continuing to take this manhunt very personally—and also told him that she didn't want anyone to see that, perhaps him especially. Her briefly unguarded expression bespoke a wound than ran even deeper than the untimely death of her captain.

Before he could find a delicate way to probe the matter, she said, "I just wish the sensor scans we tried to take of the blast area were more conclusive one way or another. As it is, he could have been vaporized—or he might have used the explosion to cover his escape in the second auxiliary ship. With all the magnetic interference in that system, he wouldn't have had a very hard time keeping himself hidden from both *Excelsior* and the *Klothos,* and then escaping."

"I certainly hope that's not the case," Sulu said. *For your sake as well as mine, Cutler.* But he knew the smart money wouldn't wager on that possibility.

And neither would the Klingons.

Feeling helpless was probably the one thing in all the universe that Kang hated the most. And confinement in the oppressive sterility of *Excelsior*'s sickbay, however temporary it might prove to be, only exacerbated his increasingly intolerable restiveness.

"Hurghom, I have been idle here long enough," he growled. "Since Doctor Chapel finally seems to be quite finished poking and prodding us all, my convalescence would be better spent aboard the *QaD*!"

The elderly Klingon doctor moved swiftly to the side of the biobed on which Kang sat, bereft of his weapons, his armor, and much of his uniform. "The fleet is already towing the *QaD* to one of our repair facilities, Captain. Captain Kor will take us aboard the *Klothos* as soon as we are all ready to depart."

Kang scowled, feeling his smooth brow crumpling until it felt as rough as weathered granite. "I *know* all that, surgeon. But I should be on board my own vessel all the same, overseeing her repairs."

Kang knew that the sooner the *QaD* was once again spaceworthy, the sooner he would be able to make certain that the raider of Korvat faced an eternity in *Gre'thor*'s foul belly, where he belonged. Or, failing that, he could at least thwart the albino's future efforts to assemble and deploy biogenic weapons anywhere within the boundaries of Klingon space.

"Hey, keep it down over there," growled the iron-haired human woman who lay on one of the nearby beds. "There are sick people here trying to rest."

Another Klingon, a man of advanced years with an impressively textured *HemQuch* forehead, stood unsteadily beside a third biobed, his tall, broad body partly draped in an undignified hospital gown.

"Speak for yourself, Doctor Klass," Ambassador Kamarag said, accenting his words with a convivial display of his sharpened teeth. "Apart from yourself, I see no sick people here."

Klass returned Kamarag's grin. "I used to think that *doctors* made the worst patients, Mister Ambassador. But that was before I shared a sickbay with a couple of restless Klingons."

The doors that lay between Kang and freedom suddenly hissed open, and Dr. Chapel stepped into the room, followed by Commander Sulu, Captains Koloth and Kor, and Ambassador Curzon Dax.

Chapel stopped at the side of Dr. Klass's bed. "I hope our guests didn't give you too much trouble, Doctor."

"*These* guys?" Klass said wryly, hiking a thumb in Kang's direction. "They're pussycats."

Kang could only hope that "pussycats" were predators at least as fierce as the sabre bears of Qo'noS.

"Sounds like you'll be strong enough to take charge again down here any minute now," Chapel said to Klass.

Klass nodded, smiling crookedly. "At least until I finally come to my senses and take my retirement, Christine. And when that day comes I don't think I'll have to do much arm-twisting to persuade our new CO to draft *you* for this job."

Chapel blushed in the glare of Sulu's answering grin. "Thanks for letting me pitch in," she said. "But since I'm still temporarily in charge down here, I'm putting you on a diet free of life-changing decisions—at least until after you're released. Doctor's orders."

"Fair enough," Klass grumbled.

"We haven't had time yet for a formal medical briefing on everyone's condition since the Qul Tuq mission," Sulu said, facing Chapel.

Chapel's face abruptly grew very taut and grim. "I wanted to talk you about that once Doctor Hurghom and I finished double-checking the results of our preliminary biomolecular analyses."

"You scanned us all right after we came back aboard," Dax said, one eyebrow raised in evident curiosity. "I thought everyone checked out as healthy then."

"So did we," Hurghom said. "But that was before I began to notice certain . . . discrepancies in the initial readings. Discrepancies that Doctor Chapel has confirmed, at least tentatively."

Kang did not like the sound of any of this. "What *kind* of discrepancies?"

Chapel nodded as several pairs of apprehensive eyes settled squarely upon her. "Doctor Hurghom and I used the past baseline readings stored in the medical files of both our respective crews in order to make certain that no one serving aboard either *Excelsior* or the *Klothos* was exposed to any of the albino's biochemical agents during the Qul Tuq battle."

"You said that all of my personnel were cleared of any biomedical danger," Kor said, his smooth brow now nearly as striated as Kamarag's.

"And so they are," Hurghom said. He turned toward Sulu, who was clearly just as concerned about the welfare of *Excelsior*'s crew. "No Starfleet personnel show any signs of having been affected either."

"But a handful of others showed subtle but definite signs

of very recent infection by bioengineered pathogens," Chapel said. "These pathogens are engineered retroviruses, and they appear to have been individually tailored to affect only their specific hosts."

Kang liked what he was hearing less and less.

"Fortunately, the list of infected parties is quite short," Hurghom said. "There are only four names on it, in fact."

"Enough mystery," Sulu said, scowling at both physicians. "*Who* has been infected?"

"Curzon Dax," Chapel said. "Along with three Klingons."

"Let me guess," Koloth said. "I am one of the three."

"As am I," Kor said.

"And me as well, no doubt," Kang said, feeling as humorless and angry as his two fellow Klingon captains looked.

"I'm afraid so," said Chapel, her sapphire eyes taking on the aspect of a regretful yet dutiful executioner.

"Can you cure it?" Sulu asked.

Hurghom shrugged. "Given enough years of study, anything is possible. But this particular retrovirus is an extraordinarily complex one. The odds against us neutralizing it any time soon are extremely slim."

"What will it do to us?" Kor wanted to know.

"Over the long haul there's no way to know for sure," Chapel said. "It could be a very nasty, pernicious little bug, or it might end up proving harmless. All I can say for certain at this point is that is has already begun rewriting portions of your DNA at a very subtle, and maybe even fundamental, level."

"That isn't a very satisfying explanation, Doctor," Koloth said, almost snarling.

To her credit, Chapel didn't quail in the face of Koloth's fury. Taking a confident step toward him, she said, "I'm afraid that's the best you're going to get at the moment, Captain. In order to cure this thing any time soon, or even take the initial step of predicting which specific genes it will rewrite, we would first have to thoroughly understand the albino's biodesign and manufacturing processes, as well as this virus's specific purpose."

Hurghom affirmed Chapel's analysis with a vigorous nod. "Without that knowledge, attempting to neutralize this retrovirus would be like trying to decode an encrypted message without the necessary cryptography key."

Kang was becoming more determined than ever to get the *QaD* back into service quickly, the better to resume the hunt as soon as possible. "I will find the albino and force him to reveal his bioengineering secrets."

"The four of you faced the albino at close quarters," Sulu said, his gaze sweeping across Kang, Kor, Koloth, and Dax. "Just as I did."

"And you're wondering why *you* haven't been affected as well," Kang said.

"Exactly," Sulu said, his eyes again focused on Chapel. "How about it, Doctor?"

"Hard to say for sure until I do some more investigation," she said, stroking her chin thoughtfully. "But we *can* venture a few guesses. For one, you might not have been one of Qagh's specific targets."

"Or perhaps the albino was not able to acquire a DNA sample from you at an earlier time, as he must have done with the others in order to individually tailor disease organisms against them," Hurghom said.

"He might have quietly collected DNA samples from us at Korvat, just before the attack," Kang said.

"That's what Doctor Hurghom and I are assuming," Chapel said.

Kang wondered exactly how it had been done. Had the albino or one of his confederates collected hair fibers from the conference tables? Or perhaps he had drawn his victims' DNA from the trace amounts of saliva that had adhered to their drinking vessels.

He decided that the details didn't matter. Only the results.

"So you're saying that Qagh just happened not to get hold of my DNA," Sulu said, addressing both Chapel and Hurghom. "At least not in time to create a tailored bioweapon with my name on it."

"Or he might have taken your DNA as well, and then exposed you to your own personally tailored retrovirus just as he did with the others," Dr. Klass said from the biobed where she lay propped halfway up into a sitting position on a pile of pillows. "Perhaps we've simply failed to detect any signs of your infection so far."

"Sounds pretty unbelievable," Sulu said.

"I might have thought so, too," Klass said. "Until I remembered that your blood still carries traces of the Omega IV virus—a pathogen that strongly resembles the retrovirus that Dax, Kang, Koloth, and Kor are carrying."

"You mean Qagh's latest bioweapon is *based* on the Omega IV virus?" Sulu asked.

"Just like the one you found on Galdonterre," Klass said, nodding.

Chapel nodded as well. "The Omega IV virus in your blood may have spared you from infection. Your time on Omega IV could have given you an accidental but effective advance inoculation against Qagh's Omega IV–based bioweapons."

Sulu looked astonished. "You're saying that the same virus that turned the entire crew of the *Exeter* into lumps of crystal—and then later *prevented* the same thing from happening to me—might also have immunized me against Qagh's current bag of tricks?"

"The jury is still out on all the biomolecular particulars," Chapel said, spreading her hands. "But I concur with Doctor Klass and Doctor Hurghom's opinion that it's a distinct possibility."

Kang suppressed a shudder. Omega IV sounded to him like an insufferable menace to the galaxy, the sort of world to which the High Council might do well to consider dispatching Admiral Hembec's planet-obliterating fleet—once it completed its current mission of locating and sterilizing the homeworld of the fuzzy, fecund eco-menaces known as the *yIH,* of course.

A shrill whistle issued from the comm unit mounted on one of the sickbay's walls, jolting Kang out of his unpleasant reverie.

"Bridge to Captain Sulu," said the disembodied female voice that followed.

Sulu strode toward the nearest companel and activated it. "Sulu here. Go ahead, Rand."

"Incoming subspace message, Captain. It's from someone claiming to be Qagh."

Sulu wasted no time dithering. "Can you trace it to its source?" he said, a split second before Kang would have said much the same thing.

"Negative, Captain. The source is obscured, apparently by the magnetic field of the Qul Tuq magnetar."

Which means, Kang thought, *either that he is still hiding his ship in the inner Qul Tuq system, or that he is bouncing his subspace signal off the star from elsewhere.* The former scenario would make him hard enough to locate. The latter would give him an all but infinite number of places to secrete himself and whatever remained of his organization and resources.

"Record it," Sulu said, "and pipe it down here."

Chapel hastened toward one of the overhead displays attached to a nearby empty biobed and quickly tapped several manual commands directly into the screen interface. The display's orderly ranks of multicolored columns, designed to provide quick graphical reference to a patient's various systems and vital signs, suddenly went blank.

The face of a chalk-white man with vaguely Klingon features, and of an even more vague apparent age, appeared in the previously empty space.

Sulu stepped toward the screen's visual pickup. "Qagh," he said, his voice deep and authoritative. "You won't be able to stay on the run forever."

The albino favored the human captain with a haughty but humorless smile. *"Really, Commander Sulu? All the years that have passed since Ganjitsu would seem to argue rather persuasively otherwise."*

"You have attacked and destroyed Klingon military vessels and attempted to interfere with the diplomatic affairs of the Empire," Koloth said with a cold fury that seemed to lower the room's temperature perceptibly. Kang understood that anger well, for he had experienced it himself on the occasion of the destruction of one of his early commands, the battle cruiser *I.K.S. Klolode.*

"The High Council treats such affronts with far more gravity than it does mere border raids," Kang said. "Make no mistake, Qagh: You *will* be brought to book for your crimes."

To Kang's annoyance, the albino continued as though Kang had not even spoken.

"Captain Kor," the freebooter said, his demeanor calm even though his eyes fairly blazed with hatred. *"I have set a potent weapon against you, my esteemed kinsman—an unstoppable force that also targets Captains Koloth and Kang, in addition to Ambassador Dax."*

"We know all about your retrovirus, *petaQ,*" Kor said with unconcealed loathing.

The albino grinned, a mannerism that gave him an uncanny resemblance to a *HemQuch* Klingon skull shorn of all its soft parts. *"I seriously doubt that, my kinsman. But you will know all about it, in time. More than you ever wished to discover. As will Captain Sulu, once I find an opportunity to make him a target as well."*

"But *why?*" Chapel asked, appearing both angry and perplexed.

"Perhaps you should ask Captain Kor. He knows as well as I do that he is guilty of propping up the once-disgraced Klingon House that abandoned me and denied me my rightful future. I owe him an honor debt of vengeance for that, as well as retribution to your captain, to Koloth and Kang, and to Dax for abetting that crime after the fact—and for greatly inconveniencing my various enterprises through their clumsy intervention at Qul Tuq."

He lures us into traps that fail to kill us and loses a freighter and a safe house, Kang thought, disgusted. *And we're clumsy?*

Aloud, he said, "Why not simply kill us and be done with it?"

"Kill you? No. That would be too simple, and would finish too quickly, to slake the fires of vengeance."

"It is also beyond your capacity, weakling," Kor spat. "Unless it is your intention to *talk* us to death."

"Believe whatever comforts you, kinsman," the albino said, grinning. *"Regardless, I can think of no better retribution than to rob all five of you of your futures, just as I have been denied mine. And I have contrived to do so in the most painful manner imaginable."*

"Come and face us again," Koloth said. "And you will be on far more intimate terms with pain than you had ever dreamed possible."

The albino ignored Koloth's threat. *"The children shall pay for the sins of their fathers,"* he said, and then vanished from the screen before Kang or anyone else could respond.

Though the pirate's effrontery made Kang's heart blaze with the deep internal fires of the Kri'stak Volcano, his backbone experienced a sudden chill reminiscent of that sacred mountain's ice-crusted slopes.

•   •   •

Sulu stood in silence as the image on the biobed screen disappeared, to be replaced by the unit's customary array of colorful columnar readouts.

"He's bluffing," Kor said, still staring contemplatively at the screen.

Sulu wished he shared Kor's confidence. "That virus is no bluff, Kor," he said, though he was addressing Kang, Koloth, and Dax as well. "The four of you *are* infected."

Kor nodded. "Agreed. But it isn't much of a weapon, is it? Not by Klingon standards, at any rate. If it really *were* as potent as he claims, then why are we not dead already?"

Though Sulu was well acquainted with Klingon bluster, he hoped these men wouldn't make the fatal mistake of underestimating their adversary.

Dr. Hurghom was evidently thinking along similar lines. "Judging from the complexity of the albino's creations," he said, "I would not assume that very much lies outside the scope of his abilities."

Sulu nodded vigorously. "I saw someone die from one of Qagh's tailored viruses a couple of weeks ago on Galdonterre," he said, the image of the woman's flash-crystallized corpse still disturbingly green in his memory. "If that's what he really has planned for our *children* . . ." He let his words remain hanging in the air, for everyone to examine in the silent privacy of their own thoughts.

"Neither Koloth nor Kang nor I have made time as yet to start families," Kor said at length.

"Nor have I," Dax said. After a thoughtful pause, he added, "At least, not *exactly.*" Sulu was tempted to ask the Trill what he meant by that, but decided it was a matter best followed up on later.

"So if the albino was speaking truthfully, then his threat *has* no target other than the five of us," Koloth said.

A surge of fear roiled deep within Sulu's guts.

"He *does* have a target," he said very quietly. "My daughter."

Sulu tried to take comfort in the fact that Demora was now dozens of light-years away from the border regions where the albino plied his odious trade. She was attending Starfleet Academy, one of the most secure places on Earth itself, the very heart of the Federation, the seat of Starfleet's galactic military power. All he could do was contact her via subspace compic, warn her of the danger that she might face in the indeterminate future, and take whatever comfort he could from the knowledge that she was safely out of the albino's reach, at least at the moment.

But how long she would *remain* so was anybody's guess.

THIRTY-EIGHT

After seeing the still-convalescing Ambassador Kamarag, Dr. Hurghom, and Captains Kang, Koloth, and Kor safely back aboard the *Klothos,* Sulu instructed Cutler to take *Excelsior* back into Federation space without any further delay. Then he accompanied Dr. Chapel to sickbay, where he hoped that either she or Dr. Klass might provide some additional insight into the dangers posed by the albino's retroviruses.

Instead, he found himself standing ringside, along with Chapel, at a most unexpected battle.

"The scanner picked up some highly improbable readings, Ambassador Dax," Dr. Klass said. "They could be related to your retroviral infection."

"I'll let Doctor Dareel back on Trill make that determination," said Curzon Dax. "But thank you."

Dr. Klass held up a medical tricorder, carefully displaying its darkened front panel, which showed that it wasn't in operation at the moment. "Mister Ambassador," she said, gently cajoling. "Please be reasonable."

Dax folded his arms across his chest and assayed a scowl that looked incongruously curmudgeonly on someone so young. "I think I've been *more* than reasonable, Doctor. You know as well as I do that my government has given me strict instructions to submit to no invasive medical scans, other than those administered by my own physician."

"Except in the case of an emergency," Klass said with a scowl every bit as formidable as the one Dax displayed.

"The emergency clause doesn't apply in this case," Dax said. "You said yourself that the virus I'm carrying isn't casually transmissible. And it isn't as though I've just refused some vital, life-saving surgical procedure."

Chapel took a step toward Klass. "He's right, Judy. I've worked with Trill patients before. I know their medical protocols."

Klass glowered at her old friend, making Sulu glad that he wasn't the current target of his CMO's ire. "Check the shingle out in the hallway, Chris. It says that *I'm* this ship's CMO. Therefore *I'm* the one who interprets the rulebooks regarding the practice of medicine on this ship. Not you."

"You're not taking into account diplomatic privilege," Chapel said.

Klass hiked a thumb in Sulu's direction. "That's up to the discretion of this ship's current commanding officer, kiddo." Turning toward Dax, she continued. "Assuming he sees things the way I do, you're free to lodge a formal protest through Ambassador Sarek's office the minute we're done." She turned and looked inquiringly at Sulu. "Just say the word, Skipper, and I'll pull rank and kick ass."

Before Sulu could begin to think the matter through, the comm unit on the wall whistled, heralding a familiar businesslike voice. *"Ambassador Sarek to Ambassador Dax."*

Looking relieved at the interruption, the young Trill

excused himself and hastened toward the companel. "Dax here, Mister Ambassador. Go ahead."

"I wish to discuss your preliminary report regarding your recent . . . foray into Klingon space, Mister Dax. Five minutes from now in my quarters, if you please."

Although the Vulcan diplomat never actually raised his voice, his words carried a definite subtext of reprimand. The Trill must have picked up on it as well, because he no longer seemed all that pleased by Sarek's interruption.

In fact, he looked pale all of a sudden. "I'm on my way," he said before closing the channel. Without so much as another word, or even a backward glance, he strode quickly toward the exit.

Klass appeared to be ready to stop him, but Sulu waved her off. After all, there was no reason the present confrontation couldn't be postponed for a while—at least until after Dax knew whether or not he still had a job that allowed him the possibility of invoking diplomatic privilege.

Still, Sulu couldn't help but wonder why Dax had been so adamant in his refusal of Klass's request that he undergo a full medical exam. *What's gotten into him anyway?*

It was the first time since he had come aboard *Excelsior* that Curzon Dax had been asked to meet Ambassador Sarek in the Vulcan's quarters rather than in one of the starship's seemingly endless inventory of conference rooms and observation lounges.

Not a good sign, he thought as the door slid open before him.

The first thing that Dax noticed after stepping across the threshold was the hot, dry air. The second was the almost complete darkness, which entirely enfolded the ambiguously-sized space, except for the diamond-flecked jumble of stars that glowed across the gulf of night like distant campfires, and the single burning candle that cast a chiaroscuro halo around Sarek's rough-hewn features.

"Sit," said the Vulcan, who was himself seated cross-legged on the floor. He wore a simple black robe adorned only with a few white figures that Dax recognized as peace-representational characters drawn from Vulcan's dominant written language.

Dax did as Sarek directed, sitting on the floor on the candle's opposite side, his anxiety steadily mounting as the silence stretched to an almost painful tautness.

"I have been in meditation for the past several hours, Mister Dax," Sarek said after a subjective eternity, his eyes closed.

That's also *not a particularly good sign,* Dax thought. Prolonged meditation meant that the Vulcan was struggling to control his anger over Dax's insubordinate decision to accompany the Klingons on their initial attempt to bring the albino to justice.

Sarek opened his eyes, which flashed like dark pulsars in the candlelight. "Your gambit was unsuccessful."

"If by that you mean that Qagh slipped away from us, Mister Ambassador," he said, "then I suppose you're right."

"Protocols must be observed in any hierarchy, Mister Dax. Even in the diplomatic service. Perhaps *especially* in the diplomatic service."

Dax swallowed hard. "I understand, sir."

"Diplomacy requires hard, painstaking work, executed within a strong framework of rules. Success requires both wisdom and patience. I offer you the example of my ongoing negotiations with the Legarans as an illustrative case in point."

Dax blinked in surprise at this, since he could think of few races in the galaxy that resembled the Klingons less than did the Legarans. Far from being aggressive folk who had built an empire on the blood and toil of countless conquered species, the Legarans were content to laze their time away in fetid pools of goo, where they dreamed and thought and planned on timescales that encompassed many generations in the life cycles of most other sentients. Dax thought that the Legarans bore far more resemblance to the long-lived, sluglike symbionts who dwelled within the abdominal pouches of joined Trills like himself.

"I'm afraid I don't understand," Dax said.

"I have worked with the Legarans steadily for the past sixteen years, with little to show for it so far," Sarek said, entering what Dax recognized as the Vulcan's long-explanation-cum-lecture mode. "Many more years, or perhaps even decades, are likely to pass before the Federation can expect any substantive agreements to emerge. Any rash, unthinking action on my part vis-à-vis the Legarans would jeopardize the entire diplomatic process.

"Just as rash, unthinking action involving a power as volatile as the Klingon Empire could jeopardize the lives of untold millions."

Dax braced himself. *He's actually going to fire me,* he thought. *I'm about to be cashiered right out of the Diplomatic Corps.*

Though the notion carried a terrifying taint of failure, Dax also found it somehow liberating, as though the act of squarely facing his own personal and professional worst-case scenario at long last had relieved him of the burden of fear. It gave him the courage to speak plainly and directly.

And, perhaps, undiplomatically as well.

"Respectfully, Mister Ambassador," Dax said, "the Klingons aren't content to dither over their every decision for years the way the Legarans are. If you want to deal with the Klingons, they have to respect you, and the best way to gain that respect is to demonstrate qualities they admire."

Sarek raised an eyebrow, clearly unaccustomed to hearing such hard-edged candor from his protégé. "Indeed."

Dax decided he had nothing to lose by pressing his point to the end. "I stand by my decision to accompany the Klingons, regardless of whatever might have become of the albino as a consequence. It was the right thing to do then, and I'd do it again in a heartbeat. However my decision might look to you now, I think it will pay off handsomely for us in terms of détente, perhaps sooner than you think."

"You were ordered to remain on *Excelsior*," Sarek said, "in the interests of reinforcing our current peace gestures toward the Klingons."

"If I had stayed behind while the Klingons conducted their manhunt, they would probably look on our *future* peace gestures as just that—gestures."

Sarek lapsed into a silence that bespoke either deep contemplation or a renewed attempt at comprehensive anger management. Dax had already begun mentally revising his professional curriculum vitae in preparation for his next job when Sarek's facial tectonics underwent a sudden shift.

It might have been a trick of the candlelight. Or perhaps it was something that only resembled a very small, very subtle smile.

"It is now clear to me that you and my son Spock have a great deal in common, Mister Dax," the Vulcan said. "Reckless impatience, for one thing."

"Doctor Chapel taught me a particular Earth idiom that might be appropriate to quote now," Dax said, returning Sarek's smile with a broad grin of his own. "'The apple doesn't fall far from the tree.'"

Sarek raised both eyebrows in response, but otherwise allowed the saying to pass without comment. Steepling his fingers between his nose and chin, he said, "It is also clear to me that I cannot argue with positive results, particularly in regard to adversaries as important and as dangerous as the

Klingons. Despite your unorthodox approach to diplomacy, Mister Dax—which the IDIC philosophy arguably dictates that I regard as a consequence of your many long and varied symbiotic life-experiences as a joined Trill—you have demonstrated a more nuanced understanding of Klingon psychology than I possess."

Dax shifted uncomfortably on the floor and wondered how anyone could possibly sit this way for hours at a stretch. "Thank you, sir," he said.

Sarek rose to his feet, moving with supple grace. "Therefore I am willing to forgo taking any disciplinary action against you for your insubordination—at least so long as the promising relationships you have forged with Kang, Koloth, and Kor continue moving in such a productive direction."

"I'll do my best, sir," Dax said.

"Of that I have no doubt, Mister Dax," Sarek said. No trace of the earlier smile remained on his face, if it had ever been there at all. "Provided, of course, that you resist the temptation to allow one early success to make you overconfident in the future."

In spite of himself, Dax allowed his eyes to widen into an almost theatrical display of wounded surprise.

"Overconfident? *Me*?"

Sitting behind the desk in her quarters, Cutler stared at the swagger stick as though it were an ancient artifact of some kind. The blistering and discoloration along its charred shaft neatly reinforced the illusion.

Her door chime sounded. She set the burned stick down beside her computer and straightened in her chair, which she turned toward the door. "Come."

The door hissed open and Commander Sulu entered, looking tired but alert, the flap of his uniform jacket unbuttoned and hanging open. Like her late captain, she hated wearing her jacket that way anywhere outside of her quarters.

"Commander Sulu," she said, trying unsuccessfully to keep the surprise out of her voice; her new de facto CO was the last person she had expected to make a social call. She quickly got to her feet and took her own maroon jacket off the back of her chair and started to put it on over her white uniform turtleneck.

"As you were, Commander," Sulu said as he approached the desk. "Sorry to bother you so late in the evening."

"It's no bother, sir." She sat, her jacket on but unbuttoned. "What can I do for you?"

Sulu shook his head, displaying a gentle yet somehow serious expression as he followed her lead and took a seat on the low sofa next to the panoramic window. "Nothing, Commander. I came because . . . because I was concerned about you."

She blinked, momentarily speechless. "I'm afraid I don't understand, sir."

"I know that Captain Styles's death has hit you hard, Commander. Maybe harder than anybody else aboard this ship."

Cutler knew she couldn't deny that, though she had done her utmost to keep it from showing, even at the brief memorial service that she and Sulu had conducted for the crew's benefit the day after the Korvat bombing. Of course, she'd probably lowered her guard a bit too much in front of Tim Henry several hours before that, when she had no doubt still been in shock in the immediate aftermath of the attack. . . .

Either Henry has a very big goddamned mouth, or else Sulu's a much more aware CO than I've been giving him credit for being, she thought.

"Yes" was the only response that would come to her. "Lawrence—" She interrupted herself and started again. "The captain's death has been a blow to all of us."

Sulu nodded. "I agree, even though I hadn't got to know

him very well yet. I'm sorry now that I won't have any more opportunities to do that."

"At least you got command of *Excelsior* as a consolation prize," she said, the bitter words tumbling out of her mouth before she could edit herself.

His eyes narrowed with apparent anger for a moment before a look of commingled sorrow and sympathy crossed his face. The moment stretched while she awaited his response with growing unease.

"That's your pain talking, Commander," he said. "And your guilt."

Once again, he'd surprised her; the word "guilt" landed like an unexpected body blow.

"You actually think," she said when she finally caught her breath, "that I blame *myself* for what happened to the captain?"

"It sounds silly when you come right out and say it, doesn't it?" he said. "After all, you had nothing whatsoever to do with the attack on Korvat. No rational person could ever hold you responsible for what happened to the captain.

"But," Sulu continued, "*you* evidently do."

Whom had he been talking to? Judy Klass? Cutler immediately dismissed the notion; the ship's CMO was not only a good friend but also a top-notch professional who would never betray her by telling tales out of school.

"And what exactly do you base that on?" Cutler said as she rose to her feet again.

Sulu also stood, his dark, intense eyes remaining fixed on Cutler's. "On the fact that Captain Styles was planning to retire—until *you* talked him into keeping his command."

Her jaw went abruptly slack and her mouth fell open. "Who told you . . . How did you find out about that?" she said at length. She groped behind her and found the edge of her desk, which she leaned on, grateful for its solidity and for the reassuring presence of her late captain's swagger stick. "Did the captain tell you?"

Sulu held up a hand in a placating gesture. "Believe me, nobody broke any confidences, least of all Captain Styles. But I've been thinking about this ever since the day I first came aboard. You've always had his ear, so it's really the only explanation that makes sense."

She nodded. "He and Miguel Darby, his exec, were both planning to leave at the same time."

"Which just happened to be a few weeks after Starfleet formally announced the cancellation of what little remained of the transwarp drive project that began aboard *Excelsior* five years ago," he said.

The transwarp project that failed *aboard* Excelsior *five years ago,* she thought, resentful about that on Styles's behalf although she'd been serving at a different post at the time.

"Commander Darby was very operationally involved in that project, wasn't he?" Sulu said.

"Yes," Cutler said. Sulu had obviously been making good use of *Excelsior*'s personnel files. "I thought the timing of his retirement made it look like he was leaving under a cloud. Miguel wouldn't listen to me and left anyway."

"But you managed to persuade Captain Styles that leaving at the same time as his exec would have been bad for his career."

She nodded, her eyes filling with tears. "He shouldn't have listened to me."

"Captain Styles was not a man who changed his mind capriciously," Sulu said. "If you got him to reverse a major career decision—one he'd already announced publicly—then you must have made a damned fine argument."

"It doesn't look so damned fine from here. Not anymore." A single tear separated from the corner of her right eye and began making a slow, laborious transit down her cheek. She was determined not to show weakness by wiping it away in front of him.

"Maybe not." He moved toward the door, then paused momentarily in the threshold after it hissed open. "Remember, I tried to persuade him that we were walking into real danger on Korvat. Did that scare him into deciding to lead from the rear? No. And I'm not sure anything either of us might have said could have done that."

With that, Sulu exited. The door closed behind him, leaving her alone again with her thoughts and the view of infinity her panoramic window afforded her. Cutler wiped away the tear, picked up Styles's bomb-burned riding crop, and tucked it under her left arm. Then she walked to the wide window and stared out into the panoply of distant stars that lay beyond. She thought about Sulu's words, repeatedly replaying their conversation—as well as the fateful one she'd had weeks ago with Styles—in her mind. Gradually growing almost meditatively calm, she began to consider the eventual possibility of forgiving herself.

Perhaps an hour later, the intercom interrupted her reverie. *"Ensign Marquez to Commander Cutler,"* said the young gamma-shift communications officer, his usually calm tenor voice propelled by an unaccustomed urgency. *"I think you'd better come up to the bridge right away."*

Cutler crossed to the companel on top of her desk and pressed the button. "Cutler here, Ensign. Is everything all right?"

A pause. Then, *"I'm not sure, Commander. We just received a priority message from Starfleet Command, directed to your eyes only."*

My *eyes,* she thought, her earlier hard-won calm suddenly evaporating. Not *Sulu's.*

Something was very wrong. "I'm on my way."

•   •   •

Although it was nearly midnight, ship's time, Sulu was rest-less, despite a vigorous fencing workout with Janice Rand down in the ship's gymnasium. As was his custom on such occasions, he pulled a light-duty uniform vest on over his Starfleet-issue turtleneck and made his way onto the quiet, darkened observation lounge on deck three, on his way to making one final check-in on the bridge before retiring for the evening.

Unlike most nights when he came here, he found he was not alone.

"How did your meeting with Sarek go, Ambassador Dax?" Sulu asked the figure who leaned forward against the railing in front of the lounge's broad panoramic window.

Dax started slightly at the intrusion; he had evidently been lost in thought, perhaps contemplating the long, sleek lines of *Excelsior*'s glowing warp nacelles that stretched out before him, or the bright spray of warp-distorted stars scat-tered throughout the black infinitude beyond.

Turning to face Sulu, the young Trill seemed to recover his composure quickly, though he still appeared unaccount-ably tense. "I remain in the gainful employ of the Federation Diplomatic Corps. For the moment, anyway."

"Congratulations," Sulu said, relieved to hear Dax's good news. "I've heard that Ambassador Sarek can be a very by-the-book kind of diplomat. And this time you ended up hav-ing to write a whole *new* book on the fly."

Dax nodded, then resumed staring out the window and into the naked face of infinity. "I gather we were *both* forced to break a few rules on this mission, Commander. I suppose I expected at least one of us to be called on the carpet for it."

Sulu smiled grimly. "The night is still young, Mister Am-bassador," he said, despite the obvious lateness of the hour. He had yet to hear back from Starfleet Command regarding the contents of his after-action report, his logs, and the logs of Commanders Cutler and Rand, Dr. Klass, and Dr. Chapel; he knew he might receive communications from his superiors regarding any or all of the above at any time.

"I think what surprised me most of all," Dax continued, "was Sarek telling me that he thought I'd distinguish myself someday as an interstellar negotiator—provided I don't take too many more crazy risks in the meantime."

A smile spread slowly across Sulu's face as he took a quick inventory of some of the "crazy risks" to which he had been a party over the past quarter century.

"Sometimes crazy risks are the only sensible options available," Sulu said. Despite Dax's recent diplomatic coup with the Klingons, he couldn't help but wonder if the serious, tightly wound young man who stood beside him now would know what to do the next time he faced such a choice.

Sulu felt a subtle but unmistakable sensation beneath his boots then, something that resembled an intrusive sound, but which was felt rather than heard; he noticed a very slight shift in the subaural vibrations that coursed through the great ship's frame whenever she traveled at high warp, as though *Excelsior* were suddenly changing her heading or velocity.

An electronic bosun's whistle split the air, and Commander Cutler's voice issued from the lounge's comm system a moment later.

"Bridge to Commander Sulu."

Sulu crossed to the compad on the wall. "Sulu here."

"We've just received top-priority communications from Starfleet Command," Cutler said in urgent tones.

Sulu had been wondering whether Starfleet Command would look upon Sulu's own choices with as much indulgent tolerance as Ambassador Sarek had afforded those made by Curzon Dax. He was now all but certain that the answer had finally arrived.

And that he wasn't going to like it.

THIRTY-NINE

Stardate 9028.7 (Early 2290)

U.S.S. Excelsior

When he stepped onto the bridge, Sulu found both Meredith Cutler and Janice Rand waiting for him. Cutler was attired in her full uniform, while Rand was still dressed for the gym, where he presumed she had been when the communication from Starfleet had arrived.

Both of them looked anxious. And neither needed to say a word to make it crystal clear that the message from Starfleet did not contain good news.

"May we speak to you in private, Commander?" Cutler said. Whatever news had just arrived, she wasn't eager to share it indiscriminately.

"Please," Sulu said, gesturing toward the turbolift from which he'd just emerged. Their expressions sober, Cutler and Rand followed him inside.

The journey to the large, secure conference room one deck below the bridge passed in tense silence, and seemed to take an eternity. None of the trio spoke until the door had hissed shut behind them.

No one made a move to take a seat around the conference table. Sulu stood as well, looking from Cutler's face to Rand's and back again before breaking the awkward hush. "I wonder why Starfleet didn't say whatever they wanted to say directly to me," he said, though he was pretty sure he already knew the reason.

"Probably because what they had to say affects *Excelsior*'s entire chain of command, sir," Cutler said, her eyes brimming with what looked like sincere regret as she stood at attention. "Effective immediately, Admiral Cartwright has relieved you of command because of your decision to enter Klingon space contrary to orders. I've forwarded it all to the terminal in your quarters."

"Thank you," Sulu said quietly.

"Cartwright has also called a hearing on Earth," Rand said, looking miserable. "To determine whether Starfleet Command will take any further action against you. We're already under way, at warp seven."

Sulu nodded, not surprised and not particularly afraid. After all, he had been called on the carpet before, along with James Kirk and the rest of the *Enterprise*'s senior staff after the Genesis affair and the alien space probe incursion. All the charges against him had been summarily dismissed on that occasion, though he would always suspect that his subsequent career had become every bit as stalled as though he'd been sent to a penal colony instead of back to starship duty.

Now a general court-martial, and perhaps even a lengthy prison term as a consequence, was beginning to look like a disconcertingly likely possibility.

"Cartwright has made me interim CO," Cutler said. "Pending the outcome of all of this, of course."

"I've accepted the job of acting exec for the duration," Rand said.

Sulu wanted to congratulate Rand, but held his tongue

because he didn't want his old friend to think he was being snide. Instead he simply nodded, studying both women's faces as he tried to process what was happening. Rand displayed the empathetic expression of someone forced to watch a dear old friend suffer a terrible and inalterable fate.

The look in Cutler's eyes was one of pure, unalloyed guilt. Sulu recognized it instantly; he'd seen it in his own bathroom mirror, immediately after the murder of Captain Styles had landed him temporarily in *Excelsior*'s command chair.

"I suppose this means I'm in your custody now, Commander," Sulu said, squaring his shoulders as he locked his gaze with that of Cutler, whose mien grew even more miserable as she nodded.

"Where's my next stop, then?" Sulu asked, keeping his voice calm and nonconfrontational. "The brig?"

Frowning, Rand turned to face Cutler. "Is that really necessary?"

Cutler's jaw muscles grew as taut as the ancient, anti-grav-assisted cables that held up the Golden Gate Bridge. "According to my orders, Rand, he's supposed to be confined."

"But, the *brig*?" Rand said.

Cutler's eyes moved from side to side, like trapped animals seeking a means of escape. Then she relaxed slightly, and a very small smile crossed her lips. "That part of the transmission must have been garbled." Facing Sulu squarely, she said, "Will confinement to quarters do?"

Despite the grimness of the current circumstances, Sulu allowed a wry grin to appear on his face. *Maybe there's hope for you yet, Mister Cutler.*

"I'm done making trouble for the moment," he said aloud. He gestured toward the door. "Walk me home.

"And take good care of *Excelsior*."

• • •

Janice Rand was not about to take this lying down.

After escorting her old friend to his quarters cum jail cell, she made a grim beeline for her own small personal space—and for the computer terminal atop her desk, which she wasted no time activating.

Though the hour was late, she opened a channel to a specific suite located among the VIP quarters on deck eight.

"Commander Rand to Ambassador Curzon Dax. . . ."

Sulu lay on his bunk in the darkness, gazing into the distant, warp-field smeared stars that were sprinkled across the void beyond *Excelsior*'s hull. He was glad he hadn't been so presumptuous as to have his things moved into the suite of rooms officially designated as the captain's quarters. Of course, there hadn't yet been time even to pack up and store the late Captain Styles's personal effects.

There's no point wasting energy thinking about the captain's quarters anymore, he thought, opening his palm to the dim glow of starlight and *Excelsior*'s warp field. One of the rank insignia from his uniform jacket glinted faintly in his hand. Its angular silver hourglass shape, bisected by a pair of braided gold bars, identified him as a full commander. It was a rank he had been proud to attain, and an insignia that he had always worn with chest-swelling pride.

But now it seemed to represent only a barrier he might never succeed in crossing, a membrane he might never penetrate, despite a lifetime of hard work and sacrifice. It was an impregnable gate that had slammed shut, separating him from the rank of captain, perhaps forever.

All because he hadn't been able to resist chasing a ghost from more than forty years in his past.

Reaching across the bed, he tossed the insignia onto the low table beside him. He tried like hell not to think about it anymore, but failed completely.

I'm at loose ends, he thought, *all* because *of a loose end.*

Fueled by both his hard-earned fatigue and the hypnotic glow of the distant stars, sleep began slowly enfolding him in its warm embrace.

Loose ends.

As he started his descent into the weightless freefall of slumber, all he could think of was the mysterious cloaked shuttle that the albino's ship had launched when he and the Klingons had been Qagh's captives. He had never discovered its purpose or destination. Besides the albino himself and the microbial time bombs he had planted, it was the most serious loose end that both he and the Klingons had failed to track down.

He could only hope that that particular loose end wouldn't return to haunt any of them.

FORTY

Seated on one of the small lab's narrow stools, Qagh frowned deeply at the biotechnological inventory report on the padd that Nej had just handed him. The hand that held the padd shook slightly, and he quickly switched hands to conceal his momentary weakness.

But he knew he couldn't conceal his deeply angry and near-despondent state of mind as he considered the seriousness of the blow that his foes had dealt him.

"I had virtually everything I needed to create a weapon that could have leveraged the High Council into doing nearly anything I wanted it to do," he said, shaking his head ruefully as he studied the grim figures on the padd for what might have been the hundredth time. "I could have threatened to wipe out whole planetary biospheres unless they let me alone. Then came my kinsman and his motley band of brothers. Now all those years of effort might as well have been deliberately thrown down Qul Tuq's gravity well."

"You shouldn't lose hope, Qagh," Nej said, his dusky face a mask of concern.

Though the albino knew Nej was merely playing his customary role of concerned physician, he found himself snarling at the man. "I would be delighted to see some justification for that spectacularly unfounded bit of reasoning. I can never gain control of the House of Ngoj. I was foolish to believe that I could, or that I even wanted to. The whole weight of a culture that rejected me—a society of which I am not overly fond to begin with—will never permit it, no matter how many weapons I develop and deploy.

"I may not survive this, Nej. Not only has my work been set back by years—including the work that keeps my . . . *condition* at bay—but the armed forces of two galactic powers have compromised some of my best sources of raw biomaterials."

Nej lapsed into silence at this, stroking his bearded chin as he made a show of choosing his next words with extreme care. "Those two galactic powers will soon have reason to afford us both a more appropriate level of respect," he said.

Qagh's despair immediately yielded to irritated puzzlement. "What are you *talking* about, Nej?"

Nej displayed his sharpened teeth, apparently eager to ingratiate himself to the freebooter. And a strange light that Qagh saw only rarely burned behind his eyes, much more strongly than ever before.

"I speak of the blow that I have already struck, in secret, against the weaklings on the Council who would discuss capitulation with the Empire's enemies," Nej said, smiling beatifically. "I wasn't going to speak of it until I was more certain of the results. But considering your present state of mind—"

"What have you *done,* Nej?" the albino said, interrupting, all at once feeling chilled by the madness he saw emerging from behind the elderly doctor's eyes. He rose from his stool, set the padd down upon it, and approached Nej, studying him closely.

"I recently finished the design work and protein synthesis on another new retrovirus," Nej said. "And I've already deployed it."

The albino's eyes grew large with astonishment. Was this Nej's way of staging a coup, like the one Qagh himself had undertaken decades ago aboard the *Jade Lady*?

"You released a new retrovirus without clearing it with me first?"

Nej raised a placating hand. "It's just a little side project—one that Hurghom and I first began working on after the Council discommendated me as punishment for the *SermanyuQ* grain-virus fiasco."

Qagh swallowed hard and he closed his eyes. His head hurt, making him wonder if it was already time to medicate again. "What is the nature of this new virus?"

"It is highly contagious, and should prove most reliably lethal to members of those Houses that wronged me over the *SermanyuQ* affair. I trust I needn't remind you that many of those individuals also took part in humbling the House from which *you* originated."

Qagh could scarcely believe his ears. Had he been so wrapped up in the intricacies of biochemically maintaining his own existence from month to month and week to week—to say nothing of his own plans to avenge himself against his enemies—that he had missed Nej's slide into a reckless vendetta-mania of his own?

Or perhaps the old man had simply been driven mad by his long years of exposure to so many exotic bioagents. *Maybe we're* both *insane after living so much of our lives out on the margins of the frontier,* he thought.

"*You* were the one responsible for launching the small auxiliary ship," Qagh said. "The one that disappeared the first time my kinsman came aboard the *Hegh'TlhoS*."

Nej nodded enthusiastically, as though he believed he had somehow cheered his employer up. "Though the small cloaking device it carries is quite a power drain, the craft ought to reach Qo'noS quite soon, if it hasn't done so already. Once there, it will release my virus into the atmosphere. It should take but little time thereafter for the pathogen to reach its intended targets."

The Houses of the High Council, or their successors, won't take this lying down, the albino thought as his surprise and bemusement swiftly metamorphosed into a hard, cold rage. He reached for his belt, and his hand landed on the butt of the small disruptor pistol he habitually kept there.

"All I wanted to do, Nej, was to stay alive with the purpose of punishing and plundering Kor's ancestral House for abandoning me during my infancy. I wanted to hold the *big* bioweapons in reserve, to keep the Council at bay.

"But you, Nej, have gone too far."

Qagh drew his weapon then and fired it into the other man's chest in a single fluid motion. It was Nej's turn to look astonished, at least for the instant it took for his suddenly lifeless body to fall backward to the deck. The albino looked down upon the dead man in disgust, and watched as the remnants of the strange, mad light slowly faded from his eyes.

The Council might have no choice now other than to declare total war upon me, he thought as he holstered his disruptor. He had always enjoyed the warm, comforting feel of a freshly fired disruptor when he returned it to his belt. Today, however, he almost regretted it.

Almost.

Nej may have just brought the entire power structure of the Klingon Empire right down on top of me, he thought. *Unless . . .*

FORTY-ONE

Seated at the sparsely populated outdoor food gallery near the TlhIng Veng laboratory and office complex where he worked whenever the *Klothos* returned to Qo'noS for repairs, Dr. Hurghom gazed contentedly into the gray, late-afternoon sky.

A warm breeze tickled the back of his neck as he caught his first glimpse of the meteor. None of the dozen or so other diners present, most of them smooth-headed *QuchHa'* people like Hurghom himself, had taken any overt notice as yet of the slender trail of fire that crossed the sky as they conversed over trays of steaming *bregit,* hot bloodwine, cool but still-writhing *gagh,* and tankards of warm, bitter *bahgol.*

At least he'd *thought* the descending missile was a meteor, until its fiery trail abruptly changed course, as though intent on reaching the most densely populated sections of the city before completing its terminal plunge to Qo'noS's

surface. Hurghom also thought it strange that a meteor
would be pursued by military fighter craft—and this object
was being chased by a pair of the sleek, one-man vessels,
both of whose forward disruptor tubes were throwing lances
of fire in a thus-far vain attempt to shoot their quarry from
the sky.

The small crowd of diners seated at the tables nearest to
Hurghom's had finally begun to notice the drama that was
playing out just above the eastern horizon and that was approaching with the rapidity of a lowland desert gale. A few
startled exclamations escaped from the watchers as a pair of
pale red disruptor beams converged at a critical point in the
air just above the city's administrative district.

The object, which Hurghom stubbornly continued to
regard as a meteor in defiance of abundant evidence to the
contrary, suddenly exploded in a spectacular amber flash.
The swiftly dissipating nimbus of fire and smoke dropped
a fine but faintly visible rain of debris over the *qell'qams*-
distant city core.

One by one, the other diners rose and exited, perhaps to
check in with friends or family at the city core, or else returned to their interrupted meals and conversations.

Hurghom, who lacked both a mealtime companion and
an appetite, could not simply ignore what he had just seen.
Leaving a payment chit on the tray beside his half-finished
gladst salad and *chech'tluth* flask, he rose and crossed the
food gallery, following the main boulevard that led toward
the city core.

If that thing wasn't a meteor, then what was it? he wondered as he looked up and down the street, hoping to catch
an inbound hoverskimmer. Unfortunately, none were visible
at the moment among the early flurry of commuter traffic.

Could it have been a small attack ship?

Unbidden visions arose of planets suddenly shattered
by stealthy projectiles—the very fate that had befallen the

Earther-allied world Coridan about a century and a half earlier.

Ignoring the grinding aches in his bones, Hurghom forgot about the hoverskimmer and continued walking along the boulevard's walkway. He quickened his pace, weaving and dodging through and around the small clusters of tradesmen and shoppers moving between the street's various shops and offices. Vehicular traffic on the far side of the street itself was light, since few vehicles were taking the inbound lanes that emptied into the city core. Traffic in the outbound lanes on Hurghom's side, however, was beginning to proliferate as a small but steady stream of low-floating hovercars tried to beat the most congested part of the daily commute from TlhIng Veng to the metropolis's sprawling suburbs and exurbs.

Hurghom noticed that an oncoming skimmer—one headed out of the city—was moving erratically, weaving in and out of its lane, causing other vehicles to swerve to avoid collision. At least a half-dozen vehicular alert-alarms began keening shrilly, eloquently conveying the displeasure of their drivers. Hurghom was momentarily frozen in place even as several of the passing pedestrians on either side of him began to take notice and cry out.

The massive skimmer abruptly swerved across four lanes of traffic.

And it was headed straight for Hurghom.

Something struck the scientist in the back, momentarily winding him as it pushed him forward. He thought for a moment that one of the other vehicles had somehow hit him while trying to evade the skimmer, then realized he had been half-tackled by a young man who was evidently intent on getting him out of harm's way as quickly as possible, without wasting too much of his energy on gentleness.

Engines gunning, the hoverskimmer hurtled past, missing him by little more than a hand's breadth as it crashed headlong into the wide glass façade of a blademaker's shop. The skimmer came to a halt only after half-burying itself in the building. Passersby scattered and milled about, the faces of men, women, and children all presenting only slight variations on the basic theme of extreme surprise.

"You weren't fast enough, old man," said Hurghom's rescuer, whom the scientist recognized now as a warrior clad in full military regalia; perhaps he had been on his way to purchase some of the blademaker's wares. Like Hurghom, the young man's forehead was smooth, though it was creased with concern at the moment.

"Never mind me," Hurghom said, only now realizing that the young warrior was still clutching him by both biceps. He shrugged himself loose from the warrior's iron grasp and pointed at the skimmer, whose motors were now audibly shutting down, probably in response to some built-in safety protocol. "There must be people in that vehicle who require far more attention than I do."

The warrior nodded, then turned and made his way toward the front of the skimmer, carefully picking his way through the pile of tangled but still-settling debris. Although the jumble of wrecked masonry and torn metal posed a not-inconsiderable hazard to him, years of service aboard a Klingon battle cruiser forced Hurghom to follow the warrior inside.

Because the sliding door near the front of the skimmer had evidently been jammed open during the crash, it took only moments for the warrior and Hurghom to get inside the vehicle.

Immediately in front of Hurghom, the warrior knelt beside the apparently unconscious middle-aged *QuchHa'* woman who was slumped in the driver's seat. No marks were visible on her, apart from some bloody mottling across her smooth forehead.

Her eyes fluttered open and she shrieked incoherently. "It

rained down from the sky!" was all Hurghom could understand.

"What?" asked the warrior. "What rained down from the sky?"

"Death," she said, then issued another scream before becoming both silent and motionless.

"She is dead," the warrior said. "The crash was too much for her."

Groans came from the dozen or so seats behind that of the driver, from those who had sustained injuries from the crash as well as from others whose foreheads displayed the same mottling as had the driver's. Hurghom was willing to wager that many of those present who had already lapsed into motionless silence had also followed the skimmer driver into *Gre'thor*'s grasp.

"She did not die from the crash," Hurghom said. He understood now with a bedrock certainty that the missile that had just been destroyed over TlhIng Veng had nevertheless accomplished its terrible mission.

Both of Hurghom's *QiVon* cracked loudly as he knelt beside the dead driver's body. His hands trembled slightly as he removed a small glass vial from his tunic pocket and carefully filled it with a sample of the blood-tinged fluid that oozed from the sores on the woman's mottled forehead.

"What are you doing, old man?" the warrior said brusquely. "That woman is beyond help. Her body is now merely an empty shell."

Hurghom carefully capped the sample vial, then allowed the scowling warrior to help him back to his feet.

"You're right, of course," the scientist said. "But she may be able to help many others who are similarly afflicted yet still live." He held up the vial for the warrior's inspection.

"*This* is the death that rained down from the sky?" the warrior wanted to know.

"Maybe not," Hurghom said, tucking the little vial back into his tunic pocket. "If I can get this sample back to my lab quickly, that is."

And if the malady to which we have both just been exposed doesn't get the better of me first.

Glancing out the hoverskimmer's rear window, Hurghom could see another half dozen passersby beginning to stagger and fall.

Fear at last made itself evident on the young warrior's face.

"Come with me," the warrior said as he moved toward the skimmer's broken front door. "I have a vehicle parked nearby."

This has to be the work of the albino, Hurghom thought as he labored alone in his lab over the biosample he had taken in the crashed skimmer.

Thanks to the warning he had dispatched to the Klingon Defense Force, all the High Council's scientific resources were even now being brought to bear against the biological attack against TlhIng Veng.

Or so the Council's lower functionaries had told him.

Hurghom was certain, however, that only Klingons of the *HemQuch* variety, rather than smooth-headed *QuchHa'* people like himself, were welcome on the teams that were seeking a cure for the malady that was even now beginning to spread generally across Qo'noS. Otherwise, why would the Council have neglected to tap the considerable expertise of the chief medical officer of the *I.K.S. Klothos*?

Spots swam before Hurghom's eyes as he studied the pathogen sample on the microscope slide, then once again consulted the readouts of the DNA analyzer.

No, not *the albino,* he thought as he recognized a lengthy tailored DNA sequence whose occurrence due to natural, random chance was extraordinarily unlikely. *Or at least the*

*albino could not have acted alone in creating and deploying
this virus. And here is the proof.*

The lab's gene comparator quickly confirmed that this
gene sequence—with which Hurghom had several decades
of close familiarity—bore, to within tolerances nearly as
fine as those of a retina scan, the signature of its creator:
Hurghom's erstwhile associate, Dr. Nej.

Nej, or someone building directly upon Nej's work, had
written a significant fraction of this new retrovirus's DNA
sequences.

Although Hurghom felt hot and was already experiencing
some intermittent trouble with his vision, he had yet to become dizzy or otherwise incapacitated. He believed he was
still reasonably rational, in part because he understood that
he himself was in no position to make that judgment. *After
all,* he thought, *one has to remain fully rational in order to
rationally evaluate rationality.*

Doesn't one?

Hurghom chuckled as he activated the genetic resequencing equipment in preparation for altering one of
the viral samples. Once the base pairs had finished lining
up, he incorporated another genetic sequence, one that he
had long labored to develop, and which was based largely
upon the work of his late grandfather Antaak. Now seemed
an especially opportune time to try out this additional gene
sequence, given the fact that the virulent nature of the
underlying retrovirus would spread the new genes far and
wide through the general Klingon population—and given
that mass death probably awaited much of the population of
Qo'noS anyway if his frantic efforts to produce an effective
counteragent were to fail.

And given the urgency of his task, he decided to cease
worrying about whether or not his decisions remained in
any way rational.

Poor Nej, he thought as he finished grafting the new gene

sequences directly onto those that had been authored years earlier by his former colleague. To this day he felt bad for Nej, whose discommendation had come largely as punishment for the failure of the Empire's covert efforts to use a quadrotriticale virus to take *SermanyuQ* away from the Earthers a quarter century ago; Nej had abruptly lost his standing in the Empire's scientific and political hierarchies, in spite of the fact that Hurghom had done about as much work on that project as had Nej. Nej's higher *HemQuch* social status had given him the bulk of the credit when things had gone well; it had also, ironically, tarred him with a disproportionate amount of the blame for failure.

But maybe I can redeem both *our reputations now,* Hurghom thought as his new, yet-untested counteragent flowed through the chem synthesizer's tangle of hoses into a fresh set of vials. *And that of Grandfather Antaak as well.*

Antaak, who had saved the lives of millions of his people from a virulent strain of Levodian flu on Qu'Vat only by contaminating the Klingon genome with Earther DNA, consigning a segment of the Klingon population to physical deformity for nearly a century and a half. Antaak, who had also killed millions, including himself, while trying to undo that one terrible mistake.

Maybe that was because he didn't remain rational at the very end, Hurghom thought, chuckling again.

Unlike me.

Less than half a *kilaan* later, the elderly scientist carried several small vials and a palm-sized handheld aerosol sprayer down to the street, where the young warrior had left the groundcar parked before he had succumbed to the illness and died behind the controls.

Hurghom hoped he would be strong enough to shove the young man's corpse into the passenger seat, and could hold out long enough to drive his vehicle to the center of TlhIng Veng.

• • •

Kang held his wife's hand tightly, kneeling beside her as she lay on the cool flagstone floor of the open-air plaza near the heart of TlhIng Veng. Mara's eyes stared unfocused at the overcast sky, from which a hot, dry wind blew relentlessly.

A wind that bears death upon its back, Kang thought.

"Perhaps I would have led a longer life had I stayed on as your science officer," she said, simultaneously chuckling and coughing.

Although Kang had never believed that a desire for safety had motivated Mara's decision to temporarily leave Kang's command to join a three-year research project on Qo'noS, the irony of her observation did not escape his notice.

But why in the name of Kahless shouldn't *she expect to be safer on the Homeworld than in the cold depths of space?*

"Help is on the way, my love," he said as gently as he could, though he hated himself for failing to keep a slight but audible edge of fear out of his voice.

He expected himself to be better able to accept the predations of death, no matter whom it stalked. He had, after all, managed to do so on many previous occasions. When he and the other survivors of the wrecked warship *I.K.S. Klolode* had briefly seized control of the *yuQjIjDIvI'* starship *'Entepray'* more than twenty years ago, the Earthers aboard that vessel had captured Mara and threatened to kill her unless Kang agreed to a truce. Kang had actually given her up for dead that day, and even told his Earther adversary, QIrq, that she would understand and accept her fate as a casualty of war, just as he would.

But *this* death was one that befitted neither a warrior nor a warrior's wife. Nor was this death exclusive to Mara, as the random clusters of fallen and still-collapsing Klingon bodies sprawled throughout the windy plaza so grimly attested.

Kang had no doubt that his own body would be added to the growing ranks of the dead soon enough.

A sudden motion just inside the periphery of his vision interrupted Kang's musings, and he turned to see who was approaching. Though multi-hued spots had begun to move before his eyes, swelling and shrinking as they tumbled past one another, he saw a single figure moving in haste toward the plaza's open center, waving an arm over his head as he stepped over the untidy array of bodies, apparently paying special attention to the approximately half of them that were still moving, speaking, or otherwise showing signs of life.

Hurghom? Kang thought as he belatedly recognized the man, who was apparently using some sort of sprayer on each still-living body he encountered.

Kang was perplexed by the unexpected presence of Kor's CMO—out of uniform and off duty while both the *Klothos* and the *QaD* were in orbital drydock undergoing repairs—before any of the city's emergency personnel had made an appearance.

A sudden wave of dizziness nearly toppled Kang as he rose unsteadily to his feet. Through narrowed eyes, he studied Hurghom, who as yet showed no sign of having seen either him or Mara. *He must be in league with whoever did this,* he thought with a certainty that transcended logic itself.

Drawing his *d'k tahg* with a shaking, sweat-slicked hand, Kang approached Hurghom from behind as dizziness competed for his attention with memories of his grandfather's tales of Qu'Vat.

Qu'Vat, the world on which Hurghom's grandfather had slain millions while splitting the Klingon species in twain.

The last of the vials was nearly empty.

The job is done at last, Hurghom thought as he depleted the contents of the aerosol sprayer for the last time. All that remained to do was to watch and wait—and hope that the hastily synthesized counteragent would live up to its promise before he succumbed to the disease himself.

Something clamped onto his shoulder, then spun him roughly about.

The countenance into which Hurghom suddenly found himself staring was a study in ferocity. As he blinked away the spots that were increasingly obscuring his vision, he gradually came to realize that he recognized that face, just as he did the familiar dark leather-and-mail military uniform beneath it.

"What have you done, Hurghom?" Kang said, taking the empty vial and sprayer from the scientist's nerveless fingers. He raised the small apparatus to his nose and sniffed it.

"It's odorless, Captain," Hurghom said, though he knew that Kang had to have discovered that for himself already.

"Of course," Kang said, tossing the spent container over his shoulder. It made far too much noise when it clattered to the pavilion's stone floor. "Death would be at a decided disadvantage were you to give it a scent that might betray its presence, like some desert *targ*."

Confusion joined hands with fever and delirium. "Captain, I'm afraid I don't understand."

Hurghom noticed the hungry-looking silver dagger in Kang's hand. How long had the captain been holding it, drawn and apparently ready to strike?

"Then allow me to explain, Doctor," Kang said as he grabbed Hurghom's shoulder with his free hand, ungently ushering him forward.

He's lost his mind, Hurghom thought, realizing that he now stood at least as close to a violent death as he ever had before. *He's acquired the disease, and it has driven him mad.*

A public alert-klaxon of an emergency vehicle wailed nearby, growing closer even as the late-afternoon breeze began to accelerate. A few blue-smocked first-response personnel had finally appeared, and had begun moving swiftly among the sick and the dying to perform battlefield-style triage.

Kang brought Hurghom to a stop after bringing him past at least a dozen other sprawled, insensate bodies.

"Mara?" Hurghom said when he saw the deathly still woman who now lay at his feet.

"*Why*, Hurghom?" Kang rumbled into Hurghom's ear, speaking in a perilously quiet voice from almost directly behind him. "I *trusted* you, perhaps as much as Kor trusted you."

"I came here to save as many people who'd been exposed to the pathogen as possible," Hurghom said.

"And just how did you acquire such intimate knowledge of this . . . pathogen before anyone else did?"

Hurghom's blood ran as cold as the ice-choked northern reaches of the Natlh Sea. *Great Kahless. He really thinks I'm the one responsible for this massacre.*

Kang's blade swung around from behind Hurghom, entering his chest so quickly and cleanly that he felt no pain whatsoever. He noticed the *d'k tahg* that protruded from his sternum a moment after its arrival, which gave Hurghom the absurd but transitory impression that the weapon had somehow sprouted haft-first from his own insides.

Cure or no cure, I'm going to die now, he thought, pleasantly surprised by the detachment and equanimity he felt at the prospect. *And if I am remembered, it will be as either a great hero or a villain.*

Or perhaps merely as a fool.

Hurghom dropped very slowly to his knees, as though the viscosity of the very air had just increased a hundredfold. Balancing precariously on both *qIVon* for what felt like an eternity, he took a moment to study the woman who lay supine before him.

From his now much-closer vantage point, he could see

that she was still breathing; he was thankful for that, though he was uncertain whether or not his counteragent deserved any credit for that.

But it was her *forehead* that attracted his attention most.

Under the skin mottling—which appeared to be fading rapidly before his admittedly fever-plagued eyes—a healthy pattern of ridges and bumps had begun rising. It was like watching a chain of mountains thrusting upward from beneath the planet's crust, but with the requisite geological ages squeezed into the space of a dying man's last few heartbeats.

He smiled, allowing himself the luxury of hope, if only for others.

It's working.

Which meant that *QuchHa'* were transforming back into *HemQuch.* Those who had been immune to the transformative effects of the *yIH*-metabolized retrovirus two decades earlier could now recover their genetic birthright.

Antaak's sins, and by extension Hurghom's as well, would finally be paid for in full.

Hurghom turned his face up toward Kang and beamed at him, though the captain's gaze was riveted to his wife's visibly metamorphosing face.

And although the afternoon light was steadily compressing into a narrow tunnel, Hurghom could see that Kang's own forehead was rippling and moving as his own *HemQuch* traits began to resurface.

"Mara?" Hurghom heard Kang say, as though speaking from across a tremendous distance. "You're alive!"

It is indeed a good day to die, Hurghom thought.

As he pitched face forward into the embrace of the encroaching darkness, he wondered if any of *Sto-Vo-Kor's* lodgings were reserved for those who died trying to wrest the secrets of creation from the universe itself. . . .

PART V: RECKONING

I will see this game of life out
to its bitter end.

—Zane Grey (1872–1939)

FORTY-TWO

Less than twenty minutes after seeing off Ambassadors Sarek and Dax, both of whom were now on a fast transport en route to rendezvous with other starships bound for their respective homeworlds, Hikaru Sulu watched as a mournful Janice Rand ran the control console of *Excelsior*'s transporter room three. Rand, the console before her, and the entire room quickly vanished behind a shimmering curtain of light, to be replaced scant moments later by the far wider and higher spaces of Archer Auditorium at Starfleet Headquarters.

The place stood empty at the moment, from the circular central space to the raised dais that supported the padded chairs, the long curved table, and the tabletop lecterns that had been set up especially for the five adjudicators of today's hearing. Even the gallery that overlooked the whole chamber was engulfed in an eerie, pregnant silence.

As he smoothed a wrinkle from his dress uniform's maroon tunic, Sulu craned his neck to take in the high, vaulted ceiling. This place had always reminded him of the interior of a cathedral, almost as though Starfleet itself was a kind of temple to rationality, despite the occasionally inexplicable actions of some of those who wore its uniform. Through the panoramic windows in the rear of the chamber he could see portions of a unique and unmistakable city skyline, framed by a foreground silhouette of the Golden Gate Bridge enfolded in a delicate batting of early-morning fog.

San Francisco, he thought. *Everything began here for me. What better place could there be for everything to come to an end?*

The room was a somewhat smaller version of the Federation Council chamber, where he had been called on the carpet just four years earlier, along with James Kirk and the rest of the former admiral's senior officers. That tribunal had been convened shortly after a powerful alien probe had come to Earth seeking the cetaceans that had vanished from Earth's oceans some two centuries earlier. The observation gallery had overflowed with diplomats from a dozen worlds, other Starfleet officers, and members of the media, all of whom had become noisily ebullient after Federation President Hiram Roth had summarily dismissed most of the charges, having taken into account the fact that Kirk and his crew had just finished saving Earth from certain destruction.

Again, Sulu thought wryly.

As he waited for the arrival of the members of the board of inquiry to take their places on the dais, Sulu found it difficult to imagine himself encountering such good fortune today.

An impossibly young female ensign in a dress uniform entered the chamber through a discreet green-room door, raised an electronic bosun's whistle to her lips, and sounded the three piping notes that signaled the imminent arrival of senior flag officers. Sulu stood rigidly at attention as a male lieutenant entered carrying the specialized legal tricorder that identified him as the court reporter for today's proceedings; he sat unobtrusively in a chair set against the panoramic window behind the dais, directly beneath the blue-and-white expanse of the UFP flag.

The first of the Starfleet brass to enter the chamber and take his seat was Admiral Lance Cartwright, whose hard grimace made Sulu believe that the admiral had paid very close attention to every infraction Sulu had committed over the course of his long career, despite all the enthusiastic applauding he had done in another public gallery immediately after the late Federation President Hiram Roth had acquitted the *Enterprise* crew of any wrongdoing in the wake of the Genesis affair.

Next came grim-faced, silver-haired Heihachiro Nogura, the admiral whose arm James Kirk had twisted to regain command of the *Enterprise* during the V'Ger crisis of about eighteen years previously. Nogura was followed by Admiral Robert Bennett, whose usual indulgent smile had been replaced by a somber, almost grave expression. Despite their apparently dire moods, Sulu was reassured by the presence of Nogura and Bennett, both of whom had long been after-the-fact supporters of the frequently unorthodox improvised field tactics of James Kirk and his crew.

Sulu felt considerably less reassured by the entrance of the craggy-faced Admiral William Smillie. One of Starfleet's more influential flag officers, Smillie had once publicly criticized the "maverick" actions of James Kirk and his senior staff during the Genesis affair—despite the fact that those actions had literally saved the world. Sulu could only hope that the man wasn't nursing a misguided five-year-old grudge.

Admiral John Jason "Blackjack" Harriman, Starfleet's current C-in-C, was the last to be seated, taking his place at the center of the semicircular table. A broad-shouldered, aggressive-looking man with a bristly iron-gray crew cut,

Harriman picked up a pen-sized metal wand from his lectern and rang a small bell twice, perfunctorily calling the hearing to order.

Three to two against me, Sulu thought, his spirits crashing and cratering. *And that's the best-case scenario.*

"Commander Hikaru Sulu," Harriman said, his gray eyes as hard and pitiless as a pair of neutron stars.

Sulu hadn't felt quite so small and helpless since he was eleven years old, on an extremely bad day on Ganjitsu. His two sets of commander's bars, which he had placed very carefully on his uniform's right shoulder and left sleeve before he'd beamed down, seemed to have increased in mass tenfold.

He stiffened his spine, determined to offer no outward display of discomfiture.

"Today you stand charged," Harriman said, "with violating explicit Starfleet orders against entering Klingon space without the Klingon High Council's express authorization. You may face a general court-martial, depending upon the findings of this board of inquiry. Do you understand that you face the possibility of severe reduction in rank, or even imprisonment, as a consequence of your actions?"

Sulu stared straight ahead and remained at attention; if he was indeed about to go down in flames, he was determined to be a credit to the uniform if and when it happened.

"I do, sir," he said, his voice deep and even.

Admiral Cartwright spoke next, his brows creased by a deeply disapproving scowl. "And do you have any idea how badly your actions may have jeopardized the Federation Diplomatic Corps' ongoing efforts at détente with the Klingon Empire?"

I suppose that remains to be seen, Sulu thought.

"I understand, Admiral," he said aloud.

"You're aware that you have the right to retain counsel, aren't you, Commander?" Bennett said.

"If it pleases this board of inquiry, Admiral, I will waive counsel—unless and until this board calls a general court-martial."

If they really are *determined to court-martial me,* Sulu thought, *then they'll do it whether I'm "lawyered up" or not.*

"Very well," Admiral Smillie said in his deep, authoritative voice. "Then how do you plead to the charge, Commander?"

Sulu knew there was little point in entering any plea other than "guilty" or "no contest." The facts, after all, were not in dispute—only their meaning.

Sulu drew a deep breath and released it slowly. Keeping his eyes focused on a point somewhere between the skyline behind Harriman's head and infinity, he opened his mouth to speak.

A loud, echoing crash sounded from somewhere behind Sulu, interrupting him and momentarily ruining his military bearing. Sulu realized instantly that someone had thrown open one of the heavy wooden doors that led to the chamber's public gallery.

"Call security!" Cartwright shouted as he rose from his chair. The male ensign with the bosun's whistle moved quickly toward a companel mounted on a nearby wall. Though clearly rattled, the female ensign remained in her seat and continued using her tricorder to record everything that was transpiring.

As the other admirals rose, Sulu turned toward whoever had just entered the room.

"Belay that order," Harriman shouted to the male ensign. "Stand down."

"Go ahead and call your security men, Admiral!" Ambassador Kamarag said with undisguised anger. "You'll need them all, and more, if you intend to keep me out of this chamber!"

Dressed in his full Klingon diplomatic armor, Kamarag stormed directly toward the room's center, his features set and determined, his forehead ridges looking hard enough to cut dilithium even through the bandages that still partially obscured them. His large body's stomping momentum constituted an all but implacable force of nature.

"What is the meaning of this intrusion, Ambassador?" Nogura demanded with equal anger.

The Klingon ambassador came to a stop beside Sulu and addressed the board of inquiry. "Captains Kang, Koloth, and Kor have all given me full reports on Commander Sulu's recent actions in Klingon space." He paused to point a mailed index finger directly at Sulu. "Need I remind this august body that this man's deeds led *directly* to the crippling of a notorious criminal organization devoted to piracy and terror?"

Harriman's eyes blazed, though he spoke in carefully measured tones. "We are aware of the events of the past several weeks. Every member of this board of inquiry has read Commander Sulu's log entries since circumstances forced him to assume command of *Excelsior*."

"Circumstances?" Kamarag said, lowering his hand as he displayed an impressively feral-looking array of sharpened teeth. "It was the craven actions of a pirate crimelord and terrorist, not *circumstances,* that relieved *Excelsior* of her captain. Your Commander Sulu merely did what his duties required of him. His decision to step into the breach not only resulted in the capture or killing of a large number of the criminal organization's members, it also compromised one of its major staging posts—in addition to providing us with enough advance warning of an impending bioweapons attack against Qo'noS to enable my government to greatly minimize the damage that was done."

"With all due respect, Ambassador," Cartwright said, "you are out of your depth here. Commander Sulu stands accused of extremely serious offenses."

Kamarag nodded. "So my government has informed me. Knowing how highly you Earthers value peace, I had no doubt that 'jeopardizing the prospects for Klingon-Federation détente' or some other similarly worded offense would rank quite high on the list of charges."

"You're quite correct, Ambassador," Harriman said. "But this is an internal Federation matter. Neither you nor anyone else in your government may cast a vote as to the disposition of this case."

Though Kamarag acknowledged Harriman's point with another nod, he still seemed to give no ground. "That is as it may be, Admiral. You, however, must understand that no less a personage than Chancellor Kesh of the Klingon High Council credits Commander Sulu's actions with having materially contributed to *averting* a diplomatic breach between our Empire and your Federation. Therefore, the latter may expect some rather dire diplomatic fallout from the former should you decide to treat Commander Sulu in too harsh a manner."

Harriman just stood behind the lectern, stunned, blinking, and silent. Sulu could not recall ever having seen him—or any of the assembled brass, for that matter—looking quite so poleaxed as all five admirals did at this moment. Kamarag stood in patient silence beside Sulu as the board members literally closed ranks, going into a brief huddle, which Harriman dispersed after perhaps half a minute of harsh whispers.

"Commander Sulu, Ambassador Kamarag," said Harriman. "I'm calling a ten-minute recess while the board of inquiry deliberates in private."

Sulu found that more than a little confusing. "But I haven't even entered a plea yet."

"Well, now you have another ten minutes to think about it before you do," Harriman said before ringing the bell on his lectern once again, and then leading the other four admirals and both ensigns out of the chamber.

Stroking his chin thoughtfully, Sulu turned toward Kamarag, who had remained standing in the room's center.

"I'm not sure what you hoped to accomplish here, Mister Ambassador," Sulu said.

"*Justice* was what I hoped to accomplish, Commander. And the repayment of a personal debt I incurred when you and your people saved my life at Korvat, and then took decisive action against those responsible for the bombing there."

Sulu shook his head, not much more comfortable with Kamarag's praise than with Starfleet Command's opprobrium. "You don't owe me anything, Ambassador," he said. "Whatever my crew and I did in rescuing you and going after the albino, we did because we thought duty required it."

"I understand that, Commander. But *you* must understand something as well: my House is allied with that of Kang, whose life you *also* saved. Therefore Kang felt he had to—how do you humans put it?—'call in a few markers' to persuade me to speak to your superiors on your behalf."

"Thank you, Mister Ambassador," Sulu said, though he suspected that Ambassadors Sarek and Dax might have put some pressure on Kamarag to intervene as well. "And please pass my thanks along to Captain Kang."

Kamarag scowled. "Do not mistake our actions for pure altruism, Commander. Your service to Kang amounted to a blood debt owed by both our allied Houses. And I do not relish finding myself indebted to a human any more than Kang does, our current mutual peace efforts notwithstanding."

Sulu allowed a small smile to emerge. *And just when these people were finally beginning to make me feel all warm and fuzzy inside.*

"Do you think there really will be a peace effort going forward, Ambassador?" he said. "Even after everything that's happened over the past couple of weeks?"

The hulking Klingon responded with a vulpine smile of his own. "We Klingons are nothing if not tenacious. Especially when in pursuit of a worthy goal—so long as the more belligerent among us can be persuaded that a goal not achievable through warfare can indeed be a worthy one."

Sulu thought that sounded like a lot to expect, particularly from a society as aggressive as the Klingon Empire. But he also knew he didn't need to dig too deeply into the history of his own species to find barbarities that might make Kamarag weep, if he only had the tear ducts for it.

"I suspect that Curzon Dax contributed at least as much persuasion as I did," Sulu said, feeling a momentary flash of envy for the Trill junior ambassador who had apparently "won his spurs," so to speak, during the aftermath of the Korvat affair—at least in the eyes of some fairly influential figures in the Klingon Empire.

"Perhaps," Kamarag said. "I will leave such questions for future academics and historians to analyze. But it should suffice to say that I remain confident that talks between our respective governments will resume soon enough, either on Korvat or elsewhere. And more importantly, my debt to you, as well as Kang's, is now settled—in spite of the insult I suffered at the hands of your doctors."

Sulu frowned, confused. "Insult?"

"Your overly thorough healers deprived me of the battle scars I won legitimately at the Korvat conference."

With that, the ambassador began heading back toward the door through which he had made such a dramatic entrance only a few short minutes earlier. "Oh well," he said over his shoulder, "there will no doubt be other peace conferences where more such scars will be easily obtainable."

Just before he vanished from sight, Kamarag favored Sulu with a momentary but nonetheless fearsome display of teeth, as well as a deep and resounding laugh. A moment later, Sulu stood alone in the wide chamber.

When Admiral Harriman returned a few minutes later, wearing the frown of a man who'd been forced at phaser-point to pick the best of a bad lot of options, Sulu could only hope that all the kindnesses that friends and enemies alike had extended on his behalf hadn't damned him outright.

FORTY-THREE

Stardate 9049.7 (Early 2290)

U.S.S. Excelsior

Janice Rand walked quickly down the corridor alongside Lieutenant Commander Cutler, bound for transporter room three in answer to Hikaru Sulu's terse call from Starfleet Headquarters.

Sulu had requested a beam-up in five minutes' time, but hadn't said a word about how his hearing had turned out. Worse, he had signed off without allowing either Rand or Cutler to ask him any questions about how the initial session of the board of inquiry had gone—and why it had concluded so quickly.

He couldn't have assured Rand's presence in the transporter room any more successfully had he issued top priority orders to summon her there.

Still, Rand didn't think Sulu's reticence could be a very good sign, even though she couldn't dismiss the possibility that he'd simply been too busy when he'd called to have a conversation with her. She also wasn't sure what the extreme brevity of Sulu's hearing might portend. Had the assembled

Starfleet brass needed only enough time to schedule a general court-martial for a later date?

Relax, Janice, Rand told herself as the transporter room doors hissed open to admit Cutler, whom she immediately followed inside. *If Starfleet Command really has decided to throw the book at him, wouldn't they have clapped him in irons instead of letting him beam right back aboard the scene of the alleged crime?*

"Commanders," said the transporter operator, a chief petty officer named Renyck, obviously addressing them both.

Acknowledging the young man with a curt nod, Rand stepped beside him and glanced at the settings on the sleek console that fronted the transporter stage. Renyck had already established a signal lock with Starfleet Headquarters, and appeared to be about to energize the pads.

"Chief, if you don't mind, I'd like to take over here for a minute or two," she said even as she stepped directly beside him, gently but firmly nudging him out of her way.

"Of course, Commander," Renyck said in sheepish tones, withdrawing to the right side of the console.

Although pressing duties of her own awaited her up on the bridge, Rand wasn't about to delegate the retrieval of her old friend to some junior officer, however talented he might be. She gathered from Cutler's somber expression that *Excelsior*'s de facto first officer felt much the same way.

Once she finished making certain that the transporter lock was in order, she placed her hand on the three slide levers that activated the materialization sequence, then gently pressed them forward.

A narrow curtain of light suddenly stretched from one of the overhead beam emitters down to the circular pad on the raised dais directly beneath it. The light instantly metamorphosed into a luminous column of energy, then swiftly faded away in an ephemeral spray of sparkling brilliance.

Hikaru Sulu stood alone on the transporter stage, still as smartly turned out in his dress uniform as he had been when he'd beamed down about thirty minutes earlier. His neutral, almost stony facial expression gave nothing away.

"Permission to come aboard?" Sulu said.

Cutler nodded, her mien as grave as Sulu's. "Granted, Commander."

So which one of you am I going to call "Captain" from now on? Rand thought, looking first at Cutler, then at Sulu.

A smile slowly spread across Sulu's face. His gaze locking onto Cutler's, he reached toward the spot on his belt where a phaser would have been holstered had he been carrying a sidearm.

He pulled out a small, hinged case of the sort that military men have used since time immemorial to store medals and other insignia, and opened it. He held up the open case to give both Cutler and Rand a good, long look at the pair of triple-barred metal uniform insignia inside.

Cutler looked shocked, as though she had been expecting a very different outcome. Rand wasn't a bit surprised by Cutler's reaction, given all the hostility she had shown Sulu prior to the past week or so. After all, Sulu had effectively thwarted Cutler's ambition to serve as Captain Styles's first officer, just by reporting for duty aboard *Excelsior.* And now he had just taken *Excelsior* itself away from her.

But what Rand *didn't* expect was the admiring smile that suddenly lit up Cutler's formerly hard countenance.

"Welcome aboard," Cutler said. "And congratulations. Captain Sulu."

"Level, please?" the turbolift control panel said in a monotone male voice as Janice Rand and Meredith Cutler followed him into the turbolift.

"Bridge," Sulu said.

The lift surged into motion. *"Thank you."*

It occurred to Sulu then that one of his first actions as *Excelsior*'s captain ought to be to program a less obnoxious voice into the turbolift systems. He wondered idly whether Dr. Chapel, if she were still aboard, might consent to having her voiceprint adapted for that purpose. . . .

"You still haven't explained exactly how you persuaded Starfleet Command to back off, Captain," Rand said wryly as she helped Sulu apply his new captain's insignia to his dress tunic. "Much less how you got them to give you a promotion."

"Those are both excellent questions," Cutler said, obviously working hard to hold down a surprisingly companionable grin. "Blackjack Harriman in particular isn't exactly the president of your fan club, Captain."

· Sulu offered up a deliberately enigmatic smile as the decks sped past as quickly as heartbeats. He paused, as though pondering exactly how candid he wanted to be in front of Meredith Cutler.

"Let's just say it never hurts to have friends in the right places who are willing to speak up for you," he said at length.

Cutler nodded, and her smile faltered. "Now that you're assuming command formally, I suppose you'll be expecting my resignation," she said.

Despite his mostly prickly relationship with Cutler up until now, the bluntness of her comment startled him. "Why, Commander? Are you unhappy aboard *Excelsior*?"

"Respectfully, Captain, that isn't the right question to ask," Cutler said. "I suppose you could say I was happy working under Lawrence Styles, but that's now a moot point. Now that you've stepped into his job, you have to assemble a command staff that *you're* comfortable with. And I'm sure you'll want a first officer who's more . . . compatible with your style of command than I am."

Sulu couldn't deny that Cutler wouldn't have been his first choice for the exec job. In fact, the one person he'd most often imagined at his right hand was Pavel Chekov, who was serving currently as Jim Kirk's tactical officer and chief of security. *But Pavel's not here,* he reminded himself. *And I really don't know for sure if he'd want to leave the* Enterprise *right now, even to become* Excelsior's *second-in-command.*

And he also couldn't deny that Cutler had risen to the occasion under some extremely difficult circumstances, wisely counseling restraint and rising above the mutual antipathy they'd felt since he'd first come aboard *Excelsior*.

"We may have had our differences, Commander," he said at length. "But you covered my back when it counted most."

Cutler chuckled ruefully as she shook her head. "When I wasn't trying to stick a knife into it, you mean."

The turbolift came to a stop and the doors opened with a pneumatic hiss onto the bridge's aft starboard side.

"Maybe we all ought to agree not to make any big changes for a little while," Rand said, hoping to disperse the tension in the air. "At least until after our new captain has had a chance to sit down in the big chair once or twice."

Sulu led the others out of the turbolift, stepped past the rear duty consoles, and finally approached the raised command chair located almost in the precise center of the bridge.

"Captain on the bridge," Cutler announced in a loud, no-nonsense tone that made everyone present snap instantly to attention. Both Lieutenant Lojur, the Halkan navigator, and Ensign Akaar, the towering Capellan relief helmsman and security officer, had risen respectfully beside their centrally located consoles.

They looked at Sulu expectantly, as did the half-dozen or so other bridge personnel who had briefly paused in their various tasks before their blinking, humming duty stations.

"As you were, everybody," Sulu said, and the bridge staff turned its collective attention back to work.

They're a good crew, he thought. *Here's hoping I'm worthy of them.*

He heard the portside turbolift hiss open, and turned to see a beaming Christine Chapel step onto the bridge.

"Chris!" he said, delighted to see another *Enterprise* alumnus on such an auspicious occasion. "I'm glad to see you're still aboard." If Dr. Klass decided to retire soon—and she'd been making noises about doing just that, particularly lately—he hoped very much that Chapel would consider signing on to replace her as *Excelsior*'s CMO.

"I wanted to make sure that Doctor Klass was completely back on her feet before I went back to the Diplomatic Corps," she said as she gathered him up in a *to-hell-with-bridge-decorum* bear hug. "And I got up here as soon as Chief Renyck called me with the good news. Congratulations on your promotion . . . *Captain* Sulu."

Captain, Sulu thought as Christine released him from the embrace. He looked down at the command chair beside him and ran his hand along one of its arms. *I think I like the sound of that.*

Then he sat in the chair, just as he had done many times before in Captain Styles's absence. But this simple action now took on much greater significance. At long last, after so many years of hard work, he actually held the rank of captain while in command of Starfleet's most advanced ship of the line. And he wasn't simply keeping the chair warm for someone else.

The combined sense of triumph and vindication tasted sweet indeed. *Excelsior* was *his* ship now. And his responsibility.

He felt at once overawed and exhilarated, as well as unexpectedly humbled; it was impossible for him to forget, after all, that he owed his captaincy to the chaotic vicissitudes of violence and death as much as he owed it to the lifetime's worth of effort he had expended ever since that horrible day on Ganjitsu.

He realized now that in some terrible, twisted way, he also owed a debt to the albino, though certainly not in the way that Kang, Koloth, or Kor would understand such things. The pirate had forever altered the trajectory of Sulu's life forty years ago.

Then, only three weeks ago, Qagh had rather cataclysmically emptied *Excelsior*'s center seat, giving Sulu no choice other than to take it.

"He's still out there somewhere," Sulu said, frowning into the image of the infinitude of stars that lay beyond the blue, half-shadowed Earth that *Excelsior* orbited.

"Excuse me, Captain?" Cutler said.

"The albino, Commander. He's not the kind of loose thread I like to leave hanging."

A knowing look crossed Cutler's face as she folded her arms before her. "Something tells me the Klingons will pick up the stitch on *that* particular loose thread, sooner or later. If there's one thing they excel at, it's the art of the karmic follow-through."

"Good point," Sulu said, nodding as he recalled the renowned Klingon preference for serving up revenge as a cold entrée. "So what's next on our agenda, Commander?"

"Captain's discretion," Cutler said with a shrug. "There was no telling in advance how long *Excelsior* would have to stay in Earth orbit, so I cleared our schedule. And our three-year exploration mission in the Reydovan sector isn't due to begin until stardate 9090.1."

"So we have nearly two whole weeks to get *Excelsior* shipshape," Rand said in amusement. "Chief Henry and the rest of the engineering crew are liable to get soft with so much extra time on their hands."

"Trust me," Cutler said around a perfectly evil grin. "I'll find stuff for them to do."

Two weeks, Sulu thought as he stroked his chin thoughtfully. *Two whole weeks to take* Excelsior *wherever I want.*

There wouldn't be a lot of time to pursue vendettas. And that realization came to Sulu with an unexpected sense of relief, since quests for revenge weren't exactly enshrined in Starfleet's charter.

"Mister Lojur, lay in a course for the drydock and shore leave facilities at Xarantine," Sulu said, facing forward. "Warp eight, Mister Lojur."

"Aye, sir," said Lojur, releasing one of his rare smiles, since Xarantine was without doubt a world on which even a troubled member of an ascetic, pacifistic race could find no end of peaceful entertainments.

"Ready to engage helm, sir," Leonard James Akaar said in a voice about half an octave deeper than Sulu's, his demeanor all business; Sulu wasn't sure the giant Capellan even knew how to smile.

"Very good," he said, turning his chair back toward starboard so that he faced Cutler again. "Chief Henry can evaluate and fine-tune our repair and maintenance needs along the way."

Cutler nodded, her enthusiasm almost palpable as she immediately began moving toward the nearest turbolift. "I'll see to it, Captain."

His eyes once again riveted to the main viewer, Sulu said, "Gentlemen . . . let's hit the road."

After a brief exchange of quizzical looks in response to their captain's peculiar human idiom, the navigator and helmsman both set about their tasks with enviable efficiency. Within moments, the sapphire globe of Sulu's birthworld had fallen away into the interstellar darkness.

The faint vibrations beneath his boots told him more

eloquently than any console readout that *Excelsior* had just gone to warp.

Don't worry, Lawrence, he thought, silently looking around the mighty starship's comfortingly busy bridge. *As long as I'm in charge here, I promise to take very, very good care of her.*

FORTY-FOUR

With her new deep-space assignment officially starting at 0600 the next morning, Ensign Demora Sulu knew she should have been happy. Literally over-the-moon happy, in fact, and filled to overflowing with anticipation for the adventure to come.

Instead, she felt the weight of the cosmos itself settling onto her shoulders as she contemplated the depths of her glass of chardonnay.

"To new frontiers," Commander Pavel Chekov said over his raised glass of Stolichnaya. "And new ships named *Enterprise*."

"May there always be a Sulu at the helm," added Captain Montgomery Scott, who held aloft a clear, sloshing tankard that contained something that was green, toxic-looking, and mercifully unidentified.

"Speech!" said fair-haired Ensign Michael Thomas Paris, who grinned over a frothy stein of blue Andorian ale, one of the signature specialties of the Quantum Café, and a favorite of many of the establishment's Starfleet habitués.

Commander Chekov was the first to show any sign of noticing that something wasn't quite right. "What's wrong, Demora?" he said as he set his drink down on the table and leaned forward, an expression of concern etched across his friendly, open face.

She sighed and shook her head. "It's nothing," she said, barely succeeding in stopping herself from adding "Uncle Pavel." Because both Chekov and Scott numbered among her father's dearest and oldest friends, she really did consider both of them family. But she didn't want to precipitate the barrage of needling that her fellow recent Starfleet Academy graduate, Ensign Paris, would surely unleash later if she were to be too familiar with a pair of Starfleet's most distinguished officers.

"Could have fooled me," Chekov said, his head tipped in curiosity.

Scott, however, wasn't going to allow her a graceful retreat. "Come now, Lassie. I may have been born *at* night, but I wasn't born *last* night," he said, grinning conspiratorially under his gray "cookie duster" mustache. "Something's troublin' you. Now what could be weighing down your soul the night before you're to ship out on Starfleet's new *Excelsior*-class flagship?"

Demora raised her glass and downed the remainder of its contents as if to make a show of honoring the toasts her two "uncles" had just made. Then she motioned with the empty glass toward one of the waiters to signal that she needed a refill, preferably at transwarp speed.

She turned her gaze wryly on her old "Uncle Monty," Captain Scott. "I thought you didn't much care for the *Excelsior*-class design, sir."

He chuckled. "Aye, I'll admit to a bias toward the tried and true, but that's only because I'm an old-timer. But a star-hopping whippersnapper like *you* ought to be thrilled to be going out to explore the galaxy—even if you're forced to do it in that oversized, overengineered bucket o' bolts."

The waiter approached Demora, bottle in hand, and filled her glass before withdrawing gracefully to an adjacent table where a trio of young Starfleet officers was already enthusiastically sharing a meal. For an evening immediately before a major starship departure, the Café seemed surprisingly empty, currently serving a mixed Starfleet and civilian clientele of only a dozen or so people.

"It'll be an honor and a privilege to be part of the new *Enterprise*'s crew," Demora said, staring into the depths of her newly filled glass. Then she fixed her gaze back upon Chekov before turning slightly to face Scott. "And I hope you'll both be aboard tomorrow for our big sendoff. I mean, we still have some settling in to do for a few days until we actually leave the system next Tuesday, but the official christening and all the other big media events are all scheduled for tomorrow afternoon."

"I'll be there," the engineer said with a broad smile. "With bells on."

"And I wouldn't miss it for the world either," Chekov added. "Captain Kirk promises he'll be there as well."

"If he doesn't break his neck with that orbital skydiving vice of his in the meantime," Scott said.

Chekov chuckled. "You know the captain. He's indestructible."

"What about the rest of the old crew?" Scott asked, still addressing Chekov.

"Doctor McCoy says he's too busy growing back his beard, taking crash courses in Klingon physiology, and starting up his new civilian practice to attend the ceremonies. But he *did* tell me he'd try to catch the *next* one."

"That certainly sounds like how Doctor McCoy would handle retirement. I wonder if it'll take this time," Scott said with a chuckle. That elicited a smile from Demora, who felt certain that the engineer would spend at least as many of his own retirement years building and tinkering as McCoy would practicing medicine and doing research.

"I got a message from Captain Spock this morning, too," Chekov said. "He won't be able to attend either. He's on Earth, though, for a meeting with the new diplomatic representative from Triskelion."

"Aye, I heard about that as well," said Scott. "The Triskelions sent Shahna herself. I saw her picture in the Federation News Service feed this morning, and she looks every inch the diplomat now. I almost didn't recognize her without the steel swimsuit and all the cutlery."

Although Demora had read extensively about the exploits of the *Enterprise* crew, she could only wonder about that one.

"Any word from *Excelsior*?" asked Ensign Paris.

Though Demora answered quietly, she was unable to keep the acid entirely out of her voice. "Do you mean before or after she brought the Triskelion envoy to Earth for that meeting with Captain Spock?"

Paris, who had acquired the ironic nickname "Iron Mike" during his Academy years because of his slight, willowy frame, winced noticeably at her rejoinder. Demora could see that the twenty-two-year-old ensign realized an instant too late that he was treading upon sensitive ground, and she instantly regretted not exercising more restraint. *In vino veritas,* she thought, regarding her wineglass as though it were a blood-smeared dagger.

When she noticed the inquisitive expressions that had spread across both Scott's and Chekov's faces, she said, "My father has already sent his regrets."

"*Excelsior* was called away?" Chekov asked, in the same understanding "Uncle Pavel" manner he'd used many times over the years to help her cope with Hikaru Sulu's countless other duty-related absences. Chekov's compassionate gaze momentarily transported her back a decade or more, to a time when she had first begun to believe that getting through the Academy and earning a Starfleet commission of her own would enable her, finally, to understand and forgive her perpetually elsewhere father.

But the present was simply not as she had imagined it would be back then. Now she was beginning to suspect that some old wounds simply ran too deep ever to heal adequately.

Demora nodded in Chekov's direction. "*Excelsior* received new orders as soon as the Triskelion ambassador was beamed down." She couldn't help but wonder if her father might have tried to avoid seeing her again, had *Excelsior*'s current itinerary been left to his own discretion.

"Now let's be fair, lass," Scott said gently, though she could hear a stern undercurrent surfacing beneath his convivial pub-crawler persona. "There's been trouble along the Klingon border ever since Praxis exploded. Captain Sulu's new assignment might be more of the same."

Demora's face flushed with shame at her own self-centeredness. Her unwillingness even to consider giving her father the benefit of the doubt suddenly made her feel more like a petulant child than a commissioned officer in humanity's primary instrument of civilization and exploration.

Counterfeiting a carefree smile, she raised her glass, which was still more than half full of white wine. She vowed to empty it at least twice more before returning, just for the night, to her small studio apartment in the Presidio District.

"To absent friends, family, and well-wishers," she said. "Godspeed to them all."

Whether or not they really *deserve the benefit of the doubt for being absent,* she thought as she returned her attention to the tart liquid in her cup.

•   •   •

Veret felt a single large bead of cold sweat swell against his backbone before making its swift, chilly descent along his spine. He did his best to ignore it.

There she is, he thought, watching from the drinking establishment's southeast corner as his Starfleet prey raised and lowered a delicate, transparent drinking vessel.

But Veret had a problem: a trio of other uniformed Starfleet officers surrounded his target. Veret felt confident enough that he could handle either the slender young human male or the rather hefty older male who sat near him. But he didn't like his chances should he be forced into an altercation with the apparently middle-aged, brown-haired man who shared a table with his prey—a young woman who might also prove surprisingly formidable should she happen to notice what he was about to attempt before it was too late.

He wished he could simply turn and exit the café and lose himself in the fog-shrouded night. His skills were such that he could certainly liberate whatever he needed in order to survive, even in this antiseptic so-called paradise that these Earthers so revered. Had he not already proved himself to be more than adept at quietly skimming his employer's profits? All he needed was a few hours to recover his stash of illicit latinum and bearer notes, and then disappear once and for all.

But Veret understood all too well that even his considerable skills as a freebooter were far from the only determiner of his continued survival. Were he to disobey the orders he'd been given, either the albino or one of his other operatives would most likely find him no matter where he tried to hide. The albino had made it abundantly clear how very important this particular prey was to him; Demora Sulu was one of a very few targets he had been stalking for the past three Federation standard years.

And even if the albino never so much as lifted a finger to pursue him, Veret understood that the retroviruses with which he'd been injected some five years earlier would enforce his employer's will more effectively than could a phaser-barrel aimed straight at his head. Veret knew that without the regular infusions of antidotes that only the albino could supply—drugs that his chalk-skinned taskmaster had laboriously developed in order to ensure both life and loyalty among those in his employ—he'd be dead inside of a week's time.

He knew with terrible certainty that the albino's retroviral threat was no bluff; he'd seen with his own eyes just how little was left of one of the albino's other operatives, a young woman who had tried to betray her master three years before.

The deed has to be done tonight, Veret thought, hugging the shadows in the corner of the café. *Tomorrow, she'll be billeted aboard a high-security Federation starship.*

And therefore far harder, perhaps even impossible, to reach. But the albino did not react well to his operatives telling him that any task was impossible.

As Veret looked on anxiously, the young woman he sought rose from her table and began walking straight toward his corner of the café. His heart suddenly leaped into his throat, and he felt the slickness of perspiration collecting on his neck-gills. Had he somehow given away his identity and purpose? If he had, his life would almost certainly be forfeit.

Then he noticed the restroom sign that lay between him and his victim, and flushed with embarrassment at his own obtuseness; while he was largely unfamiliar with the details of the human urinary tract, he did understand basic hydraulics enough to know that liquids not only could not be compressed, but also had to be released from the human body on a fairly regular basis.

Now is the time, Veret told himself. As the uniformed young woman approached, he reached into his cloak and stepped directly into her path.

The impact of his shoulder slamming into hers rattled his teeth, despite his already having braced himself for it. He did his best to appear surprised by this "accidental" contact— even as the contents of the small hypospray concealed in his left hand hissed home through his target's uniform jacket, emptying into her forearm.

Although she instinctively jerked away from him, she showed no immediate sign of having noticed his subtle invasion of her body.

"Apologies, ma'am," Veret said, stepping toward the young woman while doing his best to appear interested only in helping her maintain her suddenly compromised balance. "Are you all right?"

He met the young woman's indignant scowl with a calculated look of purest innocence that seemed to disarm whatever angry response seemed about to spring to her lips before she evidently thought better of it.

"I'm fine, thanks," she said, pausing to straighten her jacket before she continued toward the café's restrooms.

As she withdrew, apparently none the wiser about the death sentence he had just surreptitiously administered to her, he worked hard to suppress an unseemly urge to leap into the air in triumph.

Veret glanced momentarily toward the small table at which the young woman had been seated, where the brown-haired, middle-aged Starfleeter sat staring daggers at him while his two remaining drinking companions continued chatting amiably. The assassin breathed a silent prayer for the blessings of the gods of his homeworld, whom he implored to ensure that his deed remained undetected for at least a short while longer—at least until he made his escape from this place.

He moved toward the exit with as much quiet nonchalance as he could muster. *The fuse has been lit,* he thought.

He could only wonder precisely how much delay the

albino had programmed into the genetic time bomb he had just planted.

The enormity of what Veret had just done didn't really strike him until after he'd lifted off in his small shuttle and was well on his way back to the high orbit where the freebooter *Chu' Hegh'TlhoS* awaited, her large, boxy cargo modules arranged beneath a farrago of cobbled-together solar collectors and Bussard intakes along a slightly curving central spine that somehow made the renovated freighter resemble an angry hive-insect preparing to strike.

As his small, battered shuttle made its approach to dock with the *Chu' Hegh'TlhoS*'s complexly textured underbelly, Veret considered the irony of the name of his employer's vessel, which wasn't the first to bear the name. It took a good deal of daring to operate a ship bearing *any* Klingon name even on the fringes of Federation space, let alone in the vicinity of Earth itself, the very heart of the Federation. And to choose a Klingon name for multiple successive ships—especially the root-name *Hegh'TlhoS,* which translated, essentially, to "dead, almost" or "not quite dead"—was to tempt the fates into becoming downright malicious.

But such matters did not concern him now nearly as much as far more fundamental questions, such as what he had allowed his life to become.

I steal and kill for a man I hate, Veret accused himself as the *Chu' Hegh'TlhoS*'s docking clamps engaged with a jolting *clang!* that reverberated through the shuttle. *And I do it because I fear him.*

He knew he couldn't endure the guilt that tore at what remained of his soul for much longer. He felt he was swiftly coming to a crossroads. As he ascended the sealed gangway that connected the shuttle's dorsal surface to the belly of the *Chu' Hegh'TlhoS,* he wondered when his contempt for himself would become stronger than his craven instincts for self-preservation.

If only I could be as strong as the woman who ran from him three years ago, Veret thought, despairing because he knew he would probably rationalize the intolerable yet again. By tomorrow, he would make peace with his remaining shreds of conscience, if only temporarily. And he would resume his usual pattern of quiet scheming, secretly skimming the albino's profits whenever the pirate chieftain wasn't looking, and deluding himself into believing that he would one day leave this life behind. . . .

Moving silently, as befitted a professional thief—and now assassin—Veret wended his way past several Andorian, Tellarite, Denobulan, and Balduk crew members, some of whom busied themselves pursuing shipboard maintenance, and others who seemed to laze, apparently assuming that they were out of the captain's immediate view. Veret knew better; the albino's prying eyes were everywhere on board this vessel.

Stepping sideways through a narrow corridor, Veret entered the small but richly appointed captain's suite that the albino had made his permanent home. The pasty-white humanoid sat in semidarkness behind a heavy desk made of dark, polished Romulan sherawood, probably taken in a long-forgotten pirate raid decades ago.

"I have carried out your instructions, Captain Qagh," Veret said, swallowing hard.

Flanked by a pair of armed underlings, an Orion male named Jek and a Klingon female called B'Lor, Qagh leaned back in his chair, his dark brown leather tunic making a stark contrast with skin and hair that were both the color of old dry bones. He looked somewhat sicklier than usual, though Veret's report had buoyed the brigand leader's spirits visibly.

"That is very good news indeed," said the albino. "You ought to be rewarded properly."

"Thank you, sir," said Veret, keeping his mien carefully neutral. *Cure the disease with which you have afflicted me,* he thought. *Turn me loose.* End *this.*

"But it has just come to my attention that you have been rewarding *yourself*," Qagh said. "Out of my profits."

He raised a chalk-white hand that had hitherto been invisible beneath the desk. His bony fingers gripped the handle of a military-issue Klingon disruptor pistol. Veret saw a flash of fear in the eyes of both Jek and B'Lor, followed almost immediately by relief as both of them realized that they weren't the focus of Qagh's wrath.

At least for now.

When the weapon fired, Veret was surprised that he felt liberated rather than frightened.

EPILOGUE WA'

Sulu stood in solemn silence as the gathering around the
burial vault of young DaqS began to break up and drift
away, quickly leaving Kang and his wife Mara standing bereft and alone before the metal-plated stone monolith.

In response to Sulu's warning that they get their children
to a safe place, Koloth and Kor had walked to the periphery of the gathering, standing at opposite sides of it; Sulu
watched both men in turn as they spoke urgently into their
handheld communications devices, initiating conversations
that Sulu was too far away to overhear.

But Sulu knew they were checking on the status of their
own young children, to prevent their suffering the same horrible fate that had already befallen little DaqS, whom Kang
had come here today to bury.

Curzon Dax, who was standing beside Sulu, had evidently been making essentially the same observations. "For
once I'm glad I haven't had children yet," the Trill diplomat

said with a world-weary sadness that should have taken far longer than just the past five years to acquire. "Of course, that retrovirus the albino exposed us all to puts having children right at the top of my own personal 'worst ideas' list."

Sulu nodded, feeling fortunate that his daughter Demora had been born nearly two decades before the advent of the albino's tailored, weaponized retroviruses.

Of course, he was already bitterly aware that there was no shortage of other means by which the albino might strike at him through his only child. He wondered how much time remained before Demora succumbed to the disease that had stricken her an hour or so ago aboard the *Enterprise,* light-years away.

His communicator beeped as if on cue; he snatched the device from his belt and flipped open the antenna grid.

"Sulu here."

"Captain, I have an incoming communication from the Enterprise,*"* said Commander Rand, *Excelsior*'s communications officer.

Cold fingers of dread clutched at Sulu's guts as he excused himself and moved several long paces away from Dax.

"Thank you, Janice," he said. "Pipe it down here, please."

After a brief pause, the familiar voice of the *Enterprise*-B's current captain, the son of a man who had nearly seen Sulu cashiered from Starfleet service immediately after the albino affair, issued from the communicator. *"It's John, Hikaru."*

"Do you have news about Demora?" *Please, God. Let her live.*

"I do," Harriman said.

Though there was nowhere to sit on the rugged plain Kang had selected for the burial site, Sulu did his best to brace himself for the worst.

Don't. Let. Her. Die.

"Fortunately, it's good *news,"* Harriman continued. *"Doctor Michaels reports that the worst of Demora's illness seems to have passed already. The convulsive symptoms have stopped, and she's conscious. I imagine she'll need some time in sickbay to recover, but she already seems to be on her way to a complete recovery."*

His fingers suddenly numb, Sulu nearly allowed his communicator to fall to the rocky ground. He wanted to shout his joy and relief to Qo'noS's dark, meteor-striated night sky, but refrained in deference to the solemnity of the rituals that had just been performed here.

"Hikaru?"

"I'm here, John. I'd like to talk to her as soon as possible." *And I promise not to let so much time pass until the* next *time I speak with her.*

"I'll have to defer to Doctor Michaels on that one, Hikaru," Harriman said, and then dropped off the channel, presumably to look into Sulu's request.

Sulu stood waiting patiently while he watched Kor and Koloth, both of whom were still animatedly engaged in their own distant conversations. He hoped for their sakes that whatever news they were receiving involved outcomes that resembled Demora's more than they did that of poor DaqS.

A croaking, scratchy voice that Sulu scarcely recognized emerged from the communicator. *"Hello, Dad."*

"Demora?"

"I suppose I've sounded better. Thirsty." She paused, and Sulu heard sloshing sounds that made him imagine a camel sucking down water liters at a time after a weeklong ride across the Gobi. *"Doctor Michaels says I must have picked up a virus somewhere."*

"Sounds like some virus," Sulu said. He was beginning to hope he could chalk up his earlier suspicions about the albino to paranoia.

Another voice chimed in on the line, this one belonging

to a man that Sulu imagined as middle-aged and gray-haired. *"Rod Michaels here, Captain Sulu. I've already done some following up on what you suggested to Captain Harriman. It looks like the bug that put our helmsman on the temporarily disabled list really* was *artificially engineered—apparently by an expert."*

Of course, just because *you're paranoid,* Sulu reminded himself, *doesn't mean that somebody really isn't out to get you.*

Or your children.

"It's a retrovirus," Dr. Michaels continued. *"It's difficult to detect, perhaps impossible to screen out even with bio-filters, and extremely virulent. Fortunately, there seems to be no danger of its spreading."*

"Any idea where Demora picked it up, Doctor? Or when?"

"It's hard to say, Captain. The Enterprise *has gotten around quite a bit over the past two years. As for* when *the initial infection occurred, that could have happened at any time since Lieutenant Sulu came aboard, or perhaps even earlier, since I don't know the organism's precise incubation period. All I can say for certain now is that your daughter seems to possess a great deal of natural immunity to it."*

"Do you have any clue yet where this bug might have come from?"

"Nothing conclusive yet. But Nurse Thompson and I have done a quick cross-check using the medical files your CMO sent. My compliments to Doctor Chapel on her research skills, by the way."

"I'll be sure to tell her, Doctor," Sulu said, beginning to grow impatient. "What did you find?"

"As far as I can tell, this retrovirus is closely related to the pathogen that James Kirk encountered nearly thirty years ago on the planet Omega IV."

It's also the same one that the albino based most of his retroviral bioweapons on, Sulu thought. *As well as the one that's been in my blood ever since I visited Omega IV.*

The original retrovirus, which had killed the entire crew of the *U.S.S. Exeter* in a manner not too different from the way young DaqS had died, had to be allowed to build up to significant concentrations in the blood of each *Enterprise* crew member who had contracted it on the surface of Omega IV. Without the immunization conferred by this pathogenic buildup, the entire *Enterprise* crew would have died horribly within a few hours of retrieving the landing party, transformed into small piles of lifeless crystals, as had happened to the *Exeter*'s crew.

Sulu realized with a start that he was beginning to understand something else he had never before considered: because the original Omega IV virus was actually a *retrovirus,* it was capable of subtly altering the genes of anyone who'd been exposed to it—including those of one Hikaru Sulu.

Recombinant genetics, one generation removed, had evidently given Demora Sulu a certain level of immunity to the virus.

Young DaqS, whose Klingon genetics contained a very different pallet of strengths and weaknesses than those of humanity, apparently had not been so fortunate.

"Captain Sulu?" Dr. Michaels said. *"Are you still there?"*

"Sorry, Doctor. I'm still . . . processing all of this."

Demora's voice returned, sounding significantly less parched, but also more worried, than before. *"You warned me about this when I was still at the Academy. I guess when nothing happened right away . . . I must have let my guard down."*

"I still don't know for sure that this virus has anything to do with the albino's threat, Demora," he said. "And besides, you can't be expected to stay on Red Alert every minute of every day."

She chuckled at that. *"Tell that to my CO, Dad. But first . . . is there anything else you can tell us about this virus?"*

Sulu was still puzzling that out. He knew that young DaqS had been conceived after Qagh had exposed Kang to one of his tailored retroviruses; therefore that virus could have caused the child's death. The sons of Koloth and Kor had also been born only recently as well, which made them similarly vulnerable to inheriting a horrible, genetically preprogrammed death. Demora, however, could not have received the albino's tailored virus the same way DaqS or the other Klingon children had.

Therefore one of Qagh's people must have gotten close to her, exposing her to this pathogen sometime after the pirate had vowed to wreak vengeance against the children of his sworn enemies. The chalk-white ghost that still sometimes haunted his dreams had somehow managed to infect his only daughter with a genetic time bomb, and only a lucky and relatively recent fluke in the Sulu family DNA had prevented its detonation.

"Dad? You still there?"

"I'm here, Demora. Don't worry. I'm just happy that you're making such a good recovery. Listen, I'll call you again a little later. Sulu out." With that he flipped the communicator's grid closed and replaced the device on his belt. *This still could all be just a coincidence,* he told himself, even though he had never believed in coincidences.

He noticed only then that Dax was approaching him, followed by Kor, Koloth, and, finally, Kang. The uniformly grim expressions on the faces of both Kor and Koloth, who must have just finished calling their families on the small transceivers they still carried, made it plain that they, too, had absorbed some most unwelcome news.

Dax leaned toward Sulu. "Please tell me that what I think has just happened hasn't really just happened," the Trill said quietly, his voice pitched only for Sulu's ears.

Sulu said nothing. As the three Klingon captains came to a stop directly in front of him and Dax, Sulu knew what Kor and Koloth were going to say before either of them had even opened their mouths.

"Rynar, my firstborn son, now lies dead!" Kor said, his eyes burning with restrained fury. "From a cause very like the one that claimed the life of young DaqS—a disease that affected no one else in the House."

He was a target, Sulu thought, horrified. *And the disease was a weapon aimed only at him.*

"The same fate has just befallen *my* son as well," Koloth rumbled icily, conjuring images of snow-covered mountains beneath which brooded smoldering volcanoes. "He was my firstborn—and hardly more than an infant."

The five men settled into a pensive silence, broken only by the occasional mournful sounds of distant nocturnal predators. Sabre bear, perhaps, or *targ*.

"So we no longer have to wonder when the albino will finally make good on his parting threat," Dax said, shattering the quiet. "He's already struck his most hated enemies in the most vulnerable place imaginable."

"He also appears to have just made an unsuccessful attempt on the life of my daughter, who now serves aboard the *Enterprise*," Sulu said.

"His reach is long," Kang said. Turning toward Dax, he added, "Though he appears not yet to have reached *you,* Curzon Dax."

Dax nodded. "Only because Curzon Dax has no children."

Though Sulu thought it odd that the Trill diplomat had just referred to himself in the third person, none of the Klingons appeared to have noticed it.

"We must find the albino," Koloth said, eliciting grim affirmative nods from Kang and Koloth, as well as from Dax.

"I will cut out his beating heart and eat it while we force him to watch," Kang declared, generating still more nods.

"He has been seen recently doing business on several Klingon worlds," said Kor. "Galdonterre, Donatu V, Forcas III, and the Dorala system, among other places. Nevertheless, it will be a difficult hunt."

"It's a big Empire," Dax agreed, speaking with all the earnestness of youth. "But I will help the three of you search it any way I can."

Sulu frowned at the young Trill, whose tactical recklessness sometimes overrode his better diplomatic judgment. "Dax and I need to get back to *Excelsior*," he said, addressing the ambassador as much as the Klingons. "We'll conduct a full investigation into these attacks, using every resource at our disposal."

"I want to investigate the murders, too, Captain," Dax said, folding his arms. "But I think I can do a more thorough job of it here, assisting directly on Qo'noS. Or wherever else in Klingon space the albino's trail might lead us."

"And for however long the Federation Diplomatic Corps will put up with it?" Sulu asked with a frown.

Dax responded with a smile, though Sulu could see the burning, almost fanatical intensity beneath it. "I'll burn *that* bridge when I come to it, Captain. Kang's son was also *my* godson—Kang and Mara *named* him after me—so I have to do whatever I can to avenge him."

Sulu was having some trouble believing what he was hearing. "You're a public servant of the United Federation of Planets, Ambassador. Not a vigilante."

Dax stared at Sulu silently for a moment through angry, narrowed eyes. Then he turned toward Kang, as though dismissing Sulu from the conversation.

"I will swear the blood oath with the three of you," Dax declared flatly.

"The blood oath is a sacred rite," Koloth said, apparently as taken aback as Sulu. "And it is reserved only for Klingons."

Kang displayed his white, sharpened teeth. "But Curzon Dax has proved many times over that within his breast beats a heart as stout as that of any Klingon."

"I would welcome you into the blood oath as well," Kor said, grinning like a warrior relishing the prospect of a coming battle. Which, of course, was exactly what he was.

Koloth nodded. "Very well. I will accept him into the blood oath. None of the four of us will rest until we have found and slain the albino, and eaten his heart."

Kang turned toward Sulu, addressing him directly. "I would extend the blood oath to you as well, Hikaru Sulu. After all, the albino has also attacked your progeny, albeit unsuccessfully."

Four pairs of eyes were upon him, pinning him where he stood as surely as a converging array of tractor beams. The silence between the five men stretched awkwardly.

"I'm a Starfleet captain," Sulu said at length. "I can't undertake a mission of vengeance. But I *can* put all the resources of *Excelsior* behind an effort to bring Qagh to justice, under the precepts of Federation and interstellar law."

Sulu watched three pairs of eyes, each of them shadowed by overhanging brow ridges, looking askance at him. Dax merely watched him in silence.

"Your decision might have been different had Qagh actually succeeded in slaying your daughter," Kang said, his voice tinged with commingled grief and disappointment.

"Maybe," Sulu said. He knew the urge to exact revenge intimately enough, and understood its allure as well as any man; it was his own real, firsthand knowledge of how simple it would have been just to have gutted the albino after their *bat'leth* duel on the Qul Tuq moon that persuaded him that vengeance wasn't the path he wanted to follow.

That long-ago day on Ganjitsu notwithstanding.

"Maybe you're right," he said. "Maybe I *would* swear a vendetta against the albino if he'd actually managed to kill Demora. But—and I mean no disrespect to any of you when I say this—I think you're all wrong in wanting this."

At least I hope *you're wrong,* he thought.

"If the three of you don't mind," Dax said to the Klingons, "I'd like a moment in private to say goodbye to Captain Sulu."

Kang nodded, and the three Klingons obligingly withdrew, moving with graceful solemnity back toward little DaqS's funerary vault, beside which Mara still stood. Dax began walking in the opposite direction, and Sulu walked alongside him, matching the slightly taller man's stride easily.

"Do you really intend to go through with this?" Sulu asked.

Dax nodded. "Yes, Captain. I really do."

Sulu recognized the resolute quality in the other man's voice. Past experience with Dax had already demonstrated that he wasn't going to succeed in dissuading him. The conversation paused, although the pair continued walking at a leisurely pace across the rock-strewn hardpan.

"I have to tell you how disappointed I am," Sulu said at length.

"You could always drag me back with you to *Excelsior.*"

"No," Sulu said, shaking his head. "I wouldn't risk offending our Klingon hosts that way."

Dax grinned. "You just might have a better understanding of diplomacy than I do, Captain."

"I don't know about that," Sulu said. "But I think I have a pretty good idea why you feel such anger toward Qagh, even though you weren't actually attacked."

"We Trill are a famously reticent and enigmatic people, Captain," Dax said with a grim smile. "But I have no objection to hearing your speculations."

Sulu studied the younger man's spot-framed features as they walked, and noted that he was seeing the same paradoxically young-old face that Dax's diplomatic negotiating partners saw from across conference tables. Or was this merely the face of a master card player?

And was there a difference?

"All right," Sulu said. "You're angry because you actually *have* lost your children to Qagh."

Dax frowned. "As I already said, Captain: Curzon has no children." Once again, he spoke of himself in the third person.

"All right," Sulu said with a shrug. "So you don't. And that's because you don't want to risk bringing any children into the world, thanks to the albino's parting retroviral attack five years ago. The albino has brought you to the end of the line, at least genetically speaking. He's robbed you of children, which is the same thing he's done to Kang and Kor and Koloth. Only in your case he's done it preemptively."

Dax seemed to listen intently as Sulu delivered his psychoanalysis. Then he stopped walking, as did Sulu.

"I suppose all of that makes sense, Captain," Dax said. "But only from a strictly human perspective."

"Really?" Sulu said, folding his arms. "What have I missed about Trill psychology?"

"Quite a lot, actually. For starters, there's a great deal that you don't understand about Trill society in general."

In view of the well-known Trill penchant for secrecy, Sulu had no doubt that Dax was absolutely right about that. "Then I'd be pleased if you would enlighten me, Ambassador."

Dax responded with a faintly mischievous smile. "Let me just say that my decision to swear the blood oath was purely a matter of honor, friendship, and loyalty—in the manner that the Klingons understand it."

"You just accused me of misunderstanding your people," Sulu said. "So why do you think *you* can understand Klingon culture the way the Klingons understand it?"

Dax spread his hands. "I suppose there's no way to settle that question without the intervention of a telepath. But I *do* know that shared adversity has created an extremely strong bond between me and those three warriors, not to mention the society that produced them. And those bonds have only deepened during the five years since the albino attacked the Korvat conference."

"All right," Sulu said, holding up a placating hand. "Of course, I'm not sure that participating in a revenge scheme out of some noble principle is really any better than doing the same thing for an entirely selfish reason. And you can't convince me that you don't have one, since Qagh has denied you the only immortality that any mortal being can expect to achieve: children."

Dax looked at Sulu appraisingly, as though trying to decide how much of the renowned Trill reticence he could afford to set aside in order to explain himself. "Children don't represent the *only* form of immortality available, Captain," he said finally. "At least not among the Trill."

Sulu listened in rapt fascination as Curzon Dax finally began to explain why.

"But what about your symbiont?" Sulu asked a short while later. "Hasn't it . . . hasn't *Dax* been infected with the virus?"

The enigmatic young-old diplomat shook his head. "Over the past five years, I've undergone pretty thorough batteries of tests designed to settle that very question. As far as Doctor Dareel and the other Trill physicians who've examined me can tell, the albino's virus is simply incompatible with symbiont physiology."

Sulu nodded, understanding. "You're saying that Dax *can't* pass the virus along to a future host because it never contracted the disease in the first place."

"Exactly, Captain. So even if Curzon never manages to purge this damned virus from his body—even if Curzon Dax ends up having no chance whatsoever at fatherhood, or even marriage—Trill symbiosis will still give both partners more immortality than most people will ever experience, with or without children."

Sulu nodded, still trying to digest the Trill's surprising revelations. He felt as though he had just taken a long drink from a fire hose.

"Do the Klingons know about this?" he asked.

"They've known for the past five years," Dax said, nodding. "I hadn't intended to tell them, but circumstances demanded it. Regardless, I have always trusted their discretion. Just as I trust yours, Captain."

"Your people's secret will be safe with me as well, Ambassador," Sulu said. "I owe you at least that much for all you've done in trying to bring Qagh to justice."

"Which doesn't really amount to a whole lot, Captain. The albino is still out there, somewhere. And I'm sure that all of us who've sworn the blood oath against him would gladly accept your help should you change your mind about joining us."

Sulu thought of Ganjitsu. And the dead woman in the spaceport bar.

And Captain Styles.

But he knew that the road to revenge led to some very dark, very nasty places. And he thought it a pity that such a long-lived being as Curzon Dax had not yet accumulated sufficient wisdom to understand that.

"No," Sulu said, hoping that his emphatic tone had closed down the topic once and for all. "I'm not going to kill for revenge. But I won't make that decision for you. I won't pretend to be happy about it, though. I still wish you'd reconsider this."

Dax studied him silently, as though disappointed in Sulu's disappointment. At length, the Trill said, "It might be better if you'd just wish me luck instead. I'll find my own transportation home from here, Captain."

And with that, the no longer quite so enigmatic Trill turned and strode purposefully toward Kang, Mara, Koloth, and Kor, all of whom stood motionless some thirty meters away beneath the angry, meteor-streaked night sky of Qo'noS. The tangle of long shadows they cast in the pale light of dead, fragmentary Praxis transformed them into monuments to vengeance.

Right or wrong, he's got to make his own way, Sulu thought, hoping that Curzon Dax wasn't about to reap a bitter harvest of destruction.

With a sigh and a shake of his head, he pulled out his communicator and flipped its grid open.

"Sulu to *Excelsior.* One to beam up."

EPILOGUE CHA'

That the busy spaceport inn was run-down and in general disrepair came as no surprise to Kang. In fact, it mirrored the way he felt as it occurred to him—and not for the first time—that he was becoming far too old and far too weary to continue coming to such places.

But that was no matter; while breath remained in his body and his seven-decade-old blood oath remained unfulfilled, he would continue his search for the albino, following up on every conceivable lead. Such was the only comfort he could offer the unquiet ghosts of DaqS and two other dead children.

Today the trail had led him to the Dayos system's fourth planet, a cold, thin-aired, and only marginally habitable world located on the ragged fringes of Klingon space. Though its glory days now lay decades behind it, thanks largely to the increased law and order brought about by the Klingon-Federation alliance, the planet still served as a spaceport hub, making more than a dozen other border locales and nonaligned worlds alike mutually accessible to small, hard-to-track short-range craft.

Like the vast majority of worlds of its ilk, Dayos IV served a clientele that out of necessity worked in the shadows, just slightly beyond the scan resolution of the few overworked Klingon Defense Force units charged with tamping down the most egregious criminality in the border region; everyone here was from somewhere else, and no one passing through this frigid clime was at all eager to discuss either his next destination or his reasons for going there.

As he doffed his thermal overcoverings, crossed the worn carpet in the entry foyer, and started across the surprisingly bustling casino, Kang was struck by how closely this place resembled so many other seedy border-world hostelries he had seen during the many decades he'd spent on the ever-elusive albino's trail. With its extremely heterogeneous mix of species, which included Orions, Tagrans, Bolians, Rigelians, and four-armed Terrellians—in addition to Kriosians, Trafalmadorians, and several other assorted *jeghpu'wI'* races from various Klingon subject worlds, as well as a number of proudly brow-ridged Klingons—this inn wouldn't have been at all out of place on Galdonterre.

Galdonterre, the last place where Kang, Koloth, and Kor had faced the albino in pitched battle, on a day now some three decades past. Galdonterre, where the albino had somehow escaped the righteous vengeance of three Klingon warriors yet again. Kang's soul still burned with the heat of a *bat'leth* being beaten flat in the forge whenever he recalled how close he and his brethren-in-arms had come that day to quenching the blood oath's insatiable fires with the ichor of the cowardly childslayer.

But unlike that long-gone day on Galdonterre, Kang had come to Dayos IV alone. He had told none of his blood-oath comrades of his meeting here today, since he felt it would require a degree of finesse that neither Koloth nor Kor still possessed in sufficient measure after the passage of so many bitter years of fruitless questing. Koloth was far too angry, and Kor was far too drunk, not to scare off the woman whom Kang had come here to meet. And Curzon Dax, whose Federation diplomatic duties had long ago greatly curtailed the degree to which he could contribute to the search for the albino, was now too old and sick to participate in the hunt.

Entering the randomly furnished restaurant that was attached to the casino like a prefab afterthought, Kang took a seat at the agreed-upon corner booth, which was empty. A haughty-looking Orion waitress approached, and he ordered her to fetch a flagon of bloodwine. He hoped that he would have some real reason to raise his *HIvje'* in celebration before he had drunk his fill.

And he hoped, of course, that he hadn't just walked straight into one of the albino's cowardly traps.

The hard-eyed green waitress returned soon enough with his drink, which she'd poured into a battered pewter mug that reminded him of a piece of hull metal that had barely survived a fiery atmospheric reentry. As he drank, Kang quietly swept his dark, hooded eyes across the sparsely peopled, dimly illuminated room, in which a Tellarite and an Orion conducted a desultory conversation at one of the tables, a pair of identical Miradorn dined at another, and a razor-toothed Pahkwa-thanh devoured a bloody haunch of some large, unidentifiable creature with a ferocious gusto that made Kang smile in vicarious enjoyment.

Kang noticed something moving to his left side, and turned in time to see a woman approach his booth. Despite the room's weak illumination, he sized her up quickly. She was tall and slender, but also careworn, her strong face subtly grooved by worry lines, like channels etched by a stream into stone over time. Her clothing was old and threadbare, but she wore it with a defiant, almost regal pride.

"You are Kang?" the woman said as she reached his table.

Kang nodded and gestured toward the couch on the opposite side of the booth. "Please, sit."

Though she showed some obvious hesitation, she nevertheless complied. Her fearful yet resolute manner made him willing to believe that she posed no danger to him.

"What name shall I call you by?" Kang said, unsure as yet to which species she belonged. "You did not identify yourself in your message."

She looked furtively from side to side, as if to make certain she had not been followed. "I am Ylda," she said.

"And you say you are a former spouse of Qagh," Kang said. "The albino."

A look of revulsion crossed her face. "Believe me, I would make no such claim were it not true. He took me unwillingly from my family years ago. Then he discarded me as though I were garbage." Her eyes brimmed with unshed tears.

"This happened recently?"

She nodded miserably. "Just before I contacted you."

"Then you must know how I might find him," Kang said, his hopes of soon settling the blood oath rekindling.

Very quietly, she said, "No."

Her flat refusal took Kang aback. "You are hardly in a position to bargain with me, Ylda."

"I am not . . . *bargaining,* Kang. If I betray Qagh to you, you will just attempt to kill him."

"I thought I had already made that more than plain," Kang growled, his anger becoming roused.

"But he is likely to survive any such attack, just as he has done many times in the past," Ylda said, shrinking back into the worn upholstery. "And then he will come after *me,* to punish my betrayal."

His rage slowly intensifying, Kang favored her with a deeply toxic scowl. "If I choose to *force* you to give him up, there is little you can do to stop me."

She nodded, her expression taking on a slack, fatalistic character. "I understand. I ask only that you refrain from crippling me. After you are done, I will heal. And perhaps Qagh will spare me once he sees the scars and bruises you inflicted before I revealed his whereabouts to you."

Kang's mounting fury was beginning to give way to bemusement. "You *expected* me to torture the truth out of you, yet you still sought me out. *Why?*"

A single fat tear began rolling slowly down her cheek. "Because unlike Qagh, some of his enemies are honorable and trustworthy men. And because I had nowhere else to go."

Kang's anger dissipated like a summer squall over the mountain peak on Qo'noS that bore his name. He had never before encountered such a portrait of hopelessness as he saw now in Ylda—a woman so desperate that she had no one to turn to other than a vengeful enemy. In this woman's presence, he found it difficult to remain anchored to the hatred that had sustained him for all these years, thanks to the blood oath.

Now, to his immense surprise, he could feel very little save pity for the bedraggled woman who sat beside him. *I am indeed getting too old for this,* he thought, becoming more than a little disgusted with himself. *I have grown weary, and therefore soft. Like the Empire itself.*

Right or wrong, Kang decided to adopt a tack other than intimidation and torture. Catching the attention of the Orion waitress again, he waved her over to his booth. He reached into his armored tunic and withdrew a small coin purse, from which emerged a respectable pile of both latinum strips and Klingon darseks.

"I want you to prepare some comfortable quarters for this

woman," he said, pushing the heap of coins and slips across the table toward the waitress. "See that they are well provisioned with food and drink, and clean clothing as well. You will advise me when all is in readiness."

After the waitress had finished enthusiastically scooping up the unanticipated windfall and disappeared, Kang turned his attention back upon Ylda.

She couldn't have looked more surprised had he suddenly drawn a *mek'leth* and stabbed her through the heart with it.

"*Now* will you share the albino's whereabouts with me?"

She opened and closed her mouth several times, like a beached spikefish vainly gasping for air. "He will still find me and kill me."

"Only if I fail to find him and kill him first," Kang said. "But I have waited many, many years already to enjoy that privilege. So perhaps I can afford to abide a while longer, while you are in your room cleaning up, resting, and considering my . . . request."

Yes, he thought. *I am weary, and I am old. But I am also patient.* There would still be time aplenty to bring bloody justice to the albino; all he had to do in the meantime was to build a bridge of trust between himself and this woman.

Just as Curzon Dax once did for me, Koloth, and Kor.

"Thank you," Ylda said.

Kang watched with a mixture of fascination and envy as a second distended tear followed the trail its elder brother had blazed down her cheek. It had long been his understanding that among many sentient races, including Earthers, tears were thought either to reveal joy or to wash away sorrow. Though the Klingon people's lack of tear ducts prevented Kang from shedding tears for either reason, the hardships he had endured since DaqS's death sometimes made him wish he could weep.

"Do you have children?" Kang asked gently.

She nodded, her eyes flashing as still more tears struggled to escape.

Kang reached again into his tunic, from which he withdrew a small holocube. He activated its imaging controls with a flick of his thumb before setting the cube down in the center of the table.

The fiercely grinning face of his beloved, long-dead little boy DaqS suddenly appeared, hovering just above the cube like an apparition summoned by one of the mystics of ancient Qo'noS.

"Then let me tell you of the life and death of my firstborn son," Kang said, smiling gently as memories of pleasanter times returned. "And of the lives and deaths of the sons of my blood brothers, Kor and Koloth."

There will be time, Kang thought. Then he began to recount his tale of happiness and woe, of love and death, of outrage and revenge.

And he watched the flow of Ylda's rapidly dwindling supply of tears.

Acknowledgments

As ever, any errors or fubars contained in these pages are the sole responsibility of the authors. But even though only two names appear on the spine of this novel, legions of others contributed invaluable assistance in the work's creation. Among those who merit special commendations are: Marco Palmieri, an editor without whose inexhaustible patience and expert guidance this book could never have completed its arduous ten-year journey from brilliant initial idea (Marco's) to gigantic finished manuscript (ours); *I.K.S. Gorkon* author Keith R.A. DeCandido, who contributed his unparalleled expertise in Klingon culture, language, technology, metaphysics, and calendar calculations; the kind and indulgent folks at the Daily Market and Café, where much of Mike's portions of this novel were written; Dr. Marc Okrand, whose volumes on the Klingon language were constant companions; David Gerrold, whose furry creations (seen in "The Trouble with Tribbles" and "More Tribbles, More Troubles") played a small but pivotal role in the Klingon history depicted herein; Michael Jan Friedman, whose gorgeous 1999 hardcover volume *New Worlds, New Civilizations* provided valuable reference specific to both Klingons and tribbles; Dayton Ward, whose 2002 novel *In the Name of Honor* provided valuable literary continuity references regarding Klingon dermatology, and who (with coauthor Kevin Dilmore) enriched the Klingon vocabulary in 2006's *Star Trek Vanguard: Summon the Thunder*; Susan Wright's "Infinity" (from 1999's *The Lives of Dax*), which gave us *Excelsior* chief engineer Lahra as well as a previous visit from both Dr. Christine Chapel and Torias Dax; Majliss Larson, whose 1985 novel *Pawns and Symbols* named two vessels commanded by Kang; Vonda N. McIntyre, whose Captain Hunter (commander of the border ship *Aerfen*) and much of Hikaru Sulu's family history were referenced previously in 1981's *The Entropy Effect* and 1986's *Enterprise: The First Adventure*; Julia Ecklar, whose 1989 novel *Kobayashi Maru* debuted Hikaru Sulu's great-grandfather Tetsuo Inomata; Geoffrey Mandel for his *Star Trek Star Charts* (2002), which provided an invaluable reference to "galactic geography"; Diane Duane, whose 1997 novel *Intellivore* supplied some nifty Trill place names; Phaedra M. Weldon, whose story "The Lights in the Sky" (published in 1998 in the first *Strange New Worlds* anthology) shed some light on the time-frame of the launch of the *U.S.S. Enterprise*-B; Peter David, whose 1995 novel *The Captain's Daughter* established a great deal about Demora Sulu's relationship with her father, and whose 1994 audiobook *Cacophony* introduced Lieutenant Terra Spiro; David R. George, whose *Serpents Among the Ruins* (a 2003 novel) and "Iron and Sacrifice" (a story in 2005's *Tales from the Captain's Table* anthology) have charted the voyage of Demora Sulu for many parsecs beyond the boundaries of this tale; L. A. Graf (aka Julia Ecklar and Karen Rose Cercone), whose 1998 *Captain's Table* novel *War Dragons* debuted some of the characters found in these pages, including Transporter Chief

Renyck, engineer Tim Henry, and Dr. Judith Klass; Judy Klass, the author of the 1989 TOS novel *Cry of the Onlies*, who graciously allowed the author of *War Dragons* to drag her aboard *Excelsior* as the chief medical officer's namesake in the first place; Michael and Denise Okuda and Debbie Mirek, whose *Star Trek Encyclopedia: A Reference Guide to the Future* (1997 edition) remains indispensable even in the current age of wireless broadband internet service and hot-and-cold running wikis; Mike W. Barr, Tom Sutton, Ricardo Villagran, Peter David (again), Bill Mumy, and Gordon Purcell, whose many and varied *Star Trek* comic-book tales helped to guide our take on Captain Styles; Judith and Garfield Reeves-Stevens, whose 1990 novel *Prime Directive* also provided useful background pertinent to Styles and *Excelsior;* John M. Ford, whose 1984 novel *The Final Reflection* introduced the Klingon strategy game of *klin zha,* along with much else about *Star Trek*'s archetypal warrior race that has since become canonical; Josepha Sherman and Susan Shwartz, crafters of excellent novels and fine Romulan sherawood office furniture (as advertised since 2004 in the *Vulcan's Soul* hardcovers); Harve Bennett and Leonard Nimoy, whose respective efforts as scenarist and director of *Star Trek III: The Search for Spock* (1984) gave us the *U.S.S. Excelsior* in the first place; James B. Sikking, who breathed life into Captain Styles for the cameras in the aforementioned film; Jacqueline Kim, who provided our only canonical glimpse of Demora Sulu in *Star Trek Generations* (1994); Walter Koenig and Grace Lee Whitney, for their immortal portrayals, respectively, of Pavel Chekov and Janice Rand; Michael Ansara, William Campbell, and John Colicos, who brought the Klingon Warriors Three to life, in both "smooth" and "chunky" flavors; and George Takei, who has earned those captain's bars many, many times over.

About the Authors

MICHAEL A. MARTIN'S solo short fiction has appeared in *The Magazine of Fantasy & Science Fiction*. He has also coauthored (with Andy Mangels) several *Star Trek* comics for Marvel and Wildstorm and numerous *Star Trek* novels and eBooks, including *Enterprise: The Good That Men Do*; the USA Today bestseller *Titan: Taking Wing*; *Titan: The Red King*; the Sy Fy Genre Award–winning *Worlds of Deep Space 9 Volume Two: Trill—Unjoined*; *Enterprise: Last Full Measure*; *The Lost Era 2298: The Sundered*; *Deep Space 9 Mission: Gamma Book Three—Cathedral*; *The Next Generation: Section 31—Rogue*; *Starfleet Corps of Engineers #30 and #31* ("Ishtar Rising" Books 1 and 2, reprinted in *Aftermath*, the eighth volume of the *S.C.E.* paperback series); stories in the *Prophecy and Change, Tales of the Dominion War,* and *Tales from the Captain's Table* anthologies; and three novels based on the *Roswell* television series. His work has also been published by Atlas Editions (in their *Star Trek Universe* subscription card series), *Star Trek*

Monthly, Grolier Books, Visible Ink Press, *The Oregonian*, and Gareth Stevens, Inc., for whom he has penned several *World Almanac Library of the States* nonfiction books for young readers. He lives with his wife, Jenny, and their sons James and William in Portland, Oregon.

ANDY MANGELS is the *USA Today* bestselling author and coauthor of over a dozen novels—including *Star Trek* and *Roswell* books—all cowritten with Michael A. Martin. Flying solo, he is the bestselling author of several nonfiction books, including *Star Wars: The Essential Guide to Characters* and *Animation on DVD: The Ultimate Guide*, as well as a significant number of entries for *The Superhero Book: The Ultimate Encyclopedia of Comic-Book Icons and Hollywood Heroes* as well as for its companion volume, *The Supervillain Book: The Evil Side of Comics and Hollywood.*

In addition to cowriting more upcoming novels and contributing to anthologies, Andy has produced, directed, and scripted a series of over thirty half-hour DVD documentaries—and provided other special features—for BCI Eclipse's Ink & Paint brand, for inclusion in DVD box sets ranging from animated fare such as *He-Man, She-Ra, Flash Gordon*, and *Ghostbusters* to live-action favorites such as *Ark II, Space Academy*, and *Isis*. As "Dru Sullivan," Andy penned the exploits of "Miss Adventure, the Gayest American Hero" for the late, lamented *Weekly World News*.

Andy has written hundreds of articles for entertainment and lifestyle magazines and newspapers in the United States, England, and Italy. He has also written licensed material based on properties from numerous film studios and Microsoft, and over the past two decades his comic-book work has been published by DC Comics, Marvel Comics, Dark Horse, Image, Innovation, and many others. He was the editor of the award-winning Gay Comics anthology for eight years.

Andy is a national award-winning activist in the Gay community, and has raised thousands of dollars for charities over the years. He lives in Portland, Oregon, with his long-term partner, Don Hood, their dog Bela, and their chosen son, Paul Smalley. Visit his website at www.andymangels. com.